According to author JOHN WILCOX, an inability to do sums and a nascent talent to string words together steered him towards journalism – that and the desire to wear a trench coat, belted with a knot, just like Bogart. After a number of years working as a journalist, he was lured into industry. In the mid-nineties he sold his company in order to devote himself to his first love, writing. He has now published, to high acclaim, ten Simon Fonthill books, one Fonthill short story, a WWI novel and two works of non-fiction, including an autobiography.

johnwilcoxauthor.co.uk

By John Wilcox

The War of the Dragon Lady
Fire Across the Veldt
Bayonets Along the Border
Treachery in Tibet
Pirates – Starboard Side!
(a short story)
Dust Clouds of War

◆

Starshine

a&b

TREACHERY IN TIBET

JOHN WILCOX

Allison & Busby Limited
12 Fitzroy Mews
London W1T 6DW
allisonandbusby.com

First published in Great Britain by Allison & Busby in 2015.
This paperback edition published by Allison & Busby in 2016.

A CIP catalogue record for this book is available from
the British Library.

10 9 8 7 6 5 4 3 2 1

ISBN 978-0-7490-1982-2

Typeset in 10.5/15.5 pt Sabon by
Allison & Busby Ltd.

The paper used for this Allison & Busby publication
has been produced from trees that have been legally sourced
from well-managed and credibly certified forests.

Printed and bound by
CPI Group (UK) Ltd, Croydon, CR0 4YY

For Alison – again

CHAPTER ONE

Calcutta, India. Early November 1903.

Alice Fonthill screwed up her eyes against the glare of the sun and looked about her in wonder. On her way by rickshaw from the railway station she had ridden past a succession of white, neoclassical mansions, standing amidst carefully cultivated gardens – the homes of rich Indian merchants but also the stately offices of the bureaucrats who were making the British Raj function so smoothly at the birth of this new century. Calcutta, the capital of Imperial India, had indeed become a city of European architecture and style, even if the stately houses were a gilded carapace concealing behind them the hovels of the Indians who serviced them. Yet the building at whose entrance she stood now made her jaw drop.

As befitted an experienced journalist, Alice had done her homework. Government House, she knew, had been built in the time of Governor General Wellesley, the brother of the soldier who was to become the Duke of Wellington. It had cost the East India Company £63,291 – a huge sum that had prompted the recall of Wellesley. She had read that some 700 servants were housed within it now to attend to the cares of the Viceroy and his family. As the representative in India of the King Emperor, the man deserved nothing less, of course. The pomp and power of the Empire were encapsulated in him. He demanded, no, he *deserved* an imperial palace.

Alice gazed at the massive stone edifice that seemed to stretch for almost a mile on either side of her, as she stood at the huge archway that guarded its entrance. She took in the tall windows that gazed down on terraces, statues, gardens and, in the semi-distance, two ornate carriages drawn by magnificent horses that waited by a side doorway, presumably at the Viceroy's pleasure. It was the size of the thing that impressed. In truth, the building lacked elegance. It sat like some grey, stone battleship, a bit reminiscent of Buckingham Palace but without the Georgian symmetry.

She had asked to be dropped at the archway so that she could collect her thoughts before proceeding further. But now she rather regretted it, for she would be forced to walk some 200 yards at least in the hot sun down the gravelled driveway before reaching the entrance to the house itself. Tiring and rather demeaning, for Europeans rarely walked far during the day in Calcutta. And certainly not English memsahibs.

Never mind. Alice Fonthill, née Griffith, of *The Morning Post*, London, was never one to observe the proprieties. She adjusted her parasol slightly, hitched up her skirt and gave the giant Sikh guarding the entrance her brightest smile.

'Good morning,' she beamed. 'What a lovely day! I have an appointment with the Viceroy, Lord Curzon.' She presented to him the letter in which the Viceroy's secretary had confirmed the appointment and waited courteously while the man looked at it, certainly more impressed by the crest at the top of the notepaper rather than its contents, for it was most unlikely that he could read. If, however, he was unimpressed by the fact that the memsahib had not been driven up in style, under the archway and through the grounds of the palace, like most of its visitors, he gave no sign.

Springing smartly to attention and saluting, he gestured down the drive. 'Entrance to house is straight ahead, madam. You will be escorted.' He turned and barked an order to a younger but equally resplendent Sikh, who had materialised as if by magic, and saluted again.

Alice nodded her thanks and fell in behind her escort, marvelling at his erect bearing, and the vivid colours of his sashed uniform and towering turban. As she walked, treading delicately and slowly on the gravel so as not to perspire unbecomingly, she reflected once again on the essential colourfulness of all things Indian. Not, mind you, the eternal greyness of the hills and ravines of the North-West Frontier, where she and her husband, Simon, had fought in the great Pathan Revolt some six years before, but here, in the heart of the subcontinent, where, in the cities and villages, the bazaars and streets buzzed with life and brilliance. There, long swathes of cotton and gauze were invariably draped on display in hues which sang the skills of the dyer; garishly coloured dishes – almond curd, *balushahi* sweetmeats, boluses of spiced mutton, gleaming piles of white rice – stirred the taste buds; the brilliant saris and *salwar kameezes* of the women complemented the trinkets of silver, turquoise and even gold that they inspected so contemptuously on the stalls. And the evocative smells everywhere! Even now, as she walked towards Government House, soft fragrances of tea and spices wafted towards her from the Hooghly river.

Alice folded her parasol as she and her escort reached the house itself. The young Sikh murmured something in Hindi to the equally sumptuously caparisoned soldier at the door, who stood on guard, sabre resting on his shoulder. She tried to recall how many men were in the Viceroy's personal bodyguard – as many as 400, wasn't it? – and then she was ushered into the blessed cool of a gigantic hallway.

Blinking to become accustomed to the shade, she caught glimpses of tall rooms gilded with marble, mahogany, gold, velvet and silk, beneath huge crystal chandeliers, before a slim, young Englishman in grey morning coat came striding towards her.

'Ah, Miss Griffith, good morning,' he called, as he approached, his hand outstretched. Alice paused for a moment, then realised that, of course, as a correspondent of *The Morning Post*, she had used her maiden name. She extended her white-gloved hand and the young man bowed low over it. 'Willoughby, ma'am,' he said, 'the Viceroy's second secretary. His Lordship is expecting you, of course. Did you have a pleasant journey?'

'What? Oh, from Sibsagar, you mean? Yes, thank you. The worst part was getting to the town. From there, it took two days by rail, of course, but the train, though slow, was well on time. Sometimes we feel that Assam is rather a forgotten part of India, you know. We are rather remote.'

Willoughby smiled, revealing a flash of white teeth beneath his luxurious moustache. 'Oh good gracious no. The subcontinent would be virtually nothing without its tea. And, indeed, so would England, don'tcha know. You tea growers are certainly not forgotten here in Calcutta, ma'am, I assure you of that.'

As they chatted inconsequentially, the secretary led her through what seemed like a succession of marbled halls and Alice was conscious of turbanned attendants, their white robes slashed diagonally with scarlet sashes, bowing low like automatons from nooks and crannies as they passed. Eventually, they came to a cool, smaller anteroom and Willoughby gestured to a low couch, sumptuously cushioned in cream velvet.

'Do take a seat, Miss Griffith,' he said. 'His Lordship is detained by a . . . ahem . . . rather unexpected Indian visitor at the moment, but he is aware that you are here. He won't keep you a moment. I won't offer you tea, because I know that the Viceroy will like to receive that with you, but would you care for, say, a little lemon juice while you wait?'

Alice smiled gratefully. 'Oh, that would be ideal. Thank you.'

As Willoughby departed – he seemed to glide, rather than walk, she noted – Alice settled back in the cushions and sought in her handbag for her powder compact. She was glad to have a moment to herself before she met Curzon. Aware of the man's reputation for aloofness and his typical politician's dislike of the press, she remained surprised that he had so seemingly readily agreed to her request for an interview. She had put it down to the reputation of her newspaper as a solid supporter of the reigning Tory government back home and, perhaps . . . she smiled immodestly at the thought . . . at the fame that she and her husband had garnered over the years from their adventures throughout the Empire. Simon Fonthill had gained a following, not altogether welcomed by him, as a result of his exploits as a quite irregular army scout over the last three decades, while the redcoats of the Queen had pushed back boundaries all over the world. He had been appointed a Companion of the Order of the Bath after penetrating the Mahdi's lines at Khartoum and had risen to acting Brigadier General in the recent war against the Boers in South Africa, gaining a Distinguished Service Order. And his adventures had been shared and reported upon by his wife.

But Alice's smile broadened slightly as a possible other reason for the ease with which she seemed to have gained admission to the Viceroy's guilded presence reoccurred to her. Despite his reputation for reclusion and pomposity, Curzon, she had heard, was not above casting his eye upon a pretty face. Oh, as a married man to an American heiress now for some eight years, no hint of scandal had been attached to him. But, as a titled and handsome bachelor, his predilection for female company had become well known and his mistresses were legion.

Alice now, then, looked at herself critically in the small mirror of her powder compact. As a woman forging her career in the distinctly masculine world of journalism – she was not the only female war correspondent in London's Fleet Street, but distaff competitors were few – she had never been averse to using her looks to help her get ahead. The face that frowned back at her now from the small oval glass was no longer young, alas. But, she had to admit that, at nearing fifty, maturity had dealt her no harsh blows.

Her cheekbones were high and clear cut, her mouth full, her eyes of a rather challenging grey and the skin which most women of her age would have carefully protected from the sun with cream and powder, now glowed back at her with a sheen that reflected her outdoor life: unfashionable but by no means unattractive. Her hair betrayed only the faintest of grey streaks and remained lustrously fair. In fact, if it had not been for a rather squareness of jaw that betrayed determination, Alice Griffith could still have qualified as a beautiful woman.

Nevertheless, her frown remained as she dabbed onto her cheeks just a touch of powder to tone down that ridiculously healthy glow. Interviewing Lord Curzon of Kedleston, Viceroy of India, was not going to be easy – not with the questions and radical views she intended to put to him, anyway. She would need all the help she could get.

Alice was well aware that, beneath the notoriously haughty and supreme confidence exuded by the man, there lurked a scholar, a politician of conviction and a person whose knowledge of Central Asia and the trouble spots of the Middle and Far East was probably unsurpassed in the corridors of Westminster. His precocity had been marked when, while still at Oxford, his speeches in the Union there had been quoted in Parliament. A life-long Conservative, he had entered the Commons in 1886 by winning the seat of

Southport in Lancashire. He first visited India in the following year and then had travelled twice round the world and been published extensively. In the nineties he had journeyed 2,000 miles *alone* on horseback in Persia and later, on his way to stay with the Amir of Afghanistan, no less, he had climbed to an altitude of 14,000 feet, up to the plateau of the Pamirs, to visit the hidden valley of Hunza. Now, however, it seemed that those cold eyes of his were fixed on the strange, lost world of Tibet – and Alice was here to find out why.

She snapped the compact shut and gratefully accepted the tinkling glass of iced lemonade presented to her. She was stealing a quick look at her notes when a cough announced that Willoughby had returned.

'So sorry to have kept you waiting, Miss Griffith,' he announced. 'The Viceroy has managed to . . . er . . . get rid of his unannounced visitor and is looking forward to seeing you now. Do let me take your lemonade in for you.'

Ah, thought Alice. Young man, you will go far . . . !

She entered a much larger room that had all the grace and elegance of those that had preceded it and, as she did so, a tall, matchingly elegant man rose to greet her from behind the desk at its far end. He advanced towards her with hand extended, walking stiffly erect, as though on parade. Alice remembered that an accident in his youth had injured his spine, so leaving him in intermittent pain and forcing him to wear at all times a steel-braced corset. This, she knew, had helped to bequeath him the reputation of being lordly and condescending – perhaps undeservedly?

As Curzon bowed over her hand, Alice gave him the curtsy that was owed to him as the Queen's representative in this huge land and looked up into his face. It was, as she had been led to expect, undoubtedly handsome. Some four years younger than she, the Viceroy too had worn well, despite the pain of his injury. His fair hair had now receded somewhat and had been brushed back severely to reveal the noblest and most scholastic of brows. His cheekbones matched hers in their sharpness and his lips were chiselled, giving his face a lean and sensitive appearance. The reputation for haughtiness, she reflected quickly, was obviously enhanced by eyes of an indeterminate colour that seemed cold and unreceptive, belying the warmth of his smile.

'Mrs Fonthill.' His voice was mellifluous, of course, but quite grave and formal in tone. Then: 'Oh, but perhaps I shouldn't address you so. Are you Miss Griffith today?'

Alice produced her best smile once again. 'It really doesn't matter, Lord Curzon. It really is rather flattering for this married woman to be able to revert to . . . what shall I say . . . my maiden status, whenever she wants to.' (Dammit. The unintended double entendre made her sound coquettish. Far too early to play that card!)

She hid her momentary embarrassment with a cough. 'But perhaps, as I am here as a correspondent for *The Morning Post*, Miss Griffith would be most appropriate.'

'As you wish, dear lady. When I received your letter I realised that I had been reading with interest and admiration your despatches from various parts of the Empire for some years now and it is a pleasure to meet you at last.' He had retained her hand and she now withdrew it very slowly, perhaps even a little languorously. She had played this game before.

'Oh, that is more than kind of you, Your Excellency. And I am most grateful to you for sparing the time in what I am sure is a very busy day.'

He waved a dismissive hand. 'I am happy to be of whatever assistance to you that I can. Now, do come and sit down. Would you care for tea? Good gracious, of course you would. You and your husband now grow it, of course. You must drink it. Assam, I presume?'

Alice settled herself on a low divan before what was obviously a golden-gilt-covered French table of some antiquity. 'I must confess,' she smiled, as though sharing a guilty confidence, 'that I much prefer Darjeeling, if you have any, although it does seem rather traitorous.'

'So do I, as a matter of fact.' He strode to his desk and tinkled a small bell that sat on it. '*Chai*,' he called to a white-liveried orderly who responded. 'Darjeeling. Quickly, now.'

The man bowed and retreated. The curt tone used by Curzon brought to Alice's mind the by now famous ditty that one of his contemporaries at Oxford had composed about him:

My name is George Nathaniel Curzon,
I am a most superior person.
My cheek is pink, my hair is sleek,
I dine at Blenheim once a week.

She hid an irreverent grin. Yes, there was no doubt about it. His cheek *was* undoubtedly pink!

The tea was poured: the best Darjeeling, of course,

with that distinctive coppery colour, so popular now in the *salons* of Europe. Alice savoured it with pleasure. But the Viceroy was speaking now, with that fluidity and speed that had earned him a reputation as an orator of supreme confidence and style.

'I see that you are growing your tea in Northern Assam, very much up in the hills, by the look of it. I was surprised to hear that, after Fonthill's distinguished war against the Boers, he had taken up this most pastoral of occupations. The two of you have shown such great energy and enterprise in all your activities on the periphery of Empire that I might imagine that tea growing in Assam would be perhaps . . . what shall I say . . . perhaps a little boring? *N'est-ce pas?*'

Alice sipped her tea. 'Yes, I'm afraid it is, rather, although the work is proving rather hard and we have had a few problems with the Naga tribesmen, who live in the hills just east of our patch.'

'Ah yes. I have had some reports of that. You must tell me if things get worse. I know that Kitchener would be happy to despatch a troop of Gurkhas down from Darjeeling to sort them out.'

'Thank you, but I think Simon can handle it. Lord Kitchener, of course. He has more or less recently joined you as commander-in-chief, I believe. Neither Simon nor I knew him in the Sudan on the Gordon mission – he was only a major in intelligence then, if I remember rightly – but Simon, in particular, got to know him very well in South Africa. A most brilliant soldier, of course . . . ?'

It was hardly put as a question but Alice had heard that,

after a honeymoon period, the great soldier and the great imperialist were no longer on equable terms and she was not above a little probing into the matter.

Curzon did not rise to the bait. 'Oh, yes, of course. We are lucky to have him. Now, I am sorry that I did not know of your arrival in Assam. I would certainly have sent you both an invitation to dine at Government House. You must forgive me. How long have you been there?'

Alice waved aside the apology languidly. 'Not so very long. In fact, little more than a year. After the Boer armistice, we hurried back to our small estate in Norfolk to oversee our farming activities there. But,' she shrugged her shoulders, 'I'm afraid neither of us are cut out to spend our lives peacefully in the English countryside. I was anxious to resume writing again for the *Post* – there is little to write about in dear old Norfolk – and Simon was itching to try something new. So' – she sighed – 'we bought this small tea estate in Assam, which had been allowed to run down, and Simon has had his hands full there ever since.'

She raised the cup to her lips again. 'Perhaps I have been the happier of the two because there has been plenty to write about in India—'

'Ah,' he interrupted, 'you must forgive me. My duties here have meant that I have not been quite so assiduous a follower of your work as I was in London. And the *Post* arrives here so dashed late, you know, that the pot has boiled long before I get to take the lid off, so to speak.'

'Of course. You are forgiven, sir. But I am detaining you far too long with tittle-tattle about the Fonthills. If I may, Lord Curzon, I would like to discuss this Tibetan affair with you and seek your guidance in terms of analysing what is going on there and how the matter could develop.'

Curzon's face tightened for a moment. Then he raised an elegant eyebrow and smiled coldly. 'Having noticed over the years how your . . . er . . . rather radical views of matters concerning the Empire have been presented with great skill within the more traditional Tory editorial policies followed by the *Post*, I doubt whether I myself will be influential at all in helping you to report on the Tibetan problem. But, be assured that I shall try. Now do fire away.' He leant back in his chair, crossed one white silk-stockinged leg over the other – it seemed he always wore ceremonial dress during the day – and waved for her to begin.

Alice fumbled in her small bag and produced pencil and notebook. 'Thank you, Viceroy. But please be assured that my story will be written as a straightforward report, not an opinion piece. Not a leader, of course.'

'I understand. And so . . .' He leant forward, 'you would presumably have no objection if I cast an eye over it before you cable it? Just, of course,' he added hurriedly, 'so that I might be in a position to correct what might be the odd inaccuracies which can, I know, creep into the most carefully written pieces.'

Summoning what she hoped was a beguiling smile, Alice shook her head gently. 'I am afraid not, sir. It is not the policy of our newspaper to allow stories to be censored, so to speak. I fear that you must trust me.'

'Very well. Now, do please begin.'

Alice took a deep breath. 'Do you intend to invade Tibet?'

Curzon feigned deep astonishment. 'Good gracious no! Whatever made you think that?'

Scribbling away, Alice looked up. 'Because for some months now you have had a diplomatic mission – guarded by a military escort of remarkable size considering that the Tibetans are not a militaristic race – sitting over the border half a day's march into Tibet at a place called Khamba Jong. I understand that the Tibetans have consistently refused to negotiate with the mission and that it and its escort is now being withdrawn back into India and that a considerable number of troops is being assembled near the border, presumably with aggressive intents towards Tibet? Why?'

The Viceroy, seemingly unperturbed, raised two hands defensively. 'Most of what you say is true. What is not true is the assumption that you draw from the facts.'

'Then why, pray, assemble the troops? What have the Tibetans done to harm India or the Raj?'

'Ah.' He pressed the fingertips of both hands together and tapped them, in a meditative mode. 'We must go back a little in time, Miss Griffith, so that you understand the background.'

'Please do.'

'Very well. You will know that I have travelled extensively through these parts in the past and talked with a good many rulers long before I took up this position in Calcutta?'

Alice nodded, pencil poised.

'In fact, I may say – if a trifle immodestly – that, in addition to being the youngest viceroy to be posted here, I believe that I am almost certainly the best equipped, in terms of having studied the history of the region and its problems, both from the perspective of the British government in London and from my many discussions on the ground with people of influence throughout the subcontinent and its neighbours.'

Ah, thought Alice, now the man's conceit is beginning to reveal itself! But she nodded slowly again and said, 'Of course. I would certainly be prepared, sir, to concede that.'

'Very good of you, madam, I am sure. Now,' he leant forward, 'from all my studies and conversations, I have formed a firm conclusion that Russia has intentions towards Tibet, if not aggressive militarily, then certainly so in diplomatic terms.'

Alice frowned. 'But surely Tibet is a vassal state of China, and Russia would certainly not attempt to upset the Manchu Empire?'

'Oh, I am not speaking of direct invasion. But there is plenty of circumstantial evidence that Russia is attempting to turn Tibet against us. The Tsar's emissaries are to be seen frequently in Lhasa, I am informed, and more and more stories are reaching me that Moscow is beginning to arm Tibet. There is even a manufacturing plant being set up in Lhasa, I am told, to produce Russian rifles there.'

'Why should Russia do all this?'

'Because it covets India and wants a route through to this country. As you know, Cossacks have left a trail of havoc over the decades riding through Central Asia towards the Indian North-West frontier. They've taken the Russian double-headed eagle right up to the northern frontier of Afghanistan. We have called their bluff there and there they have stopped. Now, it is my conviction that they are seeking to find another way in. Tibet is under only a rather lacklustre form of suzerainty from Peking and I sense that the Russians see an opportunity there.'

Scribbling away, Alice spoke without looking up. 'So what do you propose to do about it?'

'Well, I intend to put a stop to their little game. We must persuade the Dalai Lama to open up his country to us to counterbalance the Russian threat.'

Alice put her pencil to her mouth. 'As I understand it, the Tibetans do not wish to establish formal relations with their neighbours. For instance, I have read that the last – and so far only – Englishman to reach Lhasa was in 1811. Their religion promotes a way of life that is contemplative and quite self-contained. China more or less leaves them alone to toddle along in what is virtually a medieval form of living. How would you change this?'

'Well, certainly not by a heavy-handed invasion. But we do have genuine grievances against the Tibetans, you know. In 1890, a Sikkim–Tibet Convention was concluded with China, whose suzerainty over Tibet we have always recognised. It was followed four years later by a set of trade regulations. The main purpose of these instruments, as far as we were concerned, was to secure formal Chinese recognition of our paramount rights in Sikkim, bordering Tibet, but they also dealt with matters of commerce, frontier delineation, etc. More tea?'

'No, thank you.'

Cuzon dabbed at his nose with a handkerchief clearly woven from the finest Egyptian cotton and leant back to ease his vertebrae. 'You see,' he continued, wincing slightly, 'the Tibetans have never formally ratified that treaty. They have just gone on their merry way, ignoring it completely. As a result, grazing rights at the border have been infringed, trade obstructed, boundary pillars overthrown and an illegal tariff imposed on the trickle of goods imported from India.

'The states that border Tibet – Bhutan, Sikkim and Nepal – are important to us. We, of course, recruit our Gurkhas from Nepal and the other two enjoy an autonomy which is underwritten by treaties with the British government. We are very sensitive to any encroachments by Tibet on these countries. We do not wish even the thinnest end of the wedge to be inserted here.'

Alice nodded. 'I understand that, but surely Tibet is not really a threat, is it? As I understand it, it is not exactly an aggressive country. On the contrary, in fact.'

Curzon frowned and a slight trace of irritation crossed his face. It was clear that he was not used to being contradicted, particularly by a journalist – and a woman at that! 'That's not the point,' he said. 'If the Russians are allowed to increase their influence in Lhasa, and without a presence there we have little chance of stopping them doing so, then Tibet, like the leopard, could change its spots. But there is another point. The Dalai Lama has shown great discourtesy to the British government. I have written to him twice on these matters and both letters have been returned unopened. We can't be flouted in this way in this region. Our reputation would be harmed.'

Alice stifled a smile. It was clear that he, Lord Curzon, was certainly not used to being treated like that. A case of *lèse majesté*, of course. But perhaps she was being unfair.

'Of course,' and she nodded. 'I quite see that. It would encourage the malcontents in India. But even so, sending in troops . . . surely a step too far?'

Curzon issued a viceregal sigh. 'We have no intention of "sending in troops", as you put it. I proposed to the government back home that we should send a commercial mission to Lhasa to begin negotiations of the widest possible scope, culminating, hopefully, with the appointment of a permanent British representative in that city.'

He paused and his sharp features resumed their air of painful disapproval. 'My colleagues in Whitehall took, ah, some time to consider this and, in the meantime, Russia protested that it had no designs on Tibet and, indeed, had no treaty concerning it with China. As a result, the government rejected the idea of a trade mission to Lhasa but agreed to my fallback suggestion of opening negotiations with China and Tibet at Khamba Jong, the nearest inhabited town on Tibetan territory to Giaogong, Sikkim's border town. As a result, as you have pointed out, we sent a frontier commission there, suitably protected, of course, to deter any question of the Tibetans attacking it.'

He forced a smile. 'I hope all this detail is not boring you, Miss Griffith, but I do feel it important to give you the background.'

'Oh, good gracious no, sir. I am most grateful to you for your patience. But now the commission has retreated back to India?'

'Indeed. It stayed at Khamba Jong – a most godforsaken place, by the way – for five months. We foresaw that negotiations might, er, languish, but I must confess that I did not think that none would take place at all. The Tibetans and the Chinese refused to open any formal negotiations, insisting that the commission must retreat from its soil.'

Alice cleared her throat and smiled at Curzon through her lashes. 'Perhaps a not unreasonable attitude, since we had entered Tibet without receiving an invitation to do so . . . .'

'I disagree. Quite unreasonable. We had displayed no aggressive intent while waiting on that arid plain. On the contrary, we traded very amicably with the local inhabitants, such as they were, and sent a succession of most courteously phrased messages to Lhasa. But there is more. While all this was going on, news reached us that two natives of India – British subjects – had been arrested in Lhasa, beaten and tortured and thrown into prison.'

Alice retained her smile. 'Ah, now, were they spies, I wonder . . . ?'

'That, madam, is neither here nor there. No civilised nation ill-treats nationals of another, friendly power and incarcerates them, without allowing them to defend themselves or approaching the government of their country. It was quite disgraceful. As a result, I am glad to say that the attitude of His Majesty's government has hardened. I have been given permission to launch – not an invasion – but a second mission into Tibet. This will advance some 200 miles into the heartland of the country to a place called Gyantse, a prominent Tibetan city and a little over halfway to Lhasa.'

'Escorted, presumably, by troops?'

'Indeed. We certainly could not risk the mission being attacked. But we have assured Lhasa that we have no aggressive intent. The mission will not lead to any occupation of Tibet or to permanent intervention in Tibetan affairs. As soon as reparation for past breakages of the treaty has been confirmed, then a withdrawal will be effected.'

A silence fell on the room as Alice, head down, scribbled quickly. Oh, how she wished she had learnt shorthand! Eventually, she looked up. 'What if they still refuse to negotiate? Will the mission advance to Lhasa?'

'That remains to be seen. At the moment, certainly the government does not wish it to do so.'

'Hmmm.' Alice sucked her pencil again. 'And what happens if the mission is attacked?'

'Then the escorting troops will defend it robustly.'

Putting down her pencil slowly, Alice frowned. 'Allow me to get this clear, Viceroy. Let me see. Where are we now? We are in November. It will clearly be some time before you can advance into Tibet. This means that, to penetrate some 200 miles into the country, the mission and its escort will have to cross some of the highest mountain passes in the world in the middle of winter. Surely this is a daunting prospect?'

Curzon nodded slowly. 'It will not be easy. But I am assured by Colonel Younghusband, who will lead the mission and who is vastly experienced in terms of travelling in the Himalayas, that it is quite possible.'

Alice felt anger stirring within her. She looked round the room with its opulent furnishings and then up at the ornate ceiling, from where the very latest electric fan was lazily

26

stirring the heavy air. Oh, the arrogance of the man, sitting in such comfort and planning to send men to fight in the depths of winter at such altitudes! So typical of the British ruling classes. So sure, even now, that the Empire could be extended on little more than a whim!

She sought to control her temper and coughed to clear her throat. 'But some of these passes must be . . . what . . . more than 14,000 feet high and blocked with snow by the time the column approaches them. Surely no force has been asked to make this sort of journey before. And what if the Tibetans dispute their passage?'

'We shall fight our way through. We shall have vastly superior firepower – if we are attacked, which I very much doubt. I am confident that the Tibetans will see sense, when they realise how determined we are.'

'I see. And when will the invasion – sorry . . . the journey – when will it begin?'

'I repeat. This is not an invasion. We estimate that the mission will set off in about the middle of December. Certainly before Christmas.'

Alice wrote and then slowly closed her notebook. She made as though to stand. 'I am most grateful to you, Lord Curzon,' she said, 'for giving me so much of your time and for explaining so carefully—' She stopped, for the Viceroy had raised a hand.

'There is one other matter, Miss Griffith,' he began. And she noticed that, for the first time, he looked just a little uneasy. He smiled again – the relaxation of the facial muscles that somehow did not communicate with the eyes. He leant forward.

'You will perhaps have noted that I do not usually give interviews of this nature to members of the press.'

'Er . . . yes. I confess that I was a little surprised that you agreed to my request – and most grateful, I must add.'

'Yes, yes. Quite. Well, there was another reason.' He leant back in his chair and his smile broadened. Alice tightened her buttocks instinctively. She sensed that the charm was being switched on. What was coming?

'You see, I have always been an admirer of your husband.'

'How kind.'

'Yes, well, although I may seem to you and, indeed, the world at large that I am . . . what shall I say . . . a conventional man whose own career has been marked by a rise to my present position via a well-ordered route: Eton, Oxford, the Commons, a junior position in government and so on.'

The Viceroy paused and Alice was not quite sure what was expected of her. So, she smiled in turn and murmured, 'Indeed.'

'Yes, well, that was quite true. But, if I may say so, I have also been quite adventurous in my own way – travelling widely in rather wild parts of the globe and that sort of thing. Not by any means so courageously as your husband, who,' he leant forward and shook his head slightly from side to side in mock astonishment, 'seems to have fought in every war, large or small, that this country has been engaged in for at least a quarter of a century. Yes. Quite remarkable – and, indeed,' he added quickly, 'matched virtually by you, step by step, or so it seemed.'

Alice smiled faintly and nodded at the compliment. What on earth was the man getting at?

'Yes. You see, this mission is quite important to me and I would give anything to be able to go on it myself. Alas,' he shrugged his shoulders and held out his hands resignedly, 'that is quite impossible. I cannot leave my post here. But . . .' He paused and then sat back. 'If your husband could go – not exactly in my place – but with my blessing, as my sort of representative, I would have much greater confidence in its success.'

'What?' Alice felt her jaw drop. 'Simon go to Tibet with the column?'

'Yes. Oh, I know it is a rather impertinent request considering that he and I have never met, but he is a man who has never shirked to answer a call to serve his country and I think he would be ideally placed to fulfil a rather unusual but important role with the mission.'

'But what . . . what would that role be? Surely Colonel Younghusband would be in command of the column?'

'Yes, and he will be joined by a splendid sapper, Brigadier James Macdonald, an old India and Africa hand, who has been recommended by Lord Kitchener and who will command the military escort. Both of these men are ideally suited to their tasks but, in my view, they would be perfectly complemented in tackling the strange and unconventional challenges presented to them by the presence of a man as widely experienced as your husband, who has been scout, soldier and diplomat all rolled into one in so many strange corners of the Empire.'

'Well,' Alice sought for words. Her mouth had dried

at the thought of the dangers that would be presented to Simon – a man no longer in his youth – in those high mountain passes if the column had to fight its way through deep snow, ice storms and, quite possibly, an army of indigenous tribesmen desperate to protect their country from invaders.

She swallowed. 'Sir, my husband is no longer a young man. He is nearing fifty, I doubt whether—'

Curzon cut her short. 'My dear Mrs Fonthill' – Alice noted that the form of address had now changed – 'I do appreciate your concern. But it is only a little over a year since Brigadier Fonthill, as he then was, was spending months in the saddle on the South African veldt in hot pursuit of those Boer generals Botha and de Wet, service for which he was awarded a DSO, to match his Companionship of the Bath. And, as you yourself have admitted, he is a man who quickly became bored at the life of a farmer back home. Kitchener himself was hugely impressed by the exploits of your husband in this late war and approves of him being approached to lend his services to help Younghusband and Macdonald in the difficult tasks ahead of them.'

'Well, I will certainly put this to him, sir.'

'No need to, ma'am. I have put my request to him in writing and I would be most grateful if you would carry my letter back to him.' Curzon raised his voice. 'Willoughby!'

'Sir.' The young secretary glided through the doorway.

'My letter to Brigadier Fonthill.'

'Very good, My Lord.'

Curzon was now beaming at his guest. Alice realised that this was a discreet form of blackmail: she had been granted the interview and been made privy to the Viceroy's thoughts on Tibet in return for acting as messenger to Simon. Her thoughts turned quickly to picture her husband, bandana wrapped round his perspiring forehead, on his knees in the dust beside some recalcitrant tea plant, cursing it and wishing that he had never invested his money in tea growing in the hills of Assam. Go? He would be off like a shot!

She suddenly smiled. Two could play at this game.

'Very well, Lord Curzon,' she said sweetly. 'I have a request to put to you.'

'Certainly, dear lady.'

'Well, if my husband accepts your request, I would like to accompany him on the mission.'

'What!' Within seconds, Curzon's smiling face had turned to thunder. 'Good gracious, no, madam. The mountains of Tibet are no place for a woman.'

'Do you know, sir,' she took a deep breath, 'that is more or less what was said to me about the deserts of Egypt, when Wolseley invaded that country, the hills of Afghanistan when Lord Roberts fought the Afghans, the jungle of northern Matabeleland when Cecil Rhodes's mercenaries created Rhodesia; the Khyber Pass when the Pathans revolted; and, indeed, the veldt of the Free State when de Wet and Botha roamed freely there. But I went anyway and reported on the deeds of our soldiers in all those places.'

'Yes, but . . . there will be no place for wives in this column.'

'Oh, I wouldn't go as a wife. You will shortly be receiving a request from the editor of *The Morning Post* that I be accredited as a war correspondent for that newspaper with the column. I shall wish to be treated as I always have been: as a journalist reporting on a matter of keen public interest. And the background facts that you have so kindly given me today will help me considerably when I come to carry out that task. I am very grateful.'

Ten minutes later, Alice leant back luxuriously onto the cushions in the viceregal carriage that Lord Curzon had insisted that she use to travel to her hotel and hoisted her parasol with a smug smile. It had been a good afternoon's work. She had gained splendid material for an exclusive story about what was undoubtedly an invasion by Britain of Tibet. She was, she knew, clever enough these days to roast the oleaginous Curzon in her story without appearing to deviate from reporting the facts, so staying within the the *Post*'s policy of supporting the Tory government through thick and thin. She would, of course, tell her unsuspecting editor that the Viceroy had certainly raised no objections to her accompanying the column as his newspaper's accredited correspondent – he had, of course, no idea that she was intent on going – and she had no doubt that Simon would accept the offer contained in the Curzon's letter, now housed safely in her handbag.'

She would write her story that evening at the hotel, despatch it to London from the cable office, send a telegram to Simon in the morning and, with any luck, catch the train and commence the long journey back to Assam and her husband tomorrow afternoon.

Ah, Simon! She smiled as she summoned up his face, then frowned at the thought of the danger he would face on those Himalyan peaks. She had not been dissembling when she had talked of his age. Yet, all those years of campaigning and farming had, she knew, left him as fit as a man half his age. What was he doing now, she wondered, at that very moment, among the tea plants in Assam, some 450 miles away?

CHAPTER TWO

In fact, Simon was fingering the butt of his Webley revolver nestling in its holster, as he stood, feet wide apart, questioning his overseer among the neat rows of tea bushes.

'Where did they go?'

The man was wide-eyed and obviously fearful. He gestured over his shoulder. 'They disappear into the trees over there, sahib. About six of them. They have knives.'

'Anyone hurt?'

'Yes, one. They stab him in arm. He all right, though. We bandage him up. But they take the few rupees the men have. Everyone frightened.'

Fonthill frowned. The workers had downed tools and were huddled together in the middle of the plantation, surrounding the wounded man who sat on the ground holding his arm. The group was well away from the trees which swept down from the hills and marked the edge of the plantation in a geometric line. Simon could see the opening in the woods from which the attackers had debouched.

He cursed silently. The labourers had been imported from Southern India, for the Assamese were notoriously averse to working on the tea plantations. The immigrants were better workers than the locals but timid and terrified of the wild men of the hills. This was not the first time that the Nagas had visited and robbed. They would have to be followed and taught a lesson, otherwise they would come calling again . . . and again.

He looking at his overseer appraisingly. 'Duleep,' he said. 'I left you with a rifle.' He gestured to the old Lee Metford that the man was now using as a prop. 'Why did you not use it?'

Duleep looked at the ground. 'Ah, sahib. I was afraid that if I use it they would come at me with their knives. So I pretended to aim it at them and blew my whistle to fetch you, as you told me. When they heard it they run away.'

'How long ago?'

'About five minutes.'

'Hmmm. Take the wounded man into the house and get Ahmed to look at the wound and treat it with antiseptic cream from the first-aid kit. But,' he held out a restraining hand, 'before you go, tell me if there is a good tracker amongst the men. Someone who could help me follow the Nagas' trail. They can't have gone far.'

The overseer thought for a moment, searching the huddled men with his yellow-balled eyes. 'Yes, I think.' He pointed. 'That one, the young one, on the edge staring up the trail, his hands on his hips. He is young and strong and came originally from Tibet but he was brought up near Madras in the south, where there is much forest. I think he knows the ways of the woods, as well as mountains. And he is brave. He tried to attack the man who stabbed. Oh yes.'

'Does he speak English?'

'Yes, he go to mission school, I think.'

'Good. Call him over.'

Simon broke open his revolver and checked that six cartridges were still in their chambers. Then he emptied the cartridges from the cardboard box that he had brought with him from the bungalow and stuffed them into the pockets of his breeches.

Sunil now stood before him, a slim young man of sixteen or so, who held his head back and looked steadily into Fonthill's eyes.

Simon held out his hand. At first the young Indian did not understand the gesture. Then, slowly – for he had never touched a white man before – he extended his hand and shook that of Fonthill limply, for he was, of course, unused to the custom.

'Sunil, I understand that you tried to attack the Naga who stabbed your friend.'

The Indian switched his gaze to the floor and spoke softly. 'Yes, sahib. Man, he stabbed my uncle. My uncle not harm him. I was angry.'

'You had every right to be. It was a good action. Thank you.'

The boy looked embarrassed. 'I did little, sahib.'

'Now, I propose to go after the Nagas. But I need someone to come with me. Someone who is not afraid of them and who can follow their trail. Can you do that, do you think?'

Sunil's face broke into a broad grin. 'Oh yes, sahib. I see the way they go. They crash through trees. I can follow. And,' he thrust his chest out, 'I not afraid of them.'

'Good man. Can you fire a rifle?'

A frown crossed the black face. 'No sahib. But I learn.'

Simon grinned. 'You certainly will. Duleep.' He spoke drily now. 'As you don't seem to want to use your rifle, please give it to Sunil here. I will show him how to use it. Pass over your bandolier, too.'

Sullenly, the overseer did so.

'Now,' Fonthill spoke to him again. 'Sunil and I will follow these Nagas, find them and teach them a lesson they will never forget. You will be in charge of the plantation while we are away. If there is any trouble, send a man to fetch Mr Jackson on the next plantation. Understand?'

'Yes, sahib.'

'Now, Sunil. Go back to the bungalow quickly and ask the cook to make sandwiches from last night's lamb – you are not vegetarian, are you?'

'No, sahib.'

'Good. Bring water bottles and fruit. We may be away overnight. Go quickly now. We have no time to lose. I will wait for you at the beginning of the trail over there.'

'Yes, sahib.'

Simon nodded to Duleep. 'Now, fetch the wounded

man and get the rest back to work. Tell them I am going to follow the Nagas and punish them so that they will never attack the plantation again.' Then he walked firmly past the men towards the opening where the narrow trail through the forest ended at the edge of the plantation.

He stood looking at it for a moment. He could see no sign of men having rushed down it. The trees stood thickly on either side of it – no broken twigs or anything of that kind. The earth of the trail itself was hard and bore no signs of footprints. God, he hoped that Sunil did indeed have tracking skills, for he doubted if he himself could detect the way the attackers had gone, if they moved off the trail. He looked upwards. The trees closed in on either side of the narrow path and seemed impenetrably dark. It would be so easy for an ambush to be launched from them.

The Nagas had knives, of course. He swallowed hard. The thought of cold steel involuntarily reminded him of Zulus and of Rorke's Drift all those years ago, where the warriors kept attacking the barricades in wave after wave through the night, howling and brandishing their assegais. He had seen stomachs ripped open by those blades that night. Damn! He should have witnessed enough blood spilt since that time to have washed away all those old fears. He shook his head and licked his lips.

If only 352 Jenkins was here! For over twenty years the stocky, immensely strong Welshman had been by his side through all the adventures he had shared with Alice, and sometimes with just the two of them, miles behind enemy lines. Known affectionately only by the last three digits of his army number – to distinguish him from the many other Jenkinses in the old 24th Regiment of Foot, that most Welsh of all British units – Jenkins had been his batman and had stood by him when he had been falsely accused of cowardice during the Zulu War. Together they had gone on to wipe away all memories of that accusation. After serving as the regimental sergeant major to the column of Mounted Infantry that Simon had commanded against the Boers, Jenkins had married at the end of the conflict and settled down to farm in South Africa.

Fonthill suddenly realised that, by going after the Naga tribesmen, he would be going into action again for the first time since 1878 without his old comrade at his side. Then the sound of footsteps made him turn his head to see a grinning Sunil running towards him, carrying a knapsack and rifle, the sun glinting from the cartridges cases in his bandolier. Well, he reflected, he had a new comrade now. He swallowed hard. Into battle once more!

He returned Sunil's grin. 'Give me the rifle. Now, watch me carefully. Before firing, make sure that there is a round inserted from the magazine into the breach, like this.' He worked the bolt.

The youth's eyes widened as he watched.

'The magazine takes ten bullets. You load it by taking cartridges from the bandolier . . .' and he went through the process of loading, aiming and firing. 'Do you think you can do that, Sunil?'

'Oh yes, sahib. I kill the man who hurt my uncle.'

'Good.' Fonthill smiled. 'Now, as I shall be walking ahead of you I don't want you to fire the gun accidently up my arse . . .'

'Arse, sahib?'

'Ah, sorry. It's a rude word for bottom. This little lever is the safety catch. Put that on until you want to fire the gun. On second thoughts, as you are tracking you must go ahead, but I shall be close behind you. We need to look particularly to see if and where they leave the trail. Understand?'

'Yes, sahib.'

'Good. Give me the haversack. Now, off we go. Quietly now. I don't think they will expect to be followed, but you never know. They could be waiting in ambush, so look very carefully about you.'

Fonthill shouldered the haversack, withdrew his revolver from its holster and gestured ahead. Together, they began the climb. The plantation was situated some 4,000 feet above sea level and, although he was long acclimatised to the altitude, the trail through the woods was steep and Simon was immediately forced to draw in his breath in short gasps. Sunil, however, despite coming from the southern lowlands, seemed to have no difficulty and his long stride began to pull him away, until Fonthill drew him back.

'Stay close,' he hissed.

They had climbed for some forty minutes and pines were beginning to outnumber the bold birches which had fringed the trail earlier when the youth held up his hand and dropped onto his hands and knees.

Fonthill stood above him, revolver in hand, breathing heavily. 'What?' he mouthed.

Sunil held his finger up to his lips and beckoned Simon

to kneel beside him. 'Look,' he whispered and pointed. At first, Fonthill could see nothing unusual in the dust and pine needles on the ground. Then, he noted that the needles had been disturbed and there, in the dust, was the impression, faint but clear, of the ball of a naked foot and of a big toe.

'This point to right,' whispered Sunil, 'which mean they go off trail. Through there.' He gestured to where the pine branches were no longer interlocked. A little further ahead, some had been snapped off to facilitate progress between the trees.

'Well done,' breathed Simon. 'We'll follow.'

Sunil held up his hand again and stood up. He put his head back and sniffed the air.

'They not far away,' he murmured. 'I smell them.'

'Smell them?' Simon was incredulous.

'Oh yes. They put oil on bodies and hair. I smell it when they hurt my uncle. They near. Perhaps they camp.'

'Or wait for us.' Fonthill swallowed hard. It was almost impossible to see beyond ten feet or so off the trail, where low bushes covered the ground between the trees. If the Nagas truly were near, then they could well be lying low there, hidden under the ground cover, waiting to pounce. Ah well, there was nothing for it but to advance.

He paused for a moment and then knelt to pick up a fist-sized piece of rock off the ground, which he retained in his left hand. Then he reached across to switch off the safety catch on Sunil's rifle, gestured to say that he would now take the lead and began cautiously to thrust his way through the faintly marked opening between the bushes and trees.

After some thirty yards a low sound ahead made him pause. He was unsure what it was – little more than a faint rustle, perhaps a small animal. He turned his head and Sunil, close behind him, his eyes wide and his pink tongue protruded between his lips, nodded and pointed ahead with the rifle, a little to the right.

Fonthill drew back his hand and lobbed the stone hard towards where Sunil had pointed. It crashed through the undergrowth and landed on something soft, eliciting a shout of pain.

Immediately, the bush came alive with six figures who sprang to their feet on either side of the trail, brandishing long knives and crashing through the undergrowth towards the two men.

It was, in fact, that density of ground cover that probably saved their lives, because it impeded the charge of the natives.

Simon fired instinctively and cursed as the bullet missed the leading man. His second shot, however, took the Naga in the breast and felled him. Dropping to one knee, Fonthill heard the crack of the rifle behind him and saw a second man fall – thank God Sunil had learnt to shoot! Then the third was upon him. He caught a glimpse of a gleaming black face and a naked torso and he ducked as the long knife swung above his head. He fired, with the barrel of the revolver almost touching the belly of his assailant. The man howled and doubled over, so that Simon was forced to thrust him aside and, panting, present the revolver again – at nothing.

There was just time to see one naked back vanish

through the trees before all was quiet again. Simon turned to Sunil. The boy had tears of frustration streaming down his cheeks as he struggled to work the bolt on the Lee Metford.

'Sorry, sahib,' he cried. 'I do not do this well. Thing is . . . what you say . . . stick.'

'Stuck. Here, let me.'

Fonthill took the rifle and eased the bolt back. He forced a smile and handed the gun back. 'You did well. I could not have shot them all with this handgun, but we got three of the varmints, anyway. Now we must see if any of them are still alive.'

In fact, all three of their assailants had been killed, with the third – the man whom Simon had shot through the stomach at close range – dying as they knelt by him. Fonthill realised that the boy was shaking and he patted him on the shoulder.

'It is not good to kill,' he said. 'I had hoped that this would not be necessary. But we had no alternative, for they attacked us and would surely have killed us if we had not brought half of them down. Sometimes, killing is the only way to survive.' He shook his head and realised that perspiration was pouring down his own cheeks. 'God knows,' he added quietly, 'I've done enough of it in my time.'

'Now,' he looked about him. 'They have clearly fled, presumably back to their village.' He took out his handkerchief and wiped his brow. 'I don't think they will try to attack us again, for they will have had the fright of their lives and seen three of their comrades killed. We have nothing to bury these chaps with, so I am afraid that we shall have to leave them here.'

Sunil leant down and plucked a leaf and used it to wipe his cheeks. 'We go back now, sahib?' he asked.

Fonthill shook his head. 'Afraid not, Sunil.' A thought occurred to him. 'Have you any idea what language these people speak?'

'Yes sahib. It is like Hindustani but different. Also like Tibetan, which I speak. But I understand them. I hear what they say when they shout at us. "Give us your money . . ."'

'Good. I want to go on to their village. Do you think you can find it?'

'Think so. More difficult to follow only three but I think they hurry now, they are frightened, so easier to see the way they go.'

'Good man. It will be a risk to enter the village when we find it, so I will still need you to come in with me, with the rifle. Then we must find the headman and talk, if you will translate for me. Pick up these chaps' knives and take them with you, for they will serve a purpose. Come on, now. I don't fancy staying out overnight.'

Sunil gathered up the three knives, cut a thong from the throat of one of the dead Nagas and tied them to his own belt, and the two began once more pushing their way through the undergrowth. Very shortly they struck another, clearly defined track through the trees and even Simon could see that it was well trammelled. After they had walked down the track for perhaps half an hour, Sunil tilted back his head and sniffed the air again.

'Village near, sahib,' he said. 'I think there are many of them. We must be careful.'

'Good.' Simon breathed heavily. 'Now,' he gestured to the rifle, 'work the bolt and enter a round into the chamber, as I showed you. Yes. Now take off the safety catch. Good. If you have to fire, for God's sake miss me – and then slide the bolt again to put another bullet up the spout, as we say.' He smiled, although he felt far from confident. 'I do not wish to kill anyone else today, only to warn them. Now, give me the knives and follow me. No need to be quiet. I want them to know we are coming.'

The two men, with Fonthill leading, revolver in hand, now strode ahead until the trail broadened out into a clearing, containing primitive huts made of bamboo and straw. In the centre of the clearing the ashes of a large fire were glowing. Simon stood for a moment, surveying the scene. There was no sign of any inhabitants. He cleared his throat, jerked his head to ensure that Sunil was following and strode into the centre.

There, he stood for a moment and then fired a shot into the air. The noise resounded back from the surrounding trees as though an artillery shell had dropped into the ashes of the fire. He turned to Sunil. 'Shout, and tell them we mean no harm. We have killed three of their people already, but we do not wish to kill more. We wish only to talk to the headman.'

The boy nodded and began talking. 'Louder,' commanded Fonthill, 'so that they can all hear. They're all out there somewhere.'

Sunil finished and silence fell on the clearing. There

was no movement from the surrounding wood.

'If the headman does not appear by the time I have counted five,' said Simon, 'tell them I shall burn all their huts and follow them and kill all their women and children. Count in Hindi. Translate the numbers as I call.'

Calmly, Fonthill selected a cartridge from his pocket, spun the chambers of the revolver and inserted it into the empty chamber, all as Sunil spoke. As silence fell again, Simon put the revolver back into its holster and called, 'One.'

Sunil repeated it, loudly, in a voice that cracked slightly.

'Two.' Still no movement from the forest.

'Three.' At this, a man materialised slowly from amongst the trees. He was naked, except for a wisp of loincloth. His hair was grey and a wispy beard clung to his chin.

'Ask if he is the headman.'

'Yes, sahib, he says he is.'

'Good. Tell him I mean him no harm and that is why I have put my revolver back into its holster. But it can be drawn quickly if we are attacked.'

Sunil translated. The chief's eyes remained fixed on Simon's.

'Good. Now tell him I want all of the villagers to come back into the clearing. They should put their weapons on the ground when they do so.'

Simon could see that the boy was now perspiring and his hand shaking. But he spoke out loudly and with seeming confidence. The headman turned and shouted something.

Slowly, men, and then women and some children, began appearing from among the trees. Some of the men carried bows and arrows and these were reluctantly lowered to the ground, followed by the long knives that all seemed to carry. Eventually, the three men in the middle were completely surrounded.

Fonthill nodded approval and looked around him. He swallowed hard. If any archers remained in the woods unseen and released their arrows, then he and Sunil were dead men. It was a risk he had to take.

'Very well.' He addressed the chief. 'Earlier today six of the men from your village attacked the men on my plantation. Then, they attacked us as we followed their trail.' Slowly, he untied the three knives hanging from his belt and, dramatically, one by one, he hurled them into the ground, blades first, so that they stood quivering.

'These,' he continued when the translation had been made, 'are the knives of three of those men. They are now all dead and their bodies lie back there in the forest, left for the wild dogs to eat them.'

He pointed back down the trail histrionically and a low murmur rose from the villagers. Some of the women began weeping.

The headman lifted his hand and spoke briefly.

'He say that men not come from this village,' said Sunil.

'That is a lie, for we followed their track to this village.' Fonthill let the words sink in then continued. 'We did not wish to kill these three men but they attacked us so they had to die.' Simon gestured to Sunil's rifle and drew out his own revolver from its holster and held it aloft. 'We have the weapons to kill all of you now, today, if we wished. But we do not wish.'

47

A sigh arose from the circle.

'I have come here,' he continued, 'to warn you all that any further attacks on my plantation will mean that I shall call the troops from Darjeeling and we will crash through this forest and kill every one of you and destroy your village. The power of the White Queen in England is as strong as the heat of the sun and it spreads as wide.'

Another murmur arose from the villagers.

'Now,' continued Fonthill, addressing the headman. 'I want two things from you. Firstly, I want an assurance that no more attacks will be made on my plantation. Secondly, I want the money that was taken from my workers returned and put at my feet now. The three men who survived the attack will not be punished, this time. If that happens, we will go in peace.'

The headman remained impassive, standing perfectly still, and Simon thought for a moment that his bluff had failed. What if this village was *not* the home of the thieves – and what if the chief gave a signal for a sudden attack to be launched on him and Sunil? They would be engulfed almost before they could fire a shot. He held his breath and willed himself not to withdraw the revolver that he had placed back in its holster. His thoughts flashed momentarily to Alice. Alice so far away. How would she know what had happened to him? What a way to be parted, after risking death together for so long!

Then the headman slowly turned, raised his hand and spoke a few words. Nothing happened for a moment, then three men broke out from the periphery and sullenly approached Fonthill, their heads down. They stood before him and fumbled in their breechcloths before throwing three bundles of rupee notes at his feet. Then they turned and resumed their places.

'Pick these up, please Sunil,' commanded Simon.

As the boy did so, awkwardly, for he still retained his rifle which he kept trained on the crowd, the sun peeped out from behind a cloud and the little clearing was illuminated with its rays, as though a signal had been given from the heavens.

'Good,' said Simon. 'Now, Chief, I want your word and then we will shake hands on it, as white men do, so that the promise must be solemnly kept.'

Sunil translated and the headman spoke slowly and clearly.

'He promise,' said the boy.

'Splendid. Now we shake.' He extended his hand and the man frowned. 'Explain what he must do to keep his oath,' Fonthill called to Sunil.

The youth did so and the two men shook hands, Simon crushing that of the chief in his own. Then he drew out his revolver, raised it in the air, fired it as though to seal the bargain and replaced it in its holster. As the echoes died down, he nodded to Sunil to go first and walked, without a backward glance, out of the clearing.

'Now, sahib, do we run?' asked the boy, once they were well down the trail.

'No. We walk a little way and then hide amongst the trees, just to make sure that we are not being followed.' He grinned and puffed out his cheeks. 'Then we go like hell back home – although I think I am too old to run, thank you very much.'

Suni gave a returning grin. 'The sahib was very brave there, in village,' he said. 'I think they too frightened to follow.'

And so it proved. The two stayed crouching in the undergrowth, just long enough to finish the sandwiches they had brought. Then, as swiftly as the trail permitted, they strode back down the hill towards the plantation and safety, reaching it just as twilight was turning the mountain tops to the east a soft pink. It had, reflected Simon, been a long and demanding day.

The next morning, Duleep reported that the wounded man had been treated and seemed no worse for the experience, although Fonthill ordered that he should do no work for the next two days. The men were all summoned to gather in the field and Simon, with a beaming Sunil at his side, addressed them.

He explained what had happened, praising Sunil for killing one of the Nagas, and then called forward all those who had lost their wages. He then solemnly reimbursed each man from the rupees they had recovered, insisting that each man count his money carefully. No man reported that he had been short-changed.

Grateful for this, for it reflected the honesty of each man, he then announced that Sunil henceforth would no longer work in the fields but would be promoted, with an increase in his wages, to stand guard and patrol the edge of the forest with the Lee Metford, with which he was now such an expert marksman, as a shield against further attacks. This brought expressions of approval from all of the workforce.

Back in the bungalow, Simon realised that he would have to write a report on the incident to the local magistrate. Men, even plantation owners, could not go around shooting natives without tendering a full explanation.

He was halfway through the task, when a runner appeared from the nearest settlement and telegraph point, carrying a telegram and a letter for him. The, telegram, of course, was from Alice. He tore it open and read:

GOOD INTERVIEW WITH GOD STOP AM ENTRAIN THIS AFTNN STOP WILL ARRIVE TWO DAYS STOP HAVE NEWS FOR YOU STOP LOVE YOU STOP A.

He grinned and then frowned. News? What could that be? Well, clearly, he would have to wait and see. Then he turned to the letter. It was, he noted, posted in Johannesburg, South Africa, and addressed in green ink in an untutored but vaguely familiar hand. Someone, perhaps, he had fought with – or even against – in the war?

He tore it open and his eyes went to the signature at the bottom. What he saw made the grin return to his face but it disappeared as he began to read. It ran:

Dear Bach Sir and Missus Alice,
I hope this finds you well as it leaves me. But I have sad news. My dear wife Nandi has died from the flu which has hit all the farms around here. We buried her four days ago. She spoke of you just before she

went. The children are at bordin schools in J'burg.
They are Nandis and not mine tho they are good
kids and Im fond of them. But I am missarable and
wonder if I could come and stay with you for a little
wile. Children will be aright at school. I could work
on the tea with you. I can afford the fair. Please reply.
Your faithful servant,
352

Nandi! His thoughts flew back twenty-six years and conjured up the picture of a small, oval face, the colour of *café au lait*, with black eyes that sparkled as they looked up at him as they sat beside a dam in Zululand. She had been the daughter of an Irishman, himself then a native *induna* or chief, and a Zulu woman of noble birth, living on King Cetshwayo's land just before the madness that became the Anglo-Zulu war broke out. Nandi, with her small white teeth and pert little breasts – she had revealed them to him with shameless innocence – had given evidence at his court martial and been the main cause of him being found not guilty. Nandi, the unspoken love of Jenkins's life, who had bought the Welshman happiness when they had found her again, as a hapless widow, and been forced to burn down her farm on the veldt. Now dead.

He fumbled, brought out a less-than-clean handkerchief and blew his nose roughly. It seemed hard to believe. He read 352's letter again and sought the date. The Welshman, who had only learnt to read and write under army tuition when they served together in the 24th, had not dated it, of course. Simon slowly put down the paper. Jenkins was 'missarable'. Well, the misery extended to his old comrade, for he too had been briefly in love with the little half-caste before Alice had come firmly into his life. But 352 had stayed unspokenly faithful to Nandi throughout the years, although they had not met again, except for a brief interlude near the Mozambique border, until the last war had brought them together. Fonthill shook his head. What rotten luck to have stayed true for so long and then have only less than two years together! He stirred himself. He must cable Jenkins immediately – and send him the money for the passage from Durban to Bombay, for the little man would have no idea how much a voyage like this would cost.

He dipped pen into ink and printed out a cable – luckily Jenkins had had the sense to put his address at the top of his letter. It said that a hundred guineas would be awaiting him *post restante* at the central post office in Durban, that he was to cable from there the date of his arrival at Bombay and that Simon would be waiting for him there to take him overland to Assam. (This was vital, for the Welshman, although brave as a buffalo, a fine horseman and an even better shot, had no sense of direction and could well have ended in Madras or, even worse, Kabul. Fonthill could only pray that Jenkins would be able to find his own way to Durban.) He then printed a second cable to his bank in Cape Town, instructing them to transfer the money, and sent a boy to fetch Duleep. The cables were too important to trust to anyone else.

Towards the end of the second day, just as the sinking

sun was performing its magical trick of transforming the mountains to the east into an extravaganza of colour, Alice arrived back, dusty, tired but happy.

Simon lifted her down from the buggy and the two embraced tenderly. As she looked up at him, Alice thought once again how lucky she was that she was married to a man who carried his forty-eight years so well. Only a few flicks of silver at his brow and a slight thickening at the waist betrayed his age, but his figure – at five foot nine he was a little over medium height – was trim and broad-shouldered and his body was firm from a lifetime of campaigning and farming. He shared with his wife high cheekbones and there was a reserve, or perhaps sadness, about his brown eyes that was unusual in an Englishman serving under a British Raj that usually bequeathed a certain arrogance to its white servants. Only a nose bent down and broken years ago by a Pathan musket reflected that Fonthill had lived on the edge of safety.

'I hope you've missed me,' said Alice.

'Certainly not. I have been visiting the girls in the bazaar every night. In fact, I am rather tired.'

She punched his chest. 'Not as tired as I am. You do realise, Simon, don't you, that we live in one of the most remote bloody corners of the Empire. It feels as though I have walked here from Calcutta.'

'Then come in and we'll have some tea. Or would you like something stronger . . . ?

'No. Tea would be fine. Although I will have you know that the Viceroy served me Darjeeling. Not our rubbish.'

'Oh, do be quiet. Come on. I have much to tell you.'

'Ah, and I you.'

Hand in hand, they walked into the bungalow, where a grinning tea wallah had already laid out the cups and saucers. Alice quickly washed and then joined Simon. 'Now,' she said. 'Who goes first with the news, although I do suppose nothing has happened here?'

Fonthill nodded sadly. 'Not quite.' First he told of the attack by the Nagas and of the expedition up into the hills to the village.

Alice frowned. 'Oh no. You had to kill three natives? Oh, for goodness' sake, Simon, you're not on campaign any more. You can't go around shooting people, my love. We will never be able to live in peace around here if you do that.'

Sighing, Simon explained the circumstances. Alice listened and nodded with approval when he told of the discovery of Sunil and his transformation into a tracker and brave fighter and of the recovery of the money and its restoration to the labourers. She wrinkled her brow, though, at the fact that the bodies of the three Nagas had been left in the forest.

'You should have told the chief where they were and led him to the spot,' she said. 'No doubt they have religious ceremonies for the burial of the dead which are important to them. You would have earned credit for that, my dear.'

'Hell, darling,' Simon snorted. 'There were about a hundred of them surrounding us. We could have been overwhelmed at any time. I couldn't act like some damned funeral director. Now,' he frowned. 'Speaking of funerals, we have had some news from South Africa. Bad news, I fear.' And he handed over Jenkins's letter.

She read it in silence but a tear slid down her cheek as she folded it and handed it back. 'She was a lovely, brave girl,' she said, sniffing. 'I am just sorry that dear old 352 couldn't have had longer with her. He must come here, of course – and he must bring the children with him.' Her eyes lit up. Their only child had died in childbirth some years before and they were resigned to being childless now. 'It would be wonderful—' Then she stopped. 'Ah, but not now. I don't think we would be able . . .' She tailed away again and she fumbled in her bag. 'I have a letter, too, my love, which affects everything. Here.'

Fonthill sat back in the chair and read Curzon's letter. Then he looked up, sipped his tea and reread it. He folded it absent-mindedly and looked steadily at his wife.

'You won't want me to go, will you?' he asked.

'I would rather you didn't, for all kinds of reasons: your age, the terrain – darling, this expedition – no, this *invasion* – will be attempting to cross the Himalyas in winter, in *midwinter*, dammit, and of course the obvious danger. But if you do decide to go, there will be one good thing about it.'

'What do you mean?'

'I am going anyway, to report on it for *The Morning Post*.'

'What! Don't be ridiculous.'

Calmly, she withdrew a cable from from her handbag and handed it to him. He read aloud:

AGREE YOU ACCOMPANY TIBET MISSION STOP AM
ARRANGING WITH C-IN-C YOUR ACCREDITATION STOP

STAY OUT OF DANGER STOP REPEAT STAY OUT OF
DANGER STOP. REGARDS BAXTER EDITOR STOP

Simon blew out his cheeks. 'The bloody fool! How can
you stay out of danger on an armed invasion! The Tibetans
are bound to resist. Of course you cannot go.'

Alice smiled sweetly. 'And *you* will go, my love . . . ?'

Fonthill squirmed slightly in his chair. 'I really think I
must. This is a direct appeal to me to help. Reading between
the lines, I think Curzon would like me, as his representative,
to be some sort of smoothing influence between this chap
Younghusband and the Brigadier, Macdonald, if things go
a bit wrong between them. Bring my . . . er . . . experience
to bear and so forth . . .' he tailed away. 'But look here,
Alice, we have had this debate so many times. You are the
best and bravest war correspondent, irrespective of gender,
in all of the world, but, my darling, this campaign would
be just one too far for you, I fear. Some of these passes
are . . . what? . . . 14,000 feet up and, as you say, we would
have to forge through them in midwinter, and probably in
the face of quite fierce opposition. A woman has no place in
that sort of territory. You would be, damn it all, you would
be, well,' he coughed, 'an embarrassment.'

A silence fell on the room broken only by a shrill call in
Hindi in the distance.

Alice spoke eventually, in icy tones. 'An embarrassment,
eh? How strange, but I don't remember you using that word
when I materialised out of that bloody desert in the Sudan
to rescue you and Jenkins from the Mahdi. If I remember
rightly, you were rather glad to see me.'

'Ah yes, well. Now, don't be silly, darling, that was different. You know. The temperature here is bound to drop below zero, I would think, and we will be under canvas. You would be . . . ahem . . . we would be the oldest people there. Even the senior officers will be younger. Think about it, darling. You were younger in the Sudan . . .'

Alice slapped the table and sent the tea cups rattling. 'And so were you, Simon. I am damned if I am going to stay here growing bloody tea while you invade Tibet. I am going with you and that's the end of it.'

The two sat scowling at each other until, eventually, Simon could no longer stop the smile from creeping across his face. He rose, bent down, kissed her and resumed his seat resignedly. 'Why do I always lose these damned arguments?' he asked of the ceiling. 'I don't know why I start arguing, I really don't.'

Alice returned the smile and, leaning across, squeezed his knee. 'A woman is always right, darling. Always. What about 352's letter?

Simon's reluctant smile was replaced for a moment by a frown. 'Terrible news about Nandi,' he said. 'I was very fond of her. Very fond.' Then his face brightened. 'But 352 must come with us. In fact, I wouldn't dream of going without him. He'll want to come, of course. Reading between the lines again, I reckon that he may well tire of farming on the veldt – particularly now that Nandi's gone.'

'And I have a feeling, my darling,' Alice's smile betrayed a little cynicism, 'that you are just as tired of growing tea in these hills. Am I right?'

Simon shrugged. 'I have to say, that I am even more certain than ever that I am not really cut out to be a farmer, whether it is pushing up wheat in dear old Norfolk or trying to persuade tea plants to poke their heads above the dust here.'

'So what will you do?'

'Jackson up the valley has had his eye on this plantation, ever since we bought it. We've made improvements here. I reckon I could persuade him to take it on, if I don't ask the world for it. And, darling, as you know, we don't need the money.' He thought for a moment. 'I have another thought.'

'Yes?'

'This young fellow I have discovered. The one who came up into the forest with me, chasing the Nagas . . .'

'What about him?'

'We could take him with us. We shall need a servant – dear old 352 is a bit long in the tooth to look after both of us now – and he would be ideal. I understand that, although he was brought up in the south, he is, in fact, Tibetan and speaks the language and knows the mountains. And he is as brave as a lion.'

'Good idea. How much time do we have?'

Simon consulted Curzon's letter. 'No precise date fixed for the beginning of the march into Tibet but he speaks of mid December – only five weeks or so away.' He read on silently. 'But he makes the point that, as this is very short notice for me, I could join the expedition a little later, before it penetrates deeply into Tibet. Good. That will give us time to pack up here, for 352 to sail across the Indian Ocean and for me to meet him in Bombay and bring him back here.'

Alice beamed across at her husband. 'The three of us off on campaign again, my love? What a refreshing thought. Do we have any champagne left in the cellar? I think we need – and deserve – a drink.'

CHAPTER THREE

Just five weeks later, a strange quartet rode wearily into the army camp at Gnatong, some twelve miles over the border into Tibet itself. In the lead rode Simon Fonthill, his rather awkward seat in the saddle reflecting not only the long journey they had just completed but also the fact that he had never been entirely happy on horseback. He wore a wide-brimmed canvas hat, a long woollen riding coat and jackboots. Alice rode behind, equally muffled against the cold and her swaying body moving sympathetically with that of her mount. Then came Sunil, riding a small pony, his black head protruding from the top of what appeared to be a blanket and his face alive with curiosity as he took in the strange sights all around him.

Bringing up the rear rode 352 Jenkins, leading their laden pack mule. It was clear that he was quite at home on horseback, although he cut a strange figure, for he was obviously short – perhaps some 5ft 4 ins in height – but looking almost as wide as he was tall. It was equally obvious, however, that he was immensely powerful. Even so, it had become clear to Simon and Alice, meeting him again after almost two years, that this was a slimmer and undoubtedly older Jenkins, for slivers of silver showed through the jet-black hair that stood up from his skull like a broom bottom. He now looked around him with contempt curling the great black moustache that spread under his nose like some dead rodent.

'Blimey,' he called out, 'this place is nothin' but a transit camp, look you. If it's a town it's one without 'ouses. Nothin' but army tents. Like Aldershot without the bleedin' glass 'ouse, see. Oh, sorry for the language, Miss Alice. Bein' on me own 'as made me a bit rough, see.'

Alice sighed. 'If you think that your bleedin' bad language is going to shock me, 352, after all these years, then you are mistaken. I am no debutante sitting on the stairs at the hunt ball – and anyway, I was always an army daughter, if you remember.' Then her frown turned into a smile as she turned round to look at him. 'But, bad language or not, it's wonderful to be with you again, 352. It really is.'

Jenkins looked abashed. Unaccustomed to compliments, he nodded and glared upwards along the trail that wound out of the little settlement to where it climbed into the mountain vastness ahead of them: the first outriders of Tibet's natural defences.

Fonthill turned back to them and jerked his head over his shoulder. 'That's the Jelep La,' he called. 'The pass is just over 14,000 feet high. That's where Younghusband and Macdonald and a whole damned army have gone.'

He looked around him. Apart from perhaps twenty or so rough huts, Gnatong had indeed become an army camp. Khaki tents stretched out onto the arid plain and the place was a-bustle with pack ponies, yaks, bullocks and mules, all being herded into separate enclosures by handlers, while other coolies stacked sacks and wooden boxes marked 'Ammunition – Handle with Care' nearby. Grazing fodder was being pitchforked into piles and firewood tied into bundles ready for loading. A handful of sapper NCOs were vainly trying to apply some sort of order, while even fewer officers observed the scene and stamped their feet to restore circulation. The sun shone from a cloudless sky but it was cold.

'Bloody 'ell, bach sir,' muttered Jenkins, 'if it's as parky as this down 'ere, what's it goin' to be like at that Jallopie Laa place up there? 'Ow 'igh did you say it was?'

'About 14,000 feet, I am told. But it gets even higher on the road to Lhasa. Something like 17,000 at a place called Karo La.' He grinned. 'Glad you joined, 352?'

'Oh instat, egstiteted . . .'

'Ecstatic?' prompted Alice.

'That's what I said. Let's find somewhere where I can put the kettle on.'

They trotted on until Fonthill found an officer who led them to where they could pitch their tents – one housing Alice and Simon and a second for Jenkins and Sunil – in the lee of a small wooden building that gave some protection from the wind. Then, while Jenkins and Sunil erected the tents and Alice sought kindling for a fire, Simon set off in search of the officer commanding the post.

He found him, a tired-looking major, huddled in a bell tent behind a trestle table piled with requisition orders and what appeared to be tables of loading weights. The man jumped to his feet when Fonthill introduced himself.

'Glad to see you have made it safely from Siliguri, sir,' he said. 'I was told to expect you.'

Simon pulled up a camp stool. 'There were no problems for us, Major. The way ahead was as plain as a pikestaff. It was clear that a bloody great army – or so it seemed – had tramped on before us.'

The Major smiled wistfully. 'Not as great as all that, actually, sir. But big enough to cause us all problems.' He jerked his head to the north-east. 'Trouble is that everything has to be carried in from the railhead at Siliguri and then loaded up here again and sent up there, higher into the mountains proper. Suitably guarded, of course.'

He sighed. 'There is no fodder up there above the treeline and no damned fuel for fires, either, so everything has to be carried on the backs of our animals, coolies and even the soldiers themselves. What's more, to get here, everything has had to come through the Tista Valley where anthrax, rinderpest and foot and mouth disease are rampant. We have already lost God knows how many animals from them eating aconite, a sort of poisonous plant known back home as monkshood or wolfsbane.' He shook his head.

Fonthill frowned. 'And all this before we meet any opposition from the Tibetans?'

'Exactly. We've seen nothing of them so far.'

'Hmmm. We are hoping to leave and start the big climb tomorrow. Is there a pack train due to go then?'

'Oh yes. It will leave at dawn. I do suggest you go along with it. It is not easy going by any means. The column will have stamped down the snow at the top but the trail is covered in packed ice and it's as slippery as all hell. You will have to lead your horses. Do any of you suffer from mountain sickness?'

Simon wrinkled his nose. 'Yes, I've been worried about that. But all three of us have roughed it high up in Afghanistan and the Hindu Kush without trouble . . .'

The Major shook his head. 'Not the same. The route to Gyantse is much higher. And . . .' he blew out his cheeks, 'if we have to go on to Lhasa – which everyone wants to, of course – we shall have to cross just under the peak of the Nojin Kang and that's a happy 24,000 feet, although the pass ain't quite that high, thank goodness.'

'Good heavens. What's the antidote to mountain sickness?'

'You will have to ask the medics but from what I have heard the best thing is to take phenacetin with brandy and purgatives, but,' he grinned ruefully, 'it ain't exactly easy to carry out normal bodily functions at that height in that cold. You don't want to have to chip ice off your arse, so to speak. Obviously, the most efficient antidote is to get down to lower altitudes as quickly as possible. But that's not easy either. The answer is probably to hang on until you are acclimatised. I presume that you have got snow goggles with you?'

'Yes, and we picked up the warmest clothing we could

find back in Siliguri.' Fonthill hitched his stool forward. 'Major, I would be most grateful if you could tell me what sort of force Younghusband and Macdonald have taken with them up into the mountains. It would help me to do my job if I had all the facts.'

The Major looked at him quizzically. He was obviously going to ask 'and what sort of job would that be?' but thought better of it. Which was just as well, mused Fonthill, because he was still not completely sure what his duties would be.

'Certainly, sir. Right. Now,' he pulled a closely printed long piece of paper towards him. 'Let's take the load-bearers first. There are just over 10,000 coolies that are going in relays up to the column and back and, let's see . . .' he added quickly, 'and just under 18,000 pack animals, ranging from mules to yaks, and even taking in,' he looked up and grinned, '138 bloody buffaloes, would you believe.'

Simon returned the grin. 'Yes, having looked around outside, I *would* believe. 'Do you think all of those animals will survive this first climb up to Jelep La?'

'Wouldn't think so for a minute. But we are summoning all of the pack animals we can find in the whole of Bengal, Nepal and Sikkim and even further afield. They are not all conditioned to working at those altitudes, you see, and we have just got to suck it and see, so to speak. Apart from that, even the mules have been slipping on the ice and plunging down God knows how many feet to their deaths.' He shook his head. 'No army has had to advance and fight at these heights and in these conditions before. It is going to be touch and go, I am afraid.'

'Hmmm. What about the fighting men. The escort?'

The Major consulted his sheet again. 'At the moment, some 1,150 soldiers, with four guns and two Maxims. Do you want the breakdown?'

'If you please.'

'Right. There is one section of the 7th Mountain Battery, with two ten-pounder screw guns . . .'

'Ah, splendid in the mountains but pretty lightweight if we have to pound down rock defences. Anything heavier?'

''Fraid not. There are two seven-pounders manned by the 8th Gurkhas.' He grinned. 'They're about as old as the late Queen and they are called Bubble and Squeak. Beautiful antiques but not more than that, I would say.'

'Lord! Go on: infantry?'

'Six companies of 8th Gurkhas . . .'

'Splendid chaps. Couldn't be better. Fought with them in Afghanistan under Roberts and then along the Khyber in the Pathan Rebellion, some years ago.'

The Major lifted his eyebrows. He had not been quite sure about Fonthill's background but it was clear that the fit-looking middle-aged civilian sitting before him was a man of some experience. He nodded. 'Quite agree, sir. First-class fighting men. The Indian army couldn't exist without them.'

'I presume there are more?'

'Oh indeed, yes. There are eight companies of the 23rd Sikh Pioneers.'

Fonthill nodded but frowned. 'Essential in this territory, of course, but not exactly fighting men.'

'Oh, I think you would be surprised, sir. They have a good

fighting record, as well as being fine swingers of a shovel.'
He consulted his list again. 'Then we have a half company
of sappers and miners, the usual backup specialists: field
hospital wallahs, field engineers, telegraph and postal
detachments. Oh – and a machine gun attachment of the
1st Battalion of the Norfolk Regiment.'

Fonthill jerked back his head. 'Are these the only white
troops?'

'Afraid so, sir. But this is only the first contingent, don't
forget. Depending on what opposition we meet, we are
bringing up reinforcements from Bengal to stand by at the
border.'

'Hmmm. I should think so.' He leant back on the stool.
'Everyone thinks that the Tibetans are not a militaristic
race, just because it is a society dominated by religion
and the monks and lamas. But, don't forget they invaded
Sikkinese territory back in '86 and it took quite an effort, I
remember, to dislodge them. By the sound of it, ours is not
exactly a meticulously prepared invading army.'

'Quite so, sir. But, as I say, so far so good. There has
been no opposition so far.'

'Good. Let's hope it stays that way. Thank you for your
help. We will join the pack train tomorrow morning.'

'One more thing, sir.'

'Yes?'

'It is a little brisk down here, although not too bad in
the sun. And the valley up ahead is not unpleasant. But
up in the mountains the temperature will plummet.' He
pulled a chit towards him and began to scribble. 'You say
you found some garments back at the railhead but you

will need the best protection there is.' He looked up. 'How many are you?'

'Four. Three men, one woman.'

'Woman?' The Major's jaw sagged for a moment.

'Yes. My wife is the accredited correspondent with the column for *The Morning Post*.' Fonthill experienced a touch of pride in hearing the words and immediately felt rather ashamed of himself. He coughed. 'No need to make special provision for her, though. She can look after herself, you know.'

'Ah yes . . . er . . . I am sure.' He continued scribbling then offered the chit. 'Do take this to the quartermaster – he's in the large tent further down on the left – if you feel you are inadequately catered for in terms of heavy gear. It is best to be careful.' He stood and held out his hand. 'Good luck, sir. I hope I shall be joining you up there soon.'

'Very kind of you, Major. Thank you.'

The next morning Fonthill and his companions were up long before the emerging sun had begun to make the mountain tops stand out in jagged relief. The Major's benevolence with warm clothing was immediately appreciated as they began dismantling the tents and loading the mule in the semi-darkness. They all now wore long sheepskin, *poshteen* coats, special, lined Gilgit boots and fur hats. As they worked, Fonthill realised that the climatic conditions would be particularly difficult for Sunil, who had been living in moist, steamy Madras in the south only a few months before.

The youth, however, seem impervious to the cold. 'I lived

in Tibet on high, big plateau until I was twelve and went with parents to India,' he grinned. 'I remember the cold and the wind and will get used to it again, sahib. But I am very glad of this big coat and hat now. Oh yes. Very glad.'

Jenkins, his breath floating out before him like a cloud, called out as he tightened the girth strap on the mule: 'The lad is goin' to be a good shot, look you. While you was talkin' to the Major last night, I was teachin' 'im on the old Lee Metford. We nearly turned out the guard, them thinkin' we was bein' attacked by the terrible Tibetans. But the lad was good. 'E would make a good soldier, I'm thinkin'.'

'Glad to hear it, Sunil. Well done.'

The youth's teeth flashed white.

The four joined the small column at its head, where it was led by a young lieutenant, riding a pony. 'Mind if we come along?' asked Fonthill.

'Good gracious, no. Name's Jones.' They shook hands.

Simon looked ahead up the stony valley, speckled by patches of snow, through which the now well-trodden trail led. 'How far up to the pass?'

'Not so much a question of how far, as how high.' The young man smiled. 'Gnatong is some 12,000 feet or so above sea level. 'Jelep La is about another 2,000 or so and,' he gestured ahead, 'it gets steeper as we go. I've done this trip about three times now and,' he gestured behind him, where laden coolies walked, heads down, in single file and a sprinkling of Indian troops led equally laden mules, 'I gain more respect for these chaps every time I go. It's damned hard work for animals and men. Mind you, I have to keep my eye on the coolies. We've lost a lot to desertion when the wind blows up there. They just disappear.'

Simon nodded and fell back to ride alongside Alice. 'All right, darling?'

'Yes, thanks. But I'm glad I am riding and not walking. I'm getting short of puff, I think.'

'Well, take your time because later on I think we shall have to lead the ponies.'

Soon the trail began to climb quite steeply upwards and the ground underfoot had had its covering of snow trampled down firmly so that it had turned to ice. The animals started to slip and slide and the order to dismount was given. As the pack train climbed upwards, some of the load-bearing animals, fresh from the hot Tista Valley and unaccustomed to the cold, began to buck in an attempt to shed their loads and their tenders began shouting and beating the beasts.

'I don't much like this postin', bach sir.' The plaintive cry came from Jenkins, whose moustache had now begun to wear a light dusting of ice. His face was drawn and waxen.

Simon remembered that his old comrade, the bravest of men in battle, had always had a fear of heights to add to his dread of water – he couldn't swim – and loathing of crocodiles. 'Sunil,' he called back, 'slow down so that Jenkins can hold on to your pony's tail. Keep an eye on him. He hates heights.'

'Yes, sahib.'

So the little column wound its way, slithering and sliding, shouting and cursing, up the mountain towards the pass. Simon, Alice and Jenkins began to find it difficult to catch their breath at the high altitude and walking became increasingly difficult for them. Sunil, however, seemed to revel in the conditions and constantly called encouragement to Jenkins, panting behind him.

It took six long hours climbing up the southern face of Jelep La, without respite, to reach the pass, merely a thin knife-edge in a narrow cleft. Here they were met with an icy blast that took their breath away. The descent to what was said to be the pleasant Chumbi Valley, some 5,000 feet below, promised to be as bad, if not worse than the ascent, so camp was set up just below the summit, where the wind blew less strongly.

Somehow, Jenkins – back to his resourceful, scavenging self now that there was no precipitous drop immediately near – managed to 'find' kindling wood and he was able to light a fire shielded between the two tents and the four of them huddled around it, cupping mugs of tea in gloved hands.

'How long was Nandi ill, 352?' asked Alice.

The Welshman's eyes immediately saddened. 'Oh, not long, was it. Not much more than a week, I think.' He shook his head slowly. 'You see, when her husband, the Boer feller, you know, kicked the bucket durin' the war, she 'ad no one to look after 'er, see, an' she was 'ard done by to look after the girls an' 'erself. There was no food to be 'ad, though the Dutch commandos,' he grinned sheepishly, 'you know, bach sir, the very blokes we was chasin' all over the bloody veldt . . .'

Simon nodded.

'Well they dropped 'er off whatever they could spare – but it wasn't much because they 'adn't got much themselves, see. We saw to that.'

'Oh dear,' Alice bit her lip. 'It must have been terrible for her. Poor Nandi. She didn't deserve that.'

'No, she didn't,' Jenkins's eyes flared in the firelight. 'She never done anythin' to 'arm anybody. She was a good, brave lass. But I think them months on that open veldt, givin' what food she 'ad to the little ones, weakened 'er, see. An' when the flu came she didn't 'ave much resistance left, like.'

Silence fell on the little gathering. Simon cleared his throat gruffly. 'Who is looking after the farm now, then, 352?'

'There's an old ex-squaddie runnin' a farm about ten miles away. After the war, 'e'd 'ad enough of the army an' bein' a non-drinkin' man,' Jenkins shook his head sadly, 'fancy that, not drinkin', funny bloke – well, 'e'd saved 'is army pay and, with nobody back 'ome, he bought the farm, from an old Dutchman who'd lost his son in the war. I asked 'im to look after my place while I'm away. Told 'im he could sell whatever cattle 'e wanted to as payment, as long as he didn't clear out the 'ole 'erd. Told 'im I would be back in about six months.'

Jenkins threw back his head and his teeth flashed under his moustache. 'Don't see much chance of that 'appenin' now, though.'

Alice frowned. 'What about the girls?'

'Well, old Jacob – that was Nandi's old man – 'ad a sister living in Jo'burg and Nandi got on very well with 'er, see. She's got girls of 'er own at this school where I've left our two. I've left 'er money to keep payin' the fees and to look after the girls 'till I get back.'

He frowned and stared at the ground. 'To tell the

truth, I feel a bit guilty about leaving 'em, because I'm very fond of 'em, them bein' Nandi's an' all. We weren't blessed with kids of our own, although,' the big grin returned, 'we 'ad a lot of fun tryin' . . . Oh sorry, Miss Alice that's a bit rude – an' I'll be remindin' you of your own . . . er . . . problems thereabouts. Sorry, really.'

Alice waved a dismissive hand.

Jenkins looked across the flickering flames to Fonthill. 'I was very low when she went an' I kept thinkin' about the great times that we – the three of us — 'ad 'ad over the years, that I wondered if you'd take me in for a bit. Never thought,' the great grin returned, 'that we'd be off again on our adventures, just like the old times. What a treat. Mind you, I never thought it would be as bloody cold as this. Thought India an' tea growin' would be nice an' warm an' that.' He looked around. 'This is not quite what I 'ad in mind, I 'ave to say.'

He turned to Sunil. 'I suppose it's all right for you, Sonny, eh. Comin' back 'ome, look you?'

The youth had been following the conversation, his mouth open. Then he grinned. A warm relationship had already built up between the Tibetan and the Welshman. 'Oh yes, bach, but it's colder than I remembered.'

Everyone laughed and Fonthill gestured to the tents. 'Time to turn in. If you take my advice, I wouldn't take much clothing off when you climb into your sleeping bag.'

'Goodness.' Alice blew out her cheeks. 'I had no intention of doing so. Goodnight everyone.'

The descent from the Jelep the next day was, indeed, worse than the ascent, for the trail was now a sheet of blue-black ice, at least for a few thousand feet from the summit. Three of the packhorses slid off the glittering surface and, screaming pitifully, fell down the mountainside, bouncing from rock to rock as they went. Their handlers hardly had time to throw themselves flat to avoid following their charges.

'Oh, dammit to hell,' shouted Lieutenant Jones. 'Why the hell didn't you keep 'em away from the edge?'

But there was little space away from the edge on that narrow trail as it zigzagged down. Jenkins now had taken to clawing his way with one hand on the face of the nearly vertical rock face as he led his pony with the other.

Simon looked back at him, biting his lip as he watched the slow progress of his comrade. Jenkins on a mountain, he knew, was an accident waiting to happen.

And happen it did.

Suddenly, the Welshman's pony reared, as a lump of ice above them broke free and fell past them to the depths below. Jenkins was forced to let go of the animal's halter and, in doing so, he slipped on the ice. In a second, he had fallen onto his stomach and, as the others watched in horror, he skidded away across the narrow path and his body slipped over the edge. Only his gloved fingers, clinging to a projecting rock, prevented him from disappearing into the abyss.

'Oh shit!' he shouted, as his body, the legs swinging, dangled over space. 'For God's sake, save me. Save me!'

Simon, his mouth open in terror, tore off the glove on his left hand, crawled gingerly to the edge and grabbed Jenkins's sleeve. 'Alice!' he screamed. 'Get that rope coiled on my saddle. Hang on old chap. I've got you. Hang on.'

Fonthill was suddenly aware that a huge, bearded Sikh was lying by his side, flat on his stomach and reaching down to take Jenkins's other arm which was waving upwards blindly. Somehow, the Indian's clutching fingers caught the edge of the fabric and exerting all his strength, pulled 352's arm and body up so that the Welshman's second hand could join the other gripping the stone. There Jenkins hung, still swinging.

Reaching behind him, Simon became aware that Alice was kneeling behind him. 'No,' he gasped, 'I can't take the rope yet, I'm still hanging on to 352. Can you form a loop at its end, with a slip knot, and then put it into my hand? Quickly now.' He turned his head to the Sikh. 'If we both pull can we get him over the edge do you think?'

The Indian shook his head. 'No, sahib. Him too heavy. We all go with him. Fix rope to a rock, then slip loop over his foot and then we pull him up.'

'Oh, bloody 'ell lads,' wheezed Jenkins, his face now completely white. 'Don't put yerselves in danger. Just let me go. I can't 'ang on much longer, see. God bless you all fer tryin'.'

'No. Hang on, dammit.' Simon felt the noose thrust into the hand stretched behind him and his fingers tightened over it. 'Is it fixed behind?' he croaked.

'Yes,' Alice's voice was equally hoarse. 'And we've got two more Sikhs hanging on. Can you loop it over his foot?'

'I'll try.' He turned his face to that of the Sikh. 'Can you grab him with your other hand?'

'I try, sahib.'

But the Sikh needed to keep his free hand jammed against the rock to prevent himself slipping over the edge. Simon gulped and rested his cheek for a moment on the cold ice as his mind raced. He dare not let go of Jenkins's sleeve for that would be putting all of his comrade's weight – thirteen stone plus? – onto 352's precarious hold on the rock and the Sikh's equally tenuous hold on his other sleeve. If he fished over the edge with the rope held in his own free hand would that send himself, too, slipping away down the mountainside? He stole a glance over the edge. Far, far below he caught a glimpse of the trail zigzagging down. He swallowed to avoid nausea. Nothing for it, but to try and hang the rope down to catch one of Jenkins's feet.

'Listen, old chap. I am going to try and dangle this rope with a loop on the end down the side of your body. Can you see if you can put your foot into the loop, make sure it's tight and then we'll pull you up?'

Simon could now only see the top of Jenkins's head but he saw him nod. Slowly, he inched the edge of the rope over the ice until it dropped level with the Welshman's face. Then, his cheek pressed hard into the ice to gain some stability, he felt someone's hands press down onto his ankles.

'Don't worry, darling,' he heard Alice gasp behind him, 'I've got you. Push the rope down.'

Slowly, he lowered the rope, unable now to see over the edge and glad that he couldn't, for his previous glimpse of the sheer drop below him had curdled his stomach. But he felt it brush down past the hanging body and then it tighten slightly, as, somehow, Jenkins managed to push his boot through the loop onto the bottom end of the rope.

'Good man,' shouted Simon. 'I think you're in. Now, behind me: gradually pull on the rope to tighten it. Gently now.'

The rope became taut as it took most of the burden of Jenkins's weight and, as it disappeared over the edge, the thought struck Fonthill that the pressure on the rock would fray and sever it. But the line was resting on polished ice, as smooth as a debutante's cheek. There would be no friction there.

'We've got him,' he shouted. 'Now pull him up, slowly now.'

Gradually, the weight on the two hands holding the tunic relaxed and, at last, the Welshman's great strength was allowed to come into play and, pushing down into the loop with his foot, he was able to haul himself upwards until, with a gasp and crash he was over the edge and lying panting on the path.

From behind and in front of the rescuers a ragged cheer went up and Simon realised that the progress of the column had been halted and that the path was lined with watchers, who had all been holding their collective breath.

'Oh my God,' breathed Jenkins, his black hair, now lank, plastered across his forehead and his face glistening with sweat. 'I thought I was gone, look you, I really did. Thanks to all of you, ever so much. Thank you, bach sir. Thank you.'

'Don't mention it, old chap. It was a pleasure to go fishing with you.' Simon realised that tears were pouring down the cheeks of Alice and Sunil, of whom the latter had been putting his puny weight to that of the two Sikhs holding the end of the rope. 'Just rest there a minute and then try and stand. Don't worry. You're not going to fall again, I promise you. We will all rope up to make sure you don't.'

Jenkins nodded and then, with infinite care began to crawl on hands and knees across the trail away from the cliff edge. Then, with Simon's help he stood.

He looked round him. 'I shall personally see that you all get the Victorian Cross, see,' he croaked. 'For great courage displayed on the edge of this fuckin' mountain. Oh, sorry, Miss Alice. Language. Language.'

Alice, wiping her tears, waved away his apology.

Fonthill now solemnly shook hands with the three Sikhs who had helped with the rescue and without whom, there was no doubt, Jenkins would have been doomed. He then retrieved the rope from where it was still tied around the Welshman's boot and carefully secured it around his waist. Then, throwing out some slack, he looped it around Sunil and, finally, around his own waist, securing it tightly.

'Now,' he said, waving to Lieutenant Jones who had been observing the rescue from the path down below, 'let us get off this . . . ahem . . . blasted mountain. But slowly, now, and carefully. We've held up the column long enough.'

Gingerly the column resumed its march down the icy trail, with Jenkins now hugging the mountainside with even greater tenacity, if that was possible. Thankfully, however, as they descended, the air grew warmer and the ice began to disappear.

It was desperately slow work and, at about 2,000 feet below the Jelep, the column halted at a place called Langram, where the main party had itself made camp on the original descent. Here, at last, the treeline began, so providing fuel for the campfires and welcome shelter among the birch and pines, where glossy green pepper ferns, bindweed and even some begonias grew at their roots, providing some happy links with home.

They met a straggling line of unladen mules, horses and bullocks returning from the invading force. From the officer in command they learnt that it was here that Younghusband on his descent had been met by Tibetan emissaries from Yatung, a little way ahead. They had pleaded with the Colonel to return over the pass to Gnatong where delegates, he was assured, would visit to talk with him. Younghusband refused. Would he then, he was asked, stay where he was for two or three months? No was the reply again. Down below at Yatung, said the Tibetans, was a great wall in a gorge which blocked the way. What, Younghusband was asked, if the gate in the wall was locked against him? Then I shall blow it open and march through, came the reply. The emissaries departed sadly.

The returning officer joined Jones and Fonthill's little party round their campfire that night – where whisky was dispensed to celebrate Jenkins's escape – and from the young subaltern they learnt that the gate in the Yatung wall had, in fact, been left open and the army had gone through without opposition. A forward supply base had been established in the Chumbi Valley some six miles or so ahead, where the main party had been joined from the north by the original expedition from Khamba Jong. The escort under Macdonald had gone forward to reconnoitre the way ahead of the base, which had been christened New Chumbi and where it was planned that Christmas would be spent.

'Good God!' exclaimed Alice. 'Is it Christmas? I had completely forgotten. Oh dear, I have bought no presents for anyone. I never gave it a thought.'

'Well,' sniffed Jenkins, 'I knew it was approachin', like.'

Simon regarded him sceptically. 'How did you know?'

'Back up there in the snow, I saw this old feller, dressed in red, with a great white beard. "Where're you goin, bach?" I called. "Back to me sledge," 'e shouted back. "It's too bloody dangerous for me up 'ere," he says, "I'm off out of it, back to Iceland, where it's warmer." Very wise, I thought. Very wise.'

Everyone sighed and grinned, although Sunil, listening intently as ever, remained with his mouth open, looking from face to face, with a puzzled frown on his face.

The next morning the two trains parted company and the descent continued. The ice had now given way completely to a brown slush which provided almost as insecure a footing as the ice, but the trail had widened and the column was able to increase its pace. Soon they advanced cautiously down a wooded gorge and, rounding a bend, their way was blocked by a stone wall over which the roofs of a small village could be glimpsed. But the gateway set in the middle of the wall was propped open and they were waved through by a grinning Gurkha.

On the other side the trail led through the mean streets of Yatung and immediately the little column was winding its way between excited men, women and children, all smiling and waving.

'Blimey,' said Jenkins, whose confidence had now been regained and who had taken to bowing from his pony and waving his hand in little gestures, 'It's like King Eddy's coronation. I think we can put away our guns.'

'We're now in Tibet proper,' called back Jones. 'But I'm told that the people of this valley are not your true Tibetans. They are not of pure Tibetan stock and they're called Tromopos. Much more friendly, I hear, than the folk further into the land. So it's not too surprising, perhaps, that our way has not been challenged so far.'

'Just as well,' muttered Fonthill. 'We could never have fought off an attack up on that damned mountain.'

The way now led down in easy stages until they were in the sunlit valley of Chumbi itself, which, at only 8,000 feet above sea level, seemed green and pleasant indeed, with the river Ammo Chu gurgling and bouncing between rocks in its middle. They plodded along, following the course of the river, until by the end of the day, they reached the base camp of New Chumbi, which had been established a few miles beyond the village of Chumbi.

The camp sprawled out onto the plain in a series of ridged tents, interspersed with mounds of provisions, which had been roughly fenced off. Fonthill could see no sign of any defence works, except for guards who patrolled the perimeter. The base, he presumed, was not far enough advanced into Tibet to be considered under danger of attack and certainly any troops advancing across the rocky plain would be seen at a distance in the thin mountain air.

The great white peak of Mount Chomolhari, at 23,950 feet looking remarkably like the Matterhorn, thought Simon, glittering and shimmering over all in the distance.

They were met by a quartermaster who directed where the pack transport should unload and sent a giant Sikh (Alice remembered hearing that Kitchener had promised Younghusband that he would select only the tallest native troops to accompany the mission, so to impress the Tibetans) to show them where to pitch their tents. Then Fonthill went in search of Younghusband.

He found the Colonel in a tent no more impressive than any other, leaning back in his camp chair, reading a book, one booted foot on a table leg to balance it. He sprang to his feet on the approach of the new arrival and stood, smiling gently, his hand outstretched. Simon took it and found his hand engulfed in the firmest of grips. He regarded Francis Younghusband keenly.

Before setting out, Fonthill had done his best to add to the little he knew about this famous frontier diplomat and explorer of the Himalayas. He knew that the man was nine years younger than himself and had been born into a very distinguished Indian army family. Gazetted into the King's Dragoon Guards, he had joined them at Meerut, India, in 1882. Despite having few private means with which to keep up with his contemporaries in this smartest of regiments, he was appointed adjutant and then given six months' leave to travel in Manchuria. An explorer was born.

Although only in his mid twenties, he rode alone through Inner Mongolia and Xinjiang and then, through a previously unexplored pass, into Kashmir. He was seconded to the Indian government and clashed amicably with the Russians in the high passes and in 1893 became the first political agent in Chitral, where he met the peripatetic Curzon, with whom he formed a bond. While home on leave, Chitral was attacked by Pathans and a British mission besieged in the capital. Younghusband had pleaded to be sent back but when permission was refused he went back anyway, to report on the uprising for *The Times*, eventually galloping on ahead of the relieving column and becoming the first man to reach the beleaguered garrison. All this adventuring was frowned upon by the Indian government and he was relegated to obscure civil service postings until Curzon rescued him and appointed him Resident in Indore, from where he had been summoned to lead the mission to Tibet.

It was, then, a man who – very like Fonthill himself – had earned almost myth-like status in the Empire, who now shook Simon's hand so firmly. He was not physically impressive, being only 5ft 6ins tall, but he had a wiry frame and rather bulbous piercing blue eyes that, usually, were kindly and sparkling, above a walrus moustache of Kitchener proportions.

'I am amazed that our paths have not crossed before, my dear fellow,' he said now, pumping Fonthill's hand. 'Although I have been shut up in these, I must say, beautiful mountains for most of the time that you have been gallivanting about the Empire doing goodness knows what splendid things.'

Simon smiled deprecatingly. 'Good gracious no,' he said. 'I have been a gadfly compared to you, sir.'

'Oh please don't "sir" me, Fonthill. I shall be covered in embarrassment. After all, I have just been given only the temporary – very temporary most probably – rank of colonel, while you ended the Boer War as a brigadier general, indeed.'

'Yes, but also very temporary. And I am now just an ordinary civilian who, to be quite frank, is a little puzzled about what My Lord Curzon wants me to do here.'

Younghusband threw back his head and chuckled. 'Yes, well, I can quite understand that. We have me, supposed to be in overall charge of the mission but particularly here to serve a diplomatic purpose, and we have Macdonald, with the also temporary rank of brigadier, in charge of the escort and therefore all military matters, and now you here as well. But, between us, if we don't get to Lhasa and put a spoke into the Russians' wheel, I shall be very surprised.'

Then he frowned and gestured into the tent. 'But I am forgetting my manners, my dear fellow. I am sure you would like some tea?'

He shouted loudly in Hindustani and the two sat down, a trifle awkwardly, opposite each other on camp stools. Fonthill felt an immediate liking for this charming and twinkle-eyed man, who seemed so definitively English and yet who had spent most of his adult life in the mountains of Central Asia.

'Curzon, of course, wrote and told me that you had accepted his invitation to join the mission,' said Younghusband.

'I do hope that you had no objection to that?'

'Of course not. Although, like you, I was a little unsure

about what exactly would be your role on this rather difficult expedition.'

'Quite so. Well . . .' Simon shifted a touch uneasily on his chair. 'Curzon wrote that I would be his special representative with the mission and suggested that I should put myself at the disposal of yourself and of General Macdonald, with . . .' he paused awkwardly again 'the suggestion that, if problems did emerge between the two of you, perhaps I could provide some sort of ameliorative influence. I'm afraid it's all rather vague.'

Younghusband regarded him quizzically for a moment, with one eyebrow raised. 'But you accepted his invitation, despite the perhaps rather nebulous nature of the brief?'

Fonthill grinned. 'Oh, like a shot. You see, I have always wanted to go to Tibet and the Himalayas have always fascinated me. Alice and I were planning to go climbing there some years ago but we got caught up in the Pathan rebellion, got . . . er . . . diverted, so to speak and the opportunity then slipped away.'

'Ah yes, your wife – the amazing Alice Griffith. I have been a committed reader of her work in *The Morning Post* for years. Her name was never on her pieces but the word spread and I grew to recognise her style and became an admirer. I presume she is with you?'

'Oh yes. She has been accredited to the column.'

'Good. I won't make the mistake of questioning her physical ability to cope with conditions on the march. Knowing her record, I expect that she is probably fitter than any soldier, well, white soldier, that is, in the ranks. She will stir us up, no doubt. It is difficult to entertain here, of course, but when you have settled in you must come and have supper.'

'That's kind of you.'

'There are three other correspondents expected soon, you know, Edmund Candler of the *Daily Mail*, Perceval Landon of *The Times*, who is supposed to know the Viceroy personally, and I believe that some feller from Reuters News Agency is also on his way. No doubt your wife will know them?'

'No doubt.'

Younghusband produced his infectious chuckle again. 'I am not at all disconcerted by the presence of press people here. But Macdonald – he's gone ahead reconnoitring the way forward, you know . . .'

Simon nodded.

'Yes, dear old Mac isn't happy with them at all. Feels that they are an intrusion and an unnecessary complication on what could be a difficult project.'

'I must confess I feel that, in this age of democratic, open government and so on, that's a rather old-fashioned view.'

'Quite so. But now, we have digressed on this important matter of your role here . . .' He was interrupted by the arrival of a rather dishevelled, Mongolian-looking native, wearing what looked like dirty sacking, who brought in a teapot and bowl of milk, placed it on the table without ceremony, grinned at the two Englishman and shuffled away.

'Tibetan,' grunted Younghusband. 'A local. Like to employ 'em when I can, although,' he smiled, 'they are not exactly overflowing with social graces. No lemon, I'm afraid. Milk?'

'Thank you.'

'Yes,' his pouring duties completed, the Colonel sat back, teacup in hand. 'Back to you. Curzon wrote to me about you in exactly the same terms as he expressed to you. Saying that your great experience in the field, both as a . . . ah . . . rather irregular soldier and sometime amateur but successful diplomat could be of invaluable help both to Mac and to me.'

Simon smiled. 'Offering me as a kind of dogsbody, by the sound of it.'

'Well, a bit more than that, I would think. But, as you have already hinted, I think there was a bit more to it than that. You see,' he paused. 'May I be frank?'

'Of course.'

'Well, although I was delighted when Macdonald was appointed – lots of experience and, as a sapper, well qualified to handle the sort of tasks that have cropped up on this excursion into most difficult terrain: road laying, bridge building and all that, you know?'

Simon nodded.

'Also, he had the backing of Kitchener, the army commander-in-chief in India, a fellow Engineer.' Younghusband sipped his tea, reflectively. 'Which brings me to the point. It is no secret, alas, that Curzon and K don't altogether see eye to eye on the breakdown of responsibilities between the army and the civil service in India. Two strong personalities and,' he smiled, 'egos, clashing here, I fear.'

Nodding again, Fonthill felt that, at last, they were getting to the nub of the affair – and a faint sense of uneasiness about the future of the expedition crept over him.

'Yes, well,' the Colonel continued, 'to some extent that split might have repercussions here with us in Tibet. There is no one person in overall command of this expedition. Macdonald has been given a rank senior to me, of course, and is formally in charge of the escort and is responsible for the safety of us all. I am the diplomatic head of the mission and, as our orders strictly give the purpose of this whole enterprise as opening up diplomatic channels with the Tibetans – with strict orders *not* to instigate military operations against them or to occupy Tibetan property or territory – it is a command situation which could prevent problems.'

A silence fell on the tent, broken only by the distant grunting of mules and the creaking of harness. 'Hmmm,' responded Fonthill. 'I see that. Although,' he smiled, 'it all depends, of course, upon the character and personalities of the . . . er . . . joint commanders.'

The Colonel put down his tea sharply and brushed the edge of his luxurious moustache. 'Absolutely!' he cried. 'You have put your finger on it exactly. There lies the problem. Now,' he leant forward, 'when he returns you will see that Macdonald will pitch his tent and that of his staff on the right-hand side of the column.' He raised an enquiring eyebrow. 'You will appreciate the significance of that?'

'Oh yes. The senior officer always takes that position in the field.'

'Quite so. Well, I have never made a fuss about that, but

I find it a little irksome. The most important thing, however, is that I am discovering that Macdonald is ridiculously cautious on the advance, to the point that he has slowed down the progress of the whole column and is constantly in opposition to me about the supplies needed to support us. He is now foraging ahead to set up supply depots for the march. We are becoming so preoccupied with our supply line that it appears to me that it will be next Christmas before we even get to Gyantse.'

'I see. Are you expecting to be challenged, militarily by the Tibetans along the way?'

'We just don't know. It has not happened so far, but we can be vulnerable, of course, in the high passes and we have more of those to surmount before we reach Gyantse. It remains to be seen.'

'Well,' Simon frowned, 'I suppose the General feels his responsibility keenly. An armed advance deeply into so-called enemy territory will throw up logistical problems. The further you go into these mountains in midwinter the longer your lines of communication – always the most vulnerable part of any advancing troops. And, of course, these mountains and plateaus are among the most inhospitable places on earth.' His frown softened into a smile. 'I have already seen enough to realise that.'

'Good. You appreciate the military situation. But, you know, I am not unaware of the problems we have in trying to approach the Tibetans and getting them to talk. They are ruled not by the Dalai Lama, as everyone thinks, but by the religious caste of monks and lamas that completely dominate the country. These are all, it seems, xenophobic medievalists who subjugate the people in the most cruel way.'

Younghusband leant forward in emphasis. 'My dear Fonthill, do you know that until Mac improvised a basic little wooden cart here on this plain to carry supplies, wheeled vehicles had never been used in Tibet! Just think of that.'

He took a gulp of tea and leant back comfortably. 'They are arrogant in the extreme and contemptuous of our power in India. Any sign of weakness on our part – our snail's pace advance, looking as though we are timorously afraid of them, or any temporary retreat, will give them heart and distance them even further from the negotiating table.

'You know,' the walrus moustache bent into a warm smile, 'I suppose that both Macdonald and I have our individual careers at stake on this mission. I want to surge on ahead, as fast as is humanly possible, to put pressure on the Tibetans to negotiate with us and give us equal, if not greater influence in Lhasa than the Russians. Mac, on the other hand, is terrified of being defeated by an attack on us by the Tibetan army. It would be the end of his career. Hence his excessive caution.

'But look here. Things are not quite as bad, perhaps, as I have painted them. These are very early days in terms of our task here. I am only pointing out embryonic problems which, I do hope, will not develop further and to illustrate to you what, I think, was in the back of Curzon's mind in asking you to join us as his . . . ah . . . what you might call "special representative". Because of K, he could not put me in overall command here, but I feel he could sense that issues, such as those I have described, could arise to threaten the success of the mission.'

The bulbous eyes twinkled. 'It's a great tribute to you, my dear fellow, that he thinks you might prove to be an ameliorative influence here, if things get worse.' He gestured towards Fonthill with both hands, as though giving some kind of benediction.

Simon sat deep in thought and was unconscious of the darkness developing within the tent as the sun disappeared quickly. Eventually, he grunted. 'I am most grateful to you for explaining things, so openly, ah . . . may I call you Francis?'

'Of course, Simon.'

'I presume that Lord Curzon did not quite put things so clearly to you?'

'He did not. It would have been difficult and even indiscreet to have done so.'

'Quite. Well, Francis, let me say now that the role you have described is one that makes me uncomfortable. For I do not think that I have the skills, nor indeed the seniority here to play it competently. What I will seek is an actual job, perhaps reporting to Macdonald, because I am more a soldier than a diplomat, I fear. I am used, for instance, to scouting ahead of an army and to advising on how to avoid specific dangers that loom before the main force.'

The Colonel nodded. 'That sounds very appropriate in terms of our advance in this wild country. I would have no apprehensions about you reporting to Macdonald.'

'Good. However, let me say that, if I can be of any assistance to you personally in terms of the possible problems you have described, I shall be only too happy to help. I am here to serve.'

'Most kind of you. Now,' Younghusband stood and extended his hand, 'you will want to settle in before it gets completely dark. There's hardly a twilight in these parts. I have much enjoyed our talk. Call on me at any time.'

'Thank you. I will.'

Fonthill walked back to where his little party's two tents had been erected, his brow wrinkled in thought. He had warmed to Younghusband but was far from sanguine about the part he could play in the column's advance. He hated the thought of becoming some kind of arbitrator, shuttling backwards and forwards between the two leaders. No, that was not for him. Ah well, the only thing to do was to wait for Macdonald's return and to suggest to him some positive role he could play. But what he had heard did not augur well for the future of the expedition.

CHAPTER FOUR

New Chumbi proved to be a delightful place to wait for the return of the forward party and one of the most pleasant sites for an army staging post that Simon and Alice could remember. All around, the giant mountains looked down, craggy, ice-bound peaks with skirts of dark pines breaking out from the snow lower down. The plain itself was a huge, flat meadow, sprinkled with the remains of the summer's wild flowers that reminded them all again of home: wild strawberries, anemones, primulas and celandines. Finches and red-legged crows chirped and croaked and larks swooped overhead, singing their more felicitous song, while the bark of a fox could be heard most mornings from the lower foothills as the sun touched the tent tops at about 7 a.m.

'I am beginnin' to feel distinctly warmer,' said Jenkins,

returning one morning from the river, holding up two brown trout.

'How did you get those, for goodness' sake?' asked Simon. 'You don't have a rod and line with you, do you?'

'Oh yes.' He held up one gnarled hand. 'Me fingers, see. These little fishes love bein' tickled, look you. Just right for breakfast, isn't it?'

Fonthill grinned, remembering that Jenkins had been brought up on a farm in North Wales and how his bucolic skills had often saved them from hunger in the wild.

'The lad got one, too.' Jenkins jerked his head to where Sunil was running towards them, a silvery fish wriggling in his fist.

The youth had now taken to shadowing the Welshman for much of the time, listening intently as the workings of the Lee Metford, and also of the more modern Lee Enfield rifles carried by Jenkins and Fonthill, were explained to him and adjusting his posture in the saddle under Jenkins's tuition. Slowly, however, he began also to form a bond with Alice, sitting watching silently as she scribbled her copy and then taking it for clearance to the Gurkha captain who, much to the latter's disgust and Alice's chagrin, had been given the task of press censor. He had become, noted Simon, almost one of the family, always there, always anxious to learn or be useful. It was clear that he had not forgotten the language of his ancestors, either, for he had slipped into the role of bargaining on their behalf for the delicacies – buckwheat and potatoes, plus fodder for the animals – that local people had taken to bringing in to the camp.

'I wish I could take him home to Norfolk,' confided Alice. 'He would be invaluable in Norwich market on Saturday mornings.'

Two days later, General Macdonald returned with his forward scouting party.

'Blimey,' muttered Jenkins, as the party came into sight far across the plain. 'It's not so much a scoutin' unit, more another bloody army.'

Indeed, it was; a force of some 800 men that the General had taken with him to reconnoitre the way ahead to the north. His objective had been the great fortress of Phari, some twenty-eight miles further up the valley, and over the pass of Tang La towards the towering mass of Mount Chomolhari and so into the interior of Tibet. As the huge scouting party entered the camp the news soon spread: another seemingly impregnable wall across a gorge had had its door opened for the troops and the defenders of Fort Phari itself had welcomed the invaders with open arms, running towards the soldiers with their tongues protruding from open mouths – the mark of friendship.

Fonthill, Alice, Jenkins and Sunil watched the arrival with interest. 'Hmmm,' muttered Simon. 'No cavalry to speak of. Look.' He pointed. 'There are only some thirty what you could call horsemen.'

It was true – and they looked completely exhausted. A young red-haired officer led what appeared to be a group of Sikhs, swathed in *poshteens*, some wearing great fur hats and others with woollen scarves tied across the top of their turbans and under their chins, walking ponies all of whom had their heads hanging low. For these men and beasts, at least, it had obviously been a testing excursion.

'Not cavalry, really,' mused Alice.

'More Mounted Infantry, I'd say,' offered Jenkins. 'An' not well trained at that.'

Simon turned towards Sunil. 'We all think about Tibet as being a land of mountains and high passes,' he said. 'Are there many more plains or plateaus like this one further inland?'

'Oh yes, sahib.' The youth nodded his head vigorously. 'Many. Only not like this one, as I remember.' He gestured around him. 'This very nice place, with flowers, etcetera, etcetera, etcetera. Not further up, through the mountains. There are flat places but very high. Not much grows. Very wide and long and stony and not nice. No, not nice at all. I live there when little.'

Jenkins nodded. 'We're goin' to need cavalry,' he said. 'At least for scoutin' an' that.'

'Exactly.' Frowning, Simon looked across at his old comrade. They had not spoken about the slip over the trail's edge after they had arrived at the camp, but it had been preying on his mind.

'I believe that,' he said, 'if we have to continue this march onto Lhasa, the capital of Tibet, there are, in all, five high passes to cross – counting the one from which we have just descended. How do you feel about that, 352?'

The Welshman returned the frown. 'Ah,' he said eventually. 'No other way round then, eh?'

'Afraid not.'

'Well, to tell you the truth, bach sir, I'd be a bit worried about that, like.'

'I thought you would be. But I don't want to leave you behind. Do you think you could manage them?'

Jenkins sucked in his moustache. 'O' course I could. Just a question of takin' a deep breath, look you, an' stayin away from the bleedin' edge, like. Nothin' to it, really, eh?'

Fonthill sighed. 'Absolutely nothing to it, old chap. Well done. We will all keep our eye on you – and we will rope up. That should make you feel better, eh?'

The Welshman frowned again and stared ahead, to the north-west away towards the towering peaks. 'Well, if it's all the same to you, bach sir,' he said, 'I'd rather not, see. I'd be worryin' all the time, like, about bringin' you all down the mountain the quick way, with me. You see . . .' His frowned deepened as he thought for a while. 'This bein' frightened of 'eights is silly, really. P'raps after I've slipped down the fifteenth mountain I'll 'ave conquered it, like. So the only way is to keep goin' with yer chin up, look you.'

'Good man. That's the spirit. But we will still keep an eye on you.'

'Now that would be kind, so it would. Thank you kindly.'

Simon decided not to pay his respects to Brigadier General James Macdonald immediately, for it was clear the man had much to do. But the next morning he sent a message, asking if he could wait upon him. The reply came back: 'Whenever you like.'

The General, who had, like Fonthill, been appointed a

Companion of the Order of the Bath, had, Simon knew, originally been ordered to join the mission as a colonel in charge of the building of roads over the border and into Tibet. Later, however, he had been promoted on the express order of his fellow sapper, Lord Kitchener, to take command of the mission's escort. He had served earlier in East Africa, somewhat controversially, and then in a more fighting role against Muslim rebels in Uganda, but his experience as an Engineer was wide. Nevertheless it was whispered he had been appointed to take military command of the expedition only because he was the most senior officer on the spot in Sikkim nine years later.

The man who stood to meet him at the entrance to his tent was of medium height and certainly looking older than his forty-one years. He was unsmiling and bent to stub out a cigarette as Fonthill approached. His head was bald and his nose, sharply pointed and tipped slightly upwards at its end, stood out above a less than luxurious but wide moustache. The General's expression, Simon, could not help but note, seemed sad and tired.

'How do you do,' he said. 'Do come inside.' He spoke with a faint but distinct Aberdeenshire accent.

'Thank you, General. I hear that you have had a most successful trip up into the mountains.'

'Ah yes. I suppose one could say that. Cigarette?' He offered an open silver cigarette box.

'No, thank you.'

Macdonald struck a match, lit his cigarette and deposited the matchstick carefully into a tray that was laden with nub ends. 'At least we met no opposition, although that is not to say that we shan't be opposed if we carry on much further into the hinterland.'

Fonthill noticed the 'if', but decided not to query the qualification. Macdonald gestured to a camp stool and sat opposite in a more comfortable folding chair. He was obviously a man of few words and sat, smoking, waiting for Simon to speak.

'Apart from paying my respects after my arrival, General,' Fonthill said, breaking the silence, 'I felt I should talk to you to see if you had any idea of the role you would like me to play in the column.'

'Hmmm.' Blue smoke curled past his nose as Macdonald put his head back and considered the tent ceiling for a moment. 'Lord Kitchener has written to me about you and has commended you warmly to me. Said you did first-class work in South Africa during the last show there.'

'That's very kind of him.'

'Yes.' He regarded Fonthill through the thin cloud of smoke, his eyes narrowed. 'I think we were both involved in the Boxer Rebellion, although we did not meet.'

'Really?' Simon scanned his brain quickly. He had no memory of encountering this wiry, rather distant man in the hothouse that was Peking during the siege of the city. Perhaps on the relief expedition?

He put the question and Macdonald nodded. 'I ended up as Director of Railways,' he said. 'Not the most glorious of postings but I knew of you, of course. You were always out there in front, getting up to all kinds of remarkable things, as I remember.'

The tone of cynicism was alleviated to some extent by a

faint smile on the Scotsman's face, but Simon did not take kindly to it. 'Well,' he said, frowning, 'my wife was locked up in that bloody city beleaguered by those fanatics and I was desperate to get in there and join her. It was a most difficult time – and I have to say that the relief expedition, you will remember, took its time reaching Peking.'

'Yes. Quite so.'

Another silence fell between them and Simon stirred again. 'I am quite sure that you have an excellent staff here, General, and I would not wish to intrude at a senior level.'

Macdonald carefully knocked the ash off his cigarette and coughed. 'Yes. I am very happy with the fellows I have, although, you know, they are all predominantly infantry officers.' There was another pause. 'Sooo . . .' He drew the word out slowly. 'Do you have any suggestions to make, Fonthill?'

'Well, I do so with reluctance, since I have only just arrived here, but I am most anxious to be of use and I agree with Younghusband that I might have rather more to offer on the military side than as some sort of diplomatic aid.' He smiled, seeking agreement, but Macdonald remained silently regarding him, through his blue smokescreen.

'Yes . . . er,' Simon sought for the right words to continue. Blast the man, he was being forced to present his qualifications for being in Tibet at all! He refused to offer the obligatory 'Sir,' and said: 'General, you may know that I ended the Boer War as a brigadier general – very temporary, I hasten to add – in command of two units of cavalry?'

Macdonald nodded.

'I spent the last two years of the war – that is when

101

the Boers took to the veldt and, organised as highly mobile commandos, conducted guerrilla warfare against us – I spent it in the saddle chasing those remarkably elusive and, to my mind, rather brilliant farmer generals all over the Free State, Natal and in the Transvaal.'

The General remained silent.

Simon cleared his throat. 'In fact, the chaps I had were never really trained cavalry at all, in that they were not from the smart regiments, like the Hussars and the Dragoons. No, my men were a rather ragtag lot from the gold fields and cities who volunteered to fight for us. In effect, given that some of them had seen service on foot, they became Mounted Infantry.'

'Yes.' Macdonald spoke slowly. 'I have about thirty of the same sort of fellows with me now, although, of course, they are Indians, mainly Sikh Pioneers.' He drew on his cigarette again. 'As far as I can see they have been spending quite a lot of their time falling out of their saddles, but I have a good young Irish chap leading them, young but good.'

Fonthill felt his heart sink. Was his idea going to be rubbished before he proposed it? 'Yes, I saw them return. They looked as though they were more or less shattered.'

'They were.'

Another silence. 'My idea is this, General,' Simon said, leaning forward. 'Although I was an infantry subaltern years ago in the old 24th Regiment of Foot in Zululand – you will remember Isandlwana, Rorke's Drift, etc?'

Macdonald nodded. Damn the man! Didn't he have a tongue?

'Yes, well,' Fonthill continued, 'I do not consider myself a regular soldier and, anyway, as you say, you have a first-class staff filling the key roles. I have always served outside commissioned ranks, acting as scout and sometimes intelligence officer. The Boer War, however, was different, I was recommissioned and had my own command. Nevertheless, my role was, what you might call, irregular. It was Kitchener's idea that I should stay with my men out in the veldt, fighting the Boers at their own game. Travelling light, without artillery or baggage, living in the saddle and attacking them wherever we could find them and harassing them when we could not attack.'

Macdonald nodded again, but there seemed to be a light of interest glowing in his dark eyes.

'Now, things will be very much different here, of course. But you will need horsemen. From what I have learnt of the terrain ahead, it will not be all high, snowbound passes but also vast, stony plateaus, very inhospitable but where you will need mobile scouts to range far ahead of you and spy out the Tibetan defences and indeed their forward movements against you.' Fonthill paused to gather breath. This was like pushing water uphill.

'At the moment,' he continued, 'you have some thirty men, not well trained by the look of them. You will need more, in my view, with good, hard-working ponies. I know these are difficult to find but you will need them, I promise. I am glad to hear that you have a good young fellow with them at the moment but he looks young and inexperienced.'

He leant forward again in emphasis. 'General, I can train those men. Sikhs are not generally regarded as good horsemen, but they can learn. I have with me my man Jenkins—'

Macdonald interrupted. 'The famous 352?'

Ah that was better! 'Yes, 352 Jenkins. He was my regimental sergeant major in South Africa and gained a bar there to the Distinguished Conduct Medal he earned with me in the Sudan. He is a splendid horseman – a damned sight better than me, I assure you – and he trained all our men in the Transvaal. If you can get more men, Sikhs or whatever, and ponies I will guarantee to train them on the hoof, so to speak, and, given the help of Jenkins and your red-haired fellow, lead them – I hope well.'

His words hung in the air. Then, Macdonald removed the cigarette from his mouth and said: 'I like the sound of it, Fonthill. It sounds to me as though you could be invaluable. But, you know,' he stubbed out the cigarette, 'you would have to have rank. Lieutenant colonel – how would that suit?' He gave a rare smile. 'A demotion, I fear, from your last post but probably the best we can do.'

'That's of no matter to me, General. I suppose that means that Jenkins must rejoin, too. Perhaps colour sergeant – we shall not exactly be cavalry, only Mounted Infantry?'

'Very well. Now I must get K's approval to this, because, although I can promote, I can't take in someone from outside the army and give him a position of such seniority without his permission. I'll telegraph him. Mind you, I don't think we need bother with uniforms out here. They can't be seen under the *poshteens* and furs anyway. I will get on with all this now and also inform Ottley – he's the young captain in charge of our so-called cavalry – that he's got a new CO.'

Macdonald rose from his chair and extended his hand. 'Now, if you will excuse me, for I have much to do. Good to have you with us, Fonthill.'

'Thank you, General.'

Fonthill strode away feeling much happier in his mind. At least he had carved out a role for him and Jenkins to play – and one with which they were reasonably familiar. They would be independent to a large extent and not having to work under the sharp nose of Macdonald. He frowned. A strange fish, indeed! He must obviously be handled with care. So too would Ottley, the young Irishman. He would not take kindly to having a very irregular soldier imposed in command over him. Simon sighed. At least it would be an irregular who had earned the CB and Distinguished Service Order. Perhaps that would mollify him somewhat.

He found the flame-haired captain instructing his Sikhs on how to groom their horses correctly; a good sign. He introduced himself and immediately Ottley's face lit up.

'Ah, delighted to meet you, sir,' he beamed. 'I read about the work you did with Mounted Infantry on the veldt in the recent bit of trouble. Wish I'd been with you then. What are you up to here, in this godforsaken place?'

Simon coughed awkwardly and then transmitted his news. 'I am sorry that you will be losing your independence, my dear fellow,' he said. 'But I promise that I am here to learn as much from you as you from me. It looks as though you have already done a good job in teaching these Sikhs how to ride.'

The young man's smile did not lessen. 'Good lord, no, sir,' he said. 'We are not exactly Horse Guards, you know.

If a rabbit leaves its hole, half of my troop are liable to fall out of their saddles. But they are good men. Basically good soldiers and I think you will become proud of them.'

Fonthill held out his hand. 'I am sure I will.' They shook hands. 'What is your Christian name?'

'William.'

'Good. I will address you so. And you must call me Simon.' He grinned. 'No Horse Guards stuff here, William. We will be a *very* irregular unit. Oh, one more thing I should tell you.' He explained Jenkins's role.

Ottley frowned at first, but when Jenkins's name was introduced his face brightened. 'Oh! 352. Goodness, sir . . . er . . . Simon, he is almost as famous as you. Got a DCM, didn't he?'

'Two, in fact. The first in the Sudan and the second against the Boers.'

'Well, he obviously knows his stuff.' He raised an eyebrow. 'Any chance of us being the first into Lhasa, do you think?'

'Wouldn't mind putting a guinea or two on it.'

'Splendid. Look forward to it. Do you want to superintend the grooming?'

'No. I have other things to do. I will meet the men in the morning.' A thought struck him. 'No. Better not yet. My position has to be confirmed by Kitchener. So let's keep this under our hats for the moment. But I don't anticipate any problems there. Carry on, William.'

'Thank you, ah, Simon.'

Fonthill walked away with a new-found spring in his step to find Alice and Jenkins. His wife, as usual, was not in their tent, for, with little hard news to transmit back to Fleet Street, she was regularly out and about watching the behaviour of the troops and the coolies, picking up facts and colour. At this point, she still had a free hand, for her colleagues from the other newspapers had still not made the difficult journey up from the border. Jenkins, however, was crouched down outside his tent at the side of Sunil, whose Lee Metford rifle he had broken down in parts and laid out on a piece of cloth on the ground.

'Good news,' cried Simon. 'We're back in the army.'

The Welshmen immediately assumed a melancholic face. 'Oh, bloody 'ell,' he grunted. 'You promised me that there would be no more of all that . . . bloody salutin' an' stuff.'

'No, nor will there be. We are going to be in charge of the Mounted Infantry. That lot that we watched coming in. And there's more reinforcements on their way, from what I hear. We will be a *very* irregular unit. Rather like what we were out on the veldt, except we won't have that bloody man Sir John French breathing down our necks. And you have been demoted to Colour Sergeant.'

'Ah well. Could 'ave been worse. Could 'ave been the Mountain Climbers Brigade. When do we start?'

'Probably tomorrow. As long as it takes Lord Kitchener to approve our appointment by telegraph. Then we shall have to start training these Sikhs. You work with Captain Ottley teaching 'em riding and I'll teach them formation work and so on – if I can remember the drill, that is.'

'I don't think we shall need much of that in these parts, bach sir. More a question of 'ow to sit in the saddle when the bleedin' 'orse is goin' straight up a mountain.'

'Yes. Something like that. Now, Sunil, can you put the kettle on?'

Kitchener's approval came back with flattering speed, relayed to Fonthill by Macdonald's orderly. The two men immediately found the mounted Sikhs' lines and the work began. In fact, it transpired that Ottley, a captain of the 23rd Pioneers, was the only man in the expeditionary force who had attended the Mounted Infantry course at Sialkot. He had had very little time to train his men before the column set off and the thirty with him now had been the only Sikhs, plus a handful of Gurkhas, who had been considered efficient enough to leave with the main force. Forty or so had had to be left behind for further training. Since then, twenty or so had come up to New Chumbi and others were expected.

Unskilled as horsemen, nevertheless the little unit had led the flying column that Macdonald had taken into the mountains. Ottley told Fonthill that his 'cavalry' had penetrated far ahead of the column, past the fortress of Phari – 'an imposing sight' – and pressed on up over the 15,200-high Tang La, 'The Clear Pass', so called because the prevailing winds kept it usually clear of snow, until they met the lower slopes of Mount Chomolhari.

'They towered above us like a perpendicular wall of snow,' recounted Ottley. 'We had gone as far as we possibly could and we and our ponies were exhausted. Also, despite the snow, there was little to drink, so we had to turn back.'

'How did the men behave?'

'Magnificently. I was proud of them. We met no opposition, of course, from the natives and those we saw at

Phari were very welcoming. But we discovered that we had one great problem.'

'What was that?'

'We have no riding breeches, of course, and the loose serge trousers worn by the men had chafed their inner thighs horribly. Many were bleeding and hardly able to walk, let alone ride. We need to get proper breeches as soon as possible.'

'Of course. I'll see to it straight away.'

'Despite all the problems – which included, by the way, the fact that the ponies became very disturbed and refused to settle down – despite all this, we managed to cover thirty-five miles in one day to get back. Pretty damned good, I'd say. Augurs well for the future. They are good men.'

'Splendid. I will telegraph back to the base camp for breeches. Oh – what happened with the Phari Fort? Younghusband has issued a promise to the Tibetans that we will not occupy territory or fortified positions. I presume the General left no garrison there?'

For the first time Ottley looked troubled. He frowned. 'Afraid so. Despite the appeals of the Tibetan commander there, the General threw out the wives and dependents of the defenders – who had offered no resistance, remember – and installed two companies of Gurkhas in the fort.'

'Oh dear. Presumably he was worried that it could prove an obstacle to the main column if the Tibetans decided to resist.'

'I suppose so. It looks a pretty formidable place from the outside, at least. I heard it was a fort that had dominated the old trading route to India and also some kind of mobilisation centre for this end of Tibet, so I suppose the General knew what he was doing.'

The habitual sunny smile returned to his face. 'But then generals are always supposed to know what they are doing, aren't they?'

Fonthill returned the grin. 'I've known a few who didn't. I'll go and telegraph about the breeches. Have you had the MO see to the men?'

'Yes. Just a bit of ointment. Don't think the Sikhs liked it but I made 'em apply it.'

'Good.'

Because of the chafing problems, the men were relieved of riding duties for the next few days and Simon, Ottley and Jenkins restricted their teaching activities to lectures on keeping formation, wheeling into line, firing from the saddle and so on. The black faces of the men wore intense expressions as they listened, both eyes and mouths wide open and Fonthill worried that little had been imparted, but Ottley assured him that all of the instructions had been taken on board.

Christmas came and went at New Chumbi with hardly a break in the routine of drill, weapon inspections and, once the riding breeches had been delivered, scouting expeditions by Fonthill's men that produced no sign of hostile troops. The biggest change was in the weather, for the smiling face of the Chumbi valley quickly disappeared when bitterly cold and strong winds swept along the plateau and winter settled in. Luxuries disappeared from the menu and the chapattis had to be made from a basic mixture of flour and water, which tasted, as one subaltern confessed, 'like mustard plaster'. The biggest hardship was when the officers' mess orderlies revealed that their normal care in cooling the champagne had been overdone and the wine was far too bitterly cold to be drunk. Beer, which had been kept under cover, had to be substituted.

'Serves you all right,' muttered Alice. 'Nobody deserves champagne so far, because nothing has happened. What are we supposed to be doing here, anyway?'

The answer seemed to be 'consolidating', while a second supply route between Gangtok and New Chumbi was opened, which cut some ten miles off the route and enabled the amount of food being brought in to rise to 40,000 pounds a day. The indigenous inhabitants of Chumbi were also now losing their reserve and were providing animal fodder, buckwheat and potatoes, for which they were paid handsomely.

Alice had now lost her exclusivity in the column for she had been joined by three other journalists representing *The Times*, the *Daily Mail* and Reuters News Agency. She dourly resented their presence and refused to join their little tented compound, preferring to mess with Simon, Jenkins and Sunil.

'We are all fighting for journalistic scraps here, anyway,' she confided to Simon, 'for there is nothing to write about. I am tired of describing the bloody sunset and the difficulties of putting up tents when you can't drive a peg into the ground. I do wish we could advance.'

Her wish was granted early in January, however, when it was announced that another flying column, with Younghusband and the diplomatic heart of the mission, would advance over the Tang La and set it up in a further advanced base high up on the plateau at a tiny hamlet called Tuna, where it would see out the rest of the winter.

It was to everyone's relief, then, when sufficient supplies had been built up to allow this second, stronger, flying column, led by Fonthill's Mounted Infantry, to set off from New Chumbi over the mountains again. Word filtered down that the move had been at the insistence of Younghusband who, it was said, had eventually won a highly charged argument with Macdonald about the dangers to be faced by advancing further into Tibet in midwinter. Simon, busily preparing his horsemen for the advance, was not involved in the argument – and he was heartily glad of it.

The journalists, who had grown increasingly restive under what Alice condemned as an unnecessarily rigid form of censorship installed by Macdonald on the plain, were now allowed to join the advance. Before setting off, Fonthill took Sunil to one side. The youth's relationship to Alice had become even closer and he had begun trying to teach her Tibetan. Simon decided to capitalise on the friendship.

'Listen,' he said. 'Now that we are advancing into Tibet proper and I shall be riding out with my men every day, I would be grateful if you would take on the responsibility of looking after the memsahib.'

Suni's eyes opened wide. 'Oh yes, sahib. What you want me to do?'

'Well, she doesn't need a nursemaid and she would be horrified at the suggestion that she could not look after herself. But,' he grinned, 'she can be a trifle headstrong, you know?'

The youth nodded gravely.

'So there is no need to tread on her coat-tails, so to speak, but I would be most grateful if you would stay close to her as soon as we go into action. Do you think you could do that?'

'Oh yes, sahib. Don't tread on skirt but stay close, yes.'

'Splendid. You still have your Lee Metford rifle, I think?'

'Oh yes. Jenkins Bach has given me lessons on shooting it.'

'Good. As soon as we meet trouble, my wife will certainly want to go to the front to take notes about the battle or whatever. Now, she will certainly ignore any attempts by you to stop her from doing so. So don't try it. But I would ask you to go with her, with your rifle, and protect her if it becomes necessary. Do you understand?'

Sunil's chest visibly swelled. 'Certainly, sahib. I will protect. Most certainly.'

'Good man. I knew I could rely on you. Now, don't tell her what I have asked you to do, because that will annoy her. Just accompany her casually, as though you are interested in all that she does. Which I think is true, anyway. Is it not?'

'Oh yes, indeed sahib. I will be journalist when this journey is finished.'

'Good. I am sure that you will make a good one.'

Simon looked into the earnest face before him and felt reassured. Alice could well look after herself but – and he frowned at the thought – she had a propensity for pushing herself into danger and, perhaps, with Sunil at her side, she might feel a sense of responsibility for him and so curtail her eagerness to get close to the action. He shook the boy's hand and strode away.

The Chumbi Valley was situated at about 10,000 feet above sea level but the climb for the column began almost immediately after leaving the encampment at New Chumbi. Once again, as the trail led ever upwards and became steeper, the Mounted Infantry, ranging far ahead, were forced to dismount and lead their ponies. The route led between masses of sharply cornered rocks, which merged later into great overhanging bare cliffs of blackened granite.

'Oh, bloody 'ell,' grunted Jenkins. ''Ere we go again.'

In fact, the trail, although steep up to the 15,200 feet high Tang La pass, was not as terrifying as that leading to the Jelep La, for it wound through rocks on either side, through which the wind howled like a thousand banshees, but offering no precipitate falls to an abyss below. Just beneath the pass, at about 14,000 feet, Fonthill and his advance guard debouched onto an open, barren stretch of upland, the first intimation that they were approaching the great northern plain, the Chang Tang, the fabled 'roof of Tibet'. Here, on the advice of Ottley, who had ridden this way days before, they waited until the main force caught up with them and the whole column camped for the night.

Fonthill sought out Alice and Sunil and asked anxiously 'any sign of mountain sickness?' Both shook their heads negatively and Simon, who, with Jenkins, had felt nothing more than tremors in his stomach as they climbed, put this down to the fact that they had acclimatised to a large extent at New Chumbi. After dark, however, a different problem faced them.

That night the temperature plummeted to minus eleven degrees Fahrenheit and it became clear that every scrap of clothing would be needed to prevent frostbite attacking. Simon and Alice shared a tent, as before, with Jenkins and Sunil in the other. They all retained their sheepskins and felt boots within their sleeping bags and stretched canvas covers over the bags, soon learning to sleep on their backs, for turning over allowed a piercing shaft of bitterly cold air to penetrate into the bags. Little sleep was had that night.

Dawn, however, brought bright sunlight, a cloudless sky and a rejuvenation of spirits all around – particularly when the news reached everyone that an officer in the main column had unwisely placed his false teeth in a tumbler of water at his side to find them frozen solid by the morning.

A march of little more than a mile and a half over half-frozen greensward led to a bluff beyond which stood the impressive Fort of Phari, a castellated virtual castle, looking like some remnant from the Crusades, from which a row of prayer flags and a Union Jack streamed in the strong wind – showing that the two companies of Gurkhas were still in possession. Here, a halt was made while mules and ponies were laden with supplies for the new base, some fourteen miles ahead at Tuna.

Alice took advantage of this to visit the fort, a wide-eyed Sunil at her side, carrying his Lee Metford. The stronghold had earlier yielded its stock of gunpowder and bullets without firing a single shot as the soldiers had advanced through the huddle of miserable huts that stood at the foot of its walls. Now, however, Alice wrinkled her nose in disgust as she walked through the hamlet. Centuries of inhabitants had thrown their rubbish outside their doors so that it had grown so high that steps had had to be dug down through it to reach the ground floor of the dwellings. Inside the fort, she found that its courtyards were strewn with similar rubbish, including old armour, matchlocks, limbers and spears and the building itself was a warren of narrow passages and dingy cells, all empty.

She made notes and retreated to the village in the hope of finding some of its inhabitants. They proved to be as unprepossessing as their surroundings. The women, who extended their tongues in a gesture of greeting, had covered their faces with a red paste that had blackened as it oxidised, obviously to protect their faces from the constant wind. From the pungent odour that accompanied them, Alice realised that they must have smeared their bodies with rancid butter. Yet everyone seemed to have a perfect set of white, gleaming teeth.

Through Sunil, she attempted to question them, to gain their opinion of this intrusion of alien soldiers from so far away. But the youth confessed that they seemed reluctant to talk and, she suspected, he was having difficulty in understanding their dialect. Shivering in the cold, she gave up and they walked back to the encampment, where she began writing a despatch to be cabled back by the new telegraph wires that had been set up as the column advanced, now linking Phari to the Indian border, Calcutta and the outside world.

She sat in the weak sun, drinking tea in an attempt to keep warm and sucking her pencil. There had been no military action to write about so far and, indeed, no enemy to describe. If this was a war, she confessed, it was a fake one, unreal – even spurious. Younghusband's Mission, with its escort bristling with weaponry, had been allowed slowly to climb, slip and plod wearily into the Tibetan uplands without deterrence. The weather and the terrain had been the enemy.

In this context, she decided to lead her story with a sad fact that she had picked up from one of the Indian coolies, who spoke excellent English. One of the Indian Post Office men, working on the telegraph lines, had contracted frostbite in his foot because the Raj had ruled that only soldiers were to be issued with the Gilgit felt-lined boots, which offered protection from the biting cold. As a result, the man's foot had to be amputated.

Alice licked her pencil with relish. This was just the sort of detail that would illustrate so well the conditions under which the 'little people', the ordinary civilians, were being forced to work on this expedition and also the inflexible bureaucracy of the Indian government and its army where its rules were concerned. And she was fairly certain that she had this small but telling detail exclusively to herself. She began scribbling quickly.

Then, however, she frowned and tore up the sheet and threw it away. This was just the sort of story that some ham-fisted censor, selected by the unimaginative, newspaper-hating Macdonald, would delete without a second thought. He would remove it because it would, of course, reflect badly to a liberal-minded audience back home on the leadership of the expedition. No. She sucked the pencil again and stared unseeingly at the distant tip of Chomolhari shimmering in the distance. She would slip it in lower down in the story, so that it would not stand out so invitingly to the censor – and she was sure that the Tory-loving foreign editor back home would let it through, because, after all, it was fact and not opinion.

The next day an event occurred which raised the eager interest, not only of Alice and her fellow scribblers, but the whole column. A delegation arrived, completely unannounced, consisting of three monks from the three great Tibetan monasteries and a senior commander in the Tibetan army, named Depon Lhadang, plus their attendants. Younghusband, unsure of their seniority, declined to meet them and sent, instead, his close aide, adviser and fluent Tibetan speaker, Captain Frank O'Connor, to parley with them.

The meeting proved inconclusive, with the Tibetans giving no ground and refusing to enter into any formal negotiations until the British Mission and its escort had turned back and returned to Yatung.

After the delegation had left, Fonthill sought out O'Connor, whom he had first met on the North-West Frontier, during the Pathan Revolt of 1897, when the latter was serving as a young subaltern. 'Were the Tibetans ameliorative at all?' he asked.

'Not a bit. Oh, the General, whom I've met before, was studiously polite but the other three, all high lamas from the Kashag, the ruling body of the country, were aggressive, snarling and using most disrespectful language. I am just glad that the Colonel was not there.'

O'Connor leant forward. 'I'll tell you something else, Fonthill. I've just heard back from a lama from Sikkim, whom we sent the other day to Lhasa with a special message from Younghusband to the Dalai Lama. The feller turned back a few miles from Tuna when he met a large force of Tibetan warriors, numbering about 2,000, who, he said, are waiting to stop us. This feller kept whispering to me: "War! War! They mean war!" So perhaps we shall see some action soon, eh?'

'Indeed.' Fonthill nodded and frowned. 'Well the sooner we get to Tuna and set up a properly defended camp the better.'

Within two days the column had crossed the Tang La without incident and arrived at Tuna, which turned out to be nothing more than three unremarkable stone buildings squatting in the middle of an empty, and quite flat plain, stretching out to the foothills of the dominating Mount Chomolhari to the south-east and encircled elsewhere by bleak hills. Tufted grass poked through the loose gravel that seemed to stretch for miles and no trees were to be seen.

Fonthill, in the vanguard, sat on his pony and looked around him in disbelief, his eyes watering in the cold wind. Apart from the three now deserted stone dwellings, there were no physical features that could be used to defend the camp: no gullies, no hillocks, not even a clump of bushes to provide cover. The rock-hard plain stretched unrelievedly all around. Certainly an attacking force could be detected from some distance, unless it advanced in a snowstorm, which was unlikely. But the ground was clearly ice-bound and looked impervious to pick or shovel. There could be no trenches to give shelter to the camp's defenders. He sucked in his frozen lips. Which idiot had chosen this godforsaken place as the site on which to see out the winter?

As the last mules arrived, the provisions were unloaded and the difficulties of the place were exposed. Efforts proved indeed that no trenches could be dug and, although a rough barricade of boxes and mealie bags were erected, if it was not for the rolls of barbed wire that had been providentially brought up from Chumbi and wound round the perimeter, there were no real defences that could be erected to protect the tented encampment. The walls of the three houses were promptly loopholed but they proved far too small to house more than a handful of defenders.

Fonthill took his Mounted Infantry out immediately to scout the surroundings and immediately found what he sought. He almost stumbled into a large force of armed Tibetans who were concealed behind piles of brushwood some twelve miles distant. Wheeling to the south, he encountered a second and larger group of the enemy encamped even nearer, at some hot springs beside the Bham Tso lake, near a small hamlet called Guru, guarding the ancient caravan trail that led to Gyantse.

Here, with Ottley and Jenkins, he left his men behind and trotted ahead to study what defences had been erected. He dismounted within easy musket range, dismounted, climbed a rock and scanned the way ahead through his binoculars. Although he was now in plain sight of the Tibetans, none attempted to fire or otherwise molest him as he studied the way ahead.

The road led to where the plain narrowed between the lake, which was frozen, and to the outlying spur of one of the mountain ranges to the left. Here, a rough stone wall had been erected across the top of which rows of matchlocks and what looked liked primitive artillery pieces, long-barrelled *jingals*, were levelled. Above where the wall met the spur, stone sangars, or rifle emplacements, had been established up the hillside to command the approach to the wall. At the other side, the wall ended in a small stone house. Beyond was an open space which clearly had once been a marsh, extending from the lake and probably impassable in warmer weather. But now it was frozen hard.

'The bloody fools,' muttered Ottley. 'They've left that side of the wall quite open and unprotected by the look of it. We could easily swing round there and take them by the rear.'

'Except,' said Jenkins, shielding his eyes and looking beyond the wall, 'that there appears to be millions of the buggers massin' there, look you.'

Fonthill lowered his glasses. 'Well,' he said, 'I've seen enough. This is the old caravan trail to Gyantse and so this is the way we shall have to advance, when and if,' he emphasised the last two words scornfully, 'we advance. We shall have to knock that wall down. But we might be attacked well before then. Let's get back and report. I have to say that I think our camp is very vulnerable.'

His report produced one quite unsuspected and potentially dangerous turn of events. Younghusband decided, on what appeared to be a sudden whim, to ride out to Guru, where the main force of Tibetans were camped, some ten miles away, to intercede with them personally. He took with him only O'Connor, to interpret, and a young subaltern, who was said to be learning the Tibetan language – no escort, not even an orderly to hold

121

their horses while they entered the Tibetan camp.

On returning, O'Connor recounted to Fonthill that no progress had been made and that, as before, the Tibetan general had been courteously polite but that the three lamas, who were ensconced in the camp, had been even more adversarial, confirming that it was they who were behind the opposition to the opening of any meaningful negotiations. At one point, he said, they became menacing and refused to let the trio return to Tuna. O'Connor related that it was only the good humour and bland impassivity of Younghusband that saved the day.

Simon shook his head in disbelief. It was clear that Younghusband did not lack courage, but that he possessed an impetuous streak that boded ill for the future.

From that moment on, there was no lack of contact between the two opposing forces. Little parties of Tibetans began visiting the British camp to repeat their mantra: the British must retreat and leave Tibetan soil before meaningful talks could begin. They were met with courtesy but blank refusal. It had become, reflected Fonthill, a ridiculous stalemate, with the British unable to advance because of a combination of foul weather and insufficient supplies to sustain the advance, and the Tibetans seemingly unable to summon the will to attack.

If they did decide to attack, he was not at all sure of the outcome. For the weather had blunted whatever advantages their modern weaponry gave the invaders. However carefully they were oiled, rifle bolts were now being frozen into their breeches. With night temperatures now dropping to four degrees below zero within the tents, the machine guns were particularly susceptible to the cold and Hadow, the young subaltern in charge of the guns, had taken to removing the locks from the Maxims and huddling them to his breast inside his sleeping bag at night. Sometimes Fonthill found that the carbines of his Mounted Infantry had frozen to the bottom of their saddle buckets on return from patrol.

The rarefied air in which they all lived now had also adversely affected the accuracy and range of the guns, causing them to overshoot in practice. Simon could not help but feel that a mass attack by the Tibetans at night could overwhelm the British camp. Yet none came.

On return from patrol one day, dismounting with his teeth chattering, Fonthill found that Macdonald was closeted with Younghusband and an aide suggested that it would be unwise to interrupt. 'I think there is a bit of an altercation going on between the two, sir,' he confided. 'I've heard raised voices. Better wait a bit, unless it's vitally urgent.'

Fonthill frowned. This was the sort of situation which, clearly, Curzon might have had in mind when he had hinted that he might have a reconciliatory role to play. But, dammit it all, he didn't cherish the thought of acting as schoolteacher in a playground argument. Let the two argue themselves out first and then perhaps he could step in. And, anyway, he was desperately in need of a cup of tea.

Later, he met O'Connor. 'Have you heard?' the Captain asked, conspiratorially.

Simon nodded glumly. 'Been a bit of a row, I gather.'

'Yes. The governor, it seems, has completely lost his

rag with Macdonald. The bloody man wants to withdraw to Chumbi. Says we can't exist here on this plain. Younghusband refuses to budge.'

'Well, I must confess that I have seen better defensive positions.'

'Yes, but the old man says that retreating now, when there are quite a few Tibetans hanging about, will mean losing face completely in their eyes and it will set us back quite a bit in this diplomatic stand-off. Younghusband says that, anyway, there is plenty of fodder about, if you really look for it, and that with our modern weapons, we can adequately defend ourselves.'

Fonthill shrugged. 'Well, Younghusband knows the terrain better than anyone. But I feel we could be pushed a bit if we are attacked and I have seen enough Tibetans to think that we might be. I am on my way to Mac to report now.'

The General heard the news of the nearby Tibetan forces with seeming equanimity, although he immediately coughed and lit a new cigarette from the stub of that still held between his fingers. 'Did it look as though they were preparing to attack?' he asked between coughs. To Fonthill, he appeared to be a sick man.

'I confess I don't think so,' he replied. 'Although we were only a handful, there was no attempt to challenge us when we met the first lot behind the brushwood. They all seemed to be having a bit of a picnic. And the bigger group at the wall – must have been well over 2,000 of them – let us approach quite close and observe them without a shot being fired.'

'Humph. Well, I don't like it. I will double the guard at night. Keep patrolling, Fonthill. We will need ample warning when they come.'

But they did not come. The days mounted as the force camped out under canvas waited and shivered in the cold wind. Fonthill and his men continually ranged the plain, keeping the Tibetans under surveillance, but the enemy showed no sign of moving. Indeed, they waved quite cheerily at the horsemen.

Nevertheless, it was a surprise when, on returning from one patrol, Simon was met by Alice with the news that Macdonald was withdrawing most of his force to New Chumbi and that Younghusband would be staying, with a considerably depleted military escort.

'What! He is going to leave Younghusband stuck out here? What's the point of that?'

Alice found a temporary home for her pencil by sticking it in her hair. 'From what we've been told, I gather that Macdonald feels that this plain can no longer sustain so large a force, the weather is too bad to continue the advance for the moment and, anyway, we haven't built up sufficient supplies to do so, Younghusband refuses to retreat, so General Mac is taking his toys and going back sixty miles to his playpen in Chumbi, where it's much warmer at only 10,000 feet up.'

'But that's bloody ridiculous. It's leaving the diplomatic mission comparatively undefended.'

'Not quite. You, dear, will be staying with your remarkably ungainly Sikh cavalry, and so will four companies of the 23rd Sikh Pioneers, the Norfolks' Maxim-gun detachment, a detail of Madras Sappers – who, coming from southern Indian, of course, are all shivering so much that they are quite useless as soldiers – and one of the Gurkhas' seven-pounder guns. About 200 so called fighting men in all.'

'What about you?'

'Oh, I am staying, of course, and so are the rest of the scribblers. Although General bloody Macdonald has refused to extend the telegraph line from Phari to here, probably because he hates us all.'

The General was quite sanguine, however, when Fonthill bearded him. 'We can't stay here in these numbers for the rest of the winter,' he growled, through a blue haze of cigarette smoke. 'Younghusband won't move so I am taking the main party back. It makes sense. We will, of course, keep bringing up supplies to Phari ready for the advance when the weather improves.'

'What if we are attacked?'

'Well,' Macdonald paused while he removed his cigarette and coughed. 'You have repeatedly assured me that the Tibetans show no sign of moving and Younghusband is perfectly happy with the defensive arrangements we have made here. We can advance Gurkhas to help you from Phari if you need them and I can move back here within a few days, weather permitting. Younghusband is quite prepared to take the risk. I must consider the overall position and a force this large can't be sustained here. And that's all there is to it.'

'Very well. Do you think the telegraph from Phari will remain uncut?'

'Oh yes. Since we flogged the local headman for cutting it, there has been no further trouble.'

'Who will remain in military command here?'

'Couldn't let you do it, we must be fair. Must have a regular. Colonel Hogge commands the 23rd Pioneers so he will do it. You will report to him, although I know you will stay close to Younghusband. Now you must excuse me. I have much to—' And he thrust a handkerchief to his mouth to herald another burst of coughing.

Two days later, Fonthill, Alice, Jenkins and Sunil stood together sombrely and watched as the greater part of the mission's military escort gradually turned its back on the little camp at Tuna and wound its way back over the mountains.

'Talk about the rats leaving the sinking whatsit . . .' muttered Jenkins.

Alice gripped her husband's hand tightly as the last trooper disappeared into the enveloping mist.

CHAPTER FIVE

The days that followed brought no attack and, although it remained bitterly cold, no deterioration in the weather. Younghusband did, indeed, find grass and fuel by sending foraging parties out across the plain, escorted by Fonthill's Sikhs, although it became increasingly difficult to find sufficient yak dung to keep the precious fires burning. Nevertheless, life became not exactly unpleasant for the defenders of Tuna.

Colonel Younghusband, that lover of the mountains, seemed quite unfazed by the lack of progress of his mission. He spent much of each day lying out on the rocks, warmly muffled, writing letters home or reading poetry.

The rising sun struck the top of the tents every morning promptly at 7 a.m., climbing into a sky that was cloudless except for a soft wisp of haze. From the little river that supplied water to the troops a soft mist rose and, as the sun climbed higher, the bare brown base of the surrounding mountains toned into a pastel delight of purples and pinks, while the snow summits turned into an ethereal blue. On the plain, plump little larks and finches ignored the cold and scurried about looking for food. Moles could be seen basking in the winter sunshine at the mouth of their holes.

'I quite like this postin',' confessed Jenkins to Fonthill one day, 'now that I'm not fallin' off the bleedin' mountains. And I'm gettin' quite good at this fishin' lark. What's more, you're gettin' to be almost adequate at ridin' on these ponies – almost, but not quite, that is.'

'Don't be impertinent, or I'll have you demoted to dung clearer.'

'Well, with respect, bach sir, we're all almost that now. We're not cavalry. We're collectors of 'orse shit.'

'Better than sliding near the edges of precipices.'

'Very, very true. When d'yer think we're goin' to advance?'

'Well, I hear that supplies are building up at Phari and it can't be long now. If we don't move soon those Tibetans will think we're here on holiday.'

Alice had become the most restless of the quartet. There had been less and less to write about as the days passed and she and her colleagues had become increasingly irked by the double censorship imposed by Macdonald on the press corps. This had arisen because the task had originally been handled by the mission staff, but Macdonald had insisted that the army should be involved so that the press telegrams were scanned twice.

'It is not as though anything that is published in London,' fumed Alice, 'is going to be eagerly read in Lhasa. The place could be on the moon as far as reading about the outside world is concerned.'

Her frustrations, however, had become ameliorated to some extent by the growth of her friendship with Sunil. The two had now become inseparable and Alice always showed him the text of her telegrams, explaining to him how the abbreviations worked, saving precious pennies, and the subtleties of the grammar.

Her main story during these inactive months came when disaster struck one of the convoys bringing up supplies from New Chumbi to Tuna. Amazingly, her story was allowed through by the censors despite her graphic description, gathered when she interviewed the survivors:

A convoy of the 12th Mule Corps, escorted by two companies of the 23rd Pioneers,' she wrote, *'were overtaken by a blizzard on their march between Phari and Tuna and camped in two feet of snow with the thermometer 18 degrees below zero. A driving hurricane made it impossible to light a fire or cook food. The officers were reduced to frozen bully beef and neat spirits, while the sepoys went without food for thirty-six hours. The drivers arrived at Tuna frozen to the waist. Twenty men of the 12th Mule Corps were frostbitten and thirty men of the 23rd Pioneers were so incapacitated that*

*they had to be carried in on mules. On the same
day there were seventy cases of snow blindness
among the 8th Gurkhas.*

Alice was particularly pleased that her disgusted
revelation that the officers were found rations to eat while
the sepoys were denied food somehow slipped through the
censors.

It was clear to her that the two companies of Pioneers
deployed in escorting the mule-train were almost
certainly below strength and that a sizeable part of the
convoy was diverted from its main purpose by the need to
carry the kit, rations and spare ammunition of the escort.
Alice had cultivated Younghusband, and his simmering
resentment of the caution of Macdonald in insisting on
what he considered to be excessively large escorts had
rubbed off on her.

'The bloody man is so scared of risking a black mark
on his career,' she confided to Simon, 'that he won't raise a
finger unless it is surrounded by three companies of sepoys.
We will never move the sixty miles to Gyantse at this rate,
let alone reach Lhasa.'

Fonthill smiled but shook his head. 'The man is cautious,
I agree, my love, but he carries a heavy responsibility. We
are invading a completely unknown country in foul weather,
with a line of supply and communications stretching behind
us about four times the length of the fighting head. You
must remember that.'

Alice scowled. 'He's supposed to be a general, isn't he?
And generals are supposed to fight, aren't they? Nobody's

had to fire a shot in anger except at mountain goats for months. What's he afraid of?'

The tension that had built all around, however, was relieved at last when, on the evening of 29th March, Macdonald arrived with his main body from New Chumbi prepared to advance on what he called another 'reconnaissance in force'. The following day, however, a piercing wind swept across the plain and engulfed the camp with what Alice described in her telegraph to London as 'a hurricane of tingling grit'. She reported that the discomfort of the men was increased by the orders of General Macdonald to strike their tents and to 'conceal themselves' in case Tibetan spies were observing their deployment from the surrounding hills.

'How can 1,000 men,' she complained to Simon, 'with mules, ponies, guns, ammunition supplies and other stores, disappear into a naked plain? The man is an idiot.'

At 8 a.m. on the 31st March Macdonald's army paraded in six inches of snow to begin the march on Guru. Because of the scarcity of ammunition, each infantryman was issued with no more than thirteen rounds. Nevertheless, the morning was bright, the sky was blue and everyone, including the little press contingent that marched with the column, was in good heart and relieved that, at last, the mission was on its way at least to Gyantse – and perhaps even to the forbidden city of Lhasa?

Despite the lack of ammunition the column was an impressive unit. It consisted of the two Pioneer regiments (misnamed in this context because these Sikhs had proved to be strong fighters); the 8th Gurkhas; two companies of Fonthill's Mounted Infantry, which had now grown to be a hundred-strong; two ten-pounders of the 7th Mountain Battery (a British unit), the Gurkha-manned seven-pounders, 'Bubble and Squeak'; the two Maxims of the Norfolks, also manned by British troops; and various ancillary units. The total strength of the column was just over 1,000 men, mainly made up of Indian sepoys, with British personnel numbering less than 200.

The destination was Guru, the little hamlet that Younghusband had visited, about ten miles away. But two miles to its south was the wall blocking the road that Fonthill had scouted while Tuna was being set up. This would have to be circumvented in the face of the Tibetans manning it.

As always, Fonthill and his Mounted Infantry rode on ahead of the column, fanning out in a wide screen between one and two miles to the front and flanks to protect the main force from a surprise attack. The fact that the Tibetans knew that they were on the march was confirmed when emissaries twice approached the column, repeating their old demands that the British should retire to Yatung. Both times, Younghusband sent them back with a message to their general, saying that the column was bound for Gyantse and would soon reach Guru and that if he wished to avoid a fight then he and his troops should clear the road and let the British through.

Implacably, the advance continued until Simon and his men drew near to the wall. He found that, as before, its top was lined with armed Tibetans and that the sangars overlooking the road were also well manned. He galloped back to report to the main column.

This halted about half a mile away from the wall and the guns – ten-pounders carried on mules and 'Bubble and Squeak' by coolies – were assembled and made ready for action and the troops lined up. Immediately, a small party, led by two generals and riding ponies, cantered around the end of the wall and approached the British lines. They were met by Younghusband, Macdonald, Fonthill and, of course, O'Connor, all sitting their ponies underneath a large Union Jack that crackled in the strong wind. Rugs were laid on the ground, the main participants dismounted and the latest parley began.

Alice, notebook and pencil in hand, edged forward and began making notes. She could not hear what was being said, although she could only presume – what was, indeed, confirmed later – that the old litany of 'Go back' and 'No' was being repeated. But she could describe the scene that lay before her. The wall in the background, the gravel-studded ground and the rocks that climbed steeply to the left, were all of a characterless grey. But the Tibetan deputation provided a bizarre splash of colour.

The general from Lhasa wore a high, domed and embroidered hat and both he and his fellow general wore gay yellow and green coats and carried long swords with richly worked hilts. The civilian notables squatted in equally colourful robes of purple and blue, their strange, fork-butted guns embossed with turquoise and coral; and their little ponies, fretting and stamping in the background, had saddlecloths worked in swastika patterns, filigree brass headbands and wide, moulded iron stirrups. It was, scribbled Alice, like a scene from the Arabian Nights, dropped into a slate-grey Himalayan amphitheatre.

Fonthill had remained in the saddle as the negotiations continued and, realising that they were once again going to end in stalemate, he edged his pony away to join Ottley and Jenkins, waiting at the head of the mounted Sikhs.

'This is going nowhere,' he whispered. Then he nodded ahead, to the right of the stone house that marked the end of the wall. 'The way is clear through there,' he said, 'but there are hundreds of armed Tibetans well beyond the rear of the wall up in the rocks to the right. When we advance, as I am sure we shall, they could enfilade our men. I intend to suggest to the General that we gallop through there, past the men manning the wall, and clear those chaps out. But we must be careful that we don't fire first. This whole thing may still just end peacefully and I don't want to start a battle. So, William, have the men ready.'

'Very good, Simon.'

Fonthill dismounted and walked back to where the little group still sat cross-legged on the sheepskins, the Tibetans talking garrulously, O'Connor listening and nodding sympathetically, while Younghusband and Macdonald, the latter smoking his cigarette, sat stony-faced. He stood back from the gathering and edged towards Alice, who was still writing quickly, Sunil, his rifle slung from his shoulder, at her side.

'What's happening?' she hissed.

'Usual stuff, by the look of it, neither side giving an inch. It's getting ridiculous and very boring.' He nodded towards the wall, the top of which was lined with what appeared to be matchlocks and strange tubes, resting on tripods, which represented the nearest approach the Tibetans had to artillery. 'We will probably have to use our guns to knock down that wall, although I am not sure they will be very effective at this range.'

He turned to Sunil. 'Make sure you take the memsahib away behind those rocks if the firing starts,' he said. 'It could turn very hot here in this defile.'

'Oh, for goodness' sake, Simon,' snorted Alice. 'I can look after myself. I have to get a good view of what's going on. Although I do hope there is not going to be a battle. It could be a massacre, you know . . .'

Before she could explain a massacre of whom she was interrupted by the end of the palaver. With a grunt and wave of his hand, the Tibetan general scrambled to his feet and stalked away haughtily to his pony, followed by his entourage. They all mounted and, talking animatedly, urged their mounts into a ragged gallop back to the wall.

Fonthill approached Younghusband and Macdonald, who were in earnest conversation. 'What has happened?' he asked.

Younghusband sighed. 'It's been like talking to that damned wall over there. I have told them we want no bloodshed but that we are determined to continue on to Gyantse and they must let us through without firing. I don't know what the hell they intend to do. I have given them fifteen minutes to clear the wall.'

'It would be safer to bring up our guns and reduce

the wall.' Macdonald's Aberdeenshire brogue sounded somehow deeper in the defile.

'No, Mac. Give them time to make up their minds to clear out.'

Fonthill explained his intention of riding through and clearing the Tibetans at the rear.

'Very well,' grunted Macdonald, 'but wait until we advance.'

The next fifteen minutes seemed an age to the three as they stood, staring intently at the enemy lining the head-high lines of stones ahead of them and in the sangars above and to the left. The Tibetans remained behind their weapons, chattering and gesticulating as though inviting the British to advance.

Eventually, Macdonald drew out his timepiece. 'Time's up,' he said. 'Do we fire?'

Younghusband's face was a picture of despair. 'No. Give them a minute or two more. I don't want us to fire the first shot.'

Despite the grimness of the situation, Fonthill could not but give an inward smile. The normal state of the relationship between the two men seemed to have been reversed. Here was the ploddingly cautious General itching to attack the enemy, while the usually impetuous Younghusband was reluctant to move.

Eventually, Macdonald grunted. 'We can't stay here forever. I must bring up the artillery.'

'No, Mac. Get your men simply to advance on the wall, withholding their fire until they are fired on.'

'What, walk into the face of that lot? They will be

advancing into the muzzles of about 1,000 guns. We shall present an unmissable target. We could be slaughtered.'

Younghusband's normally placid features twisted further to betray his agony. 'I know. But I promised that we would not come with aggressive intentions. We must not fire the first shot. Go ahead, Mac. Don't bring forward the guns, but order the advance and give instructions that the men must not fire until they are fired upon.'

Macdonald whirled round and barked a series of orders to his colonels, who doubled away to their waiting men. Whistles shrieked and, slowly, the khaki line began to move forward towards the waiting guns.

Fonthill swallowed hard. It seemed an act of ridiculous folly, also of courage, comparable to that of the Light Brigade at Balaclava just fifty years before when they charged into the Russian cannon. He mounted his pony and urged it to where his mounted Sikhs were waiting. Turning his head, he caught a glimpse of Alice mounting a rock to get a better view and angrily gestured for her to take cover, but she shook her head defiantly.

He came abreast of Ottley. 'William, when our chaps reach the wall, we charge round the end of it and to the rear. The orders remain the same, however: don't fire or use sabres until we meet resistance. We just shepherd those men off the rocks at the back there. If they fire, then we let them have it, but not until. Explain to the men.'

'Very good, sir.'

Jenkins joined Fonthill and looked down on the troops plodding forward, keeping their lines perfectly straight as though for The Trooping of the Colour, their regimental colours streaming back in the wind behind the large Union Jack. 'Bloody 'ell, bach sir,' he muttered. 'They're marchin' right up to them gun muzzles, look you. 'Ave you ever seen anythin' like it?'

Still the Tibetans refused to fire and the air of farce was complemented by the sight of the Lhasa general, with his bodyguard and staff, sitting *in front of the wall*, with his back to it, muttering to himself and waiting sullenly, it seemed, for events to take their turn. Had he given any orders? It seemed not.

Eventually, the front rank of the sepoys reached the wall and Simon and Jenkins moved their ponies forward and took their places at the head of the two companies of mounted Sikhs. Fonthill nodded to Ottley, raised his hand and shouted, 'Charge!'

In an instant they had rounded the end of the wall, where the stone house marked its edge, and were thundering over the stone-hard ground, scattering grey-clad Tibetans to either side as they headed to where figures could be seen peering over the rocks on a spur that jutted out to the right of the trail.

Still no shots were fired at them and they reined in, spreading out below the rocks. Here, for a moment, farce reigned again, as the horsemen sat, steam rising from their steeds, staring at the Tibetans who showed no sign of either firing or moving.

'Move, you stupid bastards,' shouted Simon, waving his sabre to indicate that the riflemen should leave the safety of their rocks and come down to the road. The Tibetans stared blankly back at him, so he urged his pony up between the rocks and slapped the nearest man on the back with the flat of his sword, pointing down to the road. He was aware that Jenkins was by his side, equally shouting and waving.

It was the turning point in the affair. The man, flinched, flung down his matchlock and turning, ran down onto the road. In an instant he was followed by the rest of the Tibetans who straggled down between the rocks onto the trail, some of them still carrying their muskets, but clearly having no intention of using them.

'That's it, lads,' shouted Jenkins, easing his pony down onto the trail. 'Yes, bugger off.' He pointed along the track with his sword. 'That way, you useless lot. Call yourselves soldiers! I've seen better in a school playground at Rhyl, look you. Go on. Piss off. No one's goin' to 'urt you.'

'William,' shouted Simon. 'Make sure they clear off. Get the men to ensure they dump their weapons and shepherd them back down the trail out of harm's way. I'm going back to the wall. Come on, 352.'

He looked ahead and realised that hundreds of Tibetans were thronging behind the wall, stretching back to the frozen lake that bordered the road to Guru and, beyond, Gyantse. They were standing, staring and gesticulating. Most of them carried flintlocks or waved long swords, but no shot was fired nor were the swords used menacingly. They appeared, he thought, like a Welsh rugby crowd who disputed the referee's decision on the field but could do nothing about it.

Up ahead, to his right, he saw sepoys of the 23rd Pioneers and the 8th Gurkhas moving among the sangars, shepherding the musketeers behind the rocks down to the road, like good-natured policemen. There, the Tibetans joined the ranks of the erstwhile defenders of the wall who milled about aimlessly. Now, the rifles of the 23rd Pioneers were lining the top of the wall, pointing down at the throng and the Maxims were trained on the crowd. But still no shot had been fired.

Fonthill reined in by the stone house and turned to Jenkins. 'Thank God,' he exclaimed. 'This looks as though this has been an absolutely bloodless victory. Younghusband will be delighted.'

He walked his horse to where the head of the mission and his general were standing, in conclave.

'Gentlemen,' he called, 'we have cleared the men off the rocks down the road and looks as though the way ahead to Gyantse is virtually cleared. Congratulations, General.'

'Hmmm.' Inevitably, Macdonald had lit a cigarette and he exhaled blue smoke into the clear, cold air. 'Well done, Fonthill. But this mass behind the wall show no signs of moving nor putting down their weapons. We can't advance leaving this lot behind us. We must get the men to remove their rifles.' He turned and gave an order. Immediately, sepoys began moving among the Tibetans attempting to remove their weapons.

It proved to be easier ordered than done. Their guns were obviously the men's own property, presumably mainly used for hunting, and they were certainly not going to relinquish them to the Indian troops. There were shouts and blows were exchanged as the Tibetans wrestled to retain their guns. All was confusion. Screams of abuse rose and stones were thrown.

It was at this point that the Lhasa general, still on the British side of the wall, decided to mount his pony. He screamed imprecations and forced the horse forward, round the wall, towards the melee. A tall Sikh barred his way and attempted to grab his bridle. The general drew a revolver and shot the sepoy through the jaw.

Immediately, the confusion that had marked the scene before, changed to one of deadly killing. The Pioneers lining the top of the wall opened fire on the crowds below them at point-blank range; volleys rang out from the escarpment above the wall and from the plain to its right; shrapnel from the British guns began to burst above the heads of the Tibetans at the rear of the melee and, most menacingly of all, the rattle of the Maxim was heard in earnest for the first time in Tibet.

Amazingly, the Tibetans, under such close fire, did not break and run. Instead, they turned their backs on the firing and *walked* away from it, with a strange and almost oriental dignity.

'My God,' screamed Fonthill, 'this is a massacre. Order the ceasefire, someone.' He lifted his voice. 'Cease firing, damn you! Cease firing!'

But the damage had been done. With only limited ammunition, the infantry, it was later learnt, fired only an average of twelve rounds per man. The two Maxims expended 700 rounds each, enough for just ninety seconds firing each. The Tibetan army, estimated at between 1,000 and 1,500 men, left between 600 and 700 dead on the field, among them their general. It was enough. One hundred and sixty-eight of their wounded were treated by British doctors and only twenty died. The army of the Raj sustained only half a dozen casualties.

When the firing had stopped, Fonthill surveyed the scene, tears in his eyes. 'There will be hell to pay back home when the news reaches London,' he muttered. Then, a sudden thought struck him and, calling to Jenkins, he dug in his heels and urged his pony past the wall towards the rear where his men had been urging the Tibetan riflemen along the road, away from the conflict.

He found Ottley on his knees beside several inert Sikh bodies.

The young man looked up, his face ashen. 'Our bloody shrapnel has killed three of our chaps,' he said. 'And we've lost two ponies.' He shook his head. 'Not from the Tibetans, mind you, Simon. But from our artillery. Damn them. They were firing over the enemy's heads to the rear. They must surely have known we were here.'

Fonthill dismounted and knelt by his side, putting a hand on the young man's shoulder. 'I don't think they did, William.' He sighed. 'It was all panic back there for just five minutes.' He looked up resignedly to where the mountains towered over them. 'All the frustration of those months shivering on the plain at Tuna or ploughing through the snow over the passes must have built up and exploded. That's bloody warfare for you. I think I've already had enough of it.'

He rode back and found an ashen-faced and trembling Alice, scribbling away, while Sunil stood over her, his Lee Metford in his hands.

She looked up. 'Oh Simon, it was a massacre. Some of

the Gurkhas were firing at a range of twenty yards down into the mob. I saw them. Machine guns against muskets. Macdonald and Younghusband should be ashamed of themselves.'

Fonthill sighed. 'Yes, it was a tragedy, darling, but go easy with your report. Younghusband and Mac held off for as long as they could, taking a huge risk in advancing without firing a shot. It was just a horrible accident that it all went wrong. Please be balanced in what you write.'

'Balanced! I'm lucky to be alive. If it hadn't been for Sunil here preventing me, I would have run to that bloody wall. Did you know that Candler of the *Daily Mail* was cut down by Tibetan swordsmen? His hand was completely severed and he received seventeen other wounds. He was only saved by his thick *poshteen*. There but for Sunil go I . . .' She burst into tears.

Fonthill dismounted and knelt beside her, putting his hand around her shoulders and pulling her to him. He looked up at Sunil and raised his other hand to him in acknowledgement. He mouthed 'Well done.'

Alice pushed him away and blew her nose. 'Sorry to be emotional,' she sniffed. 'It's been a long time since I've been close to a massacre. Must be getting old. Now, do leave me to get on with recording these horrible details.'

Simon nodded, stood and, trailing his pony behind him by its reins, walked away to find Jenkins. He found him helping to load the three dead men of the Mounted Infantry onto small wooden carts.

He looked up. 'Can't bury these poor buggers,' he said, 'because they're Sikhs. Got to be burnt, it seems, although

God knows where we are goin' to get the wood from.'

'Any more of our chaps wounded?'

'Seems not. Captain Ottley is just checking.'

Feeling at a loose end, Fonthill turned and walked with his pony back to the wall. The firing had lasted only a matter of minutes but the carnage was there for all to see. The bodies of the dead Tibetans lay where the volleys had cut them down, sprawled together in a mass of twisted, contorted shapes, alongside their weapons. A long line of bodies lay, marking the line of retreat for half a mile. The biting wind was already beginning to freeze them. Some of the Sikh Pioneers were picking their way between the bodies and applying their own first-aid dressings to the wounded.

He met O'Connor, the Tibetologist, and asked, 'For God's sake, Frank, was all this necessary?'

The Captain shook his head sadly. 'Not the governor's fault,' he muttered, 'nor Mac's, for that matter.' He put his hand on Fonthill's shoulder. 'You know, old chap, I have studied the ways of Tibetans as best I could for the last few years. Got to know the language, and all. But they are still almost a book of blank pages to me.'

He nodded to where a doctor in the Indian Medical Service was picking his way between the bodies, leading a small team of orderlies, looking for the wounded. 'Austine Waddell, there, knows 'em much better than me. He's the principal medical officer of the mission but he's much more of a Tibetologist than I am. He has always pointed out that just because Buddhism is supposed to be a religion of pacificism, that doesn't mean that the Tibetan leaders are not militaristic. They have a standing army, for instance, which, with its national territorial backup, hugely outnumbers the men under Mac's command.

'The Dalai Lama, of course, does not rule the country. The most powerful figures are the lamas, the monk priests, who have considerable power and run the country entirely in their own interests. This is not the gentle Buddhism of India. This is a Vajrayana form, which consists of idol worship and subjects the people completely to its power.'

He nodded again to where Dr Waddell was kneeling beside a wounded Tibetan. 'According to Austine, the priests are not even ecclesiastics, they never preach or educate the laity and they keep the country closed in ignorance for their own benefit. They are far more aggressive than the generals. That's Austine's view – and I am inclined to agree with him.'

O'Connor wiped the wind-tears from his cheeks. 'If it had been left to Depon Lhadang, the general who came to talk with us and who, tragically, started this bloody massacre, we could have negotiated, as Younghusband wished, and peacefully marched on to Gyantse or even Lhasa. It was the priests who wouldn't let him. As a result,' he jerked his head over his shoulder, 'we had this stupid stalemate, as dangerous as a tinderbox on Bonfire Night. And, as we saw, it only took a single spark to ignite it.'

He shook his head. 'Sorry. Got to go. Got to help poor old Y to write his report.'

Fonthill thanked him and, deep in thought, began to

lead his pony back to where his men were re-forming. He was stopped by Macdonald.

'A sad business, Fonthill,' he said. He looked over Simon's shoulder to where the trail to Guru led away into the distance. 'But I'm not sure it's over yet. You've lost some men, I hear.'

'Yes, friendly fire, I'm afraid. Our own shrapnel killed three of my Sikhs and two of our ponies.'

'Ah, damned sorry. That's the trouble with shrapnel. Can't quite control it, yer know. But look, quite a few of the Tibetans have retreated to Guru, a couple of miles away. Will you take a patrol and see if there is any evidence of them making a stand there in the village? We will have to march onto there and I don't want to be caught napping.'

'Very well, General.'

Simon mounted his horse and trotted to where Jenkins and Ottley were deep in conversation. 'William,' he called, nodding to where the three bodies were lying on the cart, 'make sure that these chaps are burnt properly. Get a company mounted and formed up, 352. We must go ahead to make sure that the Tibetans have not retreated to Guru and are not waiting to repulse us there.'

Within minutes, half of the Mounted Infantry were trotting along behind Simon and Jenkins as they moved up towards the little village two miles north of the wall. On the way, they passed the remnants of the wall's defenders, who completely disregarded them, walking on stoically.

Guru came into sight as soon as the horsemen rounded a bend and it soon became apparent that the village was occupied and that the Tibetans there, at least, were certainly going to dispute the way ahead. One shot rang out and then a fusillade as Simon and his men came fully into sight.

'Blimey,' swore Jenkins as they reined in. 'I thought there wasn't supposed to be any fight left in them lads. Looks as though they've been waitin' for us.' He pointed ahead.

Muskets, rifles and more of the strange tube-type blunderbusses could be seen poking through windows and above walls from the houses that lined the entrance to the village. Soon bullets and musket balls were flying over the heads of the mounted men as they paused uncertainly.

Fonthill frowned. He didn't want his to be the only command that suffered more fatalities. He turned in the saddle, pointed and shouted, 'Back round the bend. Quickly, now.'

The company galloped back the way they had come, accompanied by the jeers of the village's defenders. There, they halted, the breath of their ponies rising in the cold air.

'What now, bach sir?' asked Jenkins.

'Take six of the best marksmen in the company, get them behind whatever cover you can find round the bend and then open up fire on those chaps firing from the village. I will give you five minutes to make 'em get their heads down. Then I shall lead the rest of the company in a charge to clear the village. Understood?'

'Oh yes. Make sure you grip with your thighs when you charge, though. I'm not goin' to be with you to keep you in the saddle.'

Fonthill sighed. 'Oh, get on with you. Now, *Daffadar*.'

'Sahib.' A giant Sikh NCO, whose huge turban was

precariously kept in place on his head by a scarf tied under his chin, edged his pony forward.

'Line the men up across the road, out of the sight of the enemy, with sabres drawn. As soon as Company Sergeant Major Jenkins has kept up fire on the enemy in the village for about five minutes, I shall lead a charge with the remainder of the company. As we charge, we will shout like hell. Tell the men that.'

The *daffadar*'s teeth flashed white behind his beard. Every cavalryman, whether Mounted Infantry or not, reflected Simon, loved a charge. 'Oh yes. Very good, sahib.'

'Wait. There is more. The enemy will be behind cover in the buildings and behind walls. So we will charge straight through the village, cutting down anyone who is in our way. When I give the order, we will halt, dismount, the handlers will take the horses and then the rest of us, with our carbines, will run back and clear the enemy on foot from behind their defences. Understood?'

'Yes, sahib. Very understood.'

Fonthill watched as Jenkins, with his six men, began to crawl around the bend in the road, until they had disappeared from sight. He took out his watch and marked the time as soon as he heard their first shots. Then he remounted his pony, urged it into the centre of the road and waited as the *daffadar* lined up the company – some forty-six men – across the track behind him.

Sitting there, listening to the sharp crack of the marksmen out of sight ahead, Simon realised that his mouth had gone dry. He had never been a cavalryman but he remembered enough from his training as an infantry subaltern to know

149

that cavalry *did not* charge riflemen firing from cover, unless the situation was desperate. He gulped and wished, for a brief moment, that Jenkins was with him. The situation was always less desperate if his old comrade was by his side. But there was no alternative today. There was no way to outflank the village, so it would have to be a direct charge and Jenkins, as the best shot by far in the unit, would have to lead the sniping. He was banking that the Tibetans in the village would not be trained soldiers and that they would not fancy tangling with nearly fifty men thundering down on them, shrieking and waving their sabres.

He looked at his watch. One minute to go. Jenkins and his marksmen were still firing. Fonthill turned and looked behind him. The company was lined up, stretching across the road two deep. He could not resist a grin. The men sitting their ponies, eyes gleaming and grinning back at him, looked more like a band of brigands than soldiers. Most had now wrapped their scarves round the lower part of their faces, bandit-fashion; their long *poshteen* sheepskins draped down either side of their saddles, making their wiry little ponies look even more diminutive; and their sabres glistened in the cold sunlight. Simon was reminded of Wellington's remark about his raggle-taggle army facing Napoleon's troops in the Peninsular War: 'I don't know what they do to the enemy, but, by Gad sir, they frighten me.'

He looked at his watch again. The correct tactics for a cavalry charge, he seemed to have read somewhere, were to begin by trotting gently, then to canter and then, when near the enemy, to break into a gallop for the charge. But, what the hell! Now he was near enough to the enemy and he wanted to instil terror into them as soon as he and his men rounded the bend. So now, he slowly filled his lungs, raised his sabre, pointed it straight ahead and screamed: 'Charge!'

He dug in his heels, tugged on the right rein to wheel his pony round the bend and put his steed to full gallop. He caught a glimpse of Jenkins on his feet to his right, waving him on, and heard the thunder of hooves behind him. As he rode, head down, he saw rifle flashes from a wall to his left but heard nothing. A man with what appeared to be a pike lunged at him but he crashed it aside with his sabre. Then another appeared directly ahead of him, waving a long Tibetan sword. He pulled his pony to the left and cut at the man, slashing his arm. Then he was in the middle of what appeared to be a completely deserted village.

He allowed the pony to fall back into a trot and realised that he had been concentrating so hard on keeping his seat that he had forgotten to yell. Looking around, he saw that the buildings seemed to be untenanted. Had the villagers – or soldiers, if that was what they were – all congregated at the entry to the village? He held up his hand to halt his company and called for the horse handlers. Slipping the sabre back into its saddle sheath, he half fell from his horse and threw the reins to the trooper who ran forward. He drew his revolver and stood for a moment scanning the buildings on either side. Nothing.

In moments, he was surrounded by his men. '*Daffadar*,' he shouted.

The big man materialised at his side.

'Any casualties from the charge?'

'No, sahib. No one hit. All here.'

He sighed with relief. 'Good. Ensure your carbines are loaded. Yes? Good. Now, at the double, back to the end of the village. Run. NOW!'

Although beginning in the lead, Fonthill was soon overtaken by long-striding Sikhs who ranged out ahead of him. A musket poked over a wall and the man behind it was immediately brought down by a carbine shot. The Sikhs soon disappeared into the houses and grey-shrouded Tibetans began pouring out, their hands upraised. One tall man, with long Manderin-moustaches – a priest lama, perhaps? – sprang from a doorway and swung his sword horizontally at Simon, who ducked instinctively and fired his revolver directly into the man's chest. Not waiting to see if the man fell, Fonthill ran on. Then he realised that he had reached the end of the village and saw Jenkins and his marksmen trotting up the road to meet him.

'Ah,' puffed Jenkins. 'Thank God you're all right. You was never exactly good at chargin' on 'orseback wavin' a sword, bach sir. I'm amazed you did it without me.'

Fonthill put an arm on the Welshman's shoulder and leant on him, trying to regain his breath. 'I was never much better running up a Tibetan street at some ridiculous altitude, either,' he panted.

He turned. The Sikhs led by the *daffadar* were rounding up scores of terrified Tibetans, who soon began grinning as they realised that they were not to be killed out of hand. Then, sheepishly, women and children, all muffled to their chins, began dribbling out from the dwellings, putting out their tongues in signs of friendship.

Down the trail, a company of Gurkhas, their pillbox hats jauntily showing above their greatcoats, were trotting towards the village, their rifles at the trail.

'Well,' grunted Jenkins, 'I reckon that's the bloody end of that funny old battle, look you.'

'I reckon it is,' said Fonthill. 'Thank God for that.'

CHAPTER SIX

After Alice had sent her despatch and returned to the fire that Jenkins lit between their tents, she lifted her tin cup of steaming tea and frowned at Simon. 'Damn,' she said. 'I meant to ask if any guns of Russian make had been found amongst the dead. Did you see any?'

'Some rifles, although they didn't look Russian. Mostly they used – or tried to use – muskets. From the evidence so far, it doesn't appear that Moscow has been supplying the Tibetans with arms.'

Alice snorted. 'There you are. It looks as though Curzon has been completely wrong about the Russian influence in Lhasa. If he is, then this whole invasion is based on a myth.'

Fonthill raised a hand. 'Now, don't go jumping to conclusions. We have only had one real clash with the Tibetans so far and—'

'It wasn't a clash, more like a disgraceful massacre.'

'Well, whatever it was, we've only come up against them once. There are likely to be others and we shall see then, when we penetrate deeper into the country. And, don't forget, there are other reasons for making the Tibetans negotiate. They've broken treaties and not behaved like a civilised nation at all.'

Alice blew the steam away from her brimming mug. 'Well, what do you expect from people who live on the roof of the world, paint their faces and had never seen a wheeled vehicle until we brought one in – carrying guns, of course.'

'Oh dear, please don't go on.' Simon shrugged. 'Anyway, Younghusband is hoping that this battle – if you can call it that – will have put the fear of God into the lamas in Lhasa and that we shall meet no further opposition. Let's hope so.'

That, however, soon proved to be a pious hope.

Anxious to push on – a welcome and, most of the officers felt, probably temporary change of heart – Macdonald sent Fonthill and his Mounted Infantry scouting out ahead and widely to the flanks to flush out any further Tibetan forces before the advance recommenced. The unit had been reinforced by a number of Gurkhas, many of whom had never sat a horse in their lives until their intensive training back at the border. Nevertheless, as befitting their reputation as being among the most versatile and dedicated troops in the army of the Raj, they soon became as comfortable in the saddle as the Sikhs. In fact, 'Fonthill's Horse', as it became known, had now assumed something of the mantle of an *elite* force, widely respected throughout the invading force – and certainly its most actively employed.

It was patrolling ahead when Macdonald's 'reconnaissance in force' stoically gathered together its long tail and began to advance once more towards Gyantse. It plodded along beside the still frozen banks of the Bham Tso and Kala Tso lakes, their lush wildlife on the ice-free open patches of water contrasting starkly with the twisted corpses from the battlefield, where the iron-hard ground had resisted all attempts by the Pioneers to bury them. Alice, whose pony daintily threaded its own way between the once-human detritus, thankfully turned her head away to note the wildfowl: sheldrake, pintails, geese, teal and mallard. If she kept her eyes focussed to the left, she could have been in a wintry Norfolk.

Way ahead of the main column, however, Simon was leading the first of his two companies – he refused to call them squadrons, maintaining that his men remained Mounted *Infantry* – when he was fired upon as he approached a village called Samada. Retiring to regroup with his second company, he extended his front and, at the trot, approached the village, ready to break into a charge if fired upon again. In the event, he found that the defenders had retreated and the village was devoid of inhabitants.

'Funny bleedin' lot, these Tibeterans,' confided Jenkins. 'They can't seem to make up their minds whether to be 'eroes or cowards, see. Perhaps it's the weather up 'ere.'

Cautiously, the Mounted Infantry continued its patrol northwards along the trail, beside the Nyang Chu. The route was marked by small fields of barley and then, to a cheer from the Sikhs, a patch of stunted willow trees – the first real trees that the warriors had seen since climbing into the mountains. Then, just at the point where the river entered what was to be a fifteen-mile gorge that ended at the plain of Gyantse, Simon, Jenkins and Ottley, riding ahead, were fired on once again, from a wall that stretched across the trail at a place called Kangmar, the village of the Red Foot, so called from the surrounding spurs of toe-like red sandstone.

This time, however, it was a much more formidable proposition than the wall before Guru. It was loopholed, it extended right across the mouth of the gorge and it curled quite high up the mountains on both sides. Behind the wall, the Tibetans were gathered in considerable numbers.

'Ah,' muttered Jenkins, leaning forward in the saddle and munching his moustache, 'I suppose we now give it another of our famous charges, jump the wall and then trot on to this Gutsey place.'

'I rather fancy not,' said Fonthill. 'I don't want to be a dead hero. We are here to scout and we've found what we are looking for. Let's get back to the General.' He paused only long enough to make a sketch of the Tibetan position before ordering the return to the column.

There, he found the Macdonald ensconced with Younghusband and he reported to both, showing them the sketch. 'They seem pretty determined this time,' he said, 'and it looks as though they intend to defend in some depth. As best as I could see beyond the wall, the road

157

narrows beside the river considerably and then there is a spur across the road which offers a good, sound, second line of defence.'

The two officers scanned the sketch. 'Hmm,' murmured Macdonald, 'as far as we know, this blocks the only road to Gyantse and Lhasa, so we shall have to crack this nut if we want to get on.'

Younghusband nodded. 'And we certainly do want to get on. Good work, Fonthill.'

'We will sound reveille at 5 a.m. tomorrow morning and advance in battle formation,' Macdonald's voice was firm. 'You will scout ahead, as usual, Fonthill, so you should be out at 4 a.m.'

'Very good, gentlemen.'

Alice, of course, was concerned at the news. 'Not another bloody wall,' she hissed, 'which, presumably, Mac will knock down with his artillery and then butcher the peasants behind again with his Maxims and rifles.'

'I doubt if it will be that easy, this time. For God's sake, Alice, stay well out of the way. Remember what happened to that chap from the *Daily Mail*.'

'Oh, I shall be all right. I have the magnificent Sunil to defend me. We could invade Lhasa on our own.'

It was dark and, of course, bitingly cold, when Fonthill and his Mounted Infantry trotted away in the morning. Three hours or so later they approached Kangmar with caution, only to find that the wall now seemed completely unmanned. Fonthill, with Ottley, climbed as high as they could up the near-precipitate slopes on either side – Jenkins, of course, offering to stay with the men below, 'to make sure we're ready in case they attack.' Through their field glasses they were able to confirm that the Tibetans had abandoned their positions during the night and had retreated to the stronger position that Simon had glimpsed at the throat of the gorge.

Fonthill ordered up some of his nimble-footed Gurkhas to climb the mountainside as high as they could. Gasping for breath, he scrambled up after them with his binoculars. He had to pause some hundred feet below them and stayed there, focussing his glasses. When the little men rejoined him, they reported that a line of sangars had been built and manned high on both sides of the defile and that the muzzles of numerous *jingals*, the blunderbuss Tibetan artillery, could be seen trained on the road below.

'Hmm,' mused Simon, 'this is not going to be easy.'

And so he reported to Macdonald when, eventually, the main column came up. 'They have taken up good defensive positions and it looks to me as though they are going to stay and fight properly this time,' he said. 'Past the wall, the road along the bottom of the defile bends to the right for about a mile. Here the valley looks as though it widens out to about 150 yards. On the left the cliffs are perpendicular, solid walls of rock. On the right, though, the rocky slopes could probably be climbed by Gurkhas, with great difficulty – a fair old scramble, I would say.'

Macdonald coughed and, for once, took the cigarette from his mouth. 'Could you see what lay beyond?' he asked.

'A little, though not in great detail. After the wider bit, the road twists back to the left round a spur and narrows even to about six feet and seems to be studded with boulders. I reckon that, in addition to the men we could see up high on the sangars, this is where the main body of Tibetans will be. But I can't be sure. It is not until we advance that this will become clear.'

'Ah. Bloody difficult by the sound of it.'

Fonthill cleared his throat. 'May I make a suggestion, General?'

'Humph. Suggest away. But I don't guarantee to follow it. We can't afford to take extreme risks, Fonthill. We are far from home, with a very limited force and a line of supply that is stretched to twanging point.'

Simon struggled to suppress a smile. Typical Macdonald!

'Quite so. But I had some experience of fighting in hills something like these – though, of course, nothing like so high – on the North-West Frontier.'

Macdonald frowned. 'Very well. What do you propose?'

'I would hold back your main body and send Gurkhas – they can climb like mountain goats – up the mountain to the right, where some of my men have managed to get up quite high today. Let them clear the sangars. Then let me advance with my Mounted Infantry along the road below to draw the fire of the Tibetans along the defile so that we can test how many there are and how strong. We may even be able to clear the way for you behind us.'

The General stayed silent, puffing on his cigarette. Eventually, he nodded. 'Very well, Fonthill. But don't take on the whole Tibetan army on your own.' He let his features lapse into his sour smile. 'Dammit all, man, remember you're not a Regular soldier – and you're even older than me. So don't take undue risks. But first I must get the Pioneers to dismantle this damned wall and that will take all day, I should think. I will put the Gurkhas up the mountainside tomorrow and I will try and get the guns hauled up to a position where they can bear on the sangars. Have your men ready to go in when the little fellers have done their work. I shall give the order then.'

Fonthill nodded and turned away. Not the most supportive of responses but about as much as could be expected from the man!

For the rest of the day the 23rd Regiment of Pioneers, big Sikhs to a man, worked at pulling down the wall. They did so without a shot being fired at them and Simon wondered at one point if the Tibetans had, in fact, completely deserted their second position and fallen back on Gyantse. His scouts up the mountainside, however, reported that the sangars, at least, were still manned and their *jingals* were still in place, their wide muzzles still threatening any advance along the road.

That evening, Fonthill sought out Sunil, whom he found meticulously cleaning his rifle.

'I have just not had time to thank you for looking after the memsahib back at Guru,' he said, squatting down beside the youth. 'I am sure that if you had not been there, she would have rushed up the wall, like that fellow from the *Daily Mail*, and been seriously wounded, if not killed.'

Sunil flashed his teeth in a wide smile. 'Ah, thank you, sahib. She brave lady and don't listen to me much when I say, "don't go." But I tell her I shoot her if she leaves me, so she stayed, writing . . . always, what you say, scrobbling?'

'Scribbling. Yes, but she's a damned good reporter and she likes to get near the action. This fight tomorrow could be far worse than the scrap at Guru and I won't be able to be anywhere near her, so watch over her, that's a good chap.'

'I watch, yes. I watch.'

'Good man.'

Shortly after dawn the next day, the Gurkhas were sent scrambling up the mountainside until they disappeared into the mist.

Ottley and Fonthill stood below amongst the ruin of the wall, watching them. 'They're not going to be able to see much, let alone fight up there in this cloud,' said the Captain, his nose, almost as red now as his hair, peeping out from behind the turned-up collar of his *poshteen*. 'What's more,' he sniffed the air, 'I think there's a bloody snowstorm coming on. God help them up there.'

Simon nodded. 'Yes, I think you're right. I wish we hadn't dismantled the tents. There's precious little cover for men or horses down here.'

Within minutes the snowstorm had whirled down all about them, blotting out each man's view of anyone or anything but his close neighbour. Fonthill could only order the ponies to be covered with their blankets and the men to take what shelter they could. So they all crouched in the freezing cold, to the point where Simon wondered if anyone would be able to move if and when the order to do so came.

It was a blessed relief, then, when the storm lifted, leaving a grey-black cloud above their heads, so low that it could almost be touched – and, of course, still obscuring the Gurkhas, if they had survived up there in the heights. At that moment, a young subaltern came running up.

'General presents his compliments, sir,' he said. 'He doubts whether the Gurkhas have been able to clear the hillside but you are to take your mounted men and advance down the defile – he emphasises with caution – to test the enemy's defences and report back.'

'Thank you,' said Fonthill, his teeth chattering. 'We'll move if the ponies haven't been frozen to the ground. No,' he grinned. 'Don't tell the General that. Just say that we will move immediately.'

He found Ottley and Jenkins and relayed the order. 'We will go in single file,' he said, 'at a smart trot. Very much in extended order, with about fifteen yards between each man. I will lead A Company, with Sergeant Major Jenkins, and you will take B Company.'

'I would much rather come with you, Simon. After all, it used to be my troop.'

'Sorry, old chap. You have to be nearly ninety, like Jenkins and me, to do this job now.' He grinned. 'Let's hope the visibility clears, because I don't intend to just take a look and then bugger off back to the General. I wish to test the Tibetans – if they're still there, that is. So be prepared to gallop up if you hear shots. Keep sabres sheathed. We won't be able to charge, because they will probably be behind rocks. It will be a question of exchanging fire, I would think. Now, get the men lined up and good luck.'

Minutes later, Fonthill was sitting at the head of his Mounted Infantry – now numbering some 150 – winding back in single file behind him. At a nod from Jenkins, who had ridden back down the line and had now rejoined him, he put his whistle to his lips and blew a single, sharp note. Then he drew his revolver from its holster, dug in his heels and set off at a fast trot down the path that led by the side of the river at the bottom of the defile.

The clatter of the ponies' hooves echoed back from steep walls, but that was the only sound. It seemed as if the Tibetans had retreated completely – perhaps all the way to Gyantse? Simon scanned the rocks that climbed up on either side of him but they seemed quite uninhabited.

He trotted on, with Jenkins now riding just behind him, until he reached a point at where the defile opened out to about 150 yards, then virtually closed again with a boulder-strewn outcrop jutting out, leaving only a narrow space bending round taking the track out of sight. A perfect place for an ambush? He frowned. Only one way to find out. He dug in his heels and, head down, rounded the spur. Instantly, the whole of the mountainside seemed to erupt with flame and smoke as the hidden Tibetans opened fire on him and Jenkins. A perfect ambush indeed!

Simon blew his whistle and wheeled the head of his pony round, indicating to Jenkins to do the same. Bullets whined over his head and thudded into the rocks, pinging away into the infinite, but somehow missing him, the Welshman and a couple of Sikhs who had rounded the bend behind them.

All four, now at the gallop, rounded the spur into safety and Fonthill pulled up and shouted: 'Dismount and take cover. Handlers forward to take the horses. Quickly now!'

Ottley galloped up. 'What happened?'

Simon threw himself from the saddle, handed the reins to a handler and indicated to Ottley to do the same. 'It was a very cleverly placed ambush,' he gasped. 'The Tibetans are lined up the hillside on either side round the bend. If they had had the sense to delay their fire until the whole of our men had come round the bend, then they would have had us completely at their mercy. They lacked the discipline to do that so they missed their chance. Get the men to follow me on foot up this spur, to line the top and see if we can dislodge them with rifle fire.'

With Jenkins at his heels, Fonthill scrambled up the face of the spur and peered over the top. To his amazement, he realised that the Tibetans were relinquishing their secure positions behind the rocks up the mountainside and were spilling down onto the track.

He turned his head and indicated to his men climbing up behind him to spread out along the rocky top. He turned to Jenkins. 'They obviously felt we had run for it and are trying to pursue us,' he said. 'Bloody fools.' He turned to the Sikhs who had formed a ragged line along the top of the spur. 'Rapid fire at the enemy in front,' he ordered.

As he did so, he heard the rattle of musketry coming from high above him, where the Gurkhas had found positions to fire down on the sangars. This was then joined by the dull boom of artillery as the guns joined in. Looking up, Simon saw tiny figures pouring from the rocky emplacements and begin scrambling down the mountains in full retreat.

More of his own men now joined their fellows on the top of the spur and a rapid fire began pouring down on the dun-coloured Tibetans, running along the trail towards the bend. The fire immediately took its toll and the leaders began collapsing, crumpling and falling to the ground, their weapons clattering away from them. Immediately, the advance stopped, paused for a moment and then broke, the Tibetans running back, the way they had come, being joined now by others leaving their positions behind the rocks – all hurrying in headlong retreat to get away from the gunfire.

'Cease firing,' shouted Fonthill. 'Handlers, bring up the horses. Mount up. Quickly now.'

Within minutes, the companies were mounted and lined up. Simon brought his pony round and stood in his stirrups to address the men. He became aware that Ottley had joined him and Jenkins. No hanging back with the rear company for the Irishman this time! 'We will charge at the retreating enemy,' he shouted. 'The ground is covered in rocks so be careful. Do not use sabres. Fire from the saddle.'

He pulled his pony's head round and shouted. 'Bugler. Sound the charge!'

The clear notes bounced back from the walls on either side and Fonthill dug in his heels and his pony instinctively responded. Round the bend of the spur he raced and Simon found himself trusting to God and his steed's good judgement to pick its way between the bodies that were now strewn along the floor of the defile and the rocks that studded it. Being thrown at this speed could result in death or injury – not to mention being trampled by the two companies racing behind him.

Somehow, horse and rider reached clearer ground and Fonthill realised that the cleft had opened out and he became aware that he was thundering by two large images that had been carved in semi-relief on a giant boulder and painted in scarlet and gold leaf, before he was among the retreating Tibetans. He fired his revolver into the mob, with no apparent result, and caught a glimpse of what appeared to be two Tibetan generals trying to rally their troops. But all of the Mounted Infantry were now among them and, although the horsemen were completely outnumbered by the running men, the Tibetans had lost all desire to fight and the arrival of the cavalry increased their panic.

Simon suddenly felt a revulsion at firing at men who showed no intention of defending themselves and he allowed his pony to slow to a walk and push its way along among the fleeing crowd. He saw that many of the Tibetans were now attempting to escape into a narrow valley that came in from the left, but it offered them no succour, for the Gurkhas who had cleared the sangars had now descended into it. He drew in his breath, expecting the sepoys to open fire, so creating another massacre, but it seemed that they, too, had had enough of the killing and the little men now began rounding up the Tibetans, like shepherds with sheep.

He became aware that Jenkins was at his side. 'Good bit of gallopin' that, bach sir,' said the grinning Welshman. 'You're gettin' better at this lark.'

'Well, I don't want to make a habit of it. Rough ground that. Let's get our men to re-form. I don't want them to go on needlessly shooting. It looks as though the day is ours.'

And so it was. Fonthill found Ottley and the mounted men joined with the Gurkha infantry in pushing the defeated Tibetans into compliant groups and stacking their weapons into heaps. Once again, Simon searched through the rifles and muskets, finding a preponderance of the latter and only three rifles that seemed to have been made outside Tibet – and they were British.

By now, Macdonald and Younghusband had arrived with the main force and the latter ordered that the prisoners should be set to breaking up their weaponry. This the Tibetans did with glee, crashing their muskets against rocks and jumping up and down on the stocks to break them.

Fonthill rode up to where O'Connor was supervising the destruction. 'It looks as though the poor devils had nothing much to fight with,' he observed. 'No wonder they didn't hit us as we rounded that bend.'

The Captain nodded. 'Most of this lot are just poor peasants,' he said. 'They tell me that they were ordered to fight by those chaps,' he indicated a number of monks in red robes, who were looking on truculently as the weapons were destroyed. 'If they didn't they were told that their houses would be burnt down and their families taken from them. No wonder they are laughing.'

Most of the Tibetans were allowed to continue their retreat and about a hundred were taken as prisoners. A rough count later that day found that some 150 of the enemy had been killed and wounded, with the wounded once again being given every care and their wounds bound, much to their relief and delight. The only casualties among Macdonald's force were among Fonthill's Mounted Infantry, where three of his Sikhs had been wounded in that charge amongst the rocks.

Later that day, Simon found Alice. She had completed

her report and, with the ever-faithful Sunil, was sitting drinking tea.

'At least, it wasn't a massacre this time,' he said, squatting beside the pair.

His wife grimaced. 'No, but I don't believe that figure of 150 casualties among the Tibetans. I am more or less sure that it did not contain the number who were killed when our guns and the Gurkhas fired on the sangars. We have not been back up there to count, so I have put in a figure of an estimated 200.'

'Hmmm. Well that won't please Younghusband and Macdonald, for sure.'

'I don't damn well care.' Alice put down her cup. 'Simon, this is a ridiculous war, if that is what you can call it. The Tibetans themselves don't want to fight, that seems certain, so why don't we camp our bloody great army somewhere half decent and send a message to Lhasa saying that we won't advance further if the lamas will undertake to send their top men to parley with us about our so-called grievances?'

Simon grimaced. 'The trouble with that is that we just can't believe a word these monks say. If we stopped now, they would let us sit there for months and do nothing – just as they did earlier at Khamba Jong. Younghusband wouldn't consider that for a second. What he really wants is to press on to Lhasa.'

'Well, one thing is for sure. It looks as though Curzon was quite wrong about a Russian presence in Lhasa and about them supplying arms to the Tibetans. There's been no evidence of that at all.'

Fonthill nodded. 'You're right about that, my love.'

Alice put her head in her hands and reflected for a moment. 'Do you know,' she said eventually, 'I am getting really tired of riding with this damned army and standing by while it slaughters Tibetans.' She looked up. 'I wish to God I could do something to stop it all.'

Simon put a hand on her shoulder. 'You are doing your best by merely reporting what is happening. And no one can do that better. Your reporting must surely be having an affect back home.'

She nodded glumly. 'Up to a point. There have been questions asked in the House, of course, and a debate is promised.' She pulled a scrap of paper from within her blouse. 'This is a cable from my editor. He has sent me a caption from a cartoon by *Punch*, published just after the Guru massacre. It says: "We are sorry to learn that the recent sudden and treacherous attack by the Tibetans on our men at Guru seriously injured the photographs that the officers were taking."' She threw down the cable. 'That's what it has come down to. Fat commentators back home making fun of all this killing. It is disgraceful.'

Tears began to trickle down her cheeks and she blew her nose violently. Simon pulled her to him.

'I agree,' he said. 'But look at it this way. These two defeats that the Tibetans have suffered must surely have had some effect in Lhasa. I can't see them standing up to us again. And there is one more thing. At the moment, Younghusband doesn't have permission to push on to Lhasa. The resistance we've met may have changed the government's mind on that point and they may well now allow him to continue his advance to the capital. Once there, it will all be over.'

Alice regarded her husband steadily. 'There's a lot of ifs and buts there, darling,' she muttered. 'And there is one other development.' She picked up the cable. 'Curzon has left India for home. He is not well, I understand, and has gone home on leave. What that means I don't know.' She sighed. 'All I know is that we are stuck up here in these damned mountains surrounded by dead bodies.' She shuddered. 'And it is damned cold.'

That night, clutching each other in their tent, Fonthill and his wife made love for the first time since the advance had begun. It was not the most satisfactory lovemaking of their matrimonial life but it made them both feel much, much better.

The expedition left what had already become known as Red Idol Gorge as quickly as it could and marched on towards what was its official destination, the town of Gyantse, the third most important in Tibet. The route was slightly and most rewardingly downhill, for Gyantse was said to be lower in altitude, at 13,000 feet, than Tuna and the column debouched onto the Gyantse Valley on 11th April. The terrain now presented a most fertile and delightful vista to eyes smarting from the grey grit and granite of Guru and Kangmar. Dotted with trees and neat buildings of white-washed stone, clustered amongst groves and well-cultivated fields, the valley was, in fact, a fertile plain, through which the River Nyang danced and glistened in the sunlight. But every eye was drawn to a dominating feature rising from the middle of the plain, like Gibraltar emerging from the western Mediterranean. This was a white fort, set about 500 feet high atop a dark rock: the citadel of Gyantse, blocking the way north to Lhasa.

Its appearance was summarised, as usual, by Jenkins. 'Bloody 'ell,' he muttered to Fonthill. 'If the General wants to attack that, 'e can do it without me. I ain't climbin' that, look you.'

Indeed, it looked a formidable obstacle. As the column wound its way towards it from the south it appeared to be virtually impregnable, with the rock sides rising sheer. Near-to, however, it became plain that the fort itself was set on the southern edge of a ridge that ran north and south down the centre of the plain for about a mile and a half, with the ridge descending towards the north. Behind the fort was an ancient and famous monastery, Palkor Chode, the 'Illustrious Circle of the Religious Residence', and sprawled at its foot was a warren-like town, capable of housing at least 1,000 inhabitants.

The column camped on the banks of the river, less than two miles from the fort. From there, Fonthill examined the citadel with care through his field glasses. 'This is certainly not going to be easy,' he confided to Ottley and Jenkins. 'If the fort is manned, then I don't really see how we can take it, because we have no siege artillery and the garrison probably outnumber us, anyway.'

Ottley nodded. 'And for once,' he said, 'this is no job for the Mounted Infantry.'

Immediately, however, the fort gates were seen to be opened and through them came a colourful group of mounted delegates, trotting towards the camp, obviously with no aggressive intentions.

They were led by the *jongpen*, or commandant of the fort, and by Mo, a Chinese general, who was said to be an emissary of the *amban*, the resident Chinese agent in Lhasa, and whom Younghusband had met during previous abortive negotiations. The latter, with Macdonald, received them within the camp, O'Connor once again acting as interpreter. Fonthill, Ottley, some of the other British officers and the press corps, including Alice, crowded round to listen.

The *jongpen* was a smiling, round-faced and stout Tibetan with a submissive air who regretted that he was unable to hand over the fort because he was under strict orders from Lhasa to defend it to the death. Alas, he confided that he could not do that either, because most of the garrison had fled to the north when the British approached. He was, he said, in a difficult position, but he could not open the gates, for to do so would mean that all his family and his belongings would be seized by the lamas in the capital. Could not, perhaps, the British solve his problem by simply passing by and ignoring the fort?

Equally courteously, Younghusband explained that this would not be possible and that, if the gates were not opened by 8 a.m. the following morning, artillery would be brought up and the gates blasted open. Still smiling, but insisting that he was unable to accommodate the British, much as he would like to, the *jongpen* and his party rode back to the citadel.

The next morning, the guns were brought up laboriously within range of the fort. It was not until just before eight o'clock that the great doors were opened and, under the rueful gaze of the *jongpen* and his Chinese colleagues, two companies of the 32nd Sikh Pioneers marched into the citadel. Fonthill and Alice slipped into the fort on their tail and watched as the Union Jack was hoisted on the ramparts, to cheers from the soldiers watching below.

Exploring the warren of corridors within the empty fortress, they were astonished to find one huge chamber stacked full of barley, later found to contain thirty-six tons, and another horrendously packed with the severed heads of men, women and children.

Holding her nose, Alice staggered out. 'I thought the Buddhist code forbade the taking of human life,' she gasped. 'What the hell was that about?'

Simon shook his head. 'I have no idea. But it's clear that these monks run a very different show to those in India. I just don't understand this very strange country.'

Leaving the fort, the two walked through the labyrinthine streets of the township beneath the monastery. Here, they met another surprise. In seeming disregard of the fact that a hostile army was camped on their doorstep, the inhabitants were going about their normal business, without sign of fear or hostility: hundreds of men in cherry-coloured coats riding lean ponies, less well-dressed women chattering away and carrying children slung on their backs, and lines of donkeys, laden with grain or fodder, plodding along in single file. Below the main entrance to the monastery a thriving market was being held.

Here booths straddled the road and pavements, laden with carpets and saddle rugs, for which Alice had heard that the town was famous, as well as tea, tobacco, sugar, cotton cloth, matches, pipes, tumblers, kerosene oil and foodstuffs, including pork, fresh vegetables and barley beer.

'Hmmm,' mused Simon, 'better keep Jenkins away from here.'

Alice frowned. 'This place is so different from anything else we have seen so far,' she said. 'There is an abundance here that we've not glimpsed before. Is it because it's set in this fertile plain, with a much more pleasant climate, or what?'

'Don't know. Could be because of the fortress. It's important because it guards the entrance to the main interior of Tibet, the road to Lhasa and so on.'

'Well, as you said, Tibet is full of surprises.'

The next morning, Macdonald decided to move the camp away from the fort and the town, some 1,000 yards to a hamlet by the river, where water was freely available and where a Tibetan nobleman had set up a residence years before. The manor house, called Chang Lo, still stood and was surrounded by a few rustic dwellings.

Here the General produced another surprise. He announced that he was going to take approximately half of his troops – including his only effective artillery, the British-manned ten-pounders – back 150 miles to New Chumbi. This, he explained, was necessary 'to arrange posts and communications and convoys'. To guard the mission at Chang Lo, he left four companies of 32nd Pioneers, two companies of the 8th Gurkhas, fifty of Fonthill's Mounted Infantry, the two Maxims, Bubble and Squeak, part of a mule corps and one section of an

India field hospital; in all about five hundred men.

The General by now was clearly a sick man suffering from fevers, although he continued to chain smoke. 'Sorry I can't leave you in command, Fonthill,' he explained, 'but it has to be a line officer. So Lieutenant Colonel Brander, the CO of the Pioneers, will command. No offence meant, you know.'

'None taken, General. Brander is a good man.'

'Good. I am leaving you Ottley, of course.' He gave a wintry smile. 'If I took him back with me he'd give me a hell of a time. I am leaving the fort ungarrisoned. We just don't have enough men to man both places – and there's no water up there on that rock. Keep patrolling. We mustn't be caught napping here, although I must say the natives seem friendly hereabouts.'

Immediately, Brander set about making Chang Lo more defendable. The main house stood amidst willow trees and was large and spacious, containing a hall where Younghusband could hold his hoped-for meetings with representatives of the Dalai Lama. Some of the outhouses and trees were demolished to yield lines of fire and lines of sharpened stakes, called abattis, knocked into the ground, while a loopholed wall, some 300 yards in circumference, was erected around the main house and the remaining outbuildings. Within it was a large farmhouse, where the troops were housed, which was immediately called the Redoubt.

Macdonald set off on his long journey back to New Chumbi on 20th April, leaving three weeks rations for the mission, deemed plenty in view of the fact that the Tibetans were now freely trading with the newcomers, even setting up a standing market just outside Chang Lo, to which they brought regular supplies of food stuffs as well as souvenirs of all kinds. The Raj's Indian rupee, it became clear, was much valued in Tibet.

Fonthill tried to persuade Alice to return with Macdonald, arguing that nothing much could happen at Gyantse while he was away. She refused, however, stating that to do so would leave her with nothing to write about except, once again, retailing old descriptions of fighting through high, snowbound passes and problems of logistics. 'Besides which,' she explained, 'I am not sure I can trust you and Jenkins in the bazaars of wild Gyantse.'

Once Macdonald's column had wound out of sight along the plain a kind of peaceful serenity descended on Chang Lo. The spring weather was quite mild, the rivers provided reasonable fishing and the plain and the surrounding foothills offered plenty of game. A large Tibetan lady was happily recruited to plant a small garden within the hamlet – she was immediately christened Mrs Wiggs, after a bucolic novel of the day – and once the defences of the little hamlet had been erected, it was only Fonthill and his Mounted Infantry who were left with serious work to do, ranging out every day on patrol.

'How long do you think we shall be stuck here, with nothing but good food to eat and nothing to do but enjoy ourselves?' demanded Alice of her husband. 'Do you think there is any chance at all of the Chinese or Tibetans coming here to negotiate with old Y?'

Simon shrugged. 'I honestly have no idea. You know

that prevarication and procrastination are the Tibetans watchwords. Younghusband keeps receiving letters, I understand, from the Chinese *amban* in Lhasa, saying that he wishes to travel here to talk but that the lamas won't provide him with transport. I can't help feeling that the prospects of a negotiated settlement are as remote now as ever they were.'

'What does Y think?'

'Probably the same, I feel. I believe he has written to the acting viceroy urging that he be allowed to go on from here to Lhasa to force the issue, but that all depends upon how the government back home view things.' He sighed. 'Frankly, my love, I think the days of the great British thrusts into strange lands are over. We've become a bit of an anachronism, not to mention embarrassment, to Whitehall and the Horse Guards.'

'Quite right, too. We should never have invaded.'

The days of serenity were broken, however, when intelligence was received at the camp that a Tibetan army was being concentrated less than fifty miles to the east of Gyantse, at a 16,000-feet-high pass called Karo La, on the road to Lhasa. Inevitably, Fonthill and his fifty men were sent to investigate.

After a climb that left the mild air of the plain well behind them, they eventually reached the pass – to find yet another rock wall stretching across the defile and effectively blocking the road forward.

Jenkins pulled on his moustache. 'This lot is a nation of bricklayers, it seems to me, bach sir,' he observed, 'except that they've never discovered mortar. Do they just go about the place, look you, stickin' stones across the bloody road all the time?'

'Probably. What else is there to do up here?' He studied the wall through his binoculars. 'Seems unmanned.' He focussed up the steep mountain slopes on either side. 'Can't see any one there.' He lowered the glasses. 'Come on. Let's take a walk and have a look. William, stay here with the men.'

They dismounted and began walking warily towards the wall. At about 200 yards from it, however, a fusillade of fire sprang from along the wall and from the surrounding rocks, matched by stones hurled down on them from the side of the mountains.

Without a word, the two spun on their heels and ran back out of range, where they stood, panting.

'Another little surprise, look you,' gasped Jenkins.

Fonthill drew out his field glasses again from their case and examined the wall and the hillside. 'I can see hundreds of them now,' he murmured, focusing the lenses. 'Thank God they can't shoot straight. There must be well over 1,000.' He lowered the glasses. 'Let's get back. I've seen enough. We've found the Tibetan army, old chap.'

Back at Chang Lo, he reported to Colonel Herbert Brander, a short, bright-eyed officer, younger than Fonthill, of course, who had already distinguished himself on the march from the border.

'How many d'yer say, old man?'

'Could be as many as 1,500. And they seem well armed – though they still can't shoot straight.'

'Then I shall go and clear them out.'

'What, and leave the camp virtually undefended? You will need as many troops as you can muster to get them out from behind that wall.'

Brander grinned. 'Oh, I think we are pretty well housed here and I shall leave as many as I can spare. We can't afford, Fonthill, to have that many of the enemy hanging about as near to us as this. I want to hit 'em while they are not expecting us.'

Simon grimaced. 'Well, it's your decision, Brander. But I suppose you must get Y's agreement. And what about Macdonald?'

The Colonel's grin widened. 'I think Y will agree. He's all for getting on with things. And I shall get a telegram off to the General, although, alas, I am afraid he won't receive it until after I have set out. Unfortunately, I won't be able to wait for his reply. I would like you and your chaps to come with me, if you will?'

For a moment, Fonthill hesitated. Alice would be left in a camp which, if things went wrong, would have had its garrison severely reduced, whatever Brander said. But the Colonel would need scouts patrolling ahead of him to protect his force. There was no choice.

'Of course we will come. We and the horses will need a good night's rest, though. We had to ride pretty hard coming back here.'

'Very well. We leave at dawn.'

Alice rose at 4 a.m. to see off her husband for, as always, the Mounted Infantry had to leave before the main column to range ahead of the marching men. Brander had taken the decision to ban the correspondents from riding with him because, he explained, he needed to move fast and wished to have no additional responsibility for civilians in what could prove to be a stiff fight. Grudgingly, therefore, Alice returned to the small room she shared with Simon within the compound, turned up the wick of her lantern and began writing a report, detailing the despatch of Brander and his force.

Communications with London were now more tenuous, because the telegraph line had not been extended to Gyantse, running only to Kala Tso, some sixty miles away. She would need, then, to find a despatch rider quickly to take her story back to the telegraph station.

It was this delay in communicating, of course, that Brander had relied on in riding out immediately to fight the Tibetans. He had a pretty sure feeling that Macdonald would forbid him to leave the camp, but, of course, he would be well on his way before such an order could reach him. And so it proved.

Alice, of course, was unaware of this manoeuvring and, once she had despatched her story, she decided that, rather than sit and mope, worrying about Simon, she would offer her services to the mission's medical officer, Captain Walton, who had set up a small hospital just outside the perimeter walls and who had already built up a thriving practice, with peasants from the town as his patients.

In fact, she spent a busy and rewarding day, helping the Captain and his orderlies, applying dressings and administering doses of colic and other basic medicines. Her attendance was welcomed by Walton and Alice decided to return the following day.

That morning, however, she noticed a sudden and surprising slackening in the number of patients attending. In fact, as the day progressed, the inmates of the sickroom all picked themselves up and hobbled away, or were picked up by their relatives.

'Was it something that I said?' she joked to Walton.

He shrugged his shoulders. 'Strange, isn't it? I have had to turn people away almost every day over the last week. Now, they've all suddenly become extremely healthy overnight. They are, indeed, an unpredictable lot.'

The reason soon became apparent.

Alice was asleep in her hut when, at about four-thirty the next morning, she was awakened by a shrill howling, like that of a pack of hyenas fighting over a carcase that she recalled from her days in Africa. She realised, with a sinking stomach, that they were war cries. They were followed immediately by the sound of firing.

She threw on her clothes, picked up the Webley service revolver that Simon had left with her and ran out into the compound. All around, the perimeter wall was aflame with fire and gunshot smoke and she realised that muskets were poking through the loopholes and firing indiscriminately inwards *from outside the wall*!

Inside the compound all was confusion, with sepoys running towards the wall and officers, some of them in their nightshirts, shouting orders.

Alice caught the arm of one of them. 'What's happening?' she shouted.

'We're under attack, madam. The compound is

surrounded. There are hundreds of them. Get back into your house and take cover.'

Alice ran back into her hut, but only to grab a carton of cartridges for her revolver, thrusting the bullets into the pockets of her jodhpurs as she ran back, following three Sikhs towards the wall. As she ran, she was aware that Sunil was at her side, carrying his Lee Metford and keeping pace with her. She realised that the muskets firing through the loopholes were discharging their balls mainly over the heads of the defenders. The holes, of course, were set at shoulder level for the Sikh Pioneers, who were all much taller than the Tibetans, with the result that the muskets were harmlessly pointing up to the rapidly lightening sky.

Pushing the revolver into the waistband of her riding breeches, Alice followed a Sikh who was climbing up the side of one of the outhouses near to the perimeter. He reached down a hand and pulled her up onto the roof, Sunil scrambling up behind her, where they all three lay and looked over the wall. Below them stretched a thick line of Tibetans, all shrieking, some of them firing through the loopholes, others waving long swords aimlessly. Alice turned her head and realised that the enemy were pressing up against the wall on all sides of the compound. There must be nearly 1,000 of them. How long before the gates collapsed?

The Sikh levelled his Lee Metford and fired. Immediately, his action was taken up by Sunil and by other sepoys and officers who had similarly gained vantage points looking over the wall. Alice, too, instinctively levelled her pistol and fired into the mass below.

It was impossible to miss, so tightly packed were the Tibetans, and the crack of the rifles now began to outnumber the dull sound of the attackers' muskets. Within minutes, it seemed to Alice, the throng began to thin and then the Tibetans turned and ran, leaving behind them piles of bodies, hunched against the bottom of the wall.

From behind her somewhere, Alice heard an authoritarian voice shout, 'Open the gates. After the bastards!'

As she watched, scores of sepoys doubled out of the opened gates, knelt and delivered a series of volleys after the fleeing Tibetans. Then, the soldiers reloaded and began running after the enemy, pursuing them into a grove of poplars and then towards the river, where some had taken refuge behind the bank.

'Can I go with them, memsahib?' Sunil was looking at her with anxious eyes, a thin smear of cordite across his cheek.

Alice rested her head on her forearm and sighed. More killing! She inspected the chambers of her revolver. Two were empty. Did this mean that she had killed two Tibetans? She had no idea, for, caught up in the heat and fear of the moment, she had fired blindly into the mob.

'I think not, Sunil,' she said. 'I think we've had enough killing for one day, don't you?'

'No, miss. They try to kill us. We should see they don't do it again.'

Alice frowned. 'But aren't these your fellow countrymen? Do you want to kill your own people?'

For a moment the boy looked slightly puzzled. Then he

shook his head. 'They not my people now, memsahib. Not anymore.'

'I see. Well, I think Colonel Fonthill would want you stay here and help look after me. Which, I must say, you have done splendidly.'

She lay for a moment more along the top of the hut, not noticing that the Sikh had left his post, presumably to join in the pursuit.

Then she heard a familiar sound and looked up. Dawn had broken, touching the mountains to the east with a delicate pink, and skylarks were singing, their warbling replacing the harsh cracks of the Lee Metfords.

'Come on,' she said to Sunil. 'Let's see if we can find some breakfast.'

The two scrambled down the side of the hut, Alice cursing as she barked her shin, causing the blood to flow. She told Sunil to repair to the cookhouse and find food but she returned to her bed, put on her *poshteen* and replaced her revolver with her notebook, before walking outside to assess the number of Tibetan dead and to see what she could do to help the wounded. As far as she could detect, there were no casualties amongst the soldiers, who were now returning from their pursuit, grinning and laughing. But she lost count of the number of Tibetan dead, giving up at 200.

It was amazing. She knew that the number of riflemen defending the cantonment were less than 150 and there must have been nearly 1,000 of the Tibetans. If they had scaled the wall and used their swords instead of poking their muskets through the loopholes and blazing away indiscriminately, then that would have been the end of Younghusband's Mission.

Alice returned to her room and sat on a corner of the bed. If there were 1,000 attacking here at Gyantse, how many might there be waiting out there for Simon? She sat for a while, thinking. This stupid, one-sided killing had to stop. She was tired of reporting on it and finding reasons to diminish the tragic slaughter of the people of Tibet. Somehow, she had to do something positive to stop it . . .

CHAPTER SEVEN

It took nearly three days of hard marching before Brander's column reached the pass at Karo La, the last spent climbing hard. He had taken with him about two-thirds of the force left behind at Chang Lo by Macdonald: both of his guns and machine guns, three companies of his own 32nd Sikh Pioneers, one company of the 8th Gurkhas and virtually all of Fonthill's Mounted Infantry. Their route, which had often forced them to march in single file, had taken them to the highest source of the Nyang river, just underneath a glacier that rose above it, peaking in a vast wall of snow 24,000 feet high.

Just twenty-four hours after the attack on the mission, he and his 300 men halted at the wall, which had been built across the defile, about a mile and a half beyond the pass itself. Here, in the bitterly cold air, a little more than 16,000 feet above sea level, they paused.

Fonthill and Jenkins rode back to meet Brander and take him and his senior officers to the wall, leaving Ottley with the horsemen. The Colonel scanned it and whistled. 'Lord,' he mused. 'Worse than I thought. Toughest we've faced yet.'

It was, in fact, a little over six feet high, four feet thick and eight hundred yards long, cleverly loopholed and protected by sangars that climbed a little way up the sides of the semi-sheer walls on either side and projected forward. The situation was similar to the Red Idol Gorge, only worse, for the British force was outnumbered now by more than ten to one and the high altitude was making everyone gasp for breath.

The Tibetans had chosen their fortifications with care and skill, for this was the narrowest part of the defile, with precipitous and quite unpassable cliffs on the left and only a slightly less steep mountainside on the right.

'I can't see how you can outflank the wall this time,' said Fonthill, 'for the mountainsides look unclimbable to me.'

'And to me,' offered Jenkins quickly.

'Well, I can't hang about,' said Brander. 'I haven't got all that much ammunition and I can't afford to be away from the mission for very long. Let's see what Bubble and Squeak and the Maxims can do.'

He shouted an order and the two antiquated cannon were wheeled forward, together with the Maxims of the Norfolks, and positioned just out of the range of the Tibetans manning the wall. An order rang clear in the cold air and firing began.

It soon became clear that the Maxims could do little

against the rocks of the wall, for, although they were aimed at the puffs of smoke emerging from it, the loopholes could not be clearly defined and the bullets either sailed harmlessly over the top or pinged abortively into the stones themselves. The two small artillery pieces proved to be equally useless. Although they were serviced smartly by the Gurkha crews, under the direction of a British NCO, they were only loaded with shrapnel, which was quite ineffective against fortifications. The sergeant resourcefully switched to using the guns as mortars, aiming high to lob the shells over the wall, but it was impossible to see where they were exploding at a range of 600 yards – and they were not always falling with the explosive end foremost. It emerged later that only one of seventy rounds fired had hit its mark and exploded.

'The noise is bloody marvellous,' shouted Ottley to Fonthill, 'but it's doing no good.'

Brander rode up. 'There's nothing for it but to attack them frontally,' he said. Fonthill noted with approval that amidst the noise, frustration and danger – for if the Tibetans suddenly decided to leave their wall and swarm forward quickly, the sepoys could easily have been swamped and overwhelmed – the man remained completely cool and self-possessed.

'I am sending in my Pioneers to attack along the floor of the defile,' he said, pointing. 'I would be much obliged, Fonthill, if you would take, say, forty of your chaps and support them on foot. Sorry, might be a bit hot.'

Simon frowned. 'Very good, Colonel.'

He ordered a company and a half of his cavalry to fall in

with their carbines and, led by himself, Ottley and Jenkins, they all followed the Sikhs whose forward company was led by a Captain Bethune, whom Fonthill had come to respect as one of the most capable of the junior officers on the expedition. Immediately the fire of the Tibetans on the wall was concentrated on this company as it walked stolidly within range. It was impossible for the Sikhs to advance into that wall of flame and Bethune gestured to Fonthill to turn back and ordered his own men to follow them. He, however, with two sepoys, disappeared up the glacis to the right of the wall, attempting, it seemed, to outflank it.

The firepower of the Tibetans was clearly much greater than had been encountered before and both the Sikhs and Fonthill's men became pinned down on the floor of the defile, crouching behind whatever cover they could find. The Maxims now began to come under fire from the sangars above and either side of them and had to be withdrawn, not least because their ammunition was running low.

This was true also of the troops and it was difficult, if not impossible, to take fresh supplies up to the Sikhs pinned down on the floor of the defile. Brander had previously sent a company of Gurkhas in a desperate attempt to climb the cliffs on the left and a small party of Sikhs to try and scramble up the scree and shale on the right. The Gurkhas had disappeared from sight but the Sikhs had been forced to give up their attempt. A kind of stalemate had descended on the defile.

Fonthill was forced to watch the proceedings without

taking action. He did, however, notice that a rider had materialised and given a message to Colonel Brander. For a moment, Simon felt his heart lurch. Was it bad news from Chang Lo? He scrambled to the Colonel's side.

Not wanting to intrude on the officer commanding, he merely asked: 'Anything I can do, Herbert?'

Brander's expression did not change. 'No, thank you. Your chaps have done all they can so far.' He waved the note. 'This says that there has been an attack on the mission. Don't worry, it has been fought off and there are no serious casualties, so I am sure that your wife is all right.'

Fonthill blew out his cheeks. 'Thank God for that. Are you going to retreat back to there?'

'Certainly not. This makes it even more imperative that we knock these chaps over here. If we turned tail, they would come after us just like the Afghans did when we retreated from Kabul back in '42.' He smiled grimly. 'They would harass us every step of the three-day march until they had picked us off down to the last man. No. I've got to find a way to get round this bloody wall. Hang on here, old man. We shall need you yet.'

Fonthill looked up to his left and saw that the Gurkhas had fallen back down the steep side of the cliff to, it seemed, regroup. Then half a dozen of them tried a new route, climbing straight up the cliff face, until they disappeared from view. Down below, Simon saw that Brander had wormed his way forward to where his pioneers were pinned down and was talking to a native *subadar*. As he watched, he saw the *subadar* gesticulate to about a dozen men, who, with him at their head, then wriggled to where a vertical cleft or chimney in the virtually sheer cliff wall offered not only cover from the Tibetan fire but, conceivably, a way upwards. Slowly, the Sikhs began to haul their way up the cleft until they, too, disappeared from sight.

Simon realised that Jenkins was by his side. 'I would 'ave volunteered to lead 'em up there,' said the Welshman, 'but I thought I'd better not. I would 'ave climbed a bit too quickly for 'em, see, an' it would be a bit embarrassin' for 'em, like.' He had the grace to give a rueful grin.

The stalemate continued for at least another hour and Fonthill realised that the only hope Brander had of breaking it was if either of the handful of climbers could manage, somehow, to haul themselves up above the sangars so that they could direct fire down on to their defenders and onto the Tibetans on the wall itself. But the cliffs on either side seemed unclimbable.

Unclimbable, that is, until a small cheer from the sheltering Pioneers made Fonthill look up, to his left. He raised his glasses and the tiny figure of one of the Gurkhas came into view, carrying a miniature rifle. Then a second appeared and together the two began firing down onto the sangars, followed shortly by the rest of the small party who had made the climb. The effect on the Tibetans behind the sangars was immediate. Men began leaping over the stone walls of these defences and scrambling down the mountainside, now in plain view of the attackers. Immediately, the two Maxims reopened fire and sent the retreating Tibetans tumbling away down the precipitous slope.

Anxious eyes were now directed up to the top of the other side of the valley. Within minutes they were rewarded by the appearance of tiny figures surmounted by the distinctive turbans of the Sikhs and the sound of rifle fire from on high. The cheer this time from the Pioneers was even louder. Perhaps it was this that began the rout, for it soon became apparent that the defenders of the wall were now leaving in droves.

Fonthill did not wait for orders. He sprang to his feet. 'Handlers,' he shouted, 'bring up the horses. Now is our chance. Mount up! Mount up! We must pursue. Mount up!'

Brander's bugle had also sounded the advance, but Simon's Mounted Infantry swept past the Pioneers at full tilt, galloping along the bed of the frozen stream until the wall brought them to a halt. There remained no defenders to pour fire down on them and the dismounted men frantically pulled at the loose stones until a gap had been made, allowing horses and riders to pass through singly at first and then two abreast.

Re-forming his men on the far side of the wall, Fonthill looked along the bottom of the valley, which led to a ridge where the defile opened out. There was no sign of the enemy. It was as though the defenders of the wall had disappeared into thin air.

'Could be a trap, Simon,' shouted Ottley.

'Could be, but I doubt it. We will gallop to that ridge and see what we can see.'

'Very good, sir.' The young man, his red hair sticking out from under his makeshift turban, so that he looked like some medieval bandit, waved the way forward and led the men in a fast canter, until they breasted the ridge a short way ahead. Here, Fonthill and Jenkins, breathing just a little more heavily after the exertions of clearing a way through the wall, joined them.

The sight that met their eyes would stay with them for the rest of their lives. Far away – perhaps a little over a mile – was the Tibetan army in full and undisciplined retreat, spreading across the road and choking the way as it met the cliff sides. As they watched, they saw another band of men, coming up the road to reinforce the first, being swept along by the force of the retreat.

'We will gallop until we are about 100 yards from them,' shouted Fonthill, turning in his saddle. 'Then we will rein in, dismount and give them several volleys. This time, we must teach them a lesson. Now,' he rised his arm, 'Charge!'

There were no more than forty of the Mounted Infantry but no one – not Simon, Ottley, Jenkins nor any of the riders – gave a thought to the fact that they were outnumbered by some fifty to one and that, if the Tibetans, rallied, took cover – as they had time to do – and directed a steady fire at the approaching horsemen, they would almost certainly emerge as the victors. The excitement of the chase, after the frustrations of waiting for the stalemate to end, overtook every one of them.

The Tibetans, seeing and hearing the pursuit, had now all attempted to break into a shambling run as Fonthill and his men reined in, dismounted and knelt. There was no time to call up the handlers so each man tucked his reins over his right arm and fired. It was like shooting fish in a barrel for it was impossible to miss. The rearmost ranks of the mob threw up their arms and collapsed as the volleys from the Lee Metfords ravaged them.

Five times the rifles fired and the lines of the Tibetans crumbled and thinned out, fleeing for their lives from the volleys, leaving behind a mass of bodies among the stones and rocks, until most of the enemy had disappeared around a bend in the road.

Fonthill remained standing in the road, looking at the human wreckage in disgust. Listlessly, he slipped his revolver into its holster.

'You all right, bach sir?' enquired Jenkins.

Silent for a moment, Simon then nodded. 'I suppose so,' he whispered. 'I think I've had enough of this slaughter, though.'

Ottley ran to him. 'We should pursue, Simon,' he said anxiously. 'We can't let them get away to fight another day. Permission to follow, sir?'

Fonthill nodded. 'Yes, carry on. Pursue but don't exhaust the horses nor your ammunition. Take prisoners, though, William, if you can. Don't just mow down the poor bastards.'

'What?' Ottley looked puzzled. 'Oh yes. I see. Very well, sir.' He ran to the bugler who was standing by, looking equally perplexed. 'Sound the pursuit.' Then, 'Follow me.'

The forty men of the Mounted Infantry rode behind Ottley, past Simon and Jenkins, out of sight round the bend in the road. As they sped by him, Fonthill attempted a quick count. It looked as though none of his men had been hit in the charge and he breathed a sigh of relief.

'Now what do we do, then, bach?' asked Jenkins. 'Shouldn't we 'ave gone with 'em? Isn't that what cavalry is supposed to do when the enemy buggers off in a panic, like that?'

Fonthill nodded. 'Yes, old chap, it is. But there is nothing in my non-existent commission which orders me to kill defenceless men. I'll have to leave that to Ottley. And I think he can look after himself. Let's get back and report to the Colonel.'

The two mounted and let their ponies pick their way delicately over and through the bodies that now were strewn across the frozen stream and trail, until they met the first detachment of the Pioneers, with Colonel Brander at its head.

Simon dismounted. 'Congratulations, Colonel,' he said. 'You've won the day, thanks, if I may say so, to a magnificent bit of mountaineering.'

'Thank you. Quite so. What's happened to the enemy, then?' He looked over Fonthill's shoulder at the distant bodies lying, mostly still, for at short range the Lee Metford volleys were deadly. 'Looks as though you had quite an encounter.'

'We pursued them for about a mile. Dismounted and gave them five volleys and sent them all packing. Ottley is still pursuing. One way or another, I think we've taught them a sharp lesson.'

Brander looked concerned. 'Are you all right, Fonthill?'

'Oh yes. Bit winded though and . . . er . . . we've both run out of ammunition. Ottley can pursue well enough.

I've told him not to go too far, though. We are down to our last few cartridges. So I have told him to round up rather than kill.'

'Yes, indeed. Well done, Simon, although I'm afraid we will not be able to keep many prisoners. I want to get back to Chang Lo as soon as I can. We've found the enemy's camp, by the way. Cooking pots still on fires, tents still standing and so on. They pushed off in a terrible hurry.'

Brander frowned. 'We're looking at the weapons they used now. Considering the way they kept us down for three hours or so, I felt sure they had modern rifles this time. But so far up in the sangars and along the wall, we've only found old Martinis, made in Lhasa by the look of them. Nothing from Russia.'

Fonthill nodded wearily. 'Yes, so Alice is right. She always is.'

'What?'

'Oh, nothing. I think we'll have a cup of tea, or something, if you don't want us immediately.'

'Yes, of course. You and your chaps did very well again, Fonthill, and I shall report as much. Congratulations.'

'Thank you. Come on, 352, let's find a kettle and a pinch of tea.'

Ottley, in fact, pursued the broken Tibetan army for more than ten miles, he and his men firing from the saddle and inflicting more casualties, before the remnants of the Tibetan horde melted away into the snows of the hills or the side valleys. On their way they dismantled several Tibetan camps and captured valuable ponies. This was done, however, at some cost, for the riders of the Mounted Infantry had indeed expended most of their ammunition and, by the time the British camp was regained at 9.30, their horses, which had been on half rations since they left Gyantse, were exhausted.

Brander was in a hurry to return to what sounded now like a beleaguered Chang Lo, and he deemed that there was no time to bury the Tibetan dead or even to treat their wounded, nor to dismantle the wall. The Tibetans were later to put their total casualties that day at more than six hundred but the British casualties were light: four killed and thirteen wounded, among them three of Fonthill's Mounted Infantry. The bodies of Captain Bethune and his two Sikhs, who had disappeared in a lone and desperate attempt to slip round the wall, were retrieved from where they lay. The captain's Sikhs made stretchers and bore the bodies back with them to Chang Lo.

It was an arduous march back, for a blinding blizzard sprung up, reducing visibility virtually down to nil and exhausting the troops, particularly Fonthill's men, who had ridden forty-seven miles in eight hours. They had to lead their horses, two of whom died, for the last twelve miles and they were the last to arrive at the camp, slipping in under cover of darkness.

So began a difficult time for the beleaguered defenders of Chang Lo. Despite their three defeats, the Tibetan 'tame sheep', as Younghusband once described them, seemed now to have turned into wolves. Intelligence reports said that strong forces were now converging on Gyantse. Scattered buildings surrounding Chang Lo were now occupied by the enemy and a constant, if ineffective fire, was being directed at the mission, both from these buildings and from the fort, 1,300 yards away, where *jingals* and snipers were particularly active.

The tables had been turned on the invaders. The garrison of Chang Lo was outnumbered by, it was later estimated, ten to one; they were about 150 miles away from their nearest supply base; and reinforcements were equally distant. Yet Fonthill found Younghusband quite sanguine.

He later explained to Alice the reason. 'It's the British in India thing,' he said. 'For years, the Raj has been used to having its outposts surrounded and under attack. But, with well-trained soldiers handling modern weapons manning the defences, it has usually been possible to hold out and then defeat the attacking natives.

'You will remember that we were with Roberts in 1879 when his little force in Kabul was under huge pressure, surrounded by hordes of Afghans. He retreated behind the walls of Sherpur, quite confident that he could hold out and later counter-attack. He was proved right.'

Alice gave a sour smile. 'Yes, but then Roberts had the wonderful pair of Fonthill and Jenkins with him when they were much younger. They were supreme then. Mind you . . .' she pulled the ear of her husband, 'they are still pretty magnificent – for pensioners, that is.'

Simon made to smack her bottom but she danced out of the way.

The amazing thing about the investment of Chang Lo by the Tibetans was that the telegraph line, that now had been extended to Gyantse, remained uncut. A rumour spread that it had been allowed to remain because, while engineers were working on the line, they had met two lamas who had asked the purpose of the wire. The engineers had carefully explained that the British were far from home and did not want to stay in Tibet, so they had built a line to guide them home.

The telegraph had been used, of course, by Macdonald to issue an order demanding that Brander turn back from his expedition to attack the Tibetans at Karo La. The order had arrived too late to restrain the Colonel, but now Younghusband was being reprimanded for allowing the attack to go ahead. Further oblique criticisms came his way and, as he wearily confided to Fonthill, it was clear that the governments both in India and back home were beginning to regard him as a hothead, determined to force his way to Lhasa despite the British government's anxiety not to upset the government of the Tsar.

The mission at Chang Lo was now being subjected to an incessant bombardment from the fort and its surroundings, a regular and sustained attack from the guns which, while they killed only a handful of sepoys, began to become more dangerous as the days went by and wore down the nerves of the defenders. They worked out that there were now more than twenty pieces of artillery on the *jong* capable of inflicting damage, particularly two large pieces of ordnance whose arrival had been greeted by cheers from the fort. The first of the defenders called 'William' and the other, 'William the Second'. They both had a range in excess of 2,400 yards and were capable of causing serious damage. Suddenly, the expedition had, indeed, turned into a war.

Part of the problem was that there was little effective response that could be made. Fonthill and his Mounted Infantry consistently broke out from the perimeter wall and patrolled the surrounding countryside, bringing in livestock and fodder and, once, fighting a successful but fierce engagement with a party of Tibetan horsemen. But the shrapnel of Bubble and Squeak could not reach the fort and ammunition both for them, the Maxims and the rifles of the troops was now running very low.

Since Macdonald had left a month before, the mission's escort had sustained fifty-six men killed or wounded, while a further fifty had gone down with sickness. It was, then, a huge relief when, on 24th May, reinforcements arrived: two ten-pounders of the 7th Mountain Battery, eight men of the 1st Sappers and Miners, a detachment of Mounted Infantry to swell the ranks of Fonthill's horsemen and the remaining men of the 32nd Pioneers. In all, then, the garrison now had an effective strength of 800 men.

The defenders of Chang Lo could now become more proactive and the fighting became more intense. A sortie was launched before dawn one day against Palla, a village some 1,000 yards to the south-east of the fort, on the road to Lhasa. If the British were expecting a walkover, they were quickly surprised, for the Tibetans resisted with a tenacity and savagery that had not been seen before. The fighting lasted for six hours and became a hand-to-hand battle from street to street and house to house, with walls being blown down and every brick contested. It was as if a new enemy had been created.

Fonthill and his Mounted Infantry took no part in the action, but Simon lay on a roof within the mission perimeter and watched part of the action through his field glasses. At one stage, he could see Tibetan warriors deliberately exposing themselves to British fire at the open windows of the houses and waving the sepoys on towards them. Others were dancing on the roofs of the building and hurling stones at the attackers. This was most unusual bravery from Tibetan troops and Simon was told that they were Khampa warriors, hard-bitten professional soldiers from the north-west of Tibet and the core of what was left of the Tibetan standing army. Before the hamlet was finally cleared, the British had lost an officer and three sepoys, and two officers were wounded, a total far outnumbered by the number of Tibetan casualties.

Alice glumly but carefully recorded all these dead and wounded in her reports to *The Morning Post*, to which she now had daily access, thanks to the extended telegraph line. Her attitude towards the expedition had hardened even further, as though to match the Tibetans own resistance to it.

'It's as though nobody back home cares,' she complained to Simon. 'All this killing of these people – and of our own men – all for nothing. Why doesn't anyone in Whitehall oppose it?'

Fonthill sighed. 'Well, it's not as though it's a full-scale war, my love. The British public have been accustomed for years to these battles and skirmishes on the outposts of Empire. They like to have an empire, they are used to it and they have been fed for decades on the glories of it all – including the constant price we have to pay in terms of men's lives to police it.'

'Bah.' Alice's snort could surely have been heard in the fort. 'This is not a police action. This is an *invasion*, as I keep saying, but no one will listen.'

The attack on and the besieging of Chang Lo, however, could not be ignored, either in Calcutta or London. Younghusband was instructed to issue an ultimatum to the *amban* in the fort that unless it was surrendered by 25th June there could be no question of conducting negotiations at Gyantse. However, he was also further reprimanded for his tart suggestions to his superiors that the attack on the mission should be regarded as an act of war, to end all attempts at negotiations and head for Lhasa instead. He was warned that he was showing 'undue eagerness' and causing the British Cabinet 'undue apprehension'. The exchange ended with an instruction for him to leave Chang Lo immediately, with a suitable escort, and journey to New Chumbi for consultations with General Macdonald, still sitting there, if not quite comfortably, because he was suffering from gastritis.

Fonthill immediately offered to form the escort for the Commissioner and to ride with him, but Younghusband declined, asking only for forty men of the Mounted Infantry to accompany him on the 150 mile journey back.

'It's madness,' confided Simon to Alice. 'He's brave

to the point of sanguinity. I hope the government will be suitably shamed if the man is killed on the journey.'

In fact, Fonthill's dread nearly became fulfilled on the morning after Younghusband's departure when, having taken shelter for the night at a fortified post on the road at Kangmar, garrisoned by a hundred men of the 23rd Pioneers, the Commissioner awoke to howls from some three hundred Tibetans who descended on the post. Younghusband just had time to seize a rifle and rouse the Pioneers to man the walls before the attackers were upon them. Luckily, however, the Lee Metfords once again triumphed over matchlocks and swords and the attack was beaten off. It was, however, another indication that the Tibetans were now determined to fight.

The Commissioner and his escort reached New Chumbi on 10th June and three days later set off back to Gyantse with a still unwell Macdonald (he had to be carried by coolies for the last two days of the journey), but with a vastly increased force, set on relieving the garrison at Chang Lo, taking the fort there, and so opening the road to Lhasa – if, of course, 'necessary'.

The force moved off in two columns. The first comprised 125 Mounted Infantry – the success of Fonthill and Ottley's operations had demonstrated how useful cavalry could be, even in this land of mountains – 8 guns; 1,450 infantry, including, for the first time half a battalion of white troops from the Royal Fusiliers; 950 native support followers and 2,200 animals. In the second column, there were a further 500 infantry, 1,200 followers and 1,800 animals. In six months, the mission and its escort had more than doubled in size.

Along the way, Younghusband received an unexpected telegram. An important lama and one of the four state councillors from Lhasa were on their way to Gyantse to meet him. Did the Tibetans at last seriously intend to negotiate? It seemed so. Accordingly, the Commissioner was authorised to reply that the ultimatum to the *amban* at Gyantse would be extended by a further five days, to accommodate the meeting.

On the evening of the 26th June the relieving force arrived at Gyantse, and pitched its tents on the plain between Chang Lo and the fort itself, just beyond the range of the fort's artillery, which kept up its firing at the mission, despite the imminent negotiations. It became clear, however, that 'imminent' did not translate well into the Tibetan tongue, for there was no sign of the arrival of the important negotiators from Lhasa.

It was a difficult period for the defenders. Younghusband was not at all optimistic about the outcome of this new round of talks and was anxious for Macdonald to attack the fort and remove it as a threat to the expedition's line of communications, dominating, as it did, the road to Lhasa. Fonthill had now withdrawn his Mounted Infantry from patrolling the plain and, with the rest of the mission and its escort, he awaited the arrival of the emissaries. The atmosphere within Chang Lo was tense, for the bombardment continued.

Some relief was provided on 28th June, when the Tsechen monastery at the rear of the fort was captured and the villages around it cleared. Reports began to come in that desertions were taking place from the fort, but the firing from it showed no sign of diminishing.

Jenkins had resumed his previous master and pupil relationship with Sunil. Although the youth remained close to Alice, there was little for him to do because she, too, had fallen victim to the general malaise. With very little happening, there was little to write about. So Jenkins took it upon himself to improve Sunil's marksmanship.

Every afternoon, the two would repair to the far side of the perimeter wall – although remaining within it – while the old soldier would allocate a precious number of cartridges for the practice.

'Now the first thing to remember, Sunshine,' said Jenkins, 'is that this is an old rifle and probably won't fire accurately. So what do we do, eh?'

The young man's eyes widened in concentration. 'See if it fires up or down?'

Jenkins beamed. 'Absolutely. Or right or left. So, let us fire at this bit of card I 'ave nailed to that tree, aim at the circle in the middle, and see what 'appens. Three shots will do. Carry on, then, soldier.'

Sunil aimed with care and fired. Together, the two then walked to the card.

'Ah, as I thought,' said Jenkins. 'Firin' too low. Well grouped, though. Shows you've got an eye. Now, let's try again, adjustin' the sight so that the end of the gun points a bit 'igher. 'Ardly a touch, though, at this short range. That's all that it needs. Try again. Just two shots this time.'

The boy fumbled with the sight and then raised the rifle to his shoulder. He stood, for a moment, the muzzle swaying slightly.

Jenkins intervened straight away. 'Ah now, lad. A common mistake. If you wait too long with an 'eavy gun like the Lee Metford before firin' you'll wave it about like you're dryin' wet knickers.' He took the rifle. 'Thing to do, see, is to pick it up with a firm grip, look you, like this, an' thrust it into the shoulder, like this. Push it in with the left 'and an' 'old it steady with that 'and. The right 'and does nothin' until you pull the trigger. Then sight it. An' above all, don't jerk when you pull the trigger. Just squeeze it, nice an' gentle, like.'

And so it went on, until Sunil was handling the rifle with confidence and hitting the roundel in the middle of the cardboard with nine out of ten shots.

Fonthill watched from afar and slowly nodded with approval. Since they had talked round the fireside on the trek over the mountains, Jenkins had never again mentioned his adopted children. Was Sunil becoming a surrogate son? Could this lead to complications? The subject of the boy had been on his mind, anyway, during these days of inactivity. He knew that Alice had become fond of him. What to do with him when this present adventure was over? From what Jenkins had told him and what he had observed today, it looked as though Sunil could make a good soldier, if he wished to go down that route. But what about his own family? Simon had always understood that all he had left was the uncle who had remained behind on the plantation and who had seemed not at all sad, was even delighted, that his nephew was being taken off his hands for a while. He frowned. One couldn't assume responsibility for a young life without great care. Better to cross that bridge when they came to it, for he certainly had no solution at present. He shrugged his shoulders and turned away.

At last, on 29th June a large white flag was seen being carried from the fort. The man bearing it asked for an armistice until the arrival of the Ta Lama from Shigatse; the other emissary from Lhasa had, it appeared, already arrived and was in the fort. Younghusband curtly replied that he would grant an armistice until sunset on the following day but that the fort must be evacuated in the meantime.

The following day showed no signs of evacuation and the delegation from Lhasa had not appeared by sunset. A message was received, however, that the Ta Lama was definitely on his way and that the ruler of the neighbouring, pro-British state of Bhutan – with the improbable name of Tonsa Penlop (the British troops immediately called him 'The Tonsil', to match the soubriquet of 'Hambone' they had given the *amban*, the commander of the fort) – was also nearing, bearing with him a message from the Dalai Lama himself, so Younghusband prolonged the armistice.

He had to do it again when, the next day, the Ta Lama once again had not, it seemed, reached Gyantse, although the Tonsa, who had had twice as far to travel as the all-important lama from Lhasa, had already ridden in to the British camp from Bhutan, wearing a broad smile and a ceremonial grey homburg hat wedged down to just above his eyes. He did, indeed, carry a message from the Dalai Lama, but it was addressed to him and not to Younghusband. It merely asked for his help in making a peaceful settlement because 'fighting is bad for men and animals'.

At last the delegation from Lhasa appeared, ambling towards the fortress. Younghusband immediately sent a message pointing out that it was a day late and should present itself at Chang Lo without further delay. The Ta Lama replied that he proposed to pay his respects to the Tonsa on the following morning and would visit the British afterwards. This provoked a tart rejoinder from Younghusband, to the effect that unless the Ta Lama presented himself to the British Commissioner by nine o'clock in the morning the fort would be attacked.

All of this was reported to the senior British officers who were observing this game of diplomatic ping-pong with growing incredulity. Jenkins summed it up, as always.

'They're barmy,' he hissed through his moustache. 'Don't the silly buggers realise that there 'ave been – what is it – three bloody great battles, with them gettin' the worst of it and losin' 'undreds of men? What 'ave these blokes come all this way for, just a cup of tea an' a chat with old mates? We've got a bleedin' great army 'ere, look you, chompin' at the bit waitin' to 'ave a go at 'em.'

Alice shook her head sadly. 'They're from a different world, 352,' she said. 'Punctuality doesn't have the same meaning to them that it does for us. In fact, they obviously think it polite not to show any indication of undue haste. It's a culture clash, that's what it is, and Younghusband, with his knowledge of the East and as head of the mission, ought to make allowances for it.'

'I don't agree, Alice,' said Fonthill. 'Y is here, representing not just this expedition, but the King and the British Empire. He is very conscious of this and cannot allow a backward state such as Tibet to be churlish towards it. China learnt this lesson four years ago in Peking when the Boxers rose. They are supposed to have suzerainty over Tibet, they should know.'

Alice sniffed. 'I don't think the Chinese give much of a toss about Tibet. They don't seem to get involved with the country at all.'

'Yes, but they don't want another great power – such as us – getting involved, either.'

'Well, we are supposed to be here because of Russia. But from everything I have learnt so far on this trip, the Tsar is not really interested in Tibet either, despite what Curzon thinks. What the hell is everyone playing at?'

Jenkins interrupted by blowing his nose violently. 'What indeed,' he said with mock solemnity, carefully wiping his moustache. 'I am gettin' very, very bored on this postin' and am still quite cold. I shall be very glad when somethin' meaningful, like, 'appens.'

There seemed no chance of that even on the following day. Nine o'clock came and went without any sign of movement from the Tibetan camp. Shortly afterwards, however, the Ta Lama was seen heading towards Tonsa Penlop's encampment. Immediately, Younghusband instructed Fonthill to take a company of his Mounted Infantry and bring them into Chang Lo directly – by force, if necessary.

There, the diplomatic game continued. The Commissioner kept them waiting in a tent for two hours before receiving them. As Fonthill afterwards related, Younghusband then lectured the Ta Lama – a quiet, 'seemingly stupid' but quite polite old man. He told him, related Simon, that he was ready to make war or ready to make a settlement. Personally, he said that after the way he was attacked during the night he was in favour of war and that we had an army ready to advance on Lhasa tomorrow, a second army waiting in Chumbi to take this one's place and a third in India ready to come up to Chumbi. But the King Emperor in London had commanded him to make one more effort at Gyantse. They would, however, have to show that they were in earnest in wanting to negotiate or he would just march on to Lhasa.

The Ta Lama was then dismissed with orders to return to Chang Lo with his delegation for a formal durbar at noon on the following day.

Arrangements were then put in hand for this great event. Lunch was prepared and a guard of honour assembled from the Norfolk's machine gunners, tables were laid, Younghusband, Macdonald and his senior officers arrayed themselves in their full dress uniforms, Fonthill, with the aid of Alice, cobbling together something more formal than his usual jodphurs and *poshteen*, and the Commissioner appeared resplendent in a plumed cocked hat. They were all solemnly presented to Tonsa Penlop, the ruler of Bhutan, his grey homburg still screwed in place to just above his ears, who turned up pre-promptly at 11.30. There was, however, no sign of the delegation from Lhasa. All eyes stayed on the fort but the gates were not opened. So, at 1.30 lunch was taken without them – just, of course, as the delegation was seen leaving the fort.

Younghusband was coldly furious. The Ta Lama and his retinue – which included the Dalai Lama's Grand Secretary, Lobsang Trinley, already known to the Commissioner from his earlier talks at Khamba Jong and disliked by him – were ushered into a tent while the officers finished their lunch. They were left there until four in the afternoon when the British and the Tongsa Penlop eventually joined them.

Once everyone was seated, Younghusband remained silent and completely composed, staring coldly at the Tibetans. They, all robed in golden vestments, began to fidget and exchange glances until, at last, the Ta Lama broke the painful silence by apologising for their late arrival. At last, then, the durbar could begin.

It did not do so fruitfully. Younghusband began by saying that, in view of the disrespect shown to him and to the British Crown, he presumed that the Tibetan delegation was not in earnest in seeking a settlement and that he was expected therefore to march on Lhasa. This was denied and the Ta Lama earnestly vowed that a settlement was desired and that no disrespect was intended. In that case, replied the Commissioner, as a preliminary the troops who had reoccupied the fort and who had been busy building up its walls, should leave the *jong*.

It soon became apparent that the Grand Secretary still occupied hard hardline position and, despite the many and conciliatory efforts made by the amiable 'Tonsil', he dominated the Tibetan delegation. He gave no ground and neither, of course, did Younghusband as the afternoon wore on. Eventually, the Commissioner stood and declared the durbar was at an end. Unless the fort was evacuated by noon on 5th July, i.e. in two days time, the British would take it by force.

'Why on earth,' asked Alice later as she struggled to undo the collar of her husband's borrowed formal mess jacket, 'does Younghusband demand that the fort should be surrendered again before he talks? There is absolutely nothing to stop him continuing to parley here in Chang Lo, as long as there is no adversarial act made towards us from the fort. In fact, he is not negotiating at all, is he? He is just making demands. I don't understand it.'

'I think I do.' Fonthill pulled on his old shirt with a sigh of relief. 'You know that he has been rebuked from Delhi already for being too pushy and questioning of the government's policy of "take it easy?"'

'Well, yes.'

'If he continues to parley here and eventually comes out with a deal, which, given the help of Old Tonsil and the respect in which the Tibetans hold the old chap, is not beyond the bounds of possibility . . .'

'Hmm.'

'Then, I think he believes the government – in London,

if not in Delhi – will pat him on the back, call him back, replace him with someone who will report to Macdonald and then, with Mac in charge, no one will go to Lhasa and nothing will really happen. Don't forget that Curzon is, by all accounts, quite ill in England. A face-saving, anodyne treaty might ensue perhaps, but no real change of Tibet's attitude towards India or Britain. Nothing will have been gained and all this fighting and killing will have been in vain. Y won't have that.'

A silence fell on the little room. Alice eventually broke it. 'What *will* he have, then?'

'It looks as though a bit of a full-pitched battle to storm the stronghold across the way, with further loss of life on both sides and further cost to the British Exchequer. But with the great fort subdued and the road to Lhasa opened up, the British public would never countenance a full-scale retreat back to India, nor the replacement of the heroic leader of the mission. Both Delhi and London would have to let Y get on to Lhasa to subdue the lamas there. I'm afraid it's what Empire is all about, Alice.'

He gave a rueful smile and reached out for her hand, but she snatched it away.

'Well,' she hissed, 'I think it's bloody disgraceful. Russia is not entrenched in Lhasa – nobody is, not even the Chinese who are supposed to own the place – so Curzon is wrong about that. We've seen no Russian troops or Russian arms. Tibet is a backward, miserable, badly governed country which does not have its eyes on India and just wants to be left alone. Apart from which, 352 is right. It's also bloody cold.'

She grinned up at her husband ruefully through tear-wet eyelashes and he pulled her to him.

Two days later, at midday on the afternoon of the 5th July, after no response was received to Younghusband's ultimatum, the Mission Commissioner heliographed from Chang Lo to General Macdonald's headquarters in the village of Palla requesting that the attack on the great fort should begin.

CHAPTER EIGHT

Even then, the operation did not begin. Macdonald, who had sent a message to his colleague on 1st July urging him to have patience 'and I think you have a fair chance of having the game in your hands and reaping the rewards of your efforts', now heliographed back two irrelevant queries concerning diplomatic niceties before finally ordering his guns into action. It was clear that he, at least, did not exactly savour the task of attacking such a seemingly impregnable stronghold as the great fort of Gyantse.

Nevertheless, the General had laid his plans with care. Although little activity seemed to ensue from the British facing the fort after the first, exploratory shells had been launched at 2 p.m., in fact, during the afternoon Macdonald began moving troops and two guns towards the north-western bastion from where he made great ploy of capturing a village near the outworks of the fort. As darkness fell, he left his campfires burning there and moved his artillery up towards his true objective, the southern face of the fort.

Then, just before dawn on the morning of the 6th July, Macdonald launched his main assault, with three columns of infantry feeling their way forward in the darkness through the outcrop of narrow streets and houses to the base of the rock. Near disaster then ensued when, at the head of the centre column a dog was disturbed, causing it to bark and alerting the Tibetans, who opened fire. In the pitch-black, confusion reigned and the 40th Pathans collided with a company of the Royal Fusiliers behind it and the two units turned and fled, crashing into each other.

Order, however, was quickly restored and the three columns were merged into two. Some resistance continued to be offered by the Tibetans, but, with the antique Bubble at last doing good work at point-blank range, the maze of stone outbuildings was reduced by demolition parties until the whole of the southern flank of the fort was in British hands.

As soon as it was light, the artillery – the ten-pounders and the Gurkhas' pair of elderly light guns – opened up from the three positions which they had reached under cover of darkness. Initially, each battery used shrapnel, fired so that it exploded over the heads of the defenders high above. Then, they were replaced by high-explosive shells which hammered away at the walls and earthworks at the base of the fort.

Eventually, with the sun burning down, the Tibetan fire consistent but not causing great damage and the British guns seemingly to be proving equally ineffective, Macdonald dithered. The great rock on which the fort itself perched, towered above the heads of the British troops, who now held all the ground up to the point at which the rock rose from the plain. Above them a road, ascending from right to left up to a gateway had been cut diagonally into the rock. But overlooking it was a high wall, surmounted by three towers. These commanded the road and the way to the gate and the Tibetans rained down fire on anyone who attempted to use the road.

Impasse set in. How could the sepoys, with their new British colleagues, the Fusiliers, get up there?

Fonthill had only been involved in the original diversionary movement, leading one company of his Mounted Infantry to make the feint to the north. Now, tired because of little sleep, he and Jenkins wandered round to where the main force was congregated at the southern end of the rock.

There, he met an old friend from the Pathan Revolt on the North-West Frontier, Colonel Campbell of the 40th Pathans, who was in charge of the storming parties.

'Why are we stuck here?' asked Simon.

'Old Mac doesn't seem to know what the hell to do next,' growled Campbell. 'But I'll be damned if I'm going to let him keep my men sitting on their arses down here under this sun all day. Can't move without his orders, though.'

'Can you see any way up?'

'Not really. Can you?'

'There might be a way on the eastern corner. I've just walked round there. Come and have a look.'

The two men, with Jenkins tagging behind, constantly wiping his forehead with a dirty handkerchief, walked round the base of the rock, close enough to the face to avoid sniping and dodging stones that were occasionally hurled at them from up above. They eventually came to the eastern face of the rock, where the artillery fire had reduced two walls at the base of the fort itself to rubble, the second and highest of which was still being stoutly defended by a band of Tibetans. Below that wall, however, the rock face was not so sheer as elsewhere and stony projections protruded which might, just might, offer help to skilled climbers.

Fonthill pointed. 'What do you think?'

Campbell wrinkled his nose. 'My Pathans would never get up there,' he muttered, 'but Gurkhas just might.'

'From what I've seen so far,' said Simon, 'I'd back Gurkhas in full battle order to climb Everest.'

'Right, I'll suggest to the General that he gives that a try. Or . . . your idea . . . would you rather put it to him?'

Fonthill grinned. 'Good lord, no. I'm not a Regular. I'm just a part-time horseman, beyond the pale. You go and get the glory.'

'No glory in it, old man. I'm certainly not going to shin up there meself.'

Simon and Jenkins watched the Colonel stride away, casting a wary eye upwards. 'Good idea,' said the Welshman. 'I was just goin' to suggest it myself but then I thought you'd say that I should lead the climbin'.'

'You can still go up, if you want to lead.'

'No thank you. I've been up all night and I might nod off, 'angin' on with one 'and, see. An' that would set a bad example, look you.'

The two dodged back to rejoin the Fusiliers grouped amongst the rubble. Very soon the artillery opened up again, but this time concentrating on the Tibetans manning the highest of the two semi-ruined walls that formed the base of the fort's defences. The guns were laid with accuracy and soon a black hole appeared in the wall. Then, from deep inside the fort, came a dull explosion.

'We've hit a powder magazine,' declared Fonthill.

Yet the explosion seemed to have done nothing to diminish the weight of the Tibetans' fire. Even so, the bang seemed to be the signal for two companies, one from the 8th Gurkhas and one from the Royal Fusiliers, to charge across the patch of open ground between the village ruins and the base of the rock, and begin to climb.

'Splendid,' breathed Simon, 'Mac's bought the idea.'

As they watched, it became clear that the Gurkhas were easily outdistancing the Fusiliers. To protect the climbers, the guns still concentrated on the defenders up above but this was counterproductive, for the shells dislodged large lumps of rock and masonry that bounced down the almost precipitous face, hitting some of the little men in the lead and sending them plunging to the ground below.

Then the guns stopped and immediately enfilading fire opened up on the climbers from turrets on either flank and the defenders at the ruined wall reappeared and began hurling rocks at them. But the Gurkhas hung on and it became clear to the anxious watchers below that they were being led by a young English subaltern, Lieutenant John Grant, now climbing hand over hand and being followed by his Gurkha *havildar*, Karbir Pun.

A cheer rang out when it was seen that they had reached a point just below the black hole. Here the Gurkhas grouped for a moment but further progress could only be made by one man at a time, crawling on hands and knees. So Grant hauled himself up and was about to enter the breach when he was hit by a bullet and almost simultaneously another hit the *havildar*. A groan went up from the watchers as both men slid down the rock for about thirty feet. It was immediately followed by another cheer as the officer and the *havildar* immediately picked themselves up and began, agonisingly, to climb again.

They reached the gaping cavern and disappeared within it, followed hard on their heels by the waiting riflemen.

Immediately, figures high up above were seen dodging away from the battlements, others were seen running to the north and others began sliding down ropes seeking shelter in the warren of buildings there that had so far escaped the shelling.

'My God!' cried Fonthill. 'We've done it. We've recaptured the fort.' He turned to Jenkins. 'What would we do without those magnificent Gurkhas!'

The Welshman sniffed. 'Lose bloody wars, that's what. They're tough as nuts and real fighters, so they are.'

'Come on, I must go and see the General. He will probably want us to pursue the retreating soldiers and run them down. It's what I hate doing, but it's our bloody job, I suppose. Come on, Sergeant Major, smartly now.'

They half ran, half trotted in the hot sun to the hamlet of Palla, where Macdonald had his headquarters. They found the General on a rooftop, inspecting the fort with a telescope.

'Congratulations, General,' said Fonthill. 'The fort is yours. Do you want the Mounted Infantry to pursue the fleeing Tibetans?'

Macdonald wheezed, took the cigarette from his mouth and shook his head. 'Thank you, Fonthill, but I think not. I don't want to take on loads of prisoners again and I think we've done enough for one day.'

He turned and gestured to where a large Union Jack was being pulled up the flagstaff on top of the highest tower, there to flutter in the breeze. The General put his eye to the telescope again and muttered, half to himself, 'Yes, we've stormed the fort and the road to Lhasa now really is open – if we want to take it, that is . . .' His voice fell away almost to a whisper.

Fonthill nodded, relieved that he was not being asked to undertake a sabre-swinging pursuit, and turned away to find Jenkins waiting at the bottom of the stairs.

'Let's get out of here,' he said 'and find Alice.'

'Yes. I'll make us all a nice cup of tea. Victorious warriors deserve at least that, I'd say, particularly them that 'ave been up all day, like.'

On their way, however, they were met by a Royal

Fusilier warrant officer, pulling along a bedraggled Sunil and carrying the youth's rifle.

'Ah sir,' he cried. 'Glad I've found you. I believe this lad belongs to you, sort of, anyway.'

'Sort of, Sergeant Major, yes. Where did you find him?'

'He was among the ruins below the rock taking potshots at the Tibetans on the ramparts with this Lee Metford. He must have stolen it.'

'No, I did not steal,' shouted Sunil.

'No mate,' Jenkins intervened. 'It's his own. I've been teaching him to shoot.'

'Well, Taffy,' said the Sergeant Major, 'You've done a bloody good job, I'd say. While I was watchin' him, I saw him hit two of the blokes on the top. Very good shooting, indeed. And they're his own people, by the look of it.'

Sunil's face was now a dark purple. 'No, not my people. Not proper Tibetans. They Khampas. Not from here. Nasty people but fierce warriors. I happy to kill them.'

The Sergeant Major nodded. 'Ah, from what I've heard, they're the lot who gave you all a hard time in taking Palla, before we arrived. Well, if this lad wants to be a British soldier, I'll warrant the Fusiliers will take him.'

'Thank you, Sergeant Major.' Fonthill offered his hand to the old soldier, who paused for a second, unused to such a social gesture from a senior officer, and then shook it. 'We'll take the boy. I think we all deserve a cup of tea.'

'Right sir.' The warrant officer saluted smartly. 'I don't think I'll need you to sign a chit for safe receipt. Goodbye, marksman. Maybe we'll see you in the Fusiliers yet.'

Sunil glared at the back of the departing soldier. 'What is Fusiliers?' he asked.

Jenkins sniffed. 'Ah, very, very ordinary soldiers, Sunshine. They're not Welsh, y'see. Not proper soldiers like the old 24th of Foot. Now *they*—'

Fonthill interrupted smartly. 'Come on, Sunil. Let's go and find Alice.'

CHAPTER NINE

The following day it was announced that Lieutenant Grant had been recommended for the Victoria Cross and his *havildar* the Indian Order of Merit, first class – sepoys were not eligible to receive the Cross – and the General led a small force round the back of the fort to clear out the town and the monastic complex there. No further opposition was found and it was clear that what remained of the Tibetan army and the civilian population of the Gyantse had fled along the road to Lhasa. A search of the monastery, however, revealed 3,000 pounds of *atta*, or ground flour – a much prized addition to the expedition's dwindling food supplies. While some of the officers and men took part in strictly illegal looting of the fort, others were given the melancholic task of burying the dead.

Once again, the cost of the attack on the Tibetans was remarkably small: just three dead and seventeen wounded. And, as always, the intensity of the British firepower showed in the far greater number of defenders killed and wounded. As F Company of the Royal Fusiliers marched up to the fort to take over guard duty there they passed 'dead Tibetans lying in heaps'.

Ever assiduous in her reporting of the losses of both sides, Alice strode up with the Fusiliers. She stumbled upon a trench which ran the whole length of the fort and which was full of the dead defenders who must have been caught by overhead bursts of shrapnel as they sought to flee. Putting a handkerchief to her nose she carefully noted the methods used by captured prisoners to drag the dead away.

'They tie two ropes to the heels,' she scribbled, 'and two men pull while a third lifts the head by the pigtail. So the corpses are carried away.'

Later, she walked to where the monastery buildings had been demolished and picked her way delicately over a line of corpses: those of warriors from the Kham country whom she identified by what Sunil had told her about their giant physiques and long hair: 'glorious in death,' she wrote, 'lying as they fell with their crude weapons at their side and usually with a peaceful, patient look on their faces.'

She sent her despatch back down the line to be cabled to *The Morning Post* in London, sparing none of the details of the losses born by the Tibetans. Nor could she refrain from hinting at the breaking of the General's orders that no looting was to be permitted either in the ruins of the monasteries or in the fort itself.

'This expedition is becoming a disgrace,' she confided to Simon as they sat in their tiny room in the mission headquarters. 'The censor will probably strike out much of what I have written, but I don't think I can stand much more of the slaughter of these peoples and the desecration that civilised men in our army – and I speak of the British, not the sepoys – are doing to sacred sites here.'

Fonthill sighed. 'You know as well as I do, darling, that if the Tibetans continue to oppose us, there will be more killing – on both sides. And as for the pillaging, well, I suppose it is a sort of tradition in the army: the privilege of the victors, if you like. Wellington probably began it in recent times and Gordon certainly continued it in China.'

'Privilege be damned, Simon. It's against army law and as for any further killing by machine guns and artillery against muskets, I have got to think of some way of stopping it now. It simply can't go on.'

'I don't think there is anything you can do, my love. Anyway, the good news is that Lhasa is virtually within our reach now. It's about a 150 miles away and the rumour is that Y has received a message from India giving permission at last to march on the capital and, if necessary, to winter there and iron out a treaty with the Dalai Lama and his henchmen. I am told that there are plenty of monasteries lining the route and that we shall be able to buy grain from them and more or less live off the country, although we must give assurances that we shall not occupy them.'

'Nor loot them, I hope!'

Alice looked affectionately at her husband. Despite the fact that he was nearing fifty, this hard-riding life with his mounted Sikhs and Gurkhas was undoubtedly suiting him. He had lost weight and his body was hard and trim; his face and the backs of his hands were burnt dark brown by the sun and wind; and, although he wore a piratical fur hat most of the time he was in the saddle, somehow his brown hair had become bleached in the thin air to a rather becoming blonde. He was – and she hugged the thought to herself – now a very handsome, middle-aged man.

Then she frowned. But had he reverted to becoming a professional soldier again: a give-no-quarter, sabre-wielding, hunter-down of fleeing peasants? He was undoubtedly enjoying himself, as he had on the South African veldt only three years ago as he pursued those elusive Boer generals. And he was always quick to defend Younghusband and Macdonald in the face of her criticisms.

Alice sighed. Her resourceful, brave husband had always had a gentle, liberal side to him. She only hoped now that he had not lost that, here among the cold, ice-tipped mountains of Tibet.

On 14th July, under a heavy downpour that marked the beginning of the summer monsoon in India, the British force marched eastwards out of Gyentse on what everyone felt was the last lap to the Tibetan capital. Throughout the armed force, the general feeling was of hope that there would be no further attempt to delay the march by the Tibetans seeking to negotiate en route, for even the sepoys were now anxious to enter the fabled city of Lhasa.

It had been agreed between Younghusband and Macdonald that this last lap should be covered as speedily as possible, for the full column, with its supplies, could now stretch back, marching on a single-track file, a vulnerable seven miles in all. The column's flock of sheep had become a major nuisance, slowing the marching men down as they waded through the bleating animals, so they were left to straggle behind, much to the relief of the troops who had all become heartily sick of the stringy mutton and lamb, likened to 'piano wire'.

So it was a slimmed-down force – reduced, apart from the need for speed, by the necessity of leaving a garrison at Gyantse – that set off through the rain. Even so, it now included 91 British officers, 521 British NCOs and other ranks, 32 Indian native officers, 1,966 Indian and Nepali sepoys or riflemen, and approximately 1,500 orderlies, porters, transport drivers and other camp followers – in all, just over 4,000 men.

'Well,' observed Jenkins, 'it's got to be bloody obvious to even the most blind chink-eyed Tibbo that we mean business now. P'raps they won't be building any more walls in the mountains to stop us.'

That proved to be a pious hope, for, scouting ahead as usual with his two companies of Mounted Infantry – now a supremely confident, grinning ragged bunch of rough riders, looking more like brigands than soldiers – Fonthill rode cautiously up to the scene of the battle at Karo La and found that the Tibetans had strengthened their old position and were manning it once more. A second wall had been built behind the first and new sangars had been erected, even higher up the mountainside than before, to protect both flanks.

Riding back to report, however, the horsemen captured a convoy of 130 loaded yaks, together with several prisoners, which put the men in even better heart than before.

Macdonald decided to attack at once and moved into the defile on 17th July, advancing on the wall and sending up his Gurkhas once more, scrambling up the mountainsides to attack the sangars. These returned but little fire this time and these key positions were abandoned, causing the main defenders of the wall to retreat without firing a shot.

'They've had enough of our firepower to stand up to it again,' said Ottley. 'Once bitten twice shy.'

Once again it was decided, much to Fonthill's relief, that it would be useless for the Mounted Infantry to attempt to ride down the retreating Tibetans, for it would take at least a day to dismantle both walls. So it was a leisurely army that eventually debouched from Karo La and found itself looking down on a great and remote basin, filled by an immense lake. It was found to be drinkable, not salted, and its swampy shore was dotted by half-ruined castles from which screeching redshanks rose in protest as the troops ambled towards them. The lake's colour was deliciously soothing to foreign eyes accustomed to the grey shale and dirty snow of the mountains.

'It's called Yamdrok So, or the Turquoise Lake,' explained O'Connor to Fonthill. He pointed. 'See the way the white sand shows through as the shore is reached and then the water deepens to that lovely half-blue half-green colour?

I wouldn't mind betting that we are the first Europeans to see this lake since the Jesuits came this way centuries ago.'

A little ahead of the lake and immediately in their path, the trail was dominated by the fort of Nagartse and here, much to everyone's chagrin, another Tibetan delegation rode out to meet the column. Once again it was led by the Ta Lama and the still adversarial Grand Secretary. This time, however, the Gyantse team was reinforced by the Yuthok Shapé, one of the four state councillors from Lhasa.

Once again, the ceremonial rugs were laid on the floor of a large tent and hopes of the Yuthok Shapé's placatory and conciliatory interventions winning the day were crushed by the Grand Secretary's aggressive rejection of every point offered by Younghusband. The parley lasted for seven long hours, most of which Fonthill observed from a chair behind the Commissioner.

His main admiration during the long day was for O'Connor, who translated once again. Later, he reported to Alice.

'It was mind-numbing,' he said. 'The Tibetans seem to have no idea of logic or of the niceties of diplomacy. Poor old O'Connor had to strain his ears to catch the mumblings of each delegate, who, in turn, simply repeated exactly what had been said by the previous speaker in the delegation. It was, in effect, a low, continuous gabble with absolutely nothing new being said. It was as if the durbar at Gyantse and the attack on the fort had never taken place.'

Alice was scribbling. 'What about Younghusband?' she asked.

'Oh, he sat like some implacable Bhudda, no expression

231

crossing his face. I must say I admired his patience and courtesy. But, of course, he gave nothing away, repeating all that had been said before about the frontier transgressions and so on, and saying that we needed a new treaty, confirming a closer relationship between our two countries. It was all another waste of time. Nothing came of it at all.'

During the enforced stay at Nagartse, rumours reached the staff that Macdonald had once again written to Younghusband – written, his tent was only 200 yards from that of the Commissioner! – expressing his doubts about advancing on Lhasa and requesting confirmation of the need to do so. But Younghusband, it seemed, was firm. The mission *would* advance on Lhasa and if any opposition was offered to its passage the General would be expected to overcome it.

And so the mission plodded on, marching along the shores of the beautiful Yamdrok So, passing another dilapidated fortress before the route led them up to the Kamba La, which, at 15,400 feet, was the last pass on the road to Lhasa. Trouble was expected here but, once again, it proved to offer no obstacles, either from the Tibetans or from the weather, for the lake was already 14,400 feet above sea level and so the climb was comparatively short-lived. Below them ran the Tsangpo river, running through a valley much lusher and more fertile than any the troops had set their eyes on in Tibet.

The descent to it was as precipitous as any so far encountered, for the column was forced to march down into the valley along a zigzag track which descended 3,000 feet in five miles. This, however, was summer and the descent lacked any of the ice-fuelled perils that the troops had met earlier.

For the first couple of 1,000 feet the march down was through the usual bleak, grey, black, rocky hillside, after which the wood line was reached, which was welcome for it meant that firewood was plentiful. Then as the troops came into the open the most glorious sight met their eyes: thick green crops through which the yellow river meandered and large prosperous-looking villages and monasteries dotted along the riverbank, offering the prospect of good grazing for the animals and grain from the holy buildings.

Even Jenkins walked along – albeit close to the cliff face – singing the praises of the view. Not so General Macdonald, whose condition had now worsened, for dysentery was now suspected and he had to be carried down the winding track in a *dhoolie*. It was whispered again that it was his indisposition that had coloured his reluctance, expressed at Nagartse, to continue the advance to Lhasa.

The Tsangpo, however, presented a different problem. It was wide, yellow-looking and turbulent and it had to be crossed. Fonthill and his horsemen ranged on ahead to secure the crossing some ten miles upstream at a place called Chaksam, 'the Iron Bridge', at a place where the river was at its narrowest. They were just in time to see a last load of hard-fighting Khampa warriors, the remnants of the retreating Tibetan rearguard, disembarking on the far side and crying out in derision in the heavy rain at their belated pursuers.

For the bridge, an ancient – at least six centuries old, it

was rumoured – suspension affair, made of old iron chains and slats of wood, could obviously not be relied upon for a safe crossing. The main method was clearly a ferry consisting of two large rectangular boats, each capable, thought Ottley, of holding a hundred men or at least twenty mules. But these had been left on the far northern side by the retreating Khampa soldiers.

Fonthill turned and shouted an order. At last, there was a role to be played by the four Berthon, canvas and wood, folding-boats that had been brought from India for just such an occasion as this. They were brought up and, with much shouting and jocularity, assembled on the riverbank. Then, as the last of the Khampas disappeared into the distance, the boats were crewed and rowed to the other side, while the rest of Fonthill's men covered them from the riverbank. So the ferries were seized, but how to get them to the southern bank? Crewing them seemed to be a skilled business.

The riverside village, Chaksam Chori, had its statutory monastery a little further upstream. Fonthill stood in the stirrups and studied it. It seemed empty but then he caught a glimpse of movement on its walls.

'William,' he called to Ottley. 'Take six men and flush out the abbot from the monastery. I bet you will also find the ferrymen hiding there. Be sharp. We don't want to keep the main column waiting when it comes up.'

Ottley rode away and within fifteen minutes had returned, ushering a flustered-looking monk and twenty desperately frightened river boatmen.

'Tell them,' ordered Fonthill to a Tibetan that they had

brought with them from Gyantse as interpreter, 'that they will each have twenty rupees if they will cross and bring the ferries back.'

Much heated conversation ensued until the interpreter shrugged his shoulders and turned back to Simon. 'They don't go,' he said. 'They frightened that if they work for you their own people kill them.'

Fonthill drew his pistol slowly from its holster. 'Very well. Tell them that I will undoubtedly shoot every one of them now, if they do not fetch those boats.'

The effect was immediate and the ferrymen rushed to climb into the collapsible boats, with a rifleman in each to ensure that they did not run away once on the far bank. Within minutes both of the ferries had been brought back and safely moored on the southern bank.

Simon immediately ordered the abbot – happy now to be of any assistance – to fetch some *chung*, local beer, and ten sheep from the monastery. He then distributed the beer and sheep to the ferrymen and also paid them twenty rupees each. Suddenly, all was sweetness and light and the Tibetans immediately produced coracle skin boats from hiding places on the riverbank, which, as they demonstrated, proved admirable shelters from the consistent rain for the horsemen who had travelled light and therefore had no tents to provide shelter for the night.

Jenkins flicked the rain from his glistening moustache. 'Ain't it amazin' what a bit of a threat backed up by love an' kindness can do,' he observed. 'Let's feed the ponies an' then find ourselves a nice little dry boat to crawl under and drink some of that awful bloody beer.'

It was a wet and miserable night for them all, despite the coracles, but the rain eased a little in the morning and Fonthill was able to cross his men over the river in the ferry boats soon after dawn to establish a bridgehead on the far bank just as the main column came up.

The ferry boats were put into use for the main crossing straight away, but it proved to be slow work, for the river had to be crossed in two stages: first from the south bank to a sandbank in midstream, using the ferry boats, then in the yak-skin coracles to cross a shallower side channel to the far bank.

To speed things up, the engineers were able to throw a steel cable across the river and, at the same time, Major Bretherton, the column's transport officer, experimented with lashing together the Berthon boats underneath a wooden platform. Then, with another officer, Captain Moore, seven Gurkhas and two Indian camp followers, he boarded the makeshift raft and attempted the crossing.

It looked perilous and so it proved. Halfway across and before they had reached the sandbank, a strong eddy caught the craft and it upended, tipping all of the men into the surging water. Moore and five of the Gurkhas were able to reach the riverbank, but Bretherton and the remaining men, laden with packs and rifles, were swept away and drowned.

This took place while the whole column and the journalists, including Alice, were watching. Immediately a groan went up from the watchers, for Bretherton had proved to be one of the most popular officers in the whole expedition, always working to relieve the strain on his men and to think of innovative schemes to hasten the progress of the column.

Later, Alice sat sipping one of Jenkins's cups of scalding tea in the tiny, one-woman bivouac tent that she used on the march, Simon just able to crawl in and crouch beside her.

'Watching that lovely man drown was the tipping point for me,' she muttered into her cup.

'What do you mean?'

'Surely there has been enough killing on this disgraceful invasion of a hitherto peaceful country without having an accident of this kind – just because we must press on to bloody Lhasa at all cost.'

Simon looked at her sharply. They had had little opportunity to be together on these latter stages of the march, for he was consistently out riding ahead of the main column. On the rare occasions that they met, however, he had found her withdrawn, preoccupied and reluctant to talk very much.

'Oh come on, Alice,' he said now. 'You know as well as I do that these things happen on campaign. This is a war, after all – albeit a one-sided, most peculiar one – and accidents happen under pressure. And we are on the last lap now, not far from Lhasa and I am not at all sure that the Tibetans will try and stop us now.'

'Really?' She sniffed. 'What about those tough so-and-sos, the Khampas, or whatever they are called, who you said shouted at you when you arrived on the riverbank? It looks as though they haven't given up yet.'

Fonthill shrugged. 'Who's to know? But I can't see Younghusband stopping now. We have all come so far. He wants his treaty, you know.'

'To hell with his treaty.' Alice leant and threw the dregs from her tin cup out into the rain. 'Forgive me, my love, but I am very tired. I know it's early. Would you mind if I turned in now?'

'Of course not.' Her husband leant across and kissed her quickly. 'We're both a bit old for this game now, I think, darling. And you just a poor, vulnerable woman out in this freezing cold and wet. Tuck in and get a good night's sleep.'

But Alice did not. When she was sure that Simon had retreated to his own bivouac with Jenkins and his men on the far side of the camp, she pulled on her oilskin and went looking for Sunil. She found him, not far away, curled up already in the tiny tent she had procured for him back in India.

'Can I come in, Sunil?' she whispered.

'Ah, memsahib. I come out.'

'No. I will come in. There will be just about room.'

She crouched beside him under the noisy, rain-battered canvas. 'I am sorry to disturb you,' she said. 'But tell me. When you lived in Tibet as a boy did you live in Lhasa itself?'

'Oh no. I never been there.'

'Ah.' Disappointment sounded in her voice. 'Where, then, did you live? Do you remember?'

'Yes. Remember very much. I was, I think about seven when uncle take me away. Father and mother dead, you see.'

'Yes, I knew that much. But where did you live?'

'Well, strange. I think it not far from here, if I remember well. Because I know this river well. I live at place called Nethang. It is this side of Lhasa, though I never went to sacred city. It is on this road to the city, I think.'

Alice awkwardly uncrossed her aching leg. 'How far from here, do you think?'

'I don't know. But I find out.'

'Good. Do you . . . er . . . have any relatives still living there, Sunil?'

'Oh yes. I know that. I still have uncle. Brother of my father and man on your plantation in India. I know he still alive because my uncle told me when we left. He say: see Chung Li when you get to old country. Why you ask these things, memsahib?'

'Because . . . well, because it will take probably a week at least for this great army to cross this damned river and I don't want to wait here. I want you to take me tomorrow to where you used to live and find your uncle.'

'Ah!' Alice saw Sunil's black eyes open wide in the half-light. 'Why you want my uncle, then?'

'I think he may be able to help me. I will explain tomorrow. Keep what I have asked you very confidential – just between us. Yes?'

'Oh, yes, memsahib. Big secret. Yes.'

'Good. Now get a good night's sleep.'

'Goodnight, memsahib.'

Shortly after dawn, Alice was up and scribbling a note to Simon. She explained that she was having problems with the cable clerks back in Gyantse and was taking opportunity of the pause by the riverbank to ride back there with one of the supply trains to sort it out. She would be away less than a week and would easily catch up with the column. Then, she scribbled a second note, which merely said:

Sorry, Simon. Did not go Gyantse but have ridden instead on to Lhasa with Sunil. I intend to see the Tibetan high lamas and persuade them to stop this war. Don't worry. We can look after ourselves. Keep safe. A.

She gave five rupees to one of the servants and asked him to deliver the first note to Fonthill after 8 a.m. that morning. The second he was to deliver in one week's time – and, she warned, she would know if the man did not follow these instructions and he would be punished if he did not.

Then she made for the major who was the liaison officer for the correspondents. She bestowed on him one of her most radiant smiles.

'Now that the rain has stopped, Major,' she said. 'I would be most grateful if you would allow myself and my boy, Sunil, to cross to the far bank with the next ferry with our ponies, so that they can feed on that good grazing over there for an hour or two.'

'I see no reason why not, Miss Griffith. I will write you a chit for the ferry captain.'

So it was that Alice and Sunil, together with their mounts, plus food for three days tucked away in their saddlebags, crossed on that first ferry – even before Fonthill and his Mounted Infantry had mounted up for their normal daily patrol. Once on the other side, they languidly led their ponies away in the luscious pasture, until they were out of the sight of the ferrymen. Then, they mounted, dug in their heels and galloped up the road towards Lhasa to be well ahead of Simon and his first patrol.

They had trotted and cantered for two hours before Sunil, his precious rifle nestling in its saddle bucket, pulled his pony alongside that of Alice.

'Now, memsahib, you must tell me why you want see my uncle. You don't know him, do you?'

Alice grinned. 'No I don't, Sunil. But I want to ask him to guide us into Lhasa. It is only forty-three miles away from here. He will know the way and he will know the city, won't he?'

'Oh yes. But why you go before the army? Tibetans might kill us.'

'That's why I want your uncle to be with us, to explain that I am on a special mission to see the Dalai Lama. I will pay him well.'

Sunil's jaw dropped. 'You want go see Dalai Lama? Nobody sees him. Certainly not English lady. We get killed for sure.'

'I think not.' Alice's smile faded quickly. 'You see, Sunil, I am sick of being with this army of the British Raj, which is rampaging its way through Tibet, killing Tibetans with its modern weaponry. I am tired of merely reporting what happens. I want to actually do *something*, to stop this killing.'

'How you do that, then?'

'Well, you are right that I probably won't get to see the Dalai. I have heard rumours that he has fled the city, and I am not sure that he really has much control over his so-called government, anyway. But I am determined to get to see the senior lamas, perhaps all of the state councillors, who are the real decision makers.'

'What you say to them, then?'

'From what I have heard and seen of the delegates that have come to see Colonel Younghusband, they have not the faintest idea of the strength and power of the army of the Raj. Even though they have fought and lost quite a few times to the British already, with fearful losses in manpower, they still seem to think that praying and pushing forward peasants with muskets and old swords will deflect our troops. I am going to beseech them to allow Younghusband Sahib to enter Lhasa and to sit down with him to negotiate a treaty with the British. No more killing and silly talking. Proper negotiations.'

Sunil pondered this for a moment. 'You think they listen to you?'

'I don't know. Maybe not. But I have to try, don't you see?'

He nodded. 'You brave lady, memsahib.'

'It's not being brave. It's trying something, well, *different*. Something instead of Younghusband just marching in troops and making *demands*. I shall say that I am married to one of the British generals in the expedition – which is almost true – and that I am an influential writer for one of England's main newspapers, which is completely true. They would not dare to harm me, with a British army on their doorstep. Dammit, Sunil, it's worth a try.'

'You still a brave lady.'

'Well, I don't know about that. But I am well aware that I am possibly putting you in danger, so, if I can persuade your uncle to take me into Lhasa you are most welcome to stay behind in the village if you wish.'

'Oh no. I go where you go. I promise Fonthill Sahib that.' Suddenly the boy held up his hand. 'I hear. Someone coming. We go here quickly now.'

He grabbed Alice's rein and pulled it behind his own pony whom he kicked into a scramble over the shale to take both mounts and their riders behind a group of rocks, a little way up the hillside.

There they waited, hidden, and watched as a remarkable procession rounded a bend in the rocks a little more than one hundred yards ahead of them. It comprised some twenty horsemen, of which the central core were four magnificently robed lamas, one of whom Alice recognised as the Shapé who had come to negotiate with Younghusband at Nagartse.

When the retinue had wound out of sight, Sunil turned and looked, awestruck, at Alice.

'Them important people, I think. Where they go?'

Alice nodded. 'Yes. I think they have been sent to attempt one more talk with Colonel Younghusband to stop him from entering Lhasa.'

'Ah. Will Colonel Sahib stop, then?'

'Only just to listen to them. They will probably say the same thing to him as before. He will continue his advance on the city. He is determined to get there.' She paused for a moment, deep in thought. Then: 'They will do us a good turn. My husband will be scouting not far behind us. He will meet the delegation and have to escort it into our camp. That will mean that he won't be on our heels. We can move on now at a more comfortable pace. Come on, Sunshine.'

The two continued their journey, with Sunil now riding on ahead a little way to ensure that they did not stumble into the rearguard of the retreating Khampa troops, whose hoof marks straddled across the track in trampled numbers. They passed, in fact, only two shepherds, tending their scattered sheep up the mountainside. They looked down at Alice in some consternation, but she gave them a cheerful salute and a smile.

That night they made camp without a fire, tethering their horses some way off the track in a little glade and taking it in turns to keep watch. The following day was equally uneventful, although they passed more people, who gazed at them inquisitively but did not harass them. They slept out in the open again and broke camp early the next morning and set off on what Alice felt would be the last lap to the village of Nethang, which Sunil had discovered from talking to passers-by was on the outskirts of Lhasa on the road they were taking.

Alice had felt the need to change her appearance to avoid suspicion, now that they were nearing the capital, for the sight of a European woman on horseback had already caused considerable interest and she did not want to draw overt attention to herself before they had met the man whom she hoped would be their guide. Accordingly, she put a blanket loosely over her head, Tibetan style, with the ends reaching down and covering, to some extent, her boots and riding breeches. She rubbed red clay onto her face in the manner of Tibetan women and she rode now with downcast gaze. More she felt she could not do.

They reached Nethang on the late afternoon of the third day after leaving the river at Chaksam Chori. It was little more than a hamlet, off the main road, with the usual collection of one-storey, mud and stone dwellings lining the very narrow streets. The smell of yak dung and human excrement hung over the place and Alice wrinkled her nose in disgust.

'No wonder your uncle took you away,' she murmured to Sunil.

The boy looked momentarily ashamed. 'It is a stink, yes,' he muttered.

Alice felt a sudden sharp pang of doubt. What a risk they had taken! What if Sunil's uncle no longer lived here and, indeed, had died? They could not ride just blindly into the holy city. They would need some sort of guide. 'Do you know where Chung Li lives?' she asked.

'No. But I find out.'

'Very well. I think I would only draw attention to us if I came with you now into the village. I will dismount and pull under these trees here, in this gulley, and wait for you. Leave your pony here, too. Please don't be too long, Sunil. I shall feel exposed without you.'

'No, memsahib.'

In fact, the boy was away for only ten minutes when he came running back, a grin splitting his face from ear to ear.

'I find him! He glad to see me after all these years, though he not recognise me. He happy to meet you but a bit afraid of what lamas do to him if he help us. Come now. He waits.'

Alice blew out her cheeks in relief. 'Thank goodness. Lead on. I think we should lead the horses and not ride in.'

Chung Li's house, in fact, was right on the edge of the village, very near where Alice had waited. She was glad to note that it seemed rather more substantial than the dwellings surrounding it, being built of stone and timber and having some sort of second storey. Importantly, however, there was a patch of land at its back, where grazed a pair of goats and where it was possible to leave the ponies.

The old man was waiting for them, his hands folded together and thrust into the capacious sleeves of his old, cotton jacket. He was quite indistinguishable from any of the Tibetan peasants that Alice had seen on her journey so far: his features were wrinkled so that his face looked like a scroll parchment and his hair had been pulled back into a pigtail, Chinese fashion. His eyes remained quite impassive but the wrinkles on his face had fallen into a great grin, as his head bobbed up and down in greeting. Stretched behind him was an equally elderly woman, obviously his wife, and several middle-aged men and women whom Alice presumed were his children. They, too, were smiling and the women had extended their tongues in the Tibetan act of welcome.

The elderly woman now produced a piece of paper from

her sleeve and waved it in the air, while talking to Sunil.

The youth turned with an air of pride. 'This letter from my uncle on your plantation,' he said. 'He write to his brother to say that I had gone to join British army in invading Tibet and to tell him to watch for me. They heard army is near but not sure if I was with it.'

'How splendid,' said Alice. And she extended her hand to the old man.

At first, he thought she wanted the letter and he snatched it back from his wife, but Sunil intervened to explain the British way of shaking hands, so he extended his own hand and gave hers a lifeless shake. Alice then, smilingly, shook hands with the whole family.

Old wicker chairs were produced and the guests of honour made to sit while Sunil and his uncle and aunt talked in a kind of sing-song gibberish and the rest of the family squatted on the earthen floor. Then tea was produced, a fine brew that Alice felt no hesitation in nodding to her hosts enthusiastically in thanks, followed by what appeared to be sweetmeats and wrapped in little balls of dough. They, too, were delicious. It appeared that Chung Li, if not exactly rich, was a man of some substance.

'They say,' said Sunil, a touch proprietarily, 'that family is honoured to have such fine English lady in our house. We invited to stay. We eat with them tonight, but no talk business until tomorrow. That is Tibetan custom.'

'Please say,' said Alice, inclining her head to the family, 'that it is I who is honoured to be in their house and to accept their hospitality.' Then lowering her voice slightly. 'Do you think he will help us?'

'Don't know yet. See in morning.'

'Very well. Please, Sunil, would you unsaddle the horses and bring our things in. Oh, and ask if there is somewhere I could wash to take this disgusting red stuff off my face. I must try and look a little like an English memsahib.' And she inclined her head once again and smiled all around.

Chapter Ten

After the disaster of Major Bretherton's death, Fonthill's Mounted Infantry had stayed on the southern bank of the river, so Simon did not receive Alice's first note until the major part of the column had been transported over onto the other bank, where he was lining up his men in patrol order as the note was handed to him.

He read it quickly and frowned. Why on earth should she undertake the long ride back to Gyantse just to clarify some problems about cabling? Still, at least she was not riding back alone but had the good sense to go with a returning column, so she should be safe enough. He tucked the note away into his jacket and set about organising the patrol.

This was new territory, of course, and it wasn't so long since he had seen the last of the Khampa warriors crossing and hurling abuse, so maybe they were still there, somewhere up ahead, in ambush, waiting for the column to recommence its stately progress. Accordingly, he decided to spread his command: one company under Ottley pulling away to the north, away from the riverbank and the second, under his command, to continue on the road to Lhasa, which now followed a tributary of the Tsangpo called Kyi Chu, curling towards the north east.

He had not ridden far when two scouts whom he had sent on galloped in to report that a party of Tibetans, some of them gorgeously apparelled, were riding along the bank of the river towards them. Immediately, he ranged his company out away from the river, in a semicircle, and set them forward at a trot.

The Tibetans soon came in sight and he indicated to Jenkins on the extreme left wing to ride round behind the party and ahead, to ensure that they were not set up as bait to draw his men into a trap. Yet there seemed little cover ahead in which warriors could be hiding and the Welshman soon returned, giving the thumbs up.

Fonthill accordingly rode ahead and greeted the four gorgeously robed lamas in the centre of the group. One of them he immediately recognised as one of the delegates who had parleyed with Younghusband back at Nagartse and he bowed to him. Oh no! Not another durbar.

But so it proved, for the lama courteously bowed his head in acknowledgment and gestured ahead. 'Lord Younghusband,' he said, smiling. Simon nodded and, gesturing to Jenkins to hang behind with a section as rearguard, swung his pony's head round and led the way back along the riverbank towards the crossing.

The army's crossing of the river was in full flow but Younghusband greeted the lamas with his customary courtesy. The rugs were set out yet again in a hastily erected tent but, as the preparations were being made, the Commissioner pulled Fonthill to one side and told him of the latest instructions he had received from India.

'I am to impose an indemnity on the Tibetans towards the costs incurred in mounting this expedition,' he said, his eyes staring up at the cold mountains, as though speculating on whether there was time to pen an ode to them before he was forced once again to say no to pleas to turn back.

'How much will you demand?' asked Simon.

Younghusband shrugged his shoulders and gave his distant smile. 'I am to be guided by circumstances as to that,' he said. 'But it has to be a sum which it is within the power of the Tibetans to pay. I can allow them to pay in instalments but we shall occupy the Chumbi Valley until the instalments are complete.'

'I suppose that's fair.'

'Eminently fair, considering the unprovoked attack they launched on us at Chang Lo.'

Fonthill raised his eyebrows and thought how Alice would have been incensed by the use of the word 'unprovoked' but remained silent.

'The government won't hear of me demanding the imposition of a permanent agent at Lhasa,' Younghusband continued, 'but I can insist on a trade agent being established at Gyantse. So I suppose that's something.' He sighed. 'And now I must hear once again the same arguments about why we should retreat immediately back to India. Stay here, Fonthill, ready to escort this latest lot out of the camp. They will get nothing from me now until we reach Lhasa.'

He gave a smile and patted Fonthill on the back. 'Last lap, at last, old chap. Last lap, at last.'

Simon stayed to listen to the negotiations once again. As Frank O'Connor introduced the Tibetan delegates, he realised that this was probably the highest level of mediators that Lhasa had sent. In addition to the four Shapés, there were four abbots from the three great monasteries around the capital: Drepung, which housed not less than 7,700 monks, Sera (5,500) and Ganden (3,300). Fonthill marvelled once again at the grip that the religious order had on the country. Via O'Connor's translation, he heard each abbot reiterate the same plea: that these monks were all restive at the approach of the British and they might well break out and attack the column if it continued its approach.

Younghusband once again sat impassively and listened to every word and once again he repeated that his orders were to enter Lhasa and there to open negotiations with the Tibetan government and that there could be no retreat back over the passes. This time there was no state secretary from Lhasa to sound a belligerent note and smiles and politeness permeated the whole day's discussion. But the end result was the same: there would be no turning back by the mission.

At the end of the afternoon, after much bowing and smiling, Simon lined up his company of Mounted Infantry and escorted the delegation out of the camp and some seven miles along the riverside road, before he too made his salutations and returned back to the crossing, just as Ottley rode in with his company to report an uneventful patrol. There were no hostile Tibetans in the immediate vicinity of the British column to threaten it while it was vulnerable during the river crossing.

Before setting out again, Younghusband sent a letter to the Dalai Lama. In it he repeated that he must carry out his orders, which were that he must continue his journey to Lhasa. He would withdraw as soon as a satisfactory treaty had been negotiated there; his troops would not fire unless fired upon, no holy places would be occupied unless they were being used for warlike purposes and all supplies would be paid for. If any resistance was met, however, it would adversely affect the terms of the treaty.

As the last troops were ferried across the Tsangpo, Fonthill had stayed behind talking to Younghusband. Now, before leaving to catch up with his patrol, he scanned through his field glasses to where the road twisted up on the southern bank and disappeared into the mountains. There was no sign of a returning supply train nor, therefore, of Alice. He sighed and turned to overtake the column which was already now beginning its last march on Lhasa.

It was an imposing sight. The soil by the banks of the river was fecund and rich, the weather spring-like and almost warm, birds were singing overhead, despite the dust kicked up by the long column, and the forts that they passed were ruined and deserted. It seemed that the pleasant countryside was empty of all opposition.

Despite the reduction that had taken place in the ranks

of the army before leaving Gyantse, the column was still seven miles long. As always, a screen of Mounted Infantry spread out in the van, followed by the actual vanguard of Sikhs and Gurkhas, then the artillery, mounted on mountain mules, and the long line of Fusiliers and supply mounts and camp followers. Right in the middle of the column rode the fragile figure of General Macdonald, head bowed and hunched over the neck of his horse, clearly feeling that he, at least, was riding in the wrong direction.

As Fonthill trotted ahead, to catch up with his two companies of Mounted Infantry, he passed the erect and very different figure cut by Younghusband who, when on the march, always stayed writing letters or reading poetry until the rearguard began its own march, when he too would then ride gently through the plodding column until he was in the van. He gave a cheering salute to Fonthill and waved him on.

Simon was annoyed to find that, in his view, his Mounted Infantry this morning were not far enough ahead of the army and, once he had caught up with them, he ordered them once again to fan out and put at least five miles between them and the vanguard, to ensure that the main column should not be caught off guard. Then, as an afterthought he ordered Ottley once again to take his company and ride out to the north to protect that flank.

He threw out his orders – not without an obvious trace of ill temper – and settled into his creaking saddle to ride alongside Jenkins, his old companion of so many campaigns.

'Why, bach sir?' asked the Welshman. 'It's all over bar

the shoutin', ain't it? Are you expectin' more trouble, then?'

'No. But of all the units in this army, this one can't afford to relax. We're the column's eyes and ears and, indeed, the first cushion if it does ride into trouble. But I am beginning to feel that the Tibetans – or at least those big Khampas – are not just going to let us ride quietly and peacefully into their sacred city without putting up one last show.'

Jenkins nodded ruminatively. 'Why all the fuss about this bleedin' town, then? What's so special about it? It's probably a bit like Rhyl, without the seaside, like.'

'Well, to the Tibetans, I suppose it's a bit like Mecca to the Mohammedans, a very sacred place. It's full of great temples, I understand, and very few non-Tibetans and hardly any Europeans have seen it. A damned great army of non-believers moving in and camping just outside will seem as if the place will be desecrated. I can understand the point of view, although it is ridiculously old-fashioned and out of place in this twentieth century.'

'Hmm. Well, at least it'll be interesting to see it. Something to tell my girls about when I get back.'

Simon gave him a sharp glance. Jenkins now hardly ever mentioned his late wife's children but there was no doubt that the Welshman – like every man in the army, for that matter – was tired of this long journey over the mountains and into the heart of this strange, mostly barren and hostile country. His customary merry countenance was now seamed and one or two silver streaks were beginning to show through the thick thatch of his black hair. Fonthill suddenly felt an unaccustomed flash of sorrow for his old comrade, who, at fifty-three, was probably the oldest combatant in the column.

'Absolutely,' he said, 'something to tell the children, indeed. Definitely the last lap, 352, and, I hope, the quietest.'

And so the attenuated column with its cavalry eyes and ears far out ahead plodded on. The quietness that Fonthill had hoped for was maintained for the next two days until on the third day, after the river crossing, the Mounted Infantry had been riding for less than an hour, when a dust cloud materialised from the north where Ottley had been patrolling. Simon stood in the stirrups and concentrated his field glasses on the edge of the cloud. At first he could see little, then, as he focussed more carefully, he realised that the cloud was being kicked up by Ottley and his men, who were riding hard towards the rest of the Mounted Infantry.

Were they being pursued or riding back with urgent news? Within minutes Ottley had arrived, he and his company covered in dust.

'Tibetans,' he shouted, reining in. 'The big fellers. They took us by surprise. They're mounted and coming straight for you.'

'Are they coming for us or the main column?'

'For us. And they are moving fast.'

'Did you sustain casualties?'

'No. But there were too many of them to tackle so we rode away like hell. They're right behind us, though.'

'How many of them?'

'I'd say about 300 or more.'

Fonthill looked around. There was no cover in the immediate vicinity, apart from the little provided by where the riverbank fell away to the water. He turned to Jenkins.

'Send two of our best horsemen to gallop right away back to the column. Tell the general that we are about to be attacked by Khampa horsemen and that there may be more Tibetans heading towards him. We will fight them here for there is no time to fall back on the column. Tell the men to ride hard to avoid being cut off. Got that?'

'Yes, bach sir.'

'Ottley.'

'Sir?'

'I don't fancy fighting on horseback if we're to be outnumbered. Dismount the men and get the handlers up and the horses taken down to the river edge, try and find a bank. They'll get some protection there. Then spread out the men in a crescent with their backs to the river. No firing until I give the order.'

'Very good, Simon.'

Orders were barked and the two messengers galloped away, back along the riverbank. Fonthill looked back to the north where another and larger dust cloud was nearing fast. Through the field glasses he could see the Khampas clearly now. They were fanning out to cut off his escape back along the riverbank. God – he hoped the two riders would be able to get through!

He withdrew his carbine from its saddle bucket, pulled his sabre from its sheath, dismounted and handed his pony to the handler. Ensuring that the magazine in the carbine was full, he strode to where Ottley was directing the men.

'Put your company on the right, William,' he shouted, 'and command there. I will take the left side. Take out twenty men and have them wait by the riverbank in the middle as a reserve in case the Khampas break through. I will command them. It'll be carbines now but it could be sabres and kukris later. Good luck, old chap.'

'And to you, sir.'

Fonthill and Jenkins strode to where the crescent bulged out in the middle and took position among the kneeling men a little to the left of the centre. Seeing that they could not take the British by surprise, the Tibetans had now slowed their ponies to a walk and then they halted just out of range of the Lee Metfords.

Simon looked along the curve of his men. As usual, they looked a completely disreputable bunch: the Sikhs, their turbans kept in place by woollen scarves tied under their chins, looked a head taller than the Gurkhas, whose little pillbox hats poked out incongruously from their *poshteens*. The Sikhs had thrust their sabres into the ground in front of them, the Gurkhas had loosened their sheepskins the better to reach the broad-bladed kukris hanging from their belts.

At his side, as ever, stood Jenkins, a half smile bending his moustache as he looked at the host facing them. He looked up at Fonthill and winked. There was no sign of fatigue in his weathered face now. 352 Jenkins was now back in his element, facing an enemy that far outnumbered them. 'Odds about three to one, I'd say,' he said. 'Just about fair, look you. And a fine day, too. Now what could be better, eh?'

Simon forced a smile. 'My dear old 352, nothing could be better.' Then he raised his voice and addressed the line.

'From the left, NUMBER,' he screamed. The voices floated up quickly in reply and in a variety of accents: 'one, two, tree, fouer, fife . . .' and so on around the line until number seventy-seven was shouted, the Reserve, of course, being out of the line at the rear.

'On my command,' shouted Fonthill, 'we will fire in volleys. Odd numbers first, then reload and then even numbers. Now . . . wait for the command.'

He looked up at the Khampas; they had not dismounted. 'They are going to charge us on horseback,' he said to Jenkins. 'Good. They will have to jump the line.'

'Better keep our 'eads down then, eh?'

'Indeed.' Simon addressed his line again. 'They will charge us on horseback,' he shouted, enunciating each word carefully. 'Those that we don't bring down with the volleys will have to jump our line. When they do, kneel fast, just bow your heads. The Reserve will deal with them inside our line.'

He turned to the twenty men, kneeling by the riverbank under the charge of a *daffadar*. 'Reserve,' he shouted. 'Hold your fire until our line is jumped. Then bring down all those that have jumped over. Understood, *Daffadar*?'

'Yes, sahib.'

'Good.' Fonthill knelt again and worked the bolt on his rifle. 'Now we wait.'

'Not too long, I 'ope,' breathed Jenkins. 'I could do with a cup of tea. Or, better still, a beer—'

His words were cut short as an order was shouted from the ranks of the horsemen, heels were dug in, whips were slashed against horse flanks and the Khampas raised a scream as they charged against the thin line of kneeling riflemen.

Fonthill stood. 'Wait for the command,' he shouted. 'At 200 yards, in volleys, odd numbers, wait for it . . . FIRE!'

Nearly forty rifles fired as one and smoke drifted up from the kneeling men. Immediately the front rank of the horsemen collapsed in confusion, horses plunging to the ground, screaming in fear and pain and their riders hurled over their heads to lie still. But the short-barrelled carbines were not the most accurate weapons in the army of the Raj even at short range and many of the bullets sang aimlessly above the heads of the charging horsemen.

Fonthill raised his voice again. 'Odd numbers reload, even numbers FIRE!'

Again a volley rang out from the crescent and this time, given that the second rank of horsemen had to avoid their fallen comrades and this resulted in a bunching of the attackers, the target was nearer and easier. A swathe was cut through the jumbled horsemen, causing further confusion to those behind.

'Fire at will!' screamed Fonthill again above the din.

'I never could work out which one was Will, you know,' murmured Jenkins as he closed one eye and carefully sighted his carbine.

The whole line of kneeling men were now pumping their bolt mechanisms and firing as fast as they could into the mass in front of them. Blue smoke drifted up into the cold air, the flashes of the rifles breaking through it and marking where the line of the Mounted Infantry curved.

Simon stood again. 'Cease firing,' he shouted. 'They're retreating. Save your ammunition.'

Indeed, the riders, their long hair now clearly visible flowing from beneath their skullcaps, had turned and were now trotting away, as though indifferent to the losses they had sustained.

'Report on casualties, William,' shouted Fonthill. Then, '352, go along our company and give me a casualty report.'

'Very good, bach sir. But it don't look like many at this stage.'

'Never mind. They'll come again. We may have to shorten our line.'

Ottley hurried over. 'Just two chaps lightly wounded,' he reported. 'The Khampas weren't able to shoot well as they rode. Do you think they've had enough?'

Fonthill squinted to see through the pall of smoke still hanging over the line. 'It looks as though they are dismounting,' he said. 'And what's more,' he murmured as he held his binoculars to his eyes, 'dammit, I think they've got rifles. It looks as though they are going to crawl as near to us as they can and snipe at us. Trouble is,' he looked around at the curved line, 'we've got absolutely no cover here and they can crawl up behind their dead and the bodies of the horses. Well,' he shrugged his shoulders, 'we shall see what sort of marksmen they are.'

Jenkins arrived. 'Just one poor old Gurkha shot clean through the forrid,' he reported, 'an' one other wounded a bit in the shoulder.'

'Should we retreat to the riverbank, do you think?' asked Ottley.

'Problem with that,' replied Fonthill, 'is that we could have our flanks turned if they attack in force along the bank at both ends. And there's not much cover there, anyway. The bank only goes down about a foot in some places. Better hold our ground, I think, as our casualties are light. See what you can do for the wounded, William. Oh, and give me an ammunition report when you can.'

'Very good.'

He turned to Jenkins. 'Pick out our best marksmen – you will know them better than me – and see if they can pick off the leading Khampas at this long range as they try to crawl forward. No one else is to fire until I give the orders. I'm worried about our ammunition so I don't want anybody blazing away at this stage. I'm going to talk to the Reserve.'

Simon walked back to where the *daffadar* and his twenty men were crouched a little ahead of the riverbank.

'I am sorry, *Daffadar*,' he said to the beaming Sikh, 'that you haven't been in the fight yet, but I think you will be soon.'

'Yes, sahib. We have been itching to fire, you know.'

'Of course. But you are our last and perhaps the most important part of our defence. I want you to stay here without moving until you are needed. And that will be if the Tibetans break through our line. Now this could well happen because we are thinly stretched. So please keep your eye on me and when I turn and wave I want you to deliver a volley at the enemy who have broken through and then charge with your sabres. Understood?'

'Oh, very understood, sahib. We kill them all.'

'Good man. But wait for the signal.'

'Yes, sahib. Signal will be waited for.'

They exchanged grins and then Fonthill sauntered back to the line, trying to emit a confidence that he did not quite feel. Despite the many engagements he had fought since he and Jenkins had first faced the Zulus, more than a quarter of a century ago, he was never quite able to dispel the doubts about his own courage and fighting qualities that always surfaced when he faced an enemy. Now the Khampas appeared to be regrouping and still, despite their losses, well outnumbering the Mounted Infantry. Had his riders got through to the main column and would Macdonald send reinforcements? He hoped to God they would not be needed.

Ottley and Jenkins came bustling back with their ammunition reports. It seemed that the average number of rounds retained by each man was now only eleven. Fonthill gritted his teeth.

'I don't think we are going to be charged again – at least not yet,' he said. 'Tell the men to adopt the spreadeagle position and to conserve their ammunition as best they can and shoot only when they are certain they have a sure target.'

Ottley and Jenkins doubled away and Simon was left observing the enemy closely through his field glasses until a bullet whistled over his shoulder and made him fall to the ground. The sniping had begun.

Fonthill attempted to recall what he had heard about these Khampas. He knew that they were a very different breed of soldier from the pressed peasants that had mainly faced the British so far in the campaign. These warriors, virtually mercenaries from eastern Tibet, were arrogant fighters, he knew, who were feared by the ordinary people of the country because of their disregard for personal property and because they did not share the Tibetan regard for the sanctity of life. They were brave and well led – characteristics which they were displaying now.

They were now coming back into range, but, as Simon had forecast, they were crawling along to reach the small protection offered by the bodies of the horses and even those of their erstwhile comrades that lay marking the high tide of the cavalry charge. As yet, they were offering the most elusive of targets and, looking along the Mounted Infantry line, Fonthill was glad that none of the sepoys were wasting precious cartridges at this stage.

A thump at his side marked the arrival of Jenkins. 'They'll 'ave to attempt to rush us at some stage, won't they?' he asked.

'Yes. But whoever is in command there knows what he is doing. He knows we can shoot, so he is going to try and reduce our numbers first by sniping – and our chaps have no cover at all. If we had plenty of ammunition, we could keep firing to keep their heads down, but we have to be careful.'

Jenkins pulled a glum face. 'Did we not have enough rounds per man when we rode out, then?'

'We did not, because the whole column is short of ammo now. The supply line is thin and stretches back a long . . .' His voice tailed away as the mention of the supply line made him think of Alice. Where the hell was she? Had she returned and caught up with the main column yet?

His surmising was cut short as a bullet thudded into the earth at his side. 'Damn,' he muttered, 'they're getting the range now.'

'Ah . . .' Jenkins caressed the butt of his carbine with his cheek as he gently pressed the stock into his shoulder. 'I think I can see that bugger. Let's see if I can reach him.'

He waited for what seemed to Fonthill like an interminable time before, very, very gently the Welshman pressed the trigger. About 300 yards away, a bearded figure suddenly flung up his rifle and rolled onto his back.

'Good shooting, 352!'

Jenkins grinned. 'Not bad for a poor old man who keeps fallin' off mountains, was it?'

'Pretty damned good, I'd say.'

The shot was like a signal to the defenders, for at least it showed that the Tibetans were now within range, and a ragged volley rang out all along the line. It was not without effect, for the crawling Khampas had not yet reached the dubious protection of the corpses ahead of them and Simon, scanning them with his field glasses, counted seven who jerked and lay still.

'They've got guts, though,' he muttered as he put down the glasses, 'they're still coming on.'

'Yes,' Jenkins sniffed. 'But we've got to be better shots than them, look you. We're trained soldiers after all, see. If it's a game of long-range shootin' we're bound to win it, even though we're only 'idin' be'ind three grains of bloody sand.'

'I hope you're right. But I don't have much faith in these damned carbines at any sort of range. If you're not right, we may have to charge them and I wouldn't fancy that.'

The sniping duel continued for at least ten minutes and Fonthill became concerned at the expenditure of cartridges by his men. When, as seemed inevitable, the Tibetans rushed the thin line of what were now very disMounted Infantry, the sepoys would need to deliver at least one solid volley before the fighting became hand to hand.

He turned to the man on his right. 'Pass the word,' he said, 'conserve ammunition.' Then to Jenkins on his left, 'Pass it on.'

'Oh, bloody 'ell,' muttered the Welshman. 'I wish I 'ad a lunger.' No bayonets could be fixed to the carbines, so they had not been issued. He rolled over onto his side and withdrew from his belt a wicked knife that gleamed in the cold sunshine. 'Never mind,' he said, 'this old friend 'as never let me down.' And he stuck it into the sandy soil ahead of him.

Fonthill risked kneeling to take a quick look along the line to his left and right. Before a bullet whistling over his head made him plunge down again, he counted five of the Mounted Infantry lying prostrate, their rifles at their sides. Whether they were dead or merely wounded he had no way of knowing, but it was clear that they were taking no further part in the battle. He looked behind him at the Reserve. They had taken the precaution of lying face down, their rifles at the ready, and it looked as though their numbers were still intact.

The sniping continued for at least another quarter of an hour and Simon was becoming increasingly concerned that this attrition – and the fact that the Mounted Infantry's response had become severely reduced – would be adversely affecting his men's morale, when a nudge from Jenkins made him look up.

Firing from the enemy's line had now ceased. 'I think they're pluckin' up courage to come over at us,' muttered the Welshman. Figures could be glimpsed crawling up to reinforce the men behind the limited cover provided by the corpses.

Simon lifted his head and shouted to right and left. 'Men of the Mounted Infantry,' he shouted, 'the enemy are about to charge us. Empty your magazines into them as they come. Don't wait for the order. Fire at will. Then cut down the bastards with sabre and kukri.'

A ragged cheer broke out all along the line. It was met by a battle cry from the Khampas, who immediately rose from their cover, brandishing swords that flashed in the sunlight, and ran towards the defenders.

Once again the curve of the crescent was shrouded in blue smoke as the rifles of the Mounted Infantry crashed out in unison. This time, however, there was no volley firing, just a continuous crackle of gunfire as the precious last rounds in the magazines of the Lee Metfords were emptied into the mass of shrouded figures running towards them.

The Khampas fell in droves, for it was impossible to miss at that range, but still the tall warriors came on, their hair streaming behind them, their curved swords flashing above their heads.

Fonthill and Jenkins, together with all of the men who remained in the curved line, scrambled to their feet. Simon stole a quick glance behind him to see the twenty men of the Reserve also on their feet, their carbines at their shoulders. He gulped and grabbed the handle of the sabre still protruding from the soil ahead of him. At his side, he was conscious that Jenkins had ignored his sword and was now standing, legs slightly bent, his long knife glinting in his right hand, his left extended before him in that well-remembered posture, as though he was going to negotiate with his opponent.

Then the line of the Khampas was upon them. Fonthill just had time to note that it was a ragged line, showing that the cruel firing of the Lee Metfords had had its effect, before a bearded warrior lunged at him with his sword. Simon parried desperately and slashed at the man's face in return, missing as the Tibetan pulled away.

Damn! Don't slash, thrust with the point – even with a sabre! The old mantra from his Sandhurst days flashed across his mind as he parried again, this time twisting his wrist to deflect his opponent's blade away and sliding his own point along its length until, with a final lunge, it sank into the man's stomach. He extracted the blade with a twist and swung it horizontally at the neck of the man who was flailing his sword at Jenkins. The warrior sank to the ground with a sigh, blood gushing from his half-severed head.

'Watch out, bach. On your right!'

Fonthill just had time to twist his body out of the way of another sword thrust and he countered awkwardly, missing the man as he danced past him, only to meet the knife of a bloodstained Jenkins who, kneeling, thrust his knife into the warrior's groin, immediately retracting it to plunge it into his stomach.

'Are you all right, 352?' gasped Simon.

'Never been better, bach. Watch out. 'Ere's another lot.'

Simon looked up and presented his sabre – already beginning to feel double its original weight – at a huge Tibetan who made the mistake of swinging his great curved sword horizontally in huge sweeps. Dropping his point, Fonthill ducked under the flashing sword and then lunged forward. The end of the sabre took the man lightly in the breast but the impetus of his charge still carried the warrior forward, so that he impaled himself completely on the sabre, until it protruded from his back.

Unable to extricate his blade, Simon collapsed under the giant so that the hilt of his sabre hit him in the chest, winding him. He thought for a terrible moment that his adversary was still alive, for, face-to-face, as they were, it seemed as if his eyes were rolling and his teeth were clenched in a demonic grin. But his expression was a death mask and the two fell together, Fonthill underneath.

As he struggled to throw off the man, he was aware of Jenkins astride the two of them, bloodstained knife in hand, weaving from the waist like the bare-knuckle champion, Tom Sayers, but not leaving his position, parrying several sword thrusts and thrusting back adroitly.

At last Fonthill was able to squirm from under his man and struggle to his feet. 'Get yer bloody sword, quickly,' shouted Jenkins.

Simon did so, pulling it out just in time to meet yet another Khampa who came, this time, more circumspectly – so circumspectly, in fact, that, after three half-hearted thrusts, he turned and ran. Trying to regain his breath, Fonthill turned to find Jenkins now down on one knee, sucking in air himself.

'Are you all right, 352?'

'Yes. Just a bit winded. But I think they've got through, look you.'

Turning quickly, Fonthill saw that a small group of Khampas had broken through a gap in the Mounted Infantry line. He raised his arm and waved to where he could still glimpse the Reserve group. 'Reserve,' he shouted, surprising himself at the high pitch of his voice, 'Advance and fire.'

Immediately, the muzzles of the Reserve's Lee Metfords flashed with flame and, once again, a volley sounded by the banks of the river, and then another and another.

'Behind you, bach,'

Jenkins's voice again made him whirl round, to see the Welshman, now back on his feet again, catch the blade of a sword on his knife, swing it upwards and kick his boot into the unprotected groin of the assailant. The man bent over with a groan and Jenkins, bloodstained but as agile as a monkey, danced around him and sank his bloodstained knife into the back of the Tibetan.

'Thanks, 352.' Simon suddenly realised that the words pitched out into what was now a comparative silence. He squinted through the smoke that drifted past him from the Reserve's volleys and glimpsed dun-coloured figures, in twos and threes, running and limping away from the line. He turned and saw the bodies of the Khampas who had broken through the line, scattered on the ground, some moving and groaning from their wounds, but the majority lying still. Looking down the line, he saw that it now had more gaps but the men who still stood were waving their sabres and cheering.

He turned to his old comrade, 'My God, we've done it, old chap. We've beaten 'em.'

Jenkins was grinning, but was back kneeling on one knee, blood dripping down the side of his face and from the end of his great moustache from a gash in his stubbled hair and more blood oozing from a scarlet patch on his thigh.

'Course, we 'ave,' the little man gasped. 'Never doubted it. You're the best general in the British army.' Then, very slowly, he toppled over and lay on the ground.

Fonthill ran to his side, pulling out a handkerchief. 'Sword wounds or bullets?' he asked, surprised at his own coolness.

'Ah. Only sword cuts. They just 'urt a bit when I laugh, nothin' more.'

'Good.' Simon looked round. 'Give me your first-aid kit,' he demanded of a nearby Sikh who was wiping his sabre. 'Quickly, now.'

Tearing away at the cloth surrounding the leg wound, which seemed the worst of the two, Fonthill dabbed a little iodine onto the open cut, pressed a felt pad onto the wound, which was now bleeding profusely and clumsily bound a bandage tightly around the thigh. 'Lie there,' he said. 'Don't get up.'

'Oh, I was just thinkin' of runnin' after the enemy,' growled Jenkins.

The words reminded Fonthill of his duty. He stood and saw a tousle-haired Ottley running towards him.

'Glad you're all right, sir,' said the Irishman. 'Congratulations. That's the best-ordered defence I've ever been in, considering we were on open ground. Now, I think we've got enough men left to go after those bastards and the horses haven't been hurt. Permission to pursue, sir?'

'Very well, William. Well done. Yes, go after them. They must be taught a lesson, but don't ride too far. Don't pursue in more than company strength for I shall need men here in case there is another attack. Ride for say a couple of miles and then return here. We must tend to the wounded and we won't be strong enough here to try and make it back to the column without you. Understood?'

'Understood, sir. *Daffadar!*'

The horses were brought up, Ottley rounded up some fifty men and then rode off to where, in the far distance, the tiny figures of the remnants of the Khampas could just be seen riding and walking away.

'I think I can stand, bach sir, if you give me an 'and, like.' Jenkins's voice sounded less than strong.

'No. Sit there for a bit and get your strength back. It looks as though the bleeding from your leg and your head has stopped. But it would be silly to take risks.' Simon looked down at this giant of a little man, who sprawled before him. If he had ever fleetingly doubted his old friend's capacity to fight, that doubt had disappeared completely now.

'I don't know how many times you have saved my life, 352,' he said, 'but you did it again today, several times, in fact. So, thank you once more. You remain a magnificent fighter. And you are certainly not an *old* man.'

The Welshman sat up, hands on knees, and gave a crooked smile. 'Well, you're a fine one to go around thankin' people. If you 'adn't chopped off the 'ead of that big bugger, I wouldn't be sittin' 'ere, look you, enjoyin' myself so much. So I reckon that the thanks are even.'

'All right. Now stay sitting there. I must make sure we're looking after the other wounded. Don't try and stand and be heroic any more. Disregard what I just said, you're far too old for that.'

Fonthill set about the sad task of counting the dead and ensuring that the *daffadars* were tending to the wounded, as best they could, for there was no doctor with the Mounted Infantry. In all, nine had been killed and a further seventeen wounded, but only one seriously, a sword swing having almost severed his arm. Clean water was used to wash the wound and then a *daffadar* who had studied a little medicine set about sewing up the gash with needle and thread, while the Gurkha clenched his teeth and uttered not one whimper, although he did take a mouthful of brandy from Simon's flask.

The Gurkha dead were buried by the riverbank and enough driftwood was found to burn the bodies of the three Sikhs killed, in accordance with their religion. The Khampas' dead, numbering more than sixty, were left to lie where they had fallen, Fonthill feeling that their bodies would deter any other hostile Tibetans in the vicinity – and, in any case, he did not wish to burden his weary troops further.

Ottley and his men rode in some three hours after they had set off, causing Fonthill to frown, for he was anxious to set off back to join the main column before night fell. They had pursued the Khampas until what was left of them had disappeared into foothills. Despite the fact that the mounts of Ottley's men were tired, Simon insisted on moving back along the riverbank.

He arrived at the main camp just as dusk was falling, to find that Macdonald had made camp as soon as the two Mounted Infantry messengers had ridden in, setting up a defensive position by the riverbank. He listened, drawing on the inevitable cigarette, as Fonthill made his report.

'It sounds as though you did exceedingly well, despite your comparatively heavy losses,' he coughed.

'We had no cover at all,' Simon responded warmly.

'Yes, quite so. I wasn't sure, from what your riders said, about the size of the Tibetan force attacking you and, indeed, whether they would bypass you and come on to us. So I felt it judicious to set up a defensive position here, hoping that you would fall back on us. I couldn't put the main column at risk, of course.'

'No. Of course not.' But Simon felt that the deliberate irony in his tone had escaped the Scotsman.

Fonthill had expected that Alice would be waiting for him when he rode into the camp, but there was no sign of her. He sought out the officer who had taken on the role of Major Bretherton as controller of transport and supplies.

'Aren't you expecting a supply train in at any time now?' he asked.

The man shook his head. 'No. Nor do I expect one soon. Why do you ask?'

Fonthill felt his heart sink. 'But my wife left several days

274

ago, probably with her young Tibetan, to go back to the cable point with one of your supply columns.'

'Sorry, old man. We haven't sent a column back for nearly a month. We are more or less living off the country now until we get to Lhasa – and I haven't seen Mrs Fonthill for some time.'

Thanking him, Simon strode off to the small tented area where the correspondents were housed. The story was the same: no one had seen Alice for quite a few days now. They all suspected that she had ridden off with her young companion chasing some story or other.

It was when walking back from there that a rather embarrassed coolie stopped him and handed him Alice's second note. 'From memsahib again, sahib,' he said.

Simon seized it, and when he reached the phrase *I intend to see the Tibetan high lamas and persuade them to stop this war* he threw back his head and roared with anger. The coolie hung his head and stepped back a pace. 'When did she give you this?' Fonthill demanded, his face white.

'Several days ago now, sahib. I was told to wait for a week before delivering this, but I think you should have it sooner. I am sorry, sahib.'

Simon frowned and swallowed hard. 'No. You did right,' he said. He fumbled in his pocket, gave the man a handful of rupees, thrust the note into his pocket and strode away to find Jenkins.

He found the Welshman, newly bandaged at head and thigh, sitting in his tiny tent, drinking an inevitable cup of tea. Fonthill threw the note to his friend and stood drumming his fingers on the tent pole as Jenkins laboriously read the message. Then 352 looked up, a slow smile spreading across his battered face.

'You've got to admire the lass, bach sir,' he said. 'You really 'ave. Pushin' off by 'erself – well, with old Sunshine – to end the war, all by 'erself, so to speak.'

Simon sighed and sat awkwardly on the end of Jenkins's trestle bed. 'Well, that's one way of looking at it,' he said. 'Another way is to conclude that this is a certain way to have herself and young Sunil killed.' He threw back his head and stared at the low canvas above. 'Doesn't the woman know that females are not regarded highly – if at all – in this damned country and that Lhasa is a sacred city? She is more likely to be thrown into a deep pit and left to starve as to see the bloody Dalai Lama – or Santa Claus, for that matter.'

Jenkins put his head on one side and stroked his moustache. 'Ah now, bach. She's cleverer than that, an' you know it. She's been in as many difficult situations as we 'ave an' she's usually got out of it on 'er own. I reckon she'll be all right.'

A silence fell within the tent, broken only by a distant bugle call and the creaking of leather as mules were unharnessed nearby.

'What do you propose to do now, then?' asked Jenkins.

Simon frowned at his friend. 'Do? Well, go after her, of course, and bring her back – if it's not too late.'

'Very well. I'll come with you.'

'Of course you won't. You are not fit to ride.'

Jenkins sighed. 'If you think that I'm goin' to let you ride off after the missus on your own, then you don't know

Sergeant Major 352 Jenkins, just about the best wife-finder in the whole of bloody Tibet. Of course, I'm comin' with you. But we shall need more than two of us.'

'Hmm. I'm not sure about that. I'd better go and find the General – and Younghusband, for that matter. We can't just push off on our own. Now you rest a while. I promise I won't ride without you.'

'I should bloody well think not.'

CHAPTER ELEVEN

Alice awoke on the morning after her arrival at Chung Li's house to hear goats bleating and, for a second, couldn't remember where she was. Then she recalled the nature of her mission and her heart sank. Considered now, with some of the indignation that had prompted it receded, it loomed as something quixotic, with success improbable and, indeed, danger quite certain. Why the hell had she embarked on such a ridiculous journey?

Then, as she lay back on the straw-filled pillow, she recalled the sad landscape of the Tibetan bodies strewn, half frozen, after the so-called 'battles' and she saw again the desperate waving of Major Bretherton's arms as the current took him away. Yes, little chance of success but, dammit, it was worth a try!

She washed with the little tablet of soap she had

brought with her in the bowl of cold water provided, dressed and tentatively walked down the stairs. Chung Li was sitting by what appeared to be a peat fire in the main sitting room but, on seeing her, he rose, bowed briefly and left the room. His wife bustled in, tongue out in greeting, and indicated that Alice should sit at the table.

Tea was produced and a kind of porridge, which was sweet and nourishing, followed by coarse bread and some form of meat dripping which was excellent. Alice thanked her and asked, 'Sunil?'

The woman nodded and within moments Sunil had arrived to sit by her side. 'Have you had breakfast?' asked Alice.

'Oh yes, memsahib. I been grooming horses.'

'You are a splendid chap, Sunil. Thank you.' She took a spoonful of porridge. 'Have you had chance to talk to your uncle?'

Sunil frowned. 'Yes, I tell him what you want. To be taken to meet the big lamas here and maybe even Dalai Lama. He say Dalai is away and not possible to see him anyway. Nobody see him. He don't know about the boss lamas. He is going to take advice.'

Alice met his frown. 'Hmm. I'm not sure that's a good idea. The fewer people who know about me being here the better. But I suppose we have no choice. We are in the hands of Chung Li.'

'Yes, miss. I think he want to help but I am not sure.'

Alice looked at him sharply. 'Why aren't you sure?'

Sunil lowered his eyes. He was clearly embarrassed.

'I don't know, memsahib,' he said, studying the floor. 'I have feeling . . .' His voice tailed away.

'Yes, go on.'

'I have feeling that he don't like British much. There are stories about us killing Tibetans on march into this country . . .'

Alice nodded. 'Well, that's certainly true. But, you see, that's why I want to stop the fighting and persuade the lamas to sit down and negotiate with Younghusband Sahib, so that the killing will stop. I am sure I can persuade them. Perhaps I can talk to your uncle myself?'

'Of course, if you want. I ask when he returns.'

The old man was away for several hours, leaving Alice uncomfortable, with nothing to do but smile at the women, who smiled and bobbed at her in return. She was not at all happy that Chung Li had gone to consult someone on how to answer her request but all she could do was wait and see what would ensue.

She was in the little paddock, with Sunil, feeding the ponies when she heard a commotion in the house. Women's voices were raised in what sounded like indignation and then she heard male voices replying in what undoubtedly were tones of authority. She hardly had time to exchange a troubled glance with Sunil before four unusually large Tibetans with long hair and with sheathed swords hanging from their belts burst through the door, followed by Chung Li's wife and one of his daughters with tears running down their faces.

'Khampas!' The word came from Sunil who stood, his eyes wide, as two of the warriors roughly seized Alice, pinned her arms behind her back and pushed her towards the little gate in the paddock. Sunil shouted something to them in Tibetan, only to receive a fierce backhanded slap from one of the men, which sent him reeling to the ground.

'Leave the boy alone,' shouted Alice and she ducked and tore her arms away and delivered a right-handed punch to the warrior who had hit Sunil. A fierce blow to her head was her reward and, for a moment, she staggered and her ears rang with the force of the blow. Then her arms were roughly pulled behind her and this time bound.

She turned her head but there was no sign of Chung Li and she glimpsed only the two women screaming in protest and a stricken Sunil trying to regain his feet as she was dragged through the gate into the little street.

'Don't worry, memsahib,' she heard Sunil shout. 'I follow.' Then a loop was slipped over her head and body, tightened and, with one of the Khampas at the end of the rope, she was pulled through the streets, away from the house of Chung Li.

She had difficulty keeping up with the long strides of the warriors, three of whom now surrounded her and kept pushing and prodding her to keep the pace. The suddenness of it all, the barbarity of the soldiers, contrasting so sharply with the simple kindness of Chung Li's wife and daughters, brought a complete dryness to Alice's throat and mouth and she felt as though her tongue had swollen. Her head was still ringing from the blow and she forced herself to keep blinking to stop tears from running down her cheeks.

Stumbling along, being pulled by one giant warrior and closely escorted by the others, she became an object of great interest in the crowded streets, and shrouded women and high-cheeked, pigtailed Tibetan males fell away to give the party passage, a kind of hiss of . . . what? . . . interest, resentment, anger? . . . rising from them.

Alice turned her head to look behind her and thought she glimpsed the hurrying figure of Sunil following but another slap made her turn back.

A jumble of thoughts ran through her brain. Clearly Chung Li had betrayed her to the authorities. It was treachery of the basest sort, given the warm welcome that the man had extended to her and to his nephew. But then, she sighed, treachery and Tibet went together. Curzon had lied when he said that the mission to Lhasa would not be an invasion. Younghusband and Macdonald had not kept their word that the fortress at Gyantse would not be occupied by troops from the Raj. Treachery and Tibet seemed to be analogous.

Alice was getting out of breath now and was forced occasionally to break into a pathetic trot to keep up with her long-striding captors. Her thoughts continued to race. Where were they taking her? Could it be that her request to meet the high lamas was, in fact, being answered? Highly unlikely, given the roughness of the treatment. Then she remembered Simon telling her that two Indian spies sent years ago from Delhi to Lhasa had been unmasked and thrown into a dank jail in the city without trial, where they still languished – if, that is, they were still alive. The Tibetans had a morbid fear of being spied upon.

Would she be regarded as a spy? After all, she approach the sacred city in disguise. Her heart sank. What if, after all, Younghusband acceded to the Tibetans' request and negotiated without entering Lhasa? She would be left alone and forgotten in this medieval city. Forgotten? No, of course not. There was Simon, of course, he would undoubtedly come after her. Not to mention Sunil. If he had been able to follow, he could tell Simon where she was being incarcerated. If, that is, incarceration was what was intended. Feeling the headache growing from the blow she had received and looking at the harsh, primitive faces on either side of her, she couldn't help feeling that a gentle interrogation was highly unlikely. She sighed and fought back the tears again. Oh, what a damned silly fool she had been to embark on this quest! What sort of arrogance had made her feel that she, of all people, could make a difference to the conflict?

She sniffed and tried to lengthen her stride.

Alice was in no mood to look about her and note her surroundings but the thought did cross her mind that she must be the first European to enter the sacred city of Lhasa for some 200 years – and perhaps the first woman from outside Asia ever to do so. But she could catch no glimpse of the fabled temples; only rough hovels pressing in to form narrow streets.

She was beginning to stagger with the pace she was being forced to maintain when the little party abruptly turned right and then immediately into a dark, closed doorway. The Khampa pulling the rope banged onto a door which creaked open. She was pulled through into a courtyard of beaten earth, hemmed in by stone walls, lined, high up and just under the edge of the timber roof, by a row of unglazed windows, each containing six vertical bars. A most unpleasant smell assailed Alice's nostrils: human excrement was disgustingly definable but there was something else, less familiar. What was it – despair? Her heart sank further. A prison!

A door was unlocked and abruptly she was thrown through into a dark cell, with light brought only by a barred, open window, set high up in the wall. Immediately, Alice turned and looked into the narrow, implacable eyes of the soldier who had pulled her through the streets.

'You have the manners of a gutter rat and the face of a pockmarked weasel,' she hissed.

He raised his hand to hit her again but she forced herself not to duck but to remain sturdily erect, her chin thrust forward, glaring at him. He thought better of hitting her. So, instead, he kicked her in the groin.

Alice bent in pain and staggered back before collapsing onto the stone floor. The man stood looking down on her, his face quite expressionless. Then he turned, went through the door and she heard a key turn in the lock.

Grimacing in pain, Alice shouted, 'That's no way to treat a lady.' Then she let the tears flow.

Curled up, foetus-like, she realised that her hands were still bound behind her back. God! Were they going to leave her like this, bundled and trussed up like a turkey before Christmas? So much for the Buddhist respect for the sanctity of human life! She looked around her as best she could. There was absolutely no furniture of any kind in the room, except a pile of straw pushed into the corner, which is where, she supposed, she was expected to sleep.

But first, to free herself of her bonds. Her hands had been tied by a length of the same rope that had been used to encircle her body. It was of a thick diameter and hemp-like, not, thank God, thin and like a tightly woven cord. She looked around the room. One of the stones in the wall projected a little and she crawled over to it and began sawing at its edge with the rope. It took her at least fifteen minutes but, eventually, the last frayed strand gave way and she could free her hands and rub her wrists.

She stood and examined the door. It was made of heavy wood – perhaps oak – and the lock was set in the usual steel plate and looked completely impregnable. Alice thrust her hands into the pockets of her riding breeches. At least she had not been searched. What did she have that might be of use?

Turning out her pockets, she carefully laid the contents on the floor: a handkerchief, twenty rupees, a small phial of lip rouge – ah, how useful that would be! – and a small nail file. She took the latter to the door but the sharp end did not fit into any of the four sturdy screws that held the steel plate in position and, anyway, they were rusted in and probably quite immovable. The barred window was small – only perhaps a foot long and six inches deep – and set far too high up the wall for her to reach and the cell contained nothing to stand on.

Alice used the handkerchief to wipe away the tears that were starting to flow again. This would never do!

She must never give up hope. She sat on the straw then immediately jumped up again in horror. Rats? Carefully, with the nail file she poked among the pile. Nothing, thank the Lord.

Forcing herself to be rational, she considered her position. First of all, what assets did she have? Not exactly a storehouse: just the coins, the handkerchief, the lip rouge and the nail file, and of course the clothing she had put on that morning – bra, cotton vest, knickers, blouse, pullover, woollen socks, breeches and riding boots – and the remnants of the rope that had bound her wrists. Even knotted together it only reached perhaps three feet.

So . . . could she attack her jailer and stab him with her file or perhaps garrotte him with the knotted rope? Well, she considered gravely, she might stand a chance if he was only four feet tall, of slight build and extremely cowardly . . . She sighed. The prospects were not exactly encouraging. Her only hope, of course, was that the lamas – or whoever had sent the Khampas to get her – would want to interrogate her; and this would give her a chance of talking her way out of this damned cell.

But what if the lamas never learnt of her existence? Perhaps the Khampas, a law unto themselves, would just kill her out of hand as a spy and remove all trace of her existence? Her heart missed a beat. With a British army virtually on its doorstep, the government of Tibet would surely not take such extreme measures; after all, Simon had told her that the two Indians who had been held in captivity for so long were rumoured to be still alive. But it would be so simple for the Khampas to execute her and deny that she had ever entered their blasted sacred city, so removing the necessity of explaining her arrest and brutal treatment.

Yet . . . her mind raced. There was Sunil, dear Sunil, who had called 'I will follow'. Was it him she had glimpsed in the crowd behind as she was pulled through the streets? She couldn't be sure. But knowing the youth, she was sure that he would feel some sort of responsibility for his uncle's treachery. He would surely try to find out where she was incarcerated and, at the least, try and find Simon, who must now be only less than fifty miles away.

Yes, there was still hope.

Alice settled herself down in the straw and tried to relax. She began to feel hungry and, even more, thirsty. They surely wouldn't let her starve to death or die of thirst here, would they? As though in answer, the key grated in the lock and a thickset Tibetan in smock and Chinese-type skullcap stepped through the door and put a wooden cup of milk and a bowl of porridge on the floor.

'Wait,' she called as he turned to go. 'Do you speak any English?'

He said not a word but, his face impassive – did all Tibetans take a course in face muscle control? – turned, slammed shut the door and once again the key turned in the lock.

'Well thank you, anyway,' Alice called and thirstily took deep draughts of the milk and began eating the porridge with the wooden spoon provided.

Food and drink brought hope and she lay back in the

straw and closed her eyes. The strain of the last hour or so quickly introduced sleep. She did not know how long she slept – her wristwatch she had carefully removed and left with her spare clothing in Chang Li's house – and it was quite dark when she awoke. But what was it that woke her?

A faint voice was calling something from far away and he or she was repeating it. She stood under the window and strained to hear it. Luckily, whoever was calling was approaching and the voice grew slightly louder but it was clear that the person calling was doing so at little above a whisper. Then it called from under the window: 'Memsahib, are you in there?'

Alice almost screamed in delight. 'Yes, Sunil. I am here.' Then, her eyes on the door, she lowered her voice. 'Can you hear me?'

'Oh yes, miss. I hear you. I am so glad to find you.'

'Oh, Sunil, I am so glad you have. I never doubted you. I presume this is a prison I am in?'

'Yes. Nasty place, I think. Have they hurt you?'

'A little, but not much. I can survive. What time is it?'

'I am not sure. Time when most people are asleep, I think. This busy street so I can only come after dark, when people do not walk it. I did not see where you turn earlier. So I have been walking up many streets and calling up to windows.'

'You, my dear Sunil, are a jewel. Now, tell me, was it your uncle who betrayed me to the Khampas?'

For a moment, there was no reply. Then Sunil's voice was even lower. 'Yes, memsahib. I am sorry. He frightened of Khampa general who is local governor where he lives. He no longer my uncle . . .' his voice tailed away.

'Sunil, I am so sorry. I should never have put him and you in this position. Now, listen. I have to decide what to do. Have they taken all my things?'

'Yes. They know who you are, I think.'

'Did they take my Webley revolver and your rifle?'

'They take your revolver, but not,' his voice lifted a tone, 'my rifle.'

'Good. Now if you go to the room where I slept, in the corner near the window, I lifted a piece of floorboard and hid in there a small handgun I had bought at the India border before we set out. With it I hid a small box containing six rounds of ammunition for it. I doubt if the soldiers would have found it. Do you think you could bring it here tomorrow night at roughly this time, tie a line to it, throw it up through the bars and lower it down to me so you don't make a noise without anyone seeing our hearing?'

'Oh, I do that for you, I am sure.'

'Good boy. Do your uncle and aunt know you have been looking for me?'

'I don't know. I not been there since you been taken. I spend time looking for you.'

Alice felt the tears come again at the boy's loyalty, but she stifled them. 'Good. I am most grateful. Now go back to them and don't say that you have found me. Just say that you have spent the time looking. Do not upset your uncle, because it might be bad for you. When you come back tomorrow night, hopefully, I will have made a plan. Is that clear?'

'Yes, memsahib.'

'Thank you again for being such a brave and resourceful boy. You will be rewarded, I promise you.'

'I don't need reward. I get you out of there. You will see.'

'I am sure. Now go. Thank you once more and be very careful.'

'Yes, miss. Goodnight.'

'Goodnight, Sunil.'

Alice blew her nose, slumped back onto the straw and wiped away the incipient tears. What a great asset this Tibetan youth had turned out to be – and what an unthinking fool she had been to put him in danger and to expect that his uncle would have helped this strange woman from an invading force!

Now, she must think what to do. Thank goodness she had had the foresight to buy the little French handgun to back up the great clumsy Webley revolver! She had no idea of how it could be used in the prison, but it was small enough to be hidden on her person and, if the worst came to the worst, particularly if something horrible – rape or torture – threatened, she could use it to shoot her way out of the prison. But now, she must think of what to do with Sunil. He must not be placed in further danger. Sleep would help, she knew. So she lay down and closed her eyes.

She awoke when the cell door was opened and thrown back with a clang. It was clearly quite late in the morning, for light was streaming through the high window and it illuminated the striking figure that entered and strode towards her. He was very tall – perhaps 6ft 3 ins – and he stood, hands on hips, glowering down on her as she struggled to her feet. The man wore his hair long, so that it fell about his shoulders and down his back, black as a raven's wing. His face was Mongoloid, with narrow, slit eyes, and he effected a mandarin moustache that hung down either side of a cruel, firmly set mouth. He was dressed in a simple tunic that reached down to the top of his leather boots and a woollen cloak, woven finely with gold thread at the edges, hung from his shoulders.

Behind him were two of the Khampa warriors who had brought her to the jail and a small, thin, elderly Tibetan wearing pince-nez spectacles perched precariously on the end of his nose.

The big man turned and grunted something to the scholarly figure.

The small man cleared his throat and addressed Alice. 'I shall interpret, madam,' he said, in precise, clear English. 'You are either Mrs Alice Fonthill or Miss Alice Griffth. Which is it?'

'I am both.' Alice spoke loudly. She felt intimidated by the delegation – particularly by the big man – but she was determined not to show it.

The interpreter shot a quick, uneasy glance at the big man. 'Madam. You can't be both. Which are you?'

'I repeat, I am both. I am married to Brigadier Simon Fonthill, who is serving with the British column, now approaching Lhasa, so in my private life I am Mrs Fonthill. But I am also a newspaper correspondent, reporting on the . . . er . . . invasion of Tibet for *The Morning Post*,

London for which I write under my maiden name, Alice Griffith. This situation is not unusual in Europe, I assure you.'

The interpreter adjusted his spectacles and translated for the benefit of the big man, who was obviously a Khampa of some seniority.

The latter frowned and fixed Alice with a glare that seemed to light up his black eyes. Then he spoke, without taking his eyes off her.

'This is General Kemphis Jong,' the little man interpreted, 'he is general in charge of the Khampas in Tibetan army and also governor of this area of Lhasa and surrounding country. He know of your Fonthill. Your man commands British cavalry and has killed many Tibetans.'

Alice swallowed hard. They had obviously gone through her belongings and found the notes that Simon had scribbled to her when away earlier in the campaign. It seemed that Fonthill had become rather notorious in the eyes of the Khampas.

'My husband is a general in the British army,' she said, 'as your governor is in the Tibetan army. He is merely doing his duty. Soldiers are paid to fight. Your general knows that.'

The General grunted when the translation was made. Then, suddenly, without warning, he struck Alice with the back of his hand, sending her sprawling onto the straw. He towered over her and shouted something.

'He say,' translated the little man, his eyes wide now behind his glasses, 'that you here to answer questions, not to argue. You show respect or you will be hurt. Women do not answer back in Tibet.'

Alice remained lying on the straw, her face white. 'And men of honour do not strike women in England,' she said defiantly, staring up at the General.

It was clear that the interpreter considered for a moment ameliorating her response, for he paused while he sought for appropriate words, but the Khampa shouted at him to translate and the scholar gulped and did as he was told.

'Ah.' The General looked down at her and then barked a command to his Khampas. Immediately, they bent down and dragged her upright, pulling her hands high above her head. Then they frogmarched her to the wall underneath the window and bound her hands together above her head with a rope. One of the soldiers bent down and linked his fingers together, so that the other could step into them and, reaching up, pushed one end of the rope through one of the bars in the window. Then, together, they hauled on the end so that Alice was stretched high against the wall, her toes barely touching the floor.

She groaned, involuntarily, as her arms felt as though they had been pulled from their sockets and closed her eyes, dreading what was to come.

She felt her breeches being undone and roughly pulled down and then one of the Khampas roughly forced her legs apart and pushed his hand between them, wrenching upwards with his fingers. She screeched in pain and the man stepped back.

The interpreter intervened and spoke quickly, obviously now of his own accord. 'Madam,' he said, 'these men are rough barbarians from the east, even the General. They are not like ordinary Tibetans. Please do not antagonise him, or they hurt you. Tell him now that you are sorry.'

'Tell him to go to hell,' hissed Alice between clenched teeth and the little man immediately translated – but obviously not her words, for the General grunted and nodded his head. She was allowed to remain hanging, though.

The General spoke again. 'He say, why you come to Lhasa with this boy?'

At last, a chance for some sort of dialogue! Alice closed her mind against the pain and the shame of the assault and began talking. 'I have come without the permission of the British Commander or my husband. I paid the boy to take us here because I want to speak to the high lamas who control the government of Tibet. I want to plead with them not to oppose the British any more.'

The General spoke again and the scorn was obvious in what he said.

'He say, you lie and that you are British spy, come to spy out city before British approach it.'

'That is not true. Would a British general send a woman to do that work?'

She could see that the shaft had struck home and she continued quickly. 'I have witnessed all of the fighting between the British and their troops and the Tibetan army and seen the slaughter of the Tibetans and reported on it back to my newspaper, which is one of the most important in Britain.'

'I know of *The Morning Post* and have read it,' the

interpreter said quickly, not without evincing a touch of pride.

'Then you will know that I criticise the killing by the British. If the British army is opposed again before they reach Lhasa, then there will be even more Tibetans killed. I came to plead with the lamas to allow the army to approach peacefully and to sit down with them in the city to discuss a peace treaty between the two countries, like civilised people.'

She allowed the translation to take place and then continued quickly, before the pain made tears pour down her cheeks. 'Either way, if I see the lamas or not, if I am killed or violated again, then the British General and my husband will exercise fierce retribution upon the General here and upon the Khampa people. I can promise you that,' she ended fiercely.

The scholar made the translation at some length and the General stood listening, hands on his hips, his legs stretched wide. Alice observed him between half-closed eyes, praying that the torture would not be resumed.

The big man remained silent for a while. Then made his reply. 'He say we leave you here like this for a while, for your impudence,' translated the scholar. 'Then we go and get the boy and make him tell us truth. We will return.' The General nodded curtly, turned on his heels and the quartet stamped out of the cell, the little interpreter looking over his shoulder, blinking behind his spectacles and almost, Alice thought, with tears in his eyes. Then the door clanged shut.

Her first thought was one of relief that the rape that she

feared was not to follow – at least not immediately. Then, quickly, came the feeling of impotent shame that she had been violated so rudely and left, hanging now, her toes just touching the ground, but with her jodhpurs and knickers pulled down to her ankles. Now came the pain, renewed.

Her calves and her hamstrings felt that they were being stretched to breaking point as they attempted to take the strain of her weight, and her shoulders, armpits and arms seemed to be on fire. She pushed back her head and gritted her teeth. For God's sake, she had been strung up for less than five minutes. If the pain was this bad after a few minutes, what would it be like for . . . what? Hours? How long would they leave her like this and how could she bear it? Then she recalled the General's words: 'going to get the boy and make him tell us the truth'.

This time the tears poured down her cheeks as she realised that Sunil – her only hope – was about to be arrested and, no doubt, tortured, all because of her foolishness and arrogance. She sobbed at the thought and that she would now almost certainly never see Simon again. Unless . . . Had he got her second note? Surely, he would come after her? Her thoughts raced. But how to find her in this strange, labyrinth of a city? She moaned out loud in despair and pain.

Alice tried to force her aching legs to summon up a little energy to jump to take the strain off her arms, but they did not, could not, respond. She shouted to the jailer in the hope that she could promise him something, anything, if he would cut her down. But her voice echoed back to her from the walls of the cell.

She had no idea how long she had hung in this way, for blessedly, she had slumped into some sort of loss of consciousness, when she heard a voice, speaking very low, saying, 'Very sorry, madam. Forgive me if I do this.' And she felt a hand fumbling for her breeches at her ankles.

Opening her eyes, Alice realised that the little interpreter had returned. Immediately she attempted to kick him, but the power was not there. Then she realised that the cell door had been closed and that the little man seemed to be alone.

'I trying to, ah, adjust your clothing, madam,' he was saying and he somehow succeeded in pulling her knickers to cover her nudity, then hoisting her breeches to her waist. 'There,' he said, buttoning them, 'it did not please me that they did that to you.'

'Thank you,' Alice whispered through dry lips. Her tongue now felt as though it had swollen to fill her mouth. 'Do you have any . . . any water?'

'Ah yes. I think of that.' The interpreter adjusted his spectacles and fumbled in a little bag he carried and produced a small earthenware jar, removed the stopper and held it to Alice's lips.

Greedily, she gulped until the precious water ran down her chin. Carefully, the little man wiped it. 'They intend to leave you to hang like this without water or food for, I think, two days,' he whispered. 'I think this terrible thing to do, so I come back and tell the jailer that I had been sent to . . . what is the word? Ah yes. Interrogate you. So he let me in. Look I bring little meat and bread too. Can you eat?'

'Yes.' Alice licked her lips. 'But can you cut me down

first? This is very . . . it is very painful.' She cursed inwardly as she felt the tears slip down her cheeks again.

'Oh, ah, I am very sorry. But cannot do that. General would kill me if I interfere with his punishment. I am sorry. He probably kill me anyway, if he know I am here now, with food. Here, take a little bread with our butter.'

Alice shook her head in frustration. 'I am very grateful. But can't you possibly do something . . . find something to put under my feet? The pain is very, very strong. Something to take the strain away, you see.'

The interpreter pushed his pince-nez back up his nose and looked around the cell. 'Ah yes,' he muttered, 'but nothing here.' Then: 'Ah, yes. I think I see little stool outside. I get it. But be quiet now. Jailer must not hear.'

He was away for what seemed like hours to Alice, but then he returned, carrying a little three-legged stool. 'It was in corridor,' he said. 'I steal it. I hope it is not missed. Here . . . I lift your legs.'

He did so and, at last, Alice was able to stand, flat on her heels. The relief was immediate and sent from heaven, but she staggered on the precarious platform as the strain was taken from her calves and she lost her balance. The little man had to hold her for a moment.

'Oh, thank you, so much,' she gasped. 'That is such a relief. Is there . . . do you have . . . any more water?'

'Yes, of course. Here.' He lifted the jar and she drank again. 'I think I could take a little bread and whatever you have now,' she said.

He fastidiously took out meat from his haversack, then two pieces of bread, and placed the meat within the bread and held it to her lips so that she could eat. Alice munched away as best she could, hungrily now, for she had not eaten since the porridge and milk given to her, what? Probably twenty-four hours ago.

'I am very grateful to you, sir,' she said eventually. 'Pray tell me your name.'

The interpreter gave her a wan smile. 'Oh, madam. I do not think it relevant to give you my name. I am just glad to be of some small assistance to you. I teach at one of the monasteries here. Unfortunately, the General took me away from this work to interpret for him here. Although,' his smile widened a little, 'perhaps that was fortunate for you.'

'Oh, it certainly was.' Alice's voice dropped and became full of concern. 'Tell me, do you know if they have found Sunil, the Tibetan youth who came with me to Lhasa?'

'No, I do not. The soldiers go to get him but I do not know if they find him.'

'Oh, I hope to God they do not. Tell me also, do you know how many jailers or soldiers are posted here in this prison?'

'Yes. It is used also as a kind of barracks, I think. But it is really small building and has only one jailer, I think, but about ten of the Khampas, who act as General's bodyguards, live here. General lives in Governor's house, a little way up street.'

For the first time for hours, Alice felt a little ray of light open up in her mind. Only ten guards . . . ! Perhaps, if Sunil returned with her handgun, she could . . . Then despair descended again. How stupid of her to think that! The guards would almost certainly find Sunil and . . . She frowned in agony at the thought of them torturing her splendid, brave companion.

The interpreter looked over his shoulder. 'I think I must go now because jailer get suspicious.' He held up the jar. 'More water?'

'Yes please.' She took several sips, carefully this time.

He replaced the stopper. 'There is a little left. I hide this in straw in case they cut you down and you can reach it.' He tucked it away. 'I go now, lady. I hope they cut you down soon.'

Alice raised her eyebrows. 'Not as much as I do. Thank you, whoever you are. You have been kind.'

He nodded and the little smile appeared from behind his pince-nez. 'It was good to practise my English. I learn it in Calcutta, you know.'

'Yes, er, how interesting.' She tried to smile but couldn't. If he was going to stay and chat, why the hell couldn't he cut her down! 'Goodbye, and thank you again.'

He bowed, carefully put away the paper in which he had brought the bread and meat, tucked it in his bag and walked to the door, obviously left unlocked, and was gone. Alice sucked in her breath. Would her keeper notice the precious stool and take it away again? But he did not bestow a glance on her, shutting the door with a clang and locking it.

Alice sighed and then inhaled quickly as she remembered that the interpreter had said that the Khampas were going to leave her hanging for two days . . . *two days!* Thank God the stool was making her position less of a torture. But, *two days* . . . ! How much time had passed since the General's visit? She had no idea and she wished she had asked her little benefactor. She screwed her head around to try and look up at the window. Was the light fading? Yes, almost certainly. So perhaps, Sunil would come soon? Ah no! He was almost certainly captured and was probably being tortured at this very moment . . . Two days! She shook her head in confusion and frustration. Her sense of time had slipped away completely. Perhaps there would be only one more day to go. Perhaps.

She must have slipped again into some sort of sleep for she jerked awake suddenly. What was it? Someone calling? It came again: 'Memsahib, are you still there? Memsahib?'

'Oh, thank God. Sunil. Is that you?'

'Yes, miss. I keep calling but you don't answer. I thought they take you.'

'I am sorry. But, dear boy, the Khampa soldiers went to get you. Did they not find you?'

A note of pride came into the youth's voice now, almost scorn. 'Ah no. They clumsy people. Aunt hear them coming and she hide me in grain store with my rifle. They do not find me, but . . .' His voice tailed away.

'Yes, Sunil. Go on.'

The boy suddenly sounded much younger, as though the years had suddenly been torn away from him. He went on, but his voice was hardly above a whisper and Alice had to strain to hear him. 'I wait in grain store for long time. Then I creep out, with rifle, ready to shoot Khampas. But I find only bodies of my uncle, my aunt and my cousins. Khampas kill them all. Take off their heads with their swords.'

Alice realised that Sunil was sobbing now and, aching

and hitherto conscious only of her own pain, her heart went out to the boy.

'Oh, Sunil. I am so sorry. I really am. I . . . I . . . it is all my fault. I am very, very sorry.'

'Don't worry, miss.' Sunil's voice was stronger now. 'I have my rifle. I give you little gun through window and then knock on door of jail. When man comes, I shoot him, get key, let you out and then we run.'

Alice thought quickly. She had promised that when he came she would have a plan. But the events of the past few hours had confused and jumbled her mind. She had no plan – but she quickly resolved that Sunil should be exposed to no more danger.

'Ah. I think not, my dear boy. Now, listen carefully.'

'Yes, memsahib.' He sounded disappointed.

'Do you happen to have your knife with you – you know, the one which I gave you and which folds?'

'Yes. I never go without it.'

'Good. Now, if you look up to the bars on this window you will see that a rope is wound round one of them. Can you see it?'

'Yes.'

'Do you think you could climb up and cut through the rope. It is attached to my wrists, you see, and I am virtually hanging from it. It is very painful.'

'Oh goodness! I kill them for that.'

'Thank you, but can you get up to the window?'

'I look. It dirty street here. Full of rubbish. I have to find something to stand on. Back in moment.'

'Ah, please don't be long.'

He was not. Within three minutes she felt the rope tighten as his knife blade was hooked under it as it bent around the bar and he began to saw. Then he had severed it and Alice tottered for a moment on the stool and then fell headlong. The fall winded her but the relief on her arms and shoulders was wonderful. She lay for a moment, savouring it.

'Memsahib. You all right?'

'Yes, Sunil. From now on you will be known as Sunil the magnificent.'

'Yes. Good. You want gun now?'

'Yes, please. Toss it through and then lower it.'

He did so and then the cord was returned so that he could attach the little box of cartridges to it. This too was then thrown through and then lowered.

'Now, you load gun and then I go and shoot guard. Yes?'

'No, Sunil.' Alice stood with her back to the wall under the window and carefully loaded the gun. She spoke to him as she did so. 'There are eleven men – one jailer and ten soldiers – who live here in this building. As soon as you fired your rifle they would be upon you. Then we should both be killed.' She looked up at the window.

'Can you hear me?'

'Oh yes. I hear you.'

'I want you to listen carefully and do exactly as I tell you. Do you still have your pony?'

'Yes, I hide it in the gulley where you wait for me when we first arrive. Khampas take your horse.'

'Splendid. Now I want you to go from here now – don't waste any time – find the pony and ride back the way we came. If you go on that main road, ride fast and don't get

303

into trouble at all, you will eventually meet either Fonthill Sahib, coming to look for us, or the vanguard of the army. I think it will be my husband first. Explain to him exactly what has happened and bring him here.'

'What you do now, then?'

'Don't worry about me. I will be all right now that I have my little handgun. But I cannot hold out here for very long, so you must go quickly. Go now but take great care, Sunil. My life depends upon you.'

'You sure? I can kill all the soldiers with my rifle. Jenkins bach says I am good shot.'

'Yes, I am sure. Go now. And thank you, Sunil. You have been my saviour. Goodbye.'

'Goodbye, miss.'

She heard what she thought was a stifled sob, then all was silent in the cell again. Alice held the cold steel of the handgun to her cheek for a moment, as though for reassurance, and sat on the stool, deep in thought. She had absolutely no idea what she would do next, but two things were important: to get Sunil out of danger and to alert Simon about what had happened to her. With luck, Sunil's ride could accomplish both things.

She worked the mechanism of the gun to slip a cartridge into the barrel. It was a snub-nosed automatic French Chamelot-Delvigne of eleven millimetre calibre, but Alice handled it with affection. She had first come across the little weapon when she was in Egypt, covering the invasion of that country in the early 80s and had been lucky to have found one now in India. It was very small and useless at long range. But it could kill a large man at short range – and she had a large man very much in mind now as she slipped the little weapon into the pocket of her riding breeches.

She fumbled amongst the straw to find the jar of water, drained it and then lay on the straw and eased her aching shoulders. Now all she had to do was wait . . .

Chapter Twelve

Following his talk with Jenkins, Simon strode away, his mind in a whirl, to find General Macdonald, his titular superior. Of course, he must ride after Alice – but how long had she been gone? He stopped for a moment to think. The first note from her had been delivered, what – five days ago? He could not remember and he had thrown the scrap of paper away long ago. It would take her perhaps two days to reach Lhasa, so she would now have been in Lhasa for, say, three days. Long enough to get into trouble!

He had to follow her, of course, but how? Just he and Jenkins? No, they would need at least someone to interpret for them. So, what – take a company of the Mounted Infantry? No. Too many. It would seem like they were invading Lhasa, and it would take time for such a party to prepare to ride out. Better, perhaps, to take ten good men, plus an interpreter and Jenkins, of course. Even a wounded Jenkins was better than no Jenkins at all. He strode on.

He found Macdonald inevitably checking a list of supplies. Patiently, Simon explained the situation and asked permission to leave the column to ride into Lhasa and find his wife. The General removed his cigarette and regarded Fonthill through the drifting blue smoke.

'You're not proposing taking the whole of the Mounted Infantry with you, are you? I couldn't allow that, you know. They're too valuable. We might be attacked again.'

'No. Nothing like that. I thought just ten picked men: enough not to cause a disturbance when we enter Lhasa but enough to fight off any casual trouble we encounter.'

'Very well. But you'd better check with Younghusband about going into Lhasa ahead of the main column. If you get into trouble, it could upset his diplomatic approach to the lamas.'

'Very well. I will go now.'

If he was expecting a 'good luck', then it did not come. The General replaced the cigarette between his lips and returned to his column of figures. Younghusband, however, was much more animated.

'Good God!' he exclaimed. 'Gone off on her own? Whatever did she expect to achieve?'

'I'm damned if I know. But she is headstrong and brave and won't shirk danger. I must go after her.'

'Oh dear.' Younghusband frowned. 'I quite see that, old chap, but I was rather planning to enter the capital, er, peacefully, you know. Coming to negotiate, without further fighting and so on.'

'Well, I don't intend to inflame relations. That's why I will take just ten good men from the Mounted Infantry to come with me and we will do our best to enter the capital quietly, without fuss or further fighting.'

'Hmm. Where will you look to find her?'

'At this stage, I don't know. But she has taken the Tibetan youth with her. I seem to remember him saying that he had relations near Lhasa, perhaps there is a clue there. I doubt if she could just march up to the monastery where the government sits and demand entry. To start with, she would not know where to find it.'

'Quite so. Well . . .' Younghusband drummed his fingers on his trestle table. 'Under the circumstances, I can't stop you going. But, my dear fellow, I do beseech you to take great care with what you are about. You must not upset the lamas at this late stage and prejudice my negotiations. And, on the other hand, you will be entering a hornet's nest and, with such little protection, you could be in great danger. You have done magnificent service on this campaign and I would hate to lose you, not the mention the great 257.'

'352, actually, Commissioner.'

'Ah yes. I am much better at poetry than numbers.' He stood and extended his hand. 'Go off, then, Fonthill, and take whatever will help you. Most of all, take great care. Good luck to you. Bring back your wife.'

Within the hour, Ottley had been reinstated as commander of the Mounted Infantry in Fonthill's absence, ten troopers including a *daffadar* had been recruited as escort and Frank O'Connor had supplied a Tibetan who could, of course, speak the language, and who had proved a loyal servant to the column since its entry into his country. With a still-bandaged Jenkins at his side, Simon led his little band out of the camp and along the riverbank towards Lhasa.

He had been careful to ensure that the group did not go out of its way to attract attention. The Mounted Infantry, of course, did not wear uniform, as such, just their *poshteens* and bound leggings. No riding boots or pennanted lances. On reflection, he had selected only Gurkhas as his escort. Their high-cheeked, Nepalese features and their small stature gave them a Tibetan look and he ordered that their small, distinctive pillbox hats should be left behind. He could not expect them to be taken for Tibetan soldiers, for the Tibetan army contained little cavalry, but at least they would not stand out as sore thumbs in this strange country.

They rode hard, without posting outriders, and made camp well after dark. Fonthill was up well before dawn and fidgeted as breakfast and coffee were prepared.

'No good ridin' in on an empty stomach,' growled Jenkins. 'Either we're goin' to fight the whole of the Tibetan army with just ten men, or we'll get lost in this big city, ponce around for days and then get arrested for loiterin' with intent. Either way, it would be good to 'ave somethin' in our bellies, look you, before we 'it trouble.'

The sun had hardly crept above the jagged peaks before the little party was in the saddle again. Simon judged, by the number of little shacks that had begun to appear stretching away on either side of the road, that they must be nearing Lhasa. What to do when they reached the city? The question had dogged him since they had set out. Where to go? The interpreter they had brought with them had been picked up many weeks ago, near the Indian border. He had never been to Lhasa in his life and had no idea where the great monasteries and seat of government were sited.

He was deep in thought when the *daffadar* he had sent on ahead came galloping back. The Gurkha reined in amidst a flurry of dust. 'Firing up ahead, sahib,' he said.

Fonthill frowned. 'What sort of firing? Did you see anything?'

'No, sahib. It was some way down the road. I thought it better to come back and report immediately. But I recognise the sound of a Lee Metford and perhaps musket shots. But not many men.'

'A Lee Metford!' He turned to Jenkins. 'Sunil had a Lee Metford.'

'Yes. And he could use it, too.'

'Right. Let's go and take a look. *Daffadar*, you stay here with the troop and come up when we call.'

Cautiously, Fonthill and Jenkins set their ponies to the trot until they, too, could hear the sound of shots being exchanged, round a bend in the road. They tethered their horses to a bush and crept forward and peered round the edge of a boulder at the roadside.

At first they could see little, except puffs of smoke rising from three separate positions, behind rocks on the left-hand side of the road. Up a slight slope to the right they could see the body of a pony lying in a cluster of stones and someone lying behind it. It was from here that the distinctive crack of the British Lee Metford came.

Jenkins squinted his eyes to focus. 'I reckon that's old Sunshine,' he muttered.

'Damn!' exclaimed Fonthill. 'I've left my binoculars tied to the saddle.'

'Don't need 'em. That's the lad all right. And I'd say 'e's in a spot of trouble.'

'God! Can you see any sign of Alice?'

'No. I think 'e's on 'is own.'

'Right. We'll go back and bring up the troop and ride down whoever is firing at him. Come on.'

Within minutes, they had rejoined the troop. Fonthill raised his voice and explained the situation. 'We will advance at the trot and, at my command, we will charge at the men on the left of the road who are firing. They could be Khampas, so use your kukris. Right. To the front, trot.'

At the bend, Simon stood in the stirrups and drew his sabre. 'Troop will charge!' he shouted. The thirteen riders swept round the bend and thundered down the road. As they neared, Fonthill could see that it was indeed three Khampas who had taken shelter behind rocks on the left and were firing at the lone figure up the hillside.

On seeing the riders, however, the three immediately turned and fled, dodging between the rocks, their distinctive long hair flowing behind them. They reached a point where they had left their own ponies and, throwing themselves into the saddle, they set off down the road towards Lhasa.

Fonthill turned his head and shouted. '*Daffadar*. Ride down those men and kill them. Do not enter the city, but return here.'

'Sahib!'

The troop swept past Simon and Jenkins, their kukris raised and their eyes gleaming. Even the interpreter drummed his heels into his pony's sides bringing up the rear but as intent on catching the fleeing Khampas as the soldiers.

Fonthill reined in, cupped his hands and shouted up the hillside. 'Sunil. Is that you?'

A thin voice replied. 'Yes, sahib. I am very glad you come.'

'I bet you are, lad,' shouted Jenkins. 'Are you wounded?'

'No bach, but I am very tired.'

Simon threw himself off the saddle, threw the reins to Jenkins and shouted, 'Stay there. I am coming up.'

Within seconds he was crouching beside the boy, who attempted to stand beside his stricken horse, but his trembling legs would not let him. Fonthill put his arm around Sunil's shoulders and held him close. 'You are all right now. Where is Alice?'

The boy wiped his brow with a dirty finger, further smearing cordite across his face. 'She all right, I think. When I last see her.'

'When was that and where?'

'About eight or nine hours ago, I think. She in jail in Lhasa.'

Simon's eyes widened. 'In jail! But thank God she's still alive. Now, see if you can stand and we will walk down and join Jenkins. I don't want him scrambling up here. He has been wounded.'

'Oh, I am sorry.'

'He can still fight, so don't worry. Save your breath

312

until you get down there. I presume your pony is dead?'

'Oh yes. Khampas kill him.'

'Right, tell me your story when we get down. We will see if dear old 352 can brew some tea while you tell your story and we wait for the troop to return. By the look of the Khampas' old nags, I would say that they would have caught up with them by now.'

'Yes, good. They bad men.'

Slowly, Sunil related how he and Alice had found his uncle, of the old man's betrayal of them and of how he had been able to find Alice, cut her down and throw her the gun. Then, as instructed, he had run back to find his pony, mounted it without delay and ridden through the outskirts of Lhasa seeking the main road back towards the river. Unfortunately, however, in the darkness he had become lost and shortly before dawn he had ridden past a Khampas guard post on the edge of the city. They had glimpsed his rifle and shouted at him to stop. He had galloped away and somehow had stumbled on the main road ahead. But, dog-tired, just as dawn was breaking, he had pulled his mount off the road a little way up the hillside, tethered his pony where he hoped she could not be seen from the road and lay down to sleep awhile before continuing his journey. Unfortunately, however, the horse had dragged her tether and been seen by the Khampas, who had mounted their own horses to pursue him. He awoke to find them climbing towards him.

'There were four of them,' he said proudly, 'but I seize my rifle and kill one.'

'Good lad,' murmured Jenkins.

'The others ran back down the hill and began firing at me. They only have muskets but they were Khampas, so they could shoot. They kill my horse so that I could not escape.' The boy hung his head. 'I thought I was dead. I was so glad to see you charge in.' He looked up. 'I wondered if you would come.'

'Oh yes,' said Fonthill. 'We came all right. Now we must find Alice and free her.' His voice lowered. 'You say that she was tied up to a bar in the window. Had they . . . had they hurt her, do you know?'

The youth's teeth flashed. 'A little bit, I think, but she sounded very strong. She tell me what to do, exactly.'

'Thank God for that. Do you think you can find the jail again?'

'I think so, now in daylight.'

'How far are we from the city?'

'About five miles or less. I wander a bit in the dark.'

'I've made some tea,' said Jenkins quietly. And he handed out two steaming tin cups.

Sunil grabbed his and began drinking noisily. Then they all looked up as the clatter of hooves on the stony road announced the return of the troop. The *daffadar* held up a bloodstained kukri.

'We find them, sahib. They dead now.'

'Well done, *Daffadar*. They deserved that. Dismount and see if you can find brushwood and make tea. We can take a break now, I think. I know now what we must do.'

'Very good, sahib.'

The three sat in conference, while Jenkins – 'I knew I should 'ave brought three cups' – shared Simon's tea.

'Now, Sunil,' asked Fonthill, 'is the prison in the heart of the city?'

'No. I think it on the outskirts, towards where my uncle lives, er, or used to live.'

'Good. Did Alice tell you by any chance how many soldiers or guards were stationed in the prison?'

'Oh yes. She say,' he thought for a moment, 'about a dozen, I think.'

Jenkins nodded his head. 'Just right. We're not goin' to be outnumbered for once. How do you want to play this one, bach sir?'

Fonthill sighed. 'Well, I am afraid there is only one way. If Alice has her handgun with her then I only hope to God that she won't be forced to use it. Ideally, we should hide somehow, watch the prison and make a plan of attack. But we can't afford to do that. Anything could be happening to Alice as we speak. So . . .' He forced a grin. 'We ride straight up to the prison gates, knock loudly and ask if they can take any more inmates. In other words, go straight in.'

A great grin spread across Jenkins's battered face. 'What could be better? I wonder if they've got any beer in there. I could do with a sip – just a sip, mind you. After all, I am a wounded old soldier.'

And they all laughed.

After they had mounted, Fonthill addressed the troop.

'You will all know what we are doing here,' he said. 'My wife is somewhere in Lhasa and we have come to take her back to the column. We have now heard that she is in a prison on this side of the city. I intend to go straight there and free her and then ride out of the city. I do not wish to create a lot of trouble, no firing or fighting if we can help it. It is particularly important that we are allowed to get to the prison without incident.'

He cleared his throat. 'I don't want the Tibetan government to think that the General Sahib has sent just a troop of Gurkhas into the city alone to take it – although you fellows are quite capable of doing so.'

He waited until the dutiful chuckles had subsided. 'No. I want us to ride in peacefully, without fuss, as though we are all just going shopping in a bazaar back in Nepal. So carbines will remain in their saddle buckets and you will keep your kukris out of sight. In other words, we don't fight until we have to. And then, as always, as Gurkhas, we fight hard!'

At this a cheer went up from the ten soldiers. Then they formed into a compact group of five couples, with the interpreter riding behind Simon and Jenkins in the lead, and Sunil sitting at the back of Jenkins, his arm around the Welshman's waist.

They quickly passed the bodies of the three Khampas, which the Gurkhas had thrown by the side of the road. Fonthill looked enquiringly at the *daffadar*.

'Their ponies were old, sahib,' the Gurkhas said in answer to the unspoken question. 'Not worth keeping. I let them go.'

'No, *Daffadar*, you should have taken them. They will return now to their stables and the Khampas will know that their riders have been killed. They could well now come out in force looking for us.'

'Ah yes, sahib. I am sorry.'

'Very well. Ride on ahead and give us warning if you see danger.'

'Very good, sahib.'

Fonthill looked at his two companions. 'You two all right?' he asked.

Jenkins nodded. 'The wound in the thigh is throbbin' a bit but the head, where the great brain operates, like, is fine now, thank you.'

'Sunil?'

The youth gave his white, wrap-around smile. 'I am good now that we go and rescue Memsahib,' he grinned.

They were approaching Nethang, the village from which Alice was taken, when the *daffadar* came galloping back.

'Big party of Khampas on horses coming, sahib,' he reported.

'Damn! I thought as much. How far away?'

'Perhaps one-quarter mile.'

Fonthill looked around. 'I don't want to fight them now.' He turned to Sunil. 'Is there anywhere near where we can get off the road and not be seen?'

'Yes. Gulley just up here on this side.' He pointed with this right hand. 'We hid our ponies when we arrived. They can't be seen from road.'

'Good. Lead the way, 352.'

The gulley was tree-fringed and curved away into the hillside and comfortably took the troop.

'Quiet now,' ordered Fonthill and he parted the branches of a tree which hung over the entrance. Within three minutes, there was the thunder of hooves and a band of Khampa soldiers, perhaps thirty in number, galloped by, whipping their ponies, their long swords bouncing against the sides of their mounts.

'Miserable lookin' lot,' muttered Jenkins, at Simon's elbow. 'I reckon we could 'ave seen 'em off in two volleys.'

'Maybe, but I don't want to stir up trouble before we find Alice. Come on, let's get out of here before they find those bodies and start to look for our tracks.'

The little party trotted on now, bringing puzzled looks from the Tibetan peasants who were beginning to crowd the road. Fonthill looked neither to right nor left but kept his gaze fixed ahead, guiding the troop between the tables that had been set at the roadside to sell sweetmeats, lengths of cloth and a bewildering array of trinkets.

Eventually, Sunil called. 'We go right here.'

Simon led them into a narrow dark street, fringed on the right by a high stone wall in which narrow, barred, unglazed windows were set high up.

'This is place,' called Sunil.

Fonthill looked around him quickly. The street seemed deserted, although the normal Tibetan shack-like dwellings formed a terrace facing the jail. Everything was strangely quiet. He took a deep breath.

'Dismount,' he called. 'Handlers take the horses.' Two men came forward. 'Keep them here, against the wall,' Simon ordered, 'in case we have to ride away quickly. One man at the end of the street to watch for Khampa soldiers. The rest of the troop, draw kukris.'

He helped Jenkins and Sunil down from their horse, withdrew his sabre from its saddle sheath, stuck it through his belt and then took his Webley revolver from its holster.

'Where is the entrance?' he demanded of Sunil.

'Just here. It will be locked. You will need to knock loudly.'

But there was no need. The great, metal hinged door, set in its recess, hung open, revealing a dark interior. Treading carefully, Fonthill stepped forward, pulled it back with his foot and stepped inside. A small passageway opened out onto a courtyard of beaten earth, lined on all sides by blank walls, topped along the roof line by narrow, barred windows.

'Ah!' Simon drew back with a gasp. Just inside the courtyard, hung a figure, swaying gently in the breeze created by the open doorway. The rope around his neck had been fixed to a cross-beam and his feet hung only a couple of inches from the ground. Underneath his feet lay a pair of pince-nez spectacles, the glass lenses shattered, the frames twisted, as though someone had stamped upon them. Part rigor mortis seemed to have set in, so the man must have been hanging for a little time.

'My God!' exclaimed Jenkins. 'I thought at first it was Miss Alice.'

'So did I.' Fonthill levelled his revolver and looked around keenly. Nothing stirred. He stepped outside into the courtyard. All of the cell doors were hanging wide open, except one.

'Sunil, which cell was she in?'

'I can't tell from inside. Wait. I go outside and count windows.'

He returned within seconds. 'Second on the left.'

'Oh God.' Simon swallowed hard. 'That's the only one

that has been locked by the look of it. Wait. The key is still in the door on the outside.'

He stood stock-still, thinking for a moment. Then, he spoke softly. 'This may be a trap. *Daffadar*. Take the men and look into each cell. Be careful. There may be Khampas waiting in each one. Sunil and 352, come with me.'

Averting their eyes from the hanging body, the three stepped softly towards the locked cell. There, Fonthill gently turned the key, pulled open the door and stepped back.

Immediately, a Tibetan, dressed in ubiquitous smock and baggy trousers, held up both hands in the far corner of the cell and screamed something.

'He say, don't shoot,' interpreted Sunil.

'Good lord!' Once again Simon stepped back in revulsion. Two bodies, lay flat on the floor of the cell. They were obviously Khampa warriors, for their long black hair trailed behind them and they wore the washed blue smocks that were as near as these soldiers ever came to wearing uniforms. Their long swords lay, undrawn in the sheaths hanging from their belts. Two pools of blood had oozed out from a bullet wound in each of their chests and lay, half congealed, at their side. They were clearly dead.

Apart from a small heap of flattened straw lying in a corner, from which the Tibetan had obviously just risen, the rest of the cell was empty – except, that is, for a small, crumpled piece of clothing that lay against the wall near the door.

'Tell him he's not going to be shot as long as he tells us

truthfully who he is and what has happened,' said Fonthill tersely. Still keeping the man covered with his revolver, he moved to the garment and picked it up. It was a cotton garment of some sort and carried a strange, sulphurous smell, emanating from a small hole, blackened at the edges, in the centre of the fabric.

Frowning, Simon shook it out. 'Oh my God!' he exclaimed. 'It's Alice's under-vest. Look at these little primroses embroidered onto the neckline. Oh, don't say that she's been shot!' He whirled round to where Sunil was talking quietly to the man. 'What's he saying? What happened in here?'

'It's all right, sahib. She not dead. At least, not yet.'

'What happened? Tell me.'

'I do. Listen. This is jailer for the prison. He came in early this morning with these two dead men. They Khampas, part of bodyguard of Khampas General who is also governor here. It was General who ordered Memsahib's arrest and who had her tied up there to bar in window.'

'Yes. Go on. Get on with it.'

'Sorry to be slow. He keep talking. Now, he say that he let the two men in this morning. He think they going to take Memsahib to General who lives in this street for, er, further questioning – he think probably torture to make Memsahib say she really a British spy. They come into cell, but Memsahib not hanging any more because I cut her down, see. She standing facing them. The men go to her to take her but she had little pistol – I give her, you know.'

'Yes, Yes. Go on.'

'She has pistol wrapped in that cotton thing in your

hand. She fire it at each man in turn and garment reduce noise. She clever, Memsahib, of course.'

'Sunil . . . !'

'Yes, I go on. Both men die quickly because she fire into their chests very close. Jailer think she go to kill him so he falls on knees and cries for mercy. But Memsahib go to door to see if anybody who heard muffled shots is coming but nobody comes. So she takes key from jailer, makes him lie on straw and goes out, locking door behind her.'

'What a gal!' Jenkins was grinning from ear to ear. 'I told you she could look after 'erself. She's a fighter, that one.'

But Fonthill was frowning. 'What about the man hanging out there by the courtyard?'

'Ah, yes. I ask him.'

Immediately, the jailor dropped his eyes and spoke slowly, addressing the floor.

Eventually Sunil turned back. 'He say that is body of man who is professor at one of great monasteries here. He used by General to act as interpreter with Memsahib. But General finds out that he has been giving food and water to Memsahib so he has him killed, also this morning.'

'The swine. Does he have any idea of where Alice has gone?'

Sunil shook his head. He say he think Memsahib take keys to open all cell doors so that other prisoners can escape because he can hear them shouting in courtyard, but he don't know where she goes then. He worried because he thought no one would come and rescue him.'

'Ah, so the General has not come looking for his men?'

'No, sir.'

'Hmmm. That's a bad sign. Perhaps he came and took Alice himself?'

Jenkins wrinkled his face. 'No, bach sir. He would surely come and rescue the jailer, wouldn't 'e, and ask how she got out – and probably strangle the little bugger with 'is bare 'ands – 'e sounds that sort of bloke.'

They were interrupted by the return of the *daffadar*. 'Nobody in cells, sahib. Everyone empty. Whole jail seems to be empty.'

'Thank you, *Daffadar*.'

Jenkins laid a hand on Simon's arm. 'What do you intend to do now, bach sir? We've obviously got to find 'er, but where do we look in this bloody sacred city, eh?'

Fonthill nodded slowly. 'The question is . . . what would Alice have done? After acting as Mother Bountiful, that is, to the seedy dropouts of the city? Where would she have gone? To the monasteries to carry out her original mission? Maybe. But she wouldn't know where to go and wouldn't be able to ask anyone to help her.' He frowned. 'I have a feeling that this General of the Khampas can probably help us.'

He turned quickly back to Sunil. 'Find out from the jailer where the General lives and if he will have more of his bodyguard with him. I think we'd better pay him a call. I'd certainly like to make his acquaintance, anyway.'

Now it was Jenkins's turn to frown. 'You told me that old Youngfather had ordered you not to make a fuss. If you do make a fuss, it'd better be a quiet one.'

'To hell with that—'

He was interrupted by the arrival of the trooper he had left on guard at the end of the street. 'Sahib,' he cried, breathlessly, 'Khampas coming down main street.'

'Damn! *Daffadar*, get the horses in here, into this courtyard. Then shut the door behind you.'

Immediately, all was bustle as the *daffadar* rushed out, followed by his men, and then the clatter of hooves as the horses were pushed and led through the narrow archway and into the compound within.

'Sunil,' Fonthill turned to the boy. 'Come into the courtyard and bring your rifle. Interpreter, tell this jailer he is to lock the main door of the jail once the horses are inside.'

Jenkins was by his side. 'What are you goin' to do?'

'I don't want to fight unless I really have to. Perhaps if we can get everyone inside here, these fellows will pass by and we won't have any trouble.'

'Who are these blokes, anyway?'

'I should think they're probably the party that passed us on the way in and have followed our route by questioning people who saw us . . . oh damn!'

'What's the matter?'

'I've just seen that little weasel of a jailer slip through our Gurkhas and go through the doorway into the street. He's not locked it, of course. And he'll tell the Khampas where we are. *Daffadar*.'

'Sahib.' The sergeant was standing by the open gateway, ushering the last horses into the compound.

'Can you lock the door?'

'No, sahib. Don't have key. No bolts, either.'

'Very well. I think we are bound to have visitors now. Close the door and then get the men to bring the horses to the rear of this courtyard. There they must stand behind the horses. Leave the carbines in the saddle buckets. When I give the order, we will stampede the horses towards the Khampas, once they have all come into the courtyard. We will be close behind with our kukris. Quickly, now, there is little time.'

'Sahib.'

Jenkins nodded and a slow smile began to spread from under his great moustache. 'What a bloody good idea, bach sir. Set the horses on 'em in this confined space an' then go in with our koookerisdoodars. They'll be buggered. They won't know which way to turn.'

'I hope so. Now, Sunil, come with us to stand with our backs to the wall over there. You are not to fire your rifle unless it is the only way to defend yourself. I don't want gunshots to sound out. Understand?'

'Oh yes, sahib. Bloody good idea.'

'Don't swear.'

'No, sahib.'

The last pony was ushered in and the *daffadar* closed the heavy gate and sprinted back to help the Gurkhas herd the horses back to the far end of the little courtyard, where they bunched together, nervous and wide-eyed, just in front of Fonthill, Jenkins and Sunil, the total, men and beasts, taking up half of the space of the yard.

Simon drew his sabre and Jenkins his knife.

'You're not going to be much good with a wounded leg and just that knife,' said Fonthill in low voice. 'I shall lead the Gurkhas in. You stay here and look after Sunil.'

'Oh, yes. An' who's goin' to look after you, then?'

Before Simon could reply the gate was thrown open with a crash and a group of Khampas, swords drawn, broke through, ran through the passageway and then stood, hesitantly, at the entrance to the courtyard. Fonthill thrust his way between the horses towards them, stood with his legs apart, waved his sabre and shouted, 'Come on, then, you bastards. Let's see what you're made of!'

Immediately, there was a howl and the soldiers brandished their swords and set off towards him. Simon ducked back between the ponies and shouted, 'Let the horses go!'

Almost as he shouted the command, there was an answering shriek from the Gurkhas, who slapped the rumps of their steeds and set up a great howl. The horses reared, snorted and began to gallop away from their handlers. It was only a small courtyard, hardly room enough for the Gurkhas and the Khampas, let alone thirteen frightened, scampering ponies and the beasts charged straight into the new arrivals, bringing several of them down and scattering the rest.

The Gurkhas, as light and as agile on their feet as monkeys, were dancing immediately behind their mounts, cutting and thrusting at the Tibetans, slipping like quicksilver between their adversaries, slashing and shouting ancient Nepalese war cries as though fired by some strange Himalayan bloodlust.

The horses, wild with terror now, began thundering around the walled perimeters of the courtyard, to get away from the fighting. In doing so, they trampled on several of the Khampas who had previously been knocked down.

Simon and, inevitably, a limping Jenkins now joined the fray. The Khampas were in the majority but now, not knowing which way to turn, as predicted by Jenkins, they began to try and crowd back under the archway leading onto the little passageway before the open gateway. Fonthill caught a glimpse of the murdered interpreter swinging like a pendulum as he was brushed aside.

The crowded space, however, left the Khampas at an even greater disadvantage for they could not swing their long swords. Simon parried the downward swing of one man on the periphery of the crowd and countered it by thrusting the point of his sabre into the man's breast. As the man fell, he caught him and used him as a kind of battering ram to force his way along the edge of the passageway until he reached the open gateway. Luckily, the door swung outwards and he was able to pull it back and close it.

'What've you done that for?' He became aware of Jenkins at his side, blood oozing again through the bandage on his head.

'I don't want the bastards escaping and giving the alarm,' he gasped. He and Jenkins were now at the rear of the mass of Khampas and the pressure was now on the two men, who had their backs to the door. Fonthill stood parrying and thrusting with his sword into the mass of bodies before him. Jenkins was now bent almost double, his head bobbing from side to side like a boxer's as he looked for targets and then thrust selectively upwards with his long knife.

The noise in the little passageway added to the chaos,

with steel rasping on steel and the shrieks of the wounded merging with the war cries of the Gurkhas. Fonthill realised that Jenkins, crouched almost at his feet and slashing upwards ferociously, was creating a space before him, giving him time to select his targets, thrusting and withdrawing, thrusting and withdrawing.

Although savage and brave, the Khampas, were not a disciplined, well-led force. Now, fighting at front and back, and unnerved by the charge of the horses, they could not last long. In fact, the carnage was over in a remarkably short time, and Simon suddenly realised that the only people left standing in the crowded passageway and in the courtyard were his own Gurkhas, gasping for breath but wearing their beaming smiles, as though they had just returned from a native wedding.

Fonthill leant on his bloodstained sabre to get his breath. '*Daffadar!*' he panted.

'Sahib.' The man materialised as though by magic.

'Let me know the casualties.' Through the milling little men he looked anxiously to the far wall and let out a sigh of relief as he saw Sunil trying to capture some of the ponies and calm them down. He turned. 'Are you all right, 352?'

'Not as good as I used to be in this sort of a fight, see.' The little man was on his haunches, panting. ''Ave a bit of difficulty, look you, in gettin' me breath.' He levered himself upward with the help of his knife. 'All right now, though.'

'Only one casualty, sahib,' called the *daffadar* from inside the courtyard. 'The interpreter wallah. He should not have tried to fight but he did. He got killed.'

'Oh, I'm sorry. He was a brave man. But no one else?'

'No, sahib.' The *daffadar*'s smile widened. 'We too good for them. But good plan to use horses. Very clever.'

Fonthill nodded and returned the grin. 'Glad you approved. You and the men did wonderfully well. Now try and calm the horses. We are going to need them.'

'Very good, sahib.'

Jenkins stood once again at his side. 'Did you notice if many of the varmints got away?'

'No, but some of them must have done, before I got to the door. So the message that we are here and on the rampage is bound to get around, probably to the ear of the General.'

'So what do we do now, then?'

'We find that swine and have a word with him about that poor bastard swinging there on the end of the rope and, also,' his voice wavered for a brief moment, 'about my dear wife. Let's collect Sunil now, round up the horses, and find out where the General lives. Then we'll pay him a visit.'

CHAPTER THIRTEEN

After Sunil left her, Alice searched in the straw and found the little jar that the interpreter had left for her and quickly drained the water that remained within it. Her shoulders ached abominably and she shrugged and rubbed them as best she could. Then, gun in hand, she settled herself in the straw to wait. She had no great plan, but would react to circumstances. Whatever ensued, she would not let herself be taken . . .

She had not intended to let herself sleep but the strain of the last few days were too much for her and her eyes closed and she dreamt of riding away from Lhasa towards . . . she was not sure . . . almost certainly Simon. Then the grate of the key in the lock jerked her awake and she scrambled to her feet, hiding the gun behind her.

The door swung open and the hunched figure of the

jailer appeared. He seemed to be alone, for he suddenly stiffened when he saw her standing upright and not, as he expected, hanging from the bars above. He swung around and, just as she took a step forward, he swung around on his heel and pulled the door to behind him and locked it. Once again she was alone.

Light was beginning to stream in from the window, so Alice presumed that it was a little after dawn and the jailer had come, not to bring breakfast, of course, but to check to see if she was still alive. So . . . what would he do now? Go to the General, of course, and/or fetch the guards.

The danger of her position, jerked Alice out of her tiredness. She looked around her once again. There was nothing in that little cell to help her, only a few ends of the rope that had constrained her. Except, of course, for her handgun. Yet firing it would sound like a cannon in this confined space and bring all kinds of retribution upon her head. And she only had six shots. Impossible to set herself up in the cell and defend it like a fortress. They would either rush and overwhelm her or leave her to starve.

On an impulse, she whipped off her blouse and pulled off the little vest that lay beneath it. Then she rebuttoned the blouse and took the vest and bound it tightly around the hand holding the automatic pistol, so that the gun was out of sight, and the barrel completely covered by several layers of the cotton. How effective it would be in reducing the sound of the gun firing she had no idea, but it presented one possible way out of the impasse. But only if other factors slipped into place.

She estimated that the jailer would waste no time in

telling her captors that she had somehow escaped from the bonds that bound her to the window bars, so she did not trust herself to slump back on the welcoming straw, but instead, stood waiting, her back to the wall under the window.

Nothing happened for at least an hour and she was struggling to keep her eyelids from closing when two distinct sounds, one after the other, jerked her out of her reverie. The first was the well-remembered, high-pitched voice of the interpreter coming from, by the sound of it, the mid-distance beyond her door. He was arguing, or more likely pleading, by the tone of his voice. Ah! Alice bit her lip. That swine of a jailer had obviously come to the conclusion that it was he who had cut her down, as well as provided food and water for her and had betrayed him to the General. More treachery in Tibet! What was happening to him?

The second sound provided the answer. It was a high-pitched scream from just outside her door that ended in a half moan and then a kind of gurgle, followed by a creaking noise and then silence.

Alice took a deep breath and kept the bandaged pistol close to her side, her back pressed against the cold wall of the cell. Then there was the sound of laughter, again from the other side of her door, and then a regular creaking noise, as though a child was pushing a swing. The laughter, the creaking and the sound of muted voices continued for perhaps three of four minutes, when, once again the key grated in the lock, the door was swung open and the jailer entered once more.

This time, however, he was not alone. Behind him, grinning and making lewd gestures with their lifted fingers, came the two Khampa guards who had assaulted her before. For a moment they stood regarding her, grinning lasciviously, before they said something curtly to the jailer and they both stepped forward towards her.

Alice let them approach until the leading man had extended both arms to grasp her when she brought up the bandaged hand, pressed the trigger and fired into his chest at a distance of some three feet. Without a pause she turned on the other man and shot him too, symmetrically between his shoulders at a slightly longer range as the soldier paused for a moment, his mouth gaping.

Without a sound, the two men slumped to the floor. To Alice the noise of the shot seemed to boom in the confined space of the cell and she whirled around and directed the gun at the jailer. With a cry, however, he threw himself to the ground and lifted his hands beseechingly. Alice tightened her grip on the trigger but then paused. It was a very different thing, shooting two men who were about to seize her, to killing a man who was begging for mercy and grovelling at her feet.

She stepped over the two bodies and that of the jailer and put her head around the door. Nobody seemed to have heard the— She jumped back in horror. The interpreter was hanging at the entrance to the courtyard, his eyes wide open but staring sightlessly and his tongue protruding from his open mouth. His smashed spectacles lay at his feet.

Alice then realised that the poor man had been pleading for his life and that the creaking noise was that of the two

Khampas pushing him to and fro, having fun with his last struggles. She breathed hard. She mustn't faint now. She stood listening quietly. There was no sound to be heard, no obvious reaction to the muffled shots she had fired. What to do now?

She stepped back into the cell and tried not to look at the two corpses sprawled on the ground before her. Trickles of blood were forming scarlet pools on either side of them. Alice tossed aside her vest, its job done, and pointed her gun to the jailer, who immediately began wailing again.

'Oh shut up, you little worm,' she breathed. Then she gestured to the heavy key that hung from a belt around his midriff. 'Take it off,' she hissed, moving the barrel of the automatic towards the man's temple. The jailer quickly unbuckled the belt and threw it at her feet.

'Good.' She put her finger to her lips and pointed to the gun and said 'shush'. The man stared back at her speechlessly. She had no idea if she had been understood, but she picked up the belt and its appendage and backed out of the door, shutting it firmly behind her and turning the key which had remained in the lock.

Alice had briefly forgotten the interpreter and she almost walked into his hanging body. She started back and then stood still for a moment, tears springing into her eyes. 'I am so sorry, my old friend,' she whispered. 'Your very kindness to me led to your death.' And then, more brusquely, 'But I can't stop to cut you down.' She stepped around him and went into the little passageway. The doorway to the jailer's cubbyhole of an office led off it and, hesitantly in search of some more substantial weapon, she entered. There was a large cabinet hanging on one wall but little else. She fingered the key that still hung from the jailer's belt in her hand and slipped it into the keyhole in the cabinet. It swung open. Inside were two rows of similar-sized keys to that which opened her own cell.

Again she stood for a moment in thought. Then, a ghost of a smile began to spread across her features and she took down each of the keys from their hooks, noting that they were numbered. Presumably, they were the keys to the cells that fringed the courtyard and perhaps elsewhere. Tucking her automatic into the pocket of her breeches, she set out opening each of the locked cells that she found.

Some were empty but at least half were occupied – if that word could be used to describe the vacant-faced wretches, all in solitary confinement, who were sprawled on straw within. Each man struggled to his feet in his rags and looked, slack-jawed, at Alice as she stood in the doorway. 'Come on, you poor devil,' she called, 'get out. You're free now. Move yourself. Move back into the world.'

Then she moved on. As she looked back, she saw each prisoner poke his head round the door and, then, slowly, shamble out into the courtyard. Then, as she worked her way around, she heard a growing babble of voices from them all, as they stood, attempting to understand this latest, quite unexpected development in their grim, solitary lives.

Looking at them, huddled together in the churchyard, she wondered why they did not move to the jail's entrance. Then she remembered that the door was closed. After their incarceration, they lacked the initiative or courage to leave their place of imprisonment. So she pushed through them and swung the great door open, and then stood by it in the dark passageway, making ushering motions with her arms, as though she was shepherding a flock of sheep onto good grazing grounds.

'Goodbye,' she called. 'Spread out. Enjoy yourselves.'

Then Alice closed the gate and realised that she was shivering. She was not cold. It was the anticlimax, of course, and the realisation that she did not know, now, what the hell to do next. She had shot two men, locked up a third and freed the inmates of the whole bloody prison. The General would be wondering why his two henchmen had not returned with her. And hadn't she been told that ten of his bodyguard were stationed in the prison? Where the hell were they? She had to get out quickly to . . . to . . . where?

Alice took a deep breath. Having delved in for a penny she was undoubtedly in for a very deep pound. She had killed and this would bring consequences – and very soon. She was standing just behind the jail door, with her fairish and now unkempt hair straggling down her back, wearing her very English riding breeches and boots, and her dirty blouse, looking less like a Tibetan woman than was possible. If she attempted to walk down a Lhasa street in these clothes she was bound to attract attention. How to disguise herself?

She strode back into the jailer's office. There was some old woollen, hand-knitted garment hanging on a peg and also a blanket, slung over a chair. She pulled on the old cardigan, wrinkling her nose in disgust at the encrusted food stains on its front, and then wrapped the blanket round her midriff so that it hung down low like some misshapen skirt, almost hiding her riding boots. A tattered cotton scarf completed the outfit, tied over her head and under her chin, peasant-fashion. There was no mirror to study the effect but it would have to do.

Alice moved to the jail door and pulled it slightly ajar. Would the poor prisoners she had freed be milling about outside, drawing attention to themselves and to her? She peeped out, looking up and down the street. It was deserted, thank God. The inmates must have dispersed. She closed the door behind her, turned right and, head down, hurried away.

The street ended abruptly in a T-junction and, once again, she had to choose the direction to walk. For a brief moment, the thought occurred to her that to make all that had happened to her in Lhasa meaningful, she should return to her original objective and, somehow, find where one of the great monasteries stood and attempt to talk to the lamas or – what were they called? – the Chamber of Secretaries or something like that. Then, equally quickly, she realised what nonsense that would be. She had killed two Tibetans and her actions at the jail in freeing the prisoners – a spur-of-the-moment decision that she was beginning to regret – would surely count against her. Who would listen to a woman who came preaching peace and pacifism who had just killed twice?

No. She must find her way back along the main road that led south-westward towards the Indian border; the way that Simon hopefully would be taking now towards Lhasa. South-west . . . ? Which way was that, for God's sake? She looked up at the sky. The sun was hiding behind a high bank of cloud – and was she now in the southern hemisphere and, anyway, did that matter? Her brain in a whirl and anxious to avoid drawing attention to herself by her hesitation, she turned left.

At least this street seemed to be much more of a main thoroughfare than the other. Men and women, all dressed alike in the dun-coloured, long tunics of the Tibetan peasant, walked by in that nonchalant, unhurried way of their kind; going to market perhaps? But what day of the week was it? She had no idea.

Alice stole a glance behind her, hoping to catch a glance of some gilded temple that was supposed to characterise the centre of Lhasa – at least this would indicate that she was walking away from the heart of the city. But the shoddy dwellings rose too high and too close on either side to give her any kind of distance perspective. She bent her head and tried not to hurry.

It was important that she left the area of Lhasa that was controlled, she remembered hearing, by the Lhasa General, who was some sort of area governor. If she was to be apprehended again, it was better – far better – that it was not by a Khampa. Again, she fought back the desire to break into a stumbling run.

Now, market stalls were beginning to materialise on either side of the street. Oh lord! Was this, she wondered, a good or a bad sign? Did it show that she was going away from the city, perhaps into some semi-prosperous suburb, or that she was walking away from the direction she sought? At least she seemed to be attracting only the odd, inquisitive stare. Thank goodness that Lhasa was a well-populated city, at least by Tibetan standards.

The stalls, however, made Alice realise that she was ravishingly hungry. Apart from the interpreter's sandwich, she had had little to eat since leaving the house of Sunil's uncle – how long ago? She had no idea for she had lost all sense of time. But the aromas that were coming from the little trays and tables on either side of her assailed her nostrils and made her salivate.

Oh, how she wished she had mastered even a few words of Tibetan! She doubted if her very basic Hindi would be of use here. But . . . she pushed her hand underneath the blanket and fingered the handful of rupees that jingled in the pocket of her breeches. The Tibetans *loved* the rupees of the British Raj! This much she had learnt from Sunil as he had bartered for them in the little bazaars they had passed. Could she use them now? Well, they were all she had.

Alice paused and moved slowly to a stall kept by an elderly woman with a face like a wrinkled Pekingese dog. She was presiding over trays containing meatballs fried in what looked like onions and herbs, with what appeared to be local black bread at the side. Delicious . . .

The woman gave a wrinkled smile and spoke to her quickly. Alice pointed to the meatballs and, opening her mouth and pointing inside with a finger, made a negative sign, shaking her head from side to side, in what she hoped was a universal gesture indicating that she was dumb. Immediately, the woman snarled and shook her head vigorously and waved her away.

Alice then tried to smile and offered a few rupees in her hand. Immediately, the woman's manner changed. She looked up sharply but Alice kept her head down. The old woman then extended a finger and turned one of the rupees over, fastidiously. Then she grabbed all of the coins and thrust them into her apron pocket. For a terrible moment, Alice thought that that would be the end of the matter, but, still scowling, the woman scooped up some of the meatballs, loaded them onto a piece of the bread, put them onto what appeared to be a sheet of almost parchment-like paper, thrust them at Alice and then waved her away.

Gratefully, Alice grabbed the steaming bundle and did her best to melt into the passing crowd, eating the delicious half sandwich as she went. It was, she assured herself, probably the best meal she had ever had.

It had, however, been bought at a cost, for she had drawn attention to herself. Inquisitive faces now peered into hers, noticing her grey eyes, the fragments of brown hair that escaped from under her scarf and the un-oriental set of her face. Several of the men spoke to her, but she shook her head and scurried on, head bent, feeling like some figure from the lurid novels of the late Mr Dickens.

Soon, conscious of the gazes she was drawing, she turned off abruptly into a side street and, prompted by the spices contained in the meatballs, she realised that she was now as thirsty as she had been hungry. Blessedly, there to her right a little trickle of water was issuing from a tap in the wall of a more substantial house and dropping invitingly into an ornamental bowl. Tossing aside her grease-stained paper, Alice bent her head and sucked in the water. For a moment, she let it run over her face and then rubbed it into her face.

It was then that her head was pulled back and she looked

up into the black eyes of a tall man, dressed in a colour-washed blue smock. Alice's heart fell. Oh no! A Khampa!

The warrior snarled something at her. Alice immediately produced her dumb woman gestures, but the man stepped back and seized her blanket and pulled it away from her. He then stripped her of her makeshift skirt, revealing her once smart, elegantly flared riding breeches and her riding boots. Then he struck her smartly across the face and called back over his shoulder.

Immediately, two more Khampas appeared, running. Still reeling from the blow, Alice fumbled for her automatic but it was too late. Her hands were seized and a cord immediately produced and wound tightly around her wrists. The men were grinning and talking excitedly. Alice realised with a deep sense of foreboding that her freedom had ended. She had been sought and now had been found.

If she had been a subject of some small curiosity before, now she became an object of derision as she was pulled backwards through the streets by the Khampas, who had attached a longer piece of rope to the cord around her wrists. How had they traced her? Ah, of course. The rupees! This must still be a Khampa-controlled area of Lhasa, with the inhabitants completely under the sway of and fearing these brutal warriors. Alice realised that the tears were flowing. The vendor of the meatballs must have betrayed her. Treachery in Tibet again! She felt impotently but fiercely angry. To have got so far and then been recaptured!

Then she held up her head as she skipped backwards, her calves aching, as she was roughly pulled through the crowd. She still had her handgun. Well, if this was the end, she was determined to bring down some of her captors with her – particularly General Kemphis Jong. Somehow, she felt a little better at the thought.

They turned a corner and, with a sickening sense of familiarity, Alice realised that they were now in the narrow street which housed the jail – and, she now remembered the interpreter telling her, the house of the General himself. She recalled the cries of the little man and the sight of his body swinging from the cross-beam in the jail and her heart sank.

The house of General Jong seemed unimposing from the outside, but once through the door, Alice realised that it was the residence of a man of importance. Fine rugs, probably from Afghanistan, were strewn across the floor and low divans lined the walls. She strained her neck to find some images of the ubiquitous Buddha, but there were none. Did this mean that this General in the Tibetan army was a heathen? Probably. The thought did nothing to cheer her up.

She was taken to a small room that had few furnishings and left standing, with one warrior to guard her, while the other left, presumably to find the General. The man grinned and approached her, put his face close to hers and began fingering her breasts. Alice slowly drew back her head and then quickly crashed her forehead onto his nose. The soldier staggered back and then hit her with his fist, sending her reeling back against the wall. But he did not approach her again.

'Yes,' hissed Alice. 'Don't you dare do that again.' She attempted to wriggle her wrists free of her bonds, but the cord was too tightly bound. If only she could get one hand free and reach the little automatic in her pocket . . . !

She was still struggling – and realising that her eye was closing from the force of the blow – when a coterie of Khampas, led, of course, by the giant figure of the General, long sword clanking from his belt, swept into the room.

The big man came and stood quite close to her, his eyes running up and down her body. Alice realised that they were almost certainly the blackest and coldest she had ever seen. His face was quite expressionless but slowly, with finger and thumb, he examined the swelling under the right eye. With infinite care, he then pressed it hard with his thumb, extracting a cry of pain from Alice.

'Oh, you bastard,' she exclaimed through clenched teeth. She drew back one booted foot and kicked hard at the General's shins, connecting just above one ankle.

Now it was his turn to double up in pain and he swung his hand and struck her hard across the cheek, sending her brain reeling. Holding his shin, he growled an order and Alice was seized by two of the guards and bundled forward out of the room, along a dimly lit corridor into another, larger room, more, in fact, of a chamber, for there was very little furniture in it, not that Alice could take much note, for her head was still singing from the force of the blow. The General was a big, powerful man and he had hit her hard.

But now she sucked in her breath. Clearly there was more pain to come, for she glimpsed a kind of crucifix attached to the far wall. It had cords attached to the ends of the crosspieces and also to the bottom of the vertical wooden post. She closed her eyes as she was bundled across to it and silently began to pray: 'Oh God, please make it quick and don't let me suffer too long . . .'

Her wrists were untied and, just as she thought she could make a bid to extract the pistol from her pocket, her arms were pushed against the crosspieces of the crucifix and her wrists tied to their ends. Her ankles were similarly bound to the vertical post.

Alice kept her eyes firmly closed and waited for the pain to start. She was startled, then, when a heavily accented voice spoke to her in English. 'Madam, you are going to be asked some questions. It would be best for you to answer them honestly.'

She opened her eyes and realised that she was being addressed by what appeared to be a monk, dressed in a roughly woven, grey habit, the hood of which was thrown back to reveal a face, completely Oriental in appearance, with high cheekbones, a large forehead and slit-like eyes that blinked at her, expressionlessly, from behind round-framed spectacles.

Alice moistened her lips. 'Who are you?' she asked.

'It does not matter who I am, madam, I am here to interpret for General Jong. We shall ask you questions. I warn you that if you do not reply honestly pain will be inflicted upon you.'

The monk spoke with a cold imperturbability that sent a chill through Alice's heart. At his side stood the General, looming over the interpreter, his black eyes gleaming, behind them loomed two of the Khampas, knives in their hands. Knives! Were they to be the torturers? Could she appeal to this man of God – or at least, Bhudda?

'Are you a lama?' she asked.

'No. I am merely a monk who has learnt your tongue. I repeat, it does not matter who I am.'

'Oh, but it does, I assure you. The last man who interpreted between me and the General was killed by him. I saw his body hanging in the jail. This man has no time for humble interpreters, it seems.'

For the first time the shaft seemed to have hit home, for the eyebrows behind the wire frames of the spectacles rose slightly. He cleared his throat. 'I am not aware of that and I do not believe you. Now—'

Alice interrupted. 'Am I to be tortured, then?'

'Pain will be inflicted if you do not answer honestly.'

'You are a man of God. Your Bhudda did not preach that harm should be done to unarmed, innocent people.'

'Madam. You know nothing of the preaching of our lord. You have already killed two of our soldiers, so you are not unarmed or innocent. The Governor here is anxious to know why you are here and who sent you. He has a responsibility to defend this city against the unbelievers who are approaching it. Just answer without lying and you will not be harmed.'

At this point, the General growled and interjected. The monk nodded impassively. 'Governor say that his patience is becoming exhausted. You answer now. Why you here?'

Alice sighed. 'I have already told the General that I am the wife of a general in the British army that is approaching Lhasa now. I am also a correspondent for a leading British newspaper. I have been reporting on the invasion and have grown tired of witnessing your army – most of it comprising ordinary peasants, as far as I can see – being killed by the superior firepower and discipline of the British soldiers. I came here of my own volition to plead with your government not to oppose the British army any further and to sit down with Colonel Younghusband, the leader of the political mission, and negotiate with him . . .'

'Wait. I translate.'

He did so and his words produced a torrent of vituperation from Jong, who stamped his foot, leant forward and tore open Alice's blouse. He then wrenched away her brassiere, revealing her left breast.

The monk seemed completely unfazed. 'General say,' he continued, 'you lie. Why should you, a woman, think you could have any influence on holy men who rule our country? He think you come here, in some sort of disguise to spy on Tibetan military . . . ahh . . . dispositions for your army. Your generals think woman would not be suspected by us of doing such thing, so you slip into city unnoticed.'

Alice shook her head. 'That is not true . . .'

Without waiting for the translation, General Jong shouted an order. One of the Khampas stepped forward, knife in hand. He waved the blade under Alice's face and she shrank back and closed her eyes. A sharp, agonising pain swept through her as the blade was inserted into the lower part of her breast and, involuntarily, she screamed.

As though from afar, she heard the interpreter murmur, 'He cut off all your breast if you don't tell truth . . .'

Then, from even further away, as she bit her lip, awaiting a greater pain, she heard a distant but familiar voice cry, 'Alice, Alice, we are coming . . .'

She opened her eyes and saw the door crash open and

Simon, sword in hand, rush through, followed by a limping Jenkins, Sunil, rifle in hand, and a handful of Gurkhas, kukris gleaming in the dim light.

Fonthill's jaw dropped and momentarily he stopped, for Jong had leapt forward, thrusting both the interpreter and the knife-wielding Khampa aside. Drawing his sword, the General thrust the tip to Alice's throat and shouted something at the interpreter.

The monk quickly licked his lips and said, 'General say, he kill woman if you come nearer. He prepared to die but will take your wife with him if one man takes step nearer.'

Sunil lifted his rifle. 'I shoot him, sahib,' he said.

'No. No. You might hit Alice.'

Perspiration was now trickling down General Jong's face. Without taking his eyes off Fonthill, he said something to the interpreter. 'He ask,' translated the monk, 'if you are British general who is married to this woman?'

Ignoring the question, Simon, still standing near the door, his sabre in his hand, called in a broken voice: 'Alice, you are bleeding. What have they done to you?'

Alice tried to force a smile. 'Just a little cut, my love. You seem to have arrived just in time. Be careful. This man is a monster. You'd better answer him.'

'Yes,' Fonthill called out. 'I am her husband. And if you hurt a hair of her head I shall kill you.'

At this, the General nodded, as though contemplating his course of action. Then he answered, via the interpreter: 'I am not afraid to die. You have more men here than I have, but my guards will arrive soon. I sent them after you—'

Simon, his brain racing, interrupted: 'They will not

come. We lured thirty Khampas who had followed us into the courtyard of your prison and my men killed them all.' He nodded over his shoulder. 'You can see that these kukris are still bloodstained. Put down your sword. Let my wife go and I promise no harm will come to you, but you will be tried by the British for what you have done.'

Jong's eyes widened. Then he smiled. 'You sound as though you are a great warrior,' he said. 'I have heard of you and what your cavalry have done in your invasion of this country.' He lifted his sword point away from Alice's throat, pointed it briefly towards Fonthill, then returned it.

'You are a general,' he continued. 'I am a general. You have a sword, I have a sword. In my part of Tibet, general's fight, we don't just leave it to our soldiers. If you want your wife to live, then you fight me, with your sword, here and now. If I win, your men let me go. If you win, I don't care. I die anyway. Are you man enough to fight for your woman, General?'

The last sentence was spat out scornfully.

A silence fell on the room. It was broken by Alice. 'Don't do it, Simon,' she called. 'He is a brute. Don't fight him,'

'She's right,' said Jenkins. ''E's bigger than you, bach sir. Let me take 'im on. 'E's more my size.'

Fonthill realised that his lips were dry. He looked round the room. His Gurkhas had now edged through the doorway and were silently extending round the walls. But they were listening intently. If he gave the order they could descend upon the big man in a flash. But there were four Khampas, two of them with drawn knives, who were between the General and them. This would give Jong time to carry out his threat. He had only to flick his wrist and Alice would be dead . . .

'Let me shoot him, sahib,' whispered Sunil. 'This man kill my uncle, my aunt and my cousins.'

'No.' Simon licked his lips and answered Sunil in a monotone. 'Do not fire. I will fight him. If he wins, shoot him then. And shoot to kill.'

'Don't be daft.' Jenkins's voice was hoarse. ''E looks as though he could be 'andy, like, with that sword. You're no swordsman, bach. Let me do it.'

'No. I will fight him. He's probably a year or two older than me and he carries too much weight. I am fitter and I've become quite a hand with this sabre recently.' He addressed the interpreter. 'Tell the General to step forward and fight me.'

As the message was translated a grin crossed the Khampa's face. He beckoned one of his men forward and spoke to him in a low voice. As the General's sword was lowered, the knife of the soldier replaced it at Alice's throat.

'Just a precaution,' explained the interpreter, 'in case you shoot the General when he step away from woman.'

'Shrewd bugger,' murmured Jenkins.

Now the two men faced each other in the centre of the room. Jong looked a formidable figure alongside Fonthill. He was some four or five inches taller than Simon, with a consequent longer reach, and the breadth of his shoulder indicated his strength. His sword, slightly thicker at its point and curved in the Khampas' fashion, seemed longer and heavier than Fonthill's sabre. Yet he was certainly corpulent and heavier on his feet.

'Simon, don't . . .' Alice's voice ended in a sigh as she slumped into a faint.

It was as though Jong was waiting for her signal, for he immediately stamped forward and launched a series of slashes, horizontal and vertical at Fonthill, swinging his sword in a succession of arcs so swiftly executed that his blade seemed almost a blur.

'Oh blimey,' muttered Jenkins. ''E's done this before, all right.'

Somehow, however, Simon survived the attack, ducking and parrying and moving his feet like a dancer.

'Bloody good, bach,' Jenkins called out.

But the Tibetan was undaunted. He returned to the attack, hacking and swinging, as though the heavy sword was thistledown in his hand. Simon had no recourse but to back away, defending desperately and making no attempt at a riposte. The Khampa soldiers shouted encouragement.

It was clear, however, that the energy expended in this series of fierce attacks was taking its toll on the big man. His face was now shining with perspiration and, under its moustache, his mouth was open, gulping down air. Simon seized the opportunity and, feinting to the head, launched a low thrust at his opponent's midriff, grazing the man's side and tearing his tunic.

At this, the Gurkhas all raised a cheer and shouted encouragement in Gurkhali to their man.

'Bloody 'ell,' grunted Jenkins, 'it's like a bloody football match.'

'Let me shoot him,' cried Sunil again. 'I kill him easy.'

'No, lad. Leave him be. Don't shoot him till you 'ave to. I think the Colonel might just do this.'

The cut to his side seemed to galvanise Jong with new energy and he renewed his assault, stamping his feet flatly to the floor as he thumped forward with a new series of attacks. It seemed inevitable that his great strength and the force of his blows would bring the Khampa success in the end, for Fonthill was finding it increasingly difficult to ward off the blows. It was no surprise, then, that the big man drew blood when Simon was only able to divert one huge downward sweep away from his head and onto his left upper arm, the Tibetan's blade slicing through the jacket and cutting into flesh.

Simon was forced to cry out and the General's mouth extended into a wolfish grin as he leapt in for the kill. As he raised his sword, however, Fonthill's point, delivered in a classic low, forward lunge, took him in his left shoulder and it was the Tibetan's turn to gasp in pain as he staggered back.

But neither wound was fatal and the two men now circled each other, their breath coming in great gulps as the blood from their cuts dripped onto the floor. It was clear, however, that the Khampa was now the more tired of the two and it was Fonthill's turn now to attack and he forced the big man back to the wall in a series of thrusts.

'That's it, bach,' shouted Jenkins. 'The point, not the edge and you've got 'im.'

But Jong was by no means defeated. He had been brought up in the East of Tibet in a wild corner of the country, where the sword and the dagger ruled, unlike the pastoral, passive hinterland, and where he had come up through the ranks of the Khampa army by the force of his strong right arm. Now he summoned up all of his energy and stamped forward again in a new series of heavy swings of his great sword.

Fonthill was forced to retreat, parrying each blow as best he could until his foot slipped in a slither of blood that marked the centre of the chamber. Down on one knee, he desperately thrust his sword upwards to meet the next swing – and felt the shaft break and the blade shatter under the force of the blow.

Simon held up his wounded arm in a last form of protection and the giant Tibetan, his sweating face broken in a great grin, lifted up his sword to administer the *coup de grâce*. It was then that Sunil fired his rifle, the bullet taking the big man in the side of the head and breaking him down in a crash. At almost the same moment, Jenkins whirled and threw his knife in a whirl of flashing steel, so that the blade embedded itself deeply between the shoulder blades of the Khampa who held his knife at Alice's throat.

The other two Khampas and the interpreter threw up their hands in submission as the Gurkhas suddenly swept forward, but they were too late to prevent the kukris rising and falling, bringing them, too, to the ground in a grim silence.

Simon tried to struggle to his feet but slipped again. 'Alice,' he cried. 'See if Alice is all right.'

But Jenkins was already there, together with Sunil. Tenderly they held the still-unconscious figure as they untied the cords that bound her to the crucifix. She recovered just as they were laying her on the ground.

'Simon,' she whispered. 'Is he all right?'

'All right,' grunted the Welshman hoarsely, his eyes moist. 'All right? Yes, 'e's all right. In fact, 'e's just about the best swordsman since Robin Bloody 'Ood, I'll tell you.'

Sunil frowned. 'Who is this robinbloodyood man, bach?'

'Oh, I'll tell you later. You go and see to the General. I'll look after the missus.'

Within the hour, Simon's wound had been patched up and, with rather more difficulty, the bleeding from the incision in Alice's breast had been stemmed and she had been bandaged and cold compresses applied to the bruises on her face. She insisted on riding herself, so the horses had been fetched from where they had been left in the prison courtyard, two more ponies had been taken from the General's stables at the rear of the house for Alice and Sunil to ride and the little party set off down the still-deserted street towards the south-west and the advancing British army.

Simon decided to leave the bodies as they had fallen in the courtyard and in the General's house. 'When people find them,' he said, 'let them just believe that a well-deserved nemesis had overtaken them, as a result of all their misdeeds.'

Their pace was slow but two hours later they met a vastly relieved Captain Ottley, riding at the head of the Mounted Infantry, scouting in advance of the army, and were ushered through to the main body, just as it was preparing to camp for the night before entering Lhasa the next day.

Younghusband hailed Simon, shortly after Alice had been put to bed under a hastily erected tent. 'Well done, Fonthill,' he called. 'I heard you'd brought your wife back safely. Did you meet any trouble?'

Simon forced a faint smile. 'Hardly any really, thank you. Perhaps I may report in the morning?'

'Of course. Good night.'

CHAPTER FOURTEEN

Simon, whose wound had proved to be superficial, had dragged his sleeping bag beside Alice's cot so that he could be with her should she wake during the night. She did so once, shaking and perspiring as the horrors briefly returned, but he leant across and took her hand until she fell back into a deep slumber. Before dawn the next morning, as the bugles sounded reveille, she woke again, much refreshed this time and able to joke about the two black eyes that peered back at her from her hand mirror.

Jenkins crept into the crowded tent with three mugs of tea and sat while she sat up, sipping the refreshing beverage, listening as she recounted what had happened to her.

When she had finished, the three sat in an awkward silence. Alice broke it by exclaiming, 'I was stupid and arrogant, thinking that I could change things. I am ashamed of myself. As a result, I caused the deaths of Sunil's uncle, aunt and their children, that little, kind Tibetan interpreter, your own interpreter, darling, and God knows how many of those Khampa brutes.'

Simon shook his head. 'Well they, at least, deserved it.' He sighed. 'Alice, you acted, as always, with the very best of intentions and I am proud of you, as I always have been. Yes, you have been headstrong, but whatever else would I expect from you?'

He grinned. 'Now you just lie back and sleep awhile. We'll let the army advance without you. I'm afraid I must go with them, to be with my chaps, but 352 will stay here with you and I will leave a troop of Mounted Infantry to make sure you're all right and—'

Alice interrupted vehemently. 'Certainly not! I'm feeling fine now, after a good night's sleep. I mustn't miss the entry of the army into Lhasa. My editor would never forgive me. It's the end of this bloody invasion. I must cover it. Please hand me my valise. It's time I got into new clothes.'

'Oh, for goodness' sake!' Fonthill held up a hand. 'Oh, very well. But be careful you don't bring on the bleeding again. And don't go telling people that I've been knocking you about.'

She grinned. 'What a good idea!'

Later, as the camp broke up and the army – all 650 British and 4,000 Indian troops of it – prepared to set off on the last day of its long crawl to Lhasa, Fonthill reported first to Macdonald and then to Younghusband. He had decided that the least said about his clashes with the Khampas and of Alice's capture the better, so that Younghusband would not have to lie if, when he met the Tibetan rulers, the subject came up. After all, there was nobody left who had observed all these happenings, with the possible exception of the Tibetan jailer – and he was unlikely to tell his story to the lamas. He therefore related that there had been only a brush with a small band of Khampas and that Alice had never been able to reach any of the Tibetan dignitaries – which was true enough – and that she was on her way back to the army with Sunil when she had been waylaid and ill treated by brigands, before he had arrived and been able to free her. He would order his *daffadar* to instruct the troop to say nothing of their exploits.

Both of the commanders had too much to do on the morning of the entry to Lhasa to question his story and so Fonthill quickly made his excuses, left Jenkins and Sunil to help Alice rejoin the other correspondents and to stay with her, while he rode forward to catch up with Ottley and the Mounted Infantry, in the van of the advance, as always.

As the advance guard approached the village of Nethang at mid morning, it waited until the main army caught up with it so that the gaps between the various units could close up. At this late stage, no opposition to the advance was expected and none materialised. But there was now great competition amongst the British line officers to be first to catch a glimpse of the fabled city of gleaming spires and gilded roofs. That view was delayed, however, for there were rocky outcrops to be rounded and two miles of plain to be crossed before, at last, on the afternoon of August 3rd, those in the lead caught their first sight of the golden roofs of the pavilions which crowned the Dalai Lama's Potala Palace, glinting in the strong sunlight.

'You lucky chap, Fonthill,' called out Frank O'Connor, riding up alongside Simon, 'you must have seen all this before us in the last few days.'

'Er . . . not really. Didn't really enter the city, y'see.' Simon realised that Sunil must have taken them into Lhasa by some sort of side route, avoiding the walled entrance.

'Good.' O'Connor frowned. 'So we're the first living Europeans to set eyes on the place. Lord.' He fell silent for a moment. Then, 'This is a dream come true for me. I have always yearned to ride into Lhasa one day. Now it is happening. I can hardly believe it, you know.'

They rode forward and were joined by another group of officers and all approached an enormous whitewashed chorten, a sort of shrine containing religious antiquaries, with a gateway set within it, that stood at the intersection of two ridges, which together formed the western wall and boundary of the Forbidden City. Crowds of Tibetan peasants were now crowded around them, anxious to catch a glimpse of these pale-faced, heretical invaders.

Here, they urged their horses up onto the ridge alongside the gate and at last the full panorama of the old city came into view, looking resplendent against the background of the encircling mountains. In fact, the dwellings of the city itself – those nondescript terraces and shacks that Fonthill had witnessed at close hand – were dominated by one building: the grand palace of the High Lama himself. Nine hundred feet long and some seventy feet higher than the cross of Christopher Wren's St Paul's, the Potala was dazzlingly white-walled and golden-roofed and its central building, the Dalai Lama's residence, was painted a deep crimson. Great tumbling curtains, made of yak hair, cascaded down the sheer walls of the building, and on terraces and wide stairways hundreds of monks walked or sat sunning themselves.

The splendour of the central palace, however, was considerably diminished by the stench which rose from the narrow streets. The observers high on the ridge could see open sewers and pools of rainwater between the shabby houses and dogs competing with ravens and pigs for whatever lay in their fetid waters.

Fonthill turned to Ottley, who had now joined him on the ridge. 'God!' he exclaimed. 'This forbidden city could do with a good airing and scrubbing.'

The Irishman nodded. 'We've come 400 miles to what is just a bloody great slum with a palace in its middle. I wonder if it's going to be worth it.'

'Yes, I wonder what the Dalai Lama thinks about it all, looking at this damned great army on his doorstep.'

Rumour quickly spread, however, that the Dalai Lama was still very much out of town. Macdonald ordered that the army should camp just outside the city, on a plain just without the walls, and the tents had hardly been pitched before Younghusband received his first official visitors.

The first was the Nepalese consul, who warned that there remained a contingent among the religious hierarchy who had stated that they were prepared to die rather than allow barbaric foreigners to enter the sacred city. Then, in much more style, arrived the Chinese resident or *amban*, carried in a sedan chair – the only person in Lhasa apart from the Dalai himself, ran the rumour, to be allowed this form of personal transport – and attended by about fifty Chinese soldiers in scarlet cloaks and carrying agricultural-looking billhooks, with not even a musket in sight.

The *amban* proved to be very amiable, in fact, almost welcoming, according to Younghusband, who received him in his sombre and unornamented blue tunic of the Indian Civil Service. Later the Mission Commissioner confided to Fonthill that the *amban* clearly despised the backward and unsophisticated Tibetans and had been quite happy to hear of their repeated defeat by the British. Nevertheless, Younghusband took it as a great compliment that the Chinaman had paid the first visit to him, rather than the other way around, as international diplomacy demanded.

That evening, however, a rumour spread that 7,000 monks, drawn from the three great monasteries, were preparing to fall upon the British camp, and guards were mounted. Accordingly, when it was found that two of the sepoys from the 40th Pathans had left their posts during the night, the matter was viewed with great severity and they were court-martialled and ordered to be flogged, with all of the officers and troops paraded to witness the punishment.

Alice had joined the camp by this time and she watched the infliction of the punishment with curled lip. 'This makes the British Raj no better than the Khampas,' she snarled to her husband. 'I thought this sort of thing went out with Wellington.'

Fonthill shrugged his shoulders. He had long ago given up arguing these matters with his wife.

Protocol demanded that Younghusband return the *amban*'s visit and the Commissioner decided that he would use the occasion to make a grand entry into the city. Macdonald, cautious as ever, advised against this as being far too dangerous, but the Colonel overrode him and entered at the head of two companies of white-faced Royal Fusiliers and two of the 8th Gurkhas, preceded, as always, by the Mounted Infantry with Fonthill leading. This time, anxious to reflect something at least of the majesty of the British Raj, Younghusband wore the full dress uniform of the Indian Political Service, a dark-blue morning coat, edged with gold embroidery and with gold epaulettes on each shoulder, patent leather court shoes with gold buckles, with a beaver skin cocked hat and wearing his dress sword.

This would have been of little use in a fight but the dour Macdonald had taken the precaution of training his ten-pounders on the Potala and retained four companies of Sikh Pioneers outside the walls, ready to storm in should there be trouble.

In fact, Fonthill, riding at the head of the procession – and feeling extremely dowdy in his half uniform, which was the best he could manage – worried that the fireworks, which greeted the Commissioner's arrival at the Chinese Residency, would be mistaken by the General for an attack and that he would unleash a counter-attack. But all was quiet when the firecrackers eventually spluttered into silence.

Only a small group of officers, which included Fonthill, was allowed into the Residency to accompany the Commissioner and they were greeted by the *amban* and ten of his staff. Everyone was seated on crimson silk cushions and were given tea, cheroots and Huntley & Palmer biscuits. The meeting lasted about two hours and, reported Simon to Alice later, was very cordial and interesting.

'That's all very well,' she exclaimed, pencil poised, sitting awkwardly with the dressing on her breast still visible above her blouse, 'but what the hell did you talk about?'

'Well, mainly about the Tibetans, whom, he says, the Chinese government despises. The *amban* seems completely on our side – although he is a typical Chinese diplomat, urbane, even unctuous, and anxious to please. You remember them all in Peking, during the Boxer affair?'

Alice nodded.

'He says he will do all he can to help Younghusband achieve a favourable outcome to the negotiations, giving us all we want from a treaty. The trouble is . . .'

'Yes,' Alice leant forward eagerly.

'The Dalai himself is said to be three days away in some religious retreat, twirling his prayer wheel and all that and the Tibetan government – such as it is – seems to be in a state of great confusion and everybody within it at sixes and sevens and not knowing what to do with us. The Ta Lama, who seems to be next one down after the Dalai, is in disgrace, Kalon Yuthok, the most senior of the governing Shapé, or whatever it is called, has gone sick, and although the National Assembly is in almost continuous session it is completely at odds with itself. The lamas are all as much afraid of each other as they are of us. God knows how we are going to get any sort of agreement or treaty out of them. It could be a long haul here.'

'Oh dear,' Alice put down her pencil and eased the sling around her shoulder. 'Of one thing I am assured, my love.'

'Yes?'

'I'm just a teeny-bit tired of bloody Tibet. I've had enough of the weather – although I must say it's nice enough here now – I am tired of being knocked about by these damned great Khampas, and the thought of hanging around in this smelly city while dear old Frances argues the toss about his treaty fills me with dread. I yearn for a bit of greenery Norfolk would do nicely.'

Simon grinned. 'I share your feelings exactly. But won't the *Post* require that you stay until the bitter end?'

'It depends upon how long that bitter end is. If it goes on forever, with nothing much happening, I think my lot and most of the Fleet Street papers will withdraw their correspondents here and leave it to dear old Reuters, who will provide a damned good, bread-and-butter news service.'

'Good. Well, it certainly looks to me as though armed resistance is well and truly over and that a looming great army of occupation here will not be needed. Indeed, it is the very thing that Delhi and London is frightened to death of. It must be costing the Exchequer a fortune keeping us all here. Neither government, either on the subcontinent or back home, likes spending money.'

'Which means?'

'That my all-conquering Mounted Infantry will not be needed. And, if it is, then the excellent, much-better-commander-than-me Captain Ottley can very happily take command.'

Alice smiled. 'Then, my love, let us pray that the Tibetans continue to pussy-foot around and we can both – all four of us – go home.'

'Ah.' Simon frowned. 'Which raises the question of Sunil and, of course, dear old 352. What will they want to do?'

'Of course. It obviously must be their decision. But, darling, I do feel responsible for both of them. Old 352 has saved your life endless times, it seems, and Sunil has certainly saved mine. One gets the feeling that 352 will be at a bit of a loose end, without mountains to fall off and warriors to fight. Will he want to go back to South Africa, do you think?'

'I don't know. And Sunil. I feel even more responsible for him. He saved my life, too, of course, and I owe him so much. He will be a bit rootless now, I should think. Should we offer to take him home to Norfolk with us? – or both of them, for that matter?'

'I don't know either. We shall just have to leave it there for the moment, my love, and let events, to some extent, take their course.'

With virtually nothing of any significance happening and with Younghusband not anxious to be accused of bullying the Tibetan government, the Commissioner devoted himself to the task of finding himself a house of sufficient standing for a representative of the British Empire and his staff within Lhasa itself. He trailed his coat rather by intimating that the Summer Palace of the Dalai Lama would suit him admirably, but ended up accepting the offer of the unoccupied house of the First Duke in Tibet, known as Lhalu Mansion, just 1,000 yards from and looking out onto the Potala. It was commodious and allowed the officers of the military escort and of the mission a room to themselves and, great luxury, each window was glassed!

The military escort also moved itself onto an open stretch of land know as The Plain of Wild Asses. It was a more healthy site but, more importantly, it commanded with its artillery not only Younghusband's new home but also the Potala Palace and the great Sera Monastery. Macdonald was leaving nothing to chance. Trenches were dug and earthworks were thrown up so that the army was now settled within a veritable fortress.

Alice and the rest of the correspondents were housed within it, so that the Fonthills' cosy tent sharing arrangement was ended at last. Alice herself was met with a degree of good-natured joshing from her colleagues about her sad appearance, for the discoloured swelling about her eyes had not yet receded. She sighed, grinned and merely replied that it was 'a damned good story that went all wrong', refusing to add more. Her reputation, built over the years in the field for ferreting out exclusive reports, bolstered the response and her colleagues all sighed with relief that Alice Griffith had not this time scooped them once again.

Not all was sweetness and light, however, between the army and the town authorities. The army's supplies were now running low and although the Lhasa elders were told of the troops' requirement and payment promised, nothing was forthcoming that looked like meeting the need. After five days the shortage of grain and fodder had become acute and the mules were back on half rations. Macdonald moved in and demanded 320,500 lbs of grain from the nearby Drepung Monastery's stores. When O'Connor and a contingent of troops approached the monastery they were met by an angry crowd of monks who threatened them with stones, forcing them to withdraw.

Macdonald responded by bringing up his artillery and telling the monks that they had one hour to provide the grain or he would open fire on the monastery. Just as the guns were limbering up to fire, sacks of grain, *tsampa* and butter began to dribble out, slowly. The rest was promised within five days and the General took four of the monastery's abbots as hostages to ensure that the promise was kept.

Fonthill's accommodation within the Commissioner's headquarters had helped to renew his former semi-close relationship with Younghusband. The Colonel confided to Simon that he had now received the final draft of the agreement that he was to secure with the Tibetan government. 'That's all very well, old chap,' he said, 'but I don't know how on earth I shall get through it for no one will accept responsibility and the Dalai Lama has bolted.'

The terms that were to be asked of the Tibetans seemed, to Fonthill at least, to be quite onerous. The main demands were: the establishments of trade marts at Gyantse and Gartok, the latter in Western Tibet; the British occupation of the Chumbi Valley until reparations were paid; permission for the British agent in Gyantse to visit Lhasa; and – bound to be the most contentions to the Tibetans by far – the imposition of a fine, or reparations, to the Indian government to offset the cost of the expedition, the exact figure to be decided by the Commissioner 'in the light of circumstances', in other words, his estimation of how much the Tibetans would be able to pay.

Younghusband was determined to stay in Lhasa, with his military escort until the agreement was signed. But the signs were by no means propitious.

Macdonald's brush with the monks at Drepung was not the only flaring to the surface of hostility to the British. An ugly incident occurred on 18th August when two English medical officers, Captains Kelly and Cooke-Young were leaving the camp to breakfast at Lhalu Mansion. Without warning, they were suddenly attacked from behind by a monk wielding a large sword.

The man swung the blade and hit Cook-Young on the back of the head. The officer's forage cap, however, took most of the force of the blow and, although being knocked to the ground, he suffered no serious injury. Kelly meanwhile had seized a rifle and bayonet from a nearby soldier and ran at the monk, thrusting the bayonet through his arm and bringing him to his knees. A second thrust penetrated his cheek and pinned the man to the ground. When the bayonet was withdrawn, however, the monk sprang to his feet and ran head down at the Captain, like a bull to a matador, bringing him down.

The monk, seemingly impervious to his wounds, snatched up the rifle and bayonet and ran with them towards the camp. Captain Cook-Young bravely ran after him only to receive a second and more severe sword cut to the head. The attack had by now attracted attention from guards at the camp and the monk was laid low by a blow to the knees and overpowered.

Under his monk's robes, he was found to be wearing a suit of ancient chain mail and proved, under examination, to be a member of a fighting order of monks who mainly served as guards to the larger monasteries. At first he claimed that his action was a form of revenge for a brother killed at Gyantse but later admitted that he had been encouraged to mount the attack by colleagues anxious to find out what would happen to anyone who confronted the British.

They received their answer when the monk was tried by a special court the next morning and hanged as an example in sight of the city. He died still fighting; kicking a soldier in the face as he was forced up the ladder and spitting in the face of another. He was left hanging for twenty-four hours as an example and deterrent to any other monks who might consider breaking their vows in observing the sanctity of life.

It was no surprise, therefore, that when the Commissioner managed at last to set up a meeting at his official residence attended by the Dalai Lama's private secretary, the secretary of the Kashag, or ruling council, and two of the four Shapés who made up the council, it turned out to be a disaster. The Tibetans raised objections to every clause in the proposed treaty, particularly that demanding an indemnity from the Tibetans to meet the cost of the army's advance on Lhasa. If money had to be exchanged, they argued, it should go to the council to pay for the damage caused by the British troops.

When told of this, Alice predictably agreed. 'We have almost ravaged the damned country,' she said. 'They didn't invite us in. Why should they pay the cost of our invading their land?'

Simon began to argue: 'Well they are a defeated country . . .' but gave up quickly as Alice took a deep breath.

In his Sisyphean task, however, the Commissioner found two unexpected allies in the Tonsa Penlop of Bhutan – he of the homburg hat – who announced that he had advised the ruling council to depose the absent Dalai Lama. The second was the Nepalese Consul in Lhasa, Captain Jit Bahadur. The latter arrived one day at Lhalu Mansion bringing with him a previously withdrawn but, as it turned out, very important person in the form of the acting regent, an elderly, studious and extremely polite lama called Ti Rinpoche. It seemed that, when the Dalai Lama had fled the city, he had handed over his royal seal of office to this man, who had now been persuaded by Bahadur to step forward and meet the British delegation.

He proved to be just the sort of person to delight the equally studious Younghusband, of whom he enquired if he believed in reincarnation, adding that he hoped that 'both of us would be good during the negotiation, then we might both go to heaven'. The Commissioner replied that he had not the smallest doubt that they would both go to heaven if they achieved a satisfactory conclusion to the talks.

It was a good start and a touch further progress was made on 14th August when the two Indians, allegedly sent by Curzon to spy on Russian influence in Lhasa and imprisoned in the city, were formally handed over to Younghusband by the Tibetans. They revealed that, at first they had been beaten but latterly had been well treated.

They looked pale but bore no other marks of personal harassment.

It seemed a propitious moment for Fonthill to approach the Commissioner and the General. He and Alice had become increasingly restless at being forced to remain in a Forbidden City which had turned out to be smelly, unhygienic and to them both, now, a very boring place. It was clear that the negotiations, which had hardly begun in meaningful form, were going to stretch out for months yet. With no action to engage Simon and Jenkins and for Alice to report on, their presence there had become virtually redundant and their daily rounds tedious. The two had therefore decided to seek their release. Jenkins's approval had come quickly, prompted by the fact that he could find no beer in Lhasa worthy of the name.

Macdonald and Younghusband had offered no objections; the former brusquely and the latter with sadness.

'If and when I get what I want from these talks,' Younghusband said, 'I will, of course, be recommending that the services of those on this mission should be recognised, now that it has reached a successful conclusion. You have performed magnificently on this campaign, my dear fellow, but, as you served in a military capacity, it will be up to Mac to make the recommendation on your behalf. If it were left to me, given that you already possess a CB and a DSO, I would have put you up for a knighthood, although with you not being exactly a regular soldier, I doubt if it would have been accepted.'

Fonthill smiled. 'That's a most kind thought, Francis, but I really do not deserve any such recognition and, between you and I, I rather doubt whether Mac has ever really approved of me, so I doubt if any such move would have come from him. So let whatever promotion or gong is appropriate go to Ottley. He has been the real leader of the Mounted Infantry, for he trained the nucleus up in the first place and has been a magnificent number two to me. He certainly deserves promotion and for his career to be advanced.'

'Very well. When will you leave?'

'As soon as Alice gets permission from her editor to leave – and she thinks that he will agree that Reuters can do the reporting job quite adequately from now on. And, of course, if we can get passage in whatever column is going back to the border.'

'Oh, I am sure Mac can arrange that. Come in and say goodbye before you go.' The two shook hands and Simon left and went in search of Alice and Jenkins.

He found the two sharing a cup of tea and broke the news.

'Good,' exclaimed Alice. 'I will cable my editor immediately. I've just heard, anyway, that that pompous ass, Perceval Landon, who has been here for *The Times*, has pushed off back to India. He has always claimed to be a personal friend of Curzon and has explained to anyone who would listen that he has gone bearing personal letters from the Commissioner. But that is clearly rubbish. He is off back to London so that he can be the first to write a book about the expedition and pull in a whacking great publishing contract.'

Jenkins nodded his head sagely and looked around

him. 'I shan't be sorry to leave this bloody awful place,' he sniffed. 'Even the thought of crossin' them mountains again is better than stayin' 'ere, look you, twiddlin' our fingers and toes.'

Simon squatted down beside the two. 'What will you do, 352, when we get back to India? Go on to South Africa, presumably?'

The Welshman frowned and looked down at the ground. 'Well, I must go an' see to my girls, and all that. I must see 'ow they're gettin' on at their new school and,' he looked up with a rueful grin, 'throw a few more pennies into the kitty, so to speak.'

Alice leant forward. 'Yes, of course,' she said. 'But what after that? Will you stay in South Africa?'

Jenkins pulled at his moustache and seemed a touch discomforted. 'Well, to be honest, missus, I'm not sure.' He gave them both a smile that contained a trace of embarrassment. 'I'm not sure what to do with meself, see. Who would want a discharged street fighter an' gutter mongrel, who's good at killin' people and keeps fallin' off mountains? But I suppose I've got to stay with me girls, 'aven't I?'

Simon nodded. 'Of course. You must look after them. But I have an idea. Why don't you bring them over to us in Norfolk and stay with us for as long as you like, while you sort yourself out. We have a very good local school near us, where Alice is a governor, and it would do them good to travel a bit and learn at first-hand about good old England.' He turned to his wife. 'What do you think, darling?'

'I think it's a splendid idea,' Alice nodded enthusiastically.

'The Black Dog in the village will welcome you back with open arms. You must say yes, 352.'

Jenkins put down his tin cup and produced a grimy, huge handkerchief from his pocket and blew his nose, with a noise like a thunderclap. 'You're both very kind,' he said eventually. 'I know the girls would love it. But no charity to an old soldier, now. We can pay our way, you know.'

'And you certainly will.' Fonthill leant forward and extended his hand. 'We'll make a profit out of you.'

Bashfully, Jenkins shook hands with them both. Then he blew his nose again and asked: 'What about dear old Sunshine, eh? Don't forget, 'e's got into killin' ways out 'ere. 'E won't easily slot back into life with 'is rotten old uncle on your old tea place, now, I wouldn't think.'

Simon nodded. 'Quite right. We must ask him what he wants to do—'

'Yes, but,' Alice interrupted quickly, 'we must offer him something. We can't just cast him off. You've become closest to him out here, 352. Have you any idea what he would like to do when we get back to India? I think he's forgotten his original idea of being a journalist – too much scribbling, cabling and so on.'

'Oh yes.' Jenkins nodded emphatically. ''E wants to be a soldier in the British army. No doubt about that.'

A silence fell on the little group. Then it was broken by Simon: 'That boy saved my life. I wouldn't like to just let him join up back in Delhi or wherever. I owe him more than that. He's as bright as a button and he's become close to all of us.'

'The answer is quite clear.' Alice's tone was firm. 'He

must first come back with all of us to Norfolk. He's too young to go straight into the army.' She turned to her husband. 'Simon, we must put him into a good school, so that he improves that bright enquiring mind of his. Then, when he is ready and if he still wants to become a soldier, he would stand a good chance of getting a commission in the Indian army. What do you both think?'

Jenkins's great grin split his face. 'Wonderful! An' I could be 'is batman, eh?'

'He wouldn't get a better one.' Fonthill put a hand into the depths of his *poshteen* and produced a half bottle of whisky. 'Will you go and get him, please, 352, and bring him back here with four clean mugs, if you can find them. The boy had better begin to learn to drink, like a proper English soldier.'

Jenkins looked embarrassed. 'Ah, a bit late for that, bach sir. I've already been givin' 'im lessons. In fact, I 'ave to say that 'e's comin' on quite well in that direction.'

AUTHOR'S NOTE

This is a work of fiction although based on factual happenings. It is only fair to the reader, then, that I should delineate which is truth and which fiction in the telling of this story. In this context, Fonthill, Alice, Jenkins and Sunil are my creations as are other minor characters in the story, such as Willoughby, Curzon's ADC, Chung Li and his family and the rather more important figure of General Khemphis Jong.

The cast list of real people is longer: Curzon, Younghusband and Macdonald, of course, and officers in the expedition force such as Captain William Ottley, who actually led the Mounted Infantry throughout the campaign; Frank O'Connor, Younghusband's valued interpreter; Colonel Campbell of the 30th Pathans; Colonel Brander, who led the attack at Karo La; Major Bretherton, who perished in the Tsangpo: Captains Bethune, Walton, Kelly and Cook-Young; and Lt John Grant, VC and his *havildar*, Karbir Pun. Alice's three correspondent colleagues are as named.

The list of the tongue-twistedly named Tibetans who played a role in the real-life story is equally long: the Ta Lama; Yutop Shapé; the *amban*, who was commander of the fort at Gyantse; Lobsang Trinley, the Dalai Lama's adversarial Grand Secretary; the Chinese *amban* in Lhasa; Kalon Yuthok; Ti Rinpoche; and the two non-Tibetans who helped Younghusband make the initial breakthrough in negotiating the treaty; Captain Ja Bahadur, the Nepalese ambassador in Lhasa and the Tonsa Penlop, he of the homburg hat.

I have tried to retell the battles and main events of the invasion as accurately as studies of respected accounts of the campaign have allowed. I must confess, however, to two departures from the *actualité*. The first concerns the attack on the mission at Chang Lo. I have the journalists not accompanying Colonel Brander on his attack on Karo La, because I wanted Alice to stay and describe the attack on the mission. In reality, all three correspondents went with the Colonel to Karo La. The second is that the Mounted Infantry's heroic action at the river near the end of the march on Lhasa is a pure figment of my imagination, although in fact they experienced many more military encounters with the Tibetans than I have described. I felt that one more stirring piece of action was needed at this point in the story. Well, the book is a novel, after all!

If one discounts the disastrous episode of Suez in

1956 as being forced on the UK by events rather than territorial ambition, the invasion of Tibet in 1904 (and, despite Curzon's protestations, it *was* an invasion) can be described as the last real hurrah of British imperial expansionism. It took place only after Curzon pressed the British government hard to react to the border pinpricks and lack of respect shown to the Raj by the Tibetans and to the perceived threat of a growing Russian presence in Lhasa. Curzon never had firm evidence of the presence there of a permanent representative of the Tsar, nor of the existence of a Russian gun factory. He virtually lied about this, to support his long-held theory. The expedition, in fact, began shrouded in criticism from Westminster and it ended in quite bitter controversy.

Younghusband got his treaty in the end, only after hard months of arguments in Lhasa, with Macdonald fussing and fuming in the background and longing to return to India. But, after lauding the Commissioner's efforts initially, the British government emasculated the main elements of the agreement, reducing the amount of time the British occupied the Chumbi Valley from seventy-five years to three and cutting to a third the amount of reparations Younghusband had levied on the Tibetan government. It also revoked the clause, which Younghusband held dear, which allowed the British agent at Gyantse to visit Lhasa. In fact, the Tibetans never did pay the reparations and from attaining the status of hero, Younghusband limped back home accused of being headstrong and arrogant.

Sides were taken in the Macdonald vs Younghusband spats. At the end of the long, arduous campaign, having reached Lhasa after one of the most difficult and dangerous expeditions in British military history, Younghusband could reasonably have expected to be honoured with the knighthood of the Order of the Bath. Instead, he received the lower appointment of Knight Commander of the Indian Empire. Macdonald, however, was on the eve of being Gazetted Knight Companion of the Order of the Bath when, on the last minute intervention of the King himself – reputed to be an admirer of Younghusband – he, too, was demoted to the KCIE.

The controversy which ended the expedition seemed to obscure completely the fact that the main reason for the invasion – to counter the perceived strong influence in Lhasa of Russia – had been proven to be quite unfounded. But there was no more talk of a 'forward policy' being established to defend India.

The two protagonists of the long march virtually disappeared from public view. Thanks to his old supporter Curzon, Younghusband was appointed to the Residency of Kashmir, which he coveted. But that lasted only three years and it became clear that he had no longer any future in the Indian Civil Service and he resigned and, after an unsuccessful attempt to enter politics in the UK, he devoted the rest of his life to religious works, unembittered and rather mystical to the end. Macdonald became a major general and ended his career as GOC in Mauritius, before retiring early back to Scotland because of ill health.

Curzon, ill and burdened by the death of his beloved wife, returned to India but, worn out by constant conflict with Kitchener, resigned his Viceroyalty. He dropped out of public life for a while but married again, became Foreign Secretary during the war years and came within an ace of achieving the premiership in 1923, only to be pipped at the post by Baldwin. He died an unpopular figure, still carrying – perhaps unfairly – the reputation of being pompous and arrogant.

And Tibet? Historians have written that Younghusband at least brought it out of its medievalism. But it has remained to this day a backward, pastoral and theologically influenced state that is now dominated and occupied by a resurgent China. The present Dalai Lama now lives in exile in India. The waters of international interest now seem to have closed quietly over Lhasa, as though the Younghusband Expedition had never existed.

ACKNOWLEDGEMENTS

I am indebted to my agent, Jane Conway-Gordon, for her constant and loyal support and her commercial-literary efforts on my behalf. Why, she even supplied the title for this novel! My thanks also go to Susie Dunlop and her staff at Allison & Busby for their help and work in correcting my carelessness on detail and names. I would also have been lost without the London Library, whose staff helped me find the sources for ensuring that, as far as possible, my recreation of events from so long ago were accurate. Lastly, my love and thanks go to my wife Betty, for her proofreading, care and patience while I slogged over the high road to Lhasa with Simon, Alice and Jenkins.

The Tibet expedition certainly seemed to attract a good deal of literary attention – perhaps because of its pseudo glamour as a last echo of more successful exploits of

Empire? Many of the books about the invasion seemed to take sides in the ongoing debate about whether Macdonald's caution was justified or represented an unacceptable drag on Younghusband's energy and ambition. I have tried to tread between the daisies here, perhaps, however, coming down slightly on the side of the Commissioner, who, to me, steps out of the pages as a more charismatic person.

Readers anxious to dip more deeply into the history of the expedition may find the attached, very short bibliography of use.

Allen, Charles, *Duel in the Snows* (London, 2004)

Candler, Edmund, *The Unveiling of Lhasa* (London, 1905)

Fleming, Peter; Hart-Davis, Rupert, *Bayonets to Lhasa* (London, 1961)

Goradia, Nayana, *Lord Curzon: The Last of the British Moghuls* (Oxford, 1993)

Haythornthwaite, Philip J., *The Colonial Wars Source Book* (London, 1995)

O'Connor, Sir Frederick, *On the Frontier and Beyond* (London, 1931)

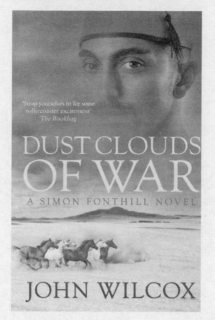

September, 1914. With the First World War already raging on the Western Front, thousands of miles away Simon Fonthill is preparing to face his most dangerous mission yet alongside his faithful companion, 352 Jenkins and his reliable tracker, Mzingeli. At the bequest of Admiral Herbert King-Hall, the trio are commanded to sink the *Königsberg*, a German cruiser ship hidden deep in the Rufiji Delta in German-occupied waters.

Meanwhile, Fonthill's wife, Alice, has been conducting investigations of her own in Mombasa – and when she thinks something is amiss within the camp, she takes matters into her own hands. Amidst the chaos of war, treachery is never far away . . .